FENTOSCIENCE

THE STARTLING DISCOVERIES OF PROFESSOR BAGDENBORG

V.S. SURY

INDIA • SINGAPORE • MALAYSIA

ISBN 979-8-89133-429-8

Dedicated to

The sweet memory of N. Raghavan, with whom I shared innumerable jokes and intimate thoughts, (and who was also Dondu, Uttam & Rock Van to those who were near and dear to him).

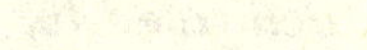

CONTENTS

Part I

Part II

Part III

What is this book about?

This book is about the astonishing discoveries in science made by Bagdenborg.

Who is Bagdenborg?

He is Professor Bagus Baglicochus Bagdenborg, a.k.a. Jestus Jesticus Jestimedes. He is a super-ultra genius. He is a polymath. He is a man of extraordinary imagination and boundless enthusiasm. He calls himself by a hundred names.

Why a hundred names?

Because, as he says, he has a hundred attributes. So, it is natural that he should have a hundred names (actually more) corresponding to the particular characteristic he would be displaying at a given moment. That is in consonance with fento-logic, he argues.

DOB? DOD?

His DOB is not known exactly. It could be somewhere before World War I. DOD must be in the far future. The professor was last seen alive a few years ago at Heathrow. He is not traceable now. But rumors surfaced at regular intervals that he was spotted in the Himalayas.

Languages known? Nationality?

Rumors again. Many say that he knows all the major languages in the world. One of his admirers insists that Herr Professor knows all the languages that ever were and are. Where Bagliochus is concerned, no piece of information can be discarded as pure rumor. He has the surprising gift of proving the impossible possible and the possible impossible. He holds the citizenship of more than two dozen countries. How he has managed it is a real mystery.

Now, what is that "fentologic" thing about the professor?

As you are well aware, nanotechnology is the latest buzzword. When a material is finely ground (reduced) to the size of nanoparticles, it exhibits new and surprising properties in that state ("nano", is smaller than "micro"). Well, Professor Bagdenborg drew inspiration from that and applied the principle in the field of logic. When logic is ground to even a finer state than "nano", to that of "fento", it transmutes into fentologic. Fentologic is thus by far superior to standard logic, thereby opening up vast vistas of knowledge.

Are the theories and discoveries of the professor true?

They are all absolutely true, as far as the professor is concerned. Unfortunately, the professor was allergic to experimentation. If you are curious enough, you can verify his theories by carrying out actual experiments. There are no objections to that.

I still have doubts to be clarified. What next?

Please contact the venerable Professor Bagdenborg if you can trace him down. Or, you may wait patiently for his promised return.

How come the world at large does not know Professor Bagdenborg?

Bagdimedes was a lone wolf. He was also very reluctant to publish his findings on a wide platform; only his group of admirers knew about his activities. Now, one admirer decided it was time that the world at large—as you said—should know about the extraordinary genius of the man. The admirer even goes to the length of comparing the professor's writings to the "notes" of the famous Renaissance man.

Why this book?

Three events impelled me to write this book:

My elderly neighbor's eyes were filled with tears, while his face bore an expression of immense sorrow. I asked him what the matter was. He pointed a weighed-down hand at the book lying on the table. By the title of the book, I knew it was the latest bestseller in popular science. My neighbor sighed and said in an almost choking voice, "I too once wanted to be a scientist. I wanted to write hundreds of books like that. It is too late now. I didn't have what it takes." The man worked all his life as a clerk. He retired from service long ago. His knowledge of science was not even at ground level. It was below the basement. But his present sorrow and regret were very real and deep.

By a strange coincidence, the next day, I was seated in the midst of a group of high-brow nerds of mixed ages. The youngest among them, a student yet, was expressing his keen desire to study modern physics and become a scientist. At which point, the oldest in the group, a mathematics (supercilious) super geek, condescendingly advised, "You study mathematics first. Not the specialized bits; the whole megillah. Study it for twenty years if you want to take up research. That is the minimum. No math, no science. Forget it." It was a very rude put-down. I could see the hurt on the student's face.

The coincidence continued to play. The third day, I had to take a young boy of six—quite brilliant for his age—to a planetarium. As we came out, I observed the glazed expression on the lad's face. He was lost to this world. His mind was roaming across intergalactic spaces, dreaming of unseen wonders. He was daydreaming intensely. He stayed thus for a week.

The three events touched something deep in my heart—something that was pushing to come out. I vowed to wipe away the tears of my neighbor and avenge the hurt of the aspiring student in one stroke. I decided to write a book on popular science! The problem was that my knowledge of mathematics was on par with that of a moron. That was where the image of the daydreaming kid came to my rescue. Go on, daydream—make up your own science, fabricate your own fictitious research!

But if science—even fictitious—is not backed up by mathematics, at least it should follow logic. Right? Fortunately, logic comes in many packages: specious, persuasive, rhetorical, fanatic, political, eristic, and even defiant. But Fentologic, developed by the beloved professor Bagdenborg, beats all types of logic hands down. I have chosen that as the medium for describing the scientific adventures of this book. As the title says, whatever ideas have been enumerated here (painstakingly) hail from a new genre, the Fi-Sci. It is not science fiction, mind you; it is fictitious science! That has been my way of satisfying the young soul of that daydreaming kid I mentioned. There is no mathematics here to restrain the "discoveries" under a tight leash. Yet, ideas have been diligently developed "logically". The logic in this book is a labor of love. It is a heady mixture of seriousness, sobriety, persuasion, and convenience, suitably impregnated with the coloring agent of humor. In fact, if the reader is not conversant with science, there is a chance that he may mistake the discoveries of Bagdimedes for real science.

The neighbor and the kid introduced at the beginning are archetypal figures. They live in the psyches of all of us. I hope this book gives a modicum of satisfaction to those archetypal figures lurking inside the readers. May the book germinate a lot more fertile ideas in the minds of adult-kids who are courageous to daydream!

How to read this book: The vision, of course, belongs entirely to Bagdenborg, a.k.a. Bagdimedes. Bagachilles had his share of myrmidons (as one of his jealous opponents called them)—the admirers. Though only Bagdenborg understood the full depth and beauty of his insights, his admirer collected, collated, and edited the contents of his notes—the interior decoration, as it were. My job has been to present their view. In order to thoroughly enjoy and appreciate the contents, you have to read the book wearing the glasses of the Admirers Club. free to join. All are welcome. Do it; it will be so much fun.

PART I

Chapter 1

SHELL SHOCK

Professor Bagdenborg firmly believed that his research in the various fields of physics was far in advance of his contemporary scientists' best efforts. More than that, he was afraid that if he published his works openly, it would attract the attention of some men of evil genius. (It was bound to happen sooner or later.) If diligent men with enough perseverance dug deeper into his theories – that too, was a certainty, given the ultra-inquisitive nature of some men – they would discover new ways of releasing sub-Planck spatial energies that were uncontrollable, that were a billion-billion times more powerful than man on Earth has ever witnessed. The fools (they would rush where angels fear to tread) would arrogantly believe they could control that immeasurable energy. The truth was that even the most sophisticated, elaborately controlled experiments would be totally ineffective in the face of the mighty release of that super energy. It would be like triggering a mini Big Bang. That would be goodbye to the Earth, which would shatter into billions and billions of pieces doomed to wander forlornly forever in the bowels of interstellar space. Ten thousand years of painstakingly built civilization and the more infinitely patiently built planet Earth, by Nature, would vanish forever in one foolish second.

Professor Bagdenborg's intention was to destroy his notebooks either upon or before his death. Obviously, he cherished his works and wanted to review them now and then – a quite understandable vanity. How, out of his enormous number of notebooks, one escaped the destruction and how it was purloined and smuggled out, how it was decrypted by one of his admirers after years of hard work; all that makes an interesting story. More of that later. Suffice it to say that his admirer too realized the danger of publishing the full contents of the notebook (remember it was just one, remaining out of many). So, only a few chosen chapters were made available to the public. The furor that the 'leaked' chapters raised lasted for a decade; it is past history now.

Let bygones be bygones. All of Professor Bagden's ideas were thrilling. Many ran against the grain of established scientific views. We give a gist of some of them, sans the encumbering (and often bewildering mathematics). Actually, what we are presenting here is a highly condensed version of the admirer's works in one volume. The admirer's admiration was over-abundant. He wrote many books on Bagdenborg's discoveries with the intention of "popularizing" them, filtering out all mathematics. That the books were ridiculed by a few members of the established scientific community, in no way detracts from the brilliant, almost blinding exposition of the admirer. We will try to preserve that zeal in this condensed version, much as it is a highly demanding task.

Enough said. Let us proceed to relish the delightful menu.

Integument

Consider an egg. If you have one in your freezer, take it out right now and place it on your table. Look at it carefully. It consists of a hard outer shell, mostly made of calcium. The inside holds things like membranes, yolks, and so on. If you are a student of biology, you can even reel out the scientific names of the contents. Okay? Now, the egg starts from the inside and ends at the outer shell. The shell is what determines and limits the empire of the egg, so to say. The shell is what separates the egg from the rest of the world, the universe. We do hope that you have no quarrel with that.

Next, consider a human being. No, we are not asking you to bring one out and place it on your table, even if you have, by chance, one in that spacious freezer you bought recently. (Most probably, it was your wife who could not resist the bargain offer at the local supermarket). The human body is made of an outer shell, like that egg on the table. Usually, it is called skin. The inside, of course, contains many more items than does an egg: bones, flesh, blood, organs like the heart, brain, liver, lungs, and so on. Now, the body too, like the egg, starts from the inside and ends at the outer surface – the skin, a living shell, so to say. That shell is what separates the body from the rest of the universe; what gives it a unique identity.

The same kind of reasoning, it is redundant to say, applies to all things: animal bodies, insects, seeds, etc.

Enough, we have given you enough broad hints. The diligent scientist in you (there are no doubts about that, we assure you) must have already caught on to where we are heading. Still, permit us to drop the bombshell (pun intended, with due apologies).

Consider the atom! Take a single atom of any of the hundred and odd elements available in the universe. An atom consists of a central nucleus around which, depending on the particular element, one or more electrons orbit. The heavier the element, the greater the number of electrons. As the population of electrons increases (in heavier elements), they occupy different "shells" – somewhat like satellites orbiting the Earth at different heights.

All this is elementary; everybody with a basic education is supposed to know it.

Here, we present the famous footnotes of Bagden himself – "Education, educated. Educated = brainwashed into numbness." If you feel these are strong words, we would like to point out that we have selected only the mildest of the professor's comments. Let us ignore those remarks for the present and proceed to the next step, the bombshell of an idea dropped by him.

There is always a demarcation between one object and another; that is the fundamental insight of Bagdenborg. Thus, he proposed ("asserted," from his point of view) that every atom is bound by an atomic shell! The atomic shell firmly maintains the individuality of each atom as a separate entity from the rest of the universe. The immediate reaction of the startled reader would be to shrug it off as an infantile fancy. After a second's thought, he may sarcastically ask, "Well, what is that shell made of? Calcium, like your egg's?" We can understand the sarcasm of the reader; the enormity of Bagdenborg's ideas arouses such emotions. The discerning question, though, deserves an answer. We will come to it soon. For now, let us take up the thread of his thoughts.

To repeat, the atom is enclosed ("protected," to use the peculiar word of Bagdenborg himself, though we do not know what deeper considerations induced him to choose that word) by a shell. The shape of the shell is naturally spherical. In his original notes, he has deduced it using abstruse concepts like super-symmetry, backing the idea all the way by employing elaborate mathematics.

– Shells, shells everywhere –

If one accepts the idea of a shell surrounding an atom, then the next natural – inevitable – progression would be to think of a shell enclosing the nucleus of the atom! That is exactly what Bagden did. The nucleus of an atom contains protons and neutrons – the exact number depending on the element chosen. This is common knowledge. The contents of the nucleus, that is, protons and neutrons, do not leave or escape from the nucleus. They do not spill out and mix with the electrons orbiting the nucleus. Also, what many may not know is the smallness of the nucleus. It is so small that the atom as a whole almost appears hollow. To get an idea, imagine the distance between the Earth and the Sun. The distance, the 'empty space' between the outer shell of the atom and the nucleus is on that comparable scale! These two facts were clear pointers, according to him. (Whenever we say 'he,' 'him,' or 'his,' it is to be understood that we are referring to Professor Bagdenborg. 'They,' invariably refers to the other scientists at large.) that the nucleus too should have a separate shell of its own. He labored on this tremendous insight for a whole year and was able to demonstrate it irrefutably through the power of mathematical analysis. It is a tribute to his immense mental powers. Albert Einstein was well-known for his thought experiments. Our man refined it and perfected it into an infallible art. No contemporary of his remembers ever seeing him entering a laboratory or conducting any sort of an experiment. "It is an idle pastime and an expensive luxury I cannot indulge in," was a famous quote of his.

The real wonder was that a good many renowned mathematicians and scientists tried to find fault with his mathematical presentation of the nucleus shell. None of them succeeded.

Here is a hint that physicists (as per Bagdenborg) have either ignored or misinterpreted. In particle physics, there is a term called mass defect. The nucleus of an atom contains protons and neutrons. Now, the masses of protons, neutrons, and the nucleus have been separately calculated. When the three are tallied (audited is the favored term), the mass of the nucleus should be equal to the sum of the masses of the protons and neutrons that it contains. But this is not so. The calculated mass of the nucleus is always greater than the added masses of its protons and neutrons. This excess difference is termed mass defect. According to the accepted explanation, this excess mass is equivalent to the energy required to hold the protons inside the nucleus. You see, protons are positively charged, and therefore, they repel one another. So, they cannot stay put inside the nucleus. Something must be holding them together. Such a force has been posited and named as the "strong force." The extra mass of the nucleus, the so-called mass defect, arises because of this "strong force." According to the most famous formula in the world, $E=mc^2$, energy and mass are equivalent, and thus, the mass defect has been shown to be equivalent to the energy content of the "strong force."

Bagus Bagliochus Bagdenborg, on the other hand, argues that the extra mass (the mass defect) of the nucleus is due to the mass of the nuclear shell he has discovered. En passant, he points his finger, with a mixture of irony and a tolerant smile, at the very same discovery he has made – that of the shell. Traditional scientists freely use that term in phrases like "electron shells of orbit," "nucleus shell," and so on, more as a metaphor than as an actual entity. When Bagden uses the word "shell," he means it literally – as a physical entity. Moreover, it is to his immortal credit that he generalized the concept thoroughly and discovered shells ranging from the electron to the universe – a magnificent achievement by any standard.

Bagdenborg's mind was exceptionally productive, inventive, and surcharged with explosive energy. Thus, in his notes, he was apt to rush in all directions of radial thoughts, once the seed of an idea caught hold of him. Consider this.

The Earth, our Earth, is a solid object of roughly spherical shape. Looking at the billions and billions (and more) objects in the universe, we do not doubt that the Earth is a separate object in its own right. Nobody thinks otherwise. "Well, think again," said Bagdenborg.

Look at the Moon, he points! So, what, you are tempted to taunt thus:-

"The Moon is a separate object hanging over there like an incandescent balloon. In the olden days, it was made of cheese. Now it is made of hardened ash, rocks, and captured meteorites. They have gone up there, do you know? They have brought back tons of Earth from the Moon. Earth from the Moon, ha-ha. It has got its own gravity too, you know that?"

To which, the unfazed Professor Bagdenborg says, "I see you have a sense of humor. I know a million jokes. I will share them with you some fine day. Now, will you please look at the Moon? Seriously."

OK, back to the Earth. The Moon is circling the Earth. It is far away from the Earth. Next, let us direct our attention to the atom. There is the nucleus (liken it to the Earth), and there is the electron (liken it to the Moon) orbiting the nucleus. What can be more explicit? The nucleus and the orbiting electrons form a single unit called the atom. Thus, the Earth and the Moon orbiting the Earth form a single unit. It cannot be otherwise.

We have been accustomed to seeing the two as separate objects because we have been conditioned to such a viewpoint. Moreover, our viewpoint has been necessarily from the Earth, all along. If you look at the Earth-Moon system from a spot far away from both, say, the surface of the Sun, then you will have not an iota of doubt that the Earth and Moon are a single object.

Any lingering doubt about the truth of this statement will vanish when one considers the fact that the Earth-Moon combination is orbiting the as a single unit. By carefully observing two apparently widely separated phenomena, we have arrived at a beautiful generalization, a profound insight, an unshakeable axiom. Thus, progress is made.

Professor Bagdenborg advises us not to stop there in smug contentment. He dared us to journey further. When we hesitated, he was the one who took the leap forward – along the chain of inductive reasoning. Remember that the atom is enclosed ("protected") by an atomic shell. Well, Bagdenborg, in his imaginative leap of inductive logic, arrived at the astounding conclusion that the Earth-Moon system too is enclosed by a shell!

Many may think that this kind of reasoning seems far-fetched. Taking advantage of the moon, his detractors may even employ the word 'lunatic' at the idea. But such people may not be aware that, most often, *a very thin line divides the boundaries of lunacy and genius.* Professor Bagdenborg's genius lay in the thoroughness with which he derived his mathematical theorems. For example, calculations that prove that the atom is enclosed in a shell fill up a space of a hundred pages. Only the most skilled people with a thorough knowledge of advanced mathematics can follow the subtle, intricate derivations of the equations. Considering the sensibilities of the lay readers, we have desisted from reproducing the math here. Even the most vehement opponents of Bagdenborg have been unable to find any chinks in his calculations. Their one and only objection has been that there has been no experimental evidence so far for the existence of the atom's shell. *So far.* But that, by itself, does not disprove his theories either. Apart from that, it is a sad fact that established laboratories across the world have shown no interest in testing Bagdenborg's theories. It is true that he has a sizeable following of admirers. Then, it is also a tragic truth that they do not have sufficient funds to take up experimental verification of Bagdenborg's theories.

Professor Bagdenborg completed his calculations of the atom's shell in two days flat. Normally, such work takes from one year to five, even in the case of gifted scientists. "The equations just flowed out of my pen. I did not cross or delete any line; I did not have to make any re-calculations," is a direct quote from his notebooks. It repeats itself at regular intervals across his notes.

Tackling the problem of the shell enclosing the Earth-moon system was apparently a more difficult task. "One week," was the laconic remark found in the notebook. To celebrate the momentous discovery, he christened the Earth-moon system as "Lunearth". The intensity, the firmness of his conviction can be gauged by the fact that, from the day he sealed his calculations, he never referred to the planet Earth as 'earth', either in his works or in his conversations. It was always – Lunearth, Lunearth, Lunearth. Such was the man.

Once Bagdenborg starts something, there is no stopping him. He gloated over his equations for one week, just for one week. His excitement was at a boiling point. His imagination was on a steady cruise. It was not wild or in a feverish pitch. (Even his admirers have admitted that when his imagination would reach a feverish pitch, they would shiver).

– And shells it shall be –

From the atom's shell to Lunearth was an enormous leap. But that was nothing compared to his next leap, which he took from the vantage point of his Earth-moon shell. He took one fantastic leap towards the Sun.

His restless finger, which was pointing at the Moon, was now wagging vigorously at the Sun. Consider the Sun, it demanded. The Sun is a big star about a hundred thousand times bigger than Earth, consisting of hydrogen, helium… No, no, his wagging finger gently admonishes you. The tip of his Zeige finger is describing a circle. Got it?

It is the solar system that his finger is asking you to behold, to visualize. Visualize it thus. The Sun is at the center. The planets forming the solar system are orbiting around the Sun – just as the electrons orbit around the nucleus of the atom. That is old hat, the reader is once again tempted to sneer in amusement. But hold your breath. Bagdenborg has declared that the solar system too is ensconced in a huge protective shell. It was not imagination at work, nor was it an idle fantasy – it was unsullied intuition.

Bagdenborg was well aware that where scientific inquiry was concerned, intuition by itself was unacceptable. Intuition surely bestowed contentment and joy on him – as it always does on the individual fortunate to have been visited by it. But convincing the scientific community at large is an entirely different matter. One needs to – no, has to – adduce faultless, rigorous mathematical proof, or irrefutable experimental evidence, or preferably both. As we said earlier, Bagdenborg took the path of mathematics. It did not take him one week this time, since he already had the basic platform of the equations developed for the Lunearth system. Within two days, he completed the task, again filling up a hundred pages with rigorous mathematics. Different people have different ways of letting off steam after a hectic period of work. Bagdenborg took to slang. "Easy peasy lemon squeezy," adorned the border of a particular page in his notebook. He was not insulting anybody either deliberately or unintentionally by that remark – he was being himself, he was talking to himself. It was a measure of his extraordinary genius. (His admirer is fond of quoting an anecdote. Professor Bagus Bagliochus had thrice spurned invitation offers of IQ tests, on the grounds that nobody had yet invented a system for testing his IQ.)

Once a concept arises, it is one's duty to stretch it to the breaking point. It was one of the professor's tenets. He had proved that atoms have shells. He had shown that, likewise, the Earth-moon system too had one, that the solar system too was bounded by a shell. Then what was left? We have to just explore, that is, stretch the shell concept a bit more, that is all. You see, the common thread running through all the three discoveries was the concept of a unit, a system, whether small or large. "Unit"; that is the pivotal word. When we think of a unit, naturally, our attention is drawn towards the fundamental constituents of matter, i.e., particles like electrons, protons, and neutrons. Bagden's laser-sharp intellect penetrated into the deep womb of matter and focused itself on those three particles. The conclusion was inevitable. All the three particles—electrons, protons, and neutrons—were found to have been equipped with ("born with" was the phrase used by him) shells.

Thus, the idea developed – the way a tiny seed, once it germinates, grows into a giant tree – into a huge, elegant synthesis. ("It is so elegant that its reality is a given". Evidently, he was taking the mickey at some of his colleagues.) It is needless to say too, that Bagden proceeded straightaway to lay a firm mathematical foundation for his latest insight. We will not mention how much time it took him; we have already provided enough hints about his prowess. In a steady progression of successive landmarks, Bagdenborg had revealed that the atoms had shells; the nucleus, the electrons, protons, and neutrons had shells. He had mathematically proved beyond doubt that the Earth-moon system (Lunearth) had a shell of its own, and beyond that, the solar system too, as a unit, had its own shell. By any standard, what he had achieved was remarkable.

It is quite possible that Bagus Baglicochus had discussed these insights with a select few of his admirers. Rather, it is the other way round – he did not care to discuss what was axiomatic to him; they must have approached him to discuss his startling concepts. He had also stopped submitting his papers to leading scientific magazines and academies. In the past, his theories had given rise to heated discussion. Most of his colleagues had greeted his extraordinary ideas with derision, many with incredulity, and very, very few with open minds.

Scattered references are available that his friends had talks with him on these and other topics. But Bagden had provided only broad hints but no specifics, no mathematics. He preferred to record everything in his notebooks.

It appears that things were quiet for a brief period – a brief period only, and quietness apparently only. Bagden's mind was actually seething restlessly at its subconscious level. Something was gnawing at him; a strong sense of dissatisfaction, a sense of having left something incomplete.

The eureka moment was not long in arriving. It struck him in his bathtub, just like it had his predecessor more than two thousand years ago, at a certain bathtub in glorious Greece. The idea was brilliant beyond measure... progressive inductive logic at its brilliant best.

In a way, it was simple and evident too. Let us go back and recall the insights of Bagliochus step by logical step. We saw that the protons and neutrons were enclosed by shells. They are contained inside the nucleus, which has a separate shell of its own. Next, we saw that the electrons orbiting the nucleus had their own shells. Rounding off the process, the system that acts as a unit, which goes by the name of 'atom', was also shown to have a unique shell. We took a big leap from the microscopic level and were astonished to discover that the Earth-moon system, a unit, was enclosed in a shell. In the next leap, we were thrilled when Bagden proved that the solar system, a unit, had a grand enclosing shell. To repeat, this was one heck of a long scientific journey. And finally... and... finally... hold your breath... sorry to repeat again but we are going to ask you to hold your breath many times more, and you better get accustomed to it... we are going to take the ultimate leap along with Professor Bagus Bagliochus Bagdenborg to the very boundary of the universe.

When Bagden (BBB) reached the edge of the universe, he found, to his infinite delight, that the cosmos too was enclosed in a shell of infinite dimensions. Not exactly infinite – almost. Bagden hated using the word 'infinity' in science; we will come to it later.

Working out the mathematics was no ordinary task, even for him. Compared to the universe, the solar system is just like a dot. There are billions and billions of similar systems: galaxies, supernovae, nebulae, pulsars, quasars, black holes; so many exotic systems in the universe. To take all of them into consideration and arrive at the defining characteristic of a cosmic shell is not a task for ordinary mortals. BBB must have sweated it out for a long time.

He was incommunicado for a long time. There is only an indirect hint in the diary of his admirer (who alone had access to Bagden). He had noted therein that Bagdenborg looked very gaunt and withdrawn. He had lost considerable weight; he must have been skipping his meals. He could have even forgotten to take food; he had done so twice previously when dealing with difficult problems. Be that as it may, JJB succeeded in formulating a complete, mathematical formulation for the cosmic shell. This must have given him immense satisfaction. But he found a more delightful bonus at the end, after he had completed his theory and was going through it for the sheer pleasure of reviewing it. The equations showed him that the cosmic shell was radiating electromagnetic energy. The real kicker was this – it was radiating energy inside! It was radiating energy outside too. The kicker's kicker (with due apologies for using the phrase) was that there was a huge, almost unimaginable, disparity between their frequencies. BBB sat down once again and wrote a separate thesis on this astonishing phenomenon. We will take up this interesting discovery later.

The shrewd reader must have already noticed that we have omitted one titbit – it was intentional, the intention being to tease the readers playfully. If you have made a list of shells enclosing various systems or units, you must have noticed that we have omitted the rest of the solar system – the sun himself! Rest assured that the sun too has a shell. Jestus Jesticus Bagdenborg guarantees that.

In the coming years, Bagdenborg refurbished his mathematical calculations, capping it off with the famous (and equally controversial) theorem – Bagden's General Theory of Shells. Briefly put, the theory states as follows:

Every system, either consisting of a single unit or of multiple units, exhibiting the behavior of a recognizable system, is enclosed by a harmonic of the cosmic shell.

We have amply illustrated this before. Electrons and protons are units. The atom, the Lunearth, and the solar systems are collections of units behaving as recognizable systems. Of course, the universe taken as a whole is the Grand System. Just a word about the "harmonic of the cosmic shell". Though JJB used the word "harmonic," he meant it in broad terms. In his notes, he described the cosmic shell as the mother shell. All the other numerous shells belong to that cosmic family and are 'spawned' from it. Aesthetically bringing in a term from biological science to illustrate a purely physical phenomena, he elegantly proved, using mathematics, that the equations for the cosmic shell ("mother") contained in their womb the seeds of all the other shells in the universe; that by properly 'germinating' the seed equations, the entire family of those shells could be developed.

Shell In a Nutshell

The shell theory was one of the many landmarks JJB built along the long road he trod in quest of scientific knowledge.

Naturally, most people who come across this idea of shells for the first time will be perplexed. The reactions of the rest may vary: amazement, curiosity, wonder, incredulity, vehement opposition, downright rejection, sarcasm, or even a supercilious sneer. Not surprising. All great ideas that are ahead of their times are usually greeted thus.

What exactly is the "shell" that Bagdenborg is talking about? What is it made of? What is its nature?

These are tough questions to answer. A complex concept like this cannot be explained in a single sentence. Especially in the field of modern science (physics), it is becoming more and more difficult to "explain" abstruse concepts. Bagdenborg could be quite laconic – even reticent – when the whim takes over, even with his few close friends. But it seems the admirer we have been referring to succeeded in penetrating Bagden's wall of silence. Even so, he was able to coax terse, compacted hints only from B. From the admirer's copious commentaries, a fairly good idea can be obtained.

If you draw two converging arrows on paper, you can pinpoint exactly where they will meet. If there are many arrows apparently converging but not at a single point, then the best thing you can do is to follow the outline of their tips. The outline will be an image that can provide you with a rough idea of what the arrows are trying to convey. We will follow that method.

Let us begin with the simplest visual analogies – an egg, a tennis ball, a ping-pong ball. Take the ping-pong ball, for example. Air is trapped inside the shell of the ball. The air is made up of millions of molecules and atoms. The behavior and properties of individual constituents vary enormously; speed, weight, direction of movement, spin, etc., are all different. But as long as the shell holds them within its boundary, all those millions of bits follow the shell as a group, as one single system. While being hit back and forth on the ping-pong table, the ball follows many trajectories that can be mathematically precisely defined. All the molecules inside the ball, taken as a whole, obediently follow the same trajectory. That is the purpose of the shell – "to preserve the identity of a system," as JJB said. "Preserve the identity" is a curious phrase.

When asked by his admirer what it meant, BBB reluctantly mumbled a couple of pithy sentences. The commentary of the admirer sheds more light on them.

The above analogy serves as a rough sketch. The shells of the egg, the tennis ball, and the ping-pong ball differ in texture, color, and chemical properties. The cosmic shell and its family of derivatives are obviously far more refined and subtle.

Consider any fundamental particle, say, an electron. Generally, when we think of such a particle (however minute it might be), we imagine it as an almost invisible tiny dot, in isolation, meaning it is surrounded by empty space, though empty space serves as a background to imagine the dot. Okay? Don't strain too hard; just try to picture the electron in your mind because the knockout punch is about to land.

Bagliochus' brilliant, irrefutable intuition surmised that if left to itself, the electron would spread out in all directions, and it would keep spreading out until it filled up the entire universe, becoming thinner and thinner in the process, until, in the end, there would be nothing left that could be called or identified as an electron! Let's reiterate – there would be nothing left that could be called or identified as an electron. Whew! When the idea hits you, it is sure to knock the breath out of you. But you will get used to such ideas by and by. Here is where fentologic will be of great help. If you have skipped the introduction part of this look, it's better to go back and get familiarized with fentologic. This is how fentologic explains the spreading out of the electron.

Place a small piece of camphor in your bedroom. Observe how the purifying scent spreads out and fills up the space inside. Keep it open, without a wrapper. A time will come when there will be no camphor left. It would have spread out throughout your house and, if the windows are open, into the town. We could have suggested petrol instead of camphor, but it is a bit dangerous (though it would have evaporated faster and convinced you more deeply). There are many more such substances that spread out – the experienced reader knows it better than we do. The point is that some substances don't stay in one place. Some spread out fast, some slowly.

The foregoing analogy will help the reader understand how the electron spreads out. The process is similar to what is called "sublimation" in chemistry. The illustration is one of the pointing arrows in the imagery we discussed earlier.

Let's examine the spreading out phenomenon from another perspective. Take a bucket and fill it halfway with water. Using your hand or a pad, stir the water round and round vigorously. You've created a mini whirlpool. Observe now that the water level in the bucket rises up the inner surface of the bucket. This is a famous experiment attributed to Sir Isaac Newton. His intention was to prove a point regarding motion and absolute space. We are not contemplating anything so grand. The point is that when the water in the bucket starts spinning, the water particles are subjected to a force called centrifugal force; a force that acts radially (similar to an infinite number of spokes on a wheel), pushing the water molecules away from the center. It is this force that pushes the water up the vertical wall of the bucket. The same principle is utilized in the operation of centrifugal pumps that supply water to the overhead tanks of your residential area.

The point of interest here is that if the wall of the bucket is not there to oppose the radially outward moving water, the water will keep spreading in wider and wider circles. A more powerful image will be that of a cyclone, which could often spread more than a thousand miles across. Let this image of the enormous force generated by spin be firmly imprinted in your mind.

Now, let's return to the electron. Electrons inside an atom are spinning too, in addition to orbiting the nucleus, and they do so at enormous speeds. Do we need to paint a more detailed picture? We believe not. The tremendous spin of the electron will create havoc. If there is no "wall" to contain it, the stuff, the essence, the mass of the electron will spread outward and outward, at least at the speed of light, long before you have finished exclaiming "oh my gosh." That "wall" which contains the spreading stuff of the electron is the electron shell.

Satisfied? Perhaps some astute readers are not. They may ask, "What about particles that do not spin?" It is customary to greet such questions with the remark, "Good question." Fentologic gently nudges these questioners to move on to the third arrow tip of the now familiar diagram.

Let's forget about the electron for a moment. Take any particle, fundamental or otherwise (fundamental being the better option because you cannot get more fundamental than the fundamental). Now, what is the most fundamental fact about the universe? Energy! Every conceivable thing in the universe, whether it's a particle, non-particle, matter, dark matter, field, wave, or anything that can be conceived as having existence, is energy in one form or another. "Existence is energy" is another famous dictum of Jestimedes, also known as Jestus and Bagdenborg. In fact, we do not even need Bagden's dictum to understand the indispensable existence of energy.

Energy is like a tiger kept on a leash. The moment you remove the leash, the tiger bounds where it wishes. Similarly, energy, if unleashed, bounds where it listeth; and it listeth to go all around, everywhere. "To the edges of the universe," as Bagdenborg was fond of saying. We make no apologies for repeating that everything is energy, especially fundamental particles ("Energy in its primordial form," another saying by Jestimedes). Therefore, if the particles (primordial energy) are not contained, chained, leashed, bound, packed, encased, or enclosed, nature itself dictates that they will spread out uniformly in all directions until they become indistinguishable from the body of the universe itself.

Pause here to admire the beautiful ("elegant") syllogism of fentologic. Existence is energy. Energy spreads out uniformly all over, tending to become formless. If there is to be a form, energy should be contained. There should be a container. That container is the shell – QED. This, in a nutshell, is Bagden's General Theory of the Cosmic Shell.

We ask you to hop to the next arrow tip so that you may glean other aspects of the shell. A little digression of an introductory nature is needed here. Initially, man observes an object in nature. The quest for more knowledge impels him to examine it more. This knowledge will be of the nature of the various properties of the object, such as its weight, size, smell, taste, and so on, and the behavior of the object under various conditions: what happens when it is heated, when it is struck, pushed, or in motion through the air, etc. These are only hints. Science grows this way—gravity, electromagnetism, thermodynamics, and so on. The descriptive part is kept to a minimum. But inevitably, especially as science is becoming more and more sophisticated, mathematics creeps in. It is like the proverbial camel being permitted to put its head inside the tent. There comes a stage when mathematics dominates the field of study to such an enormous extent that most often the illusion is created as if the mathematics of the object under study is more real than the object itself. This statement is not an exaggeration. Bagdenborg would have said that the mathematician, as far as his solutions and equations are perfect, logically consistent, and 'elegant,' will not care whether the object under study exists physically or not! JJB has used more acerbic words in his notebooks. We want to dilate a bit on this; please be tolerant. We want to bring home what we are going to state in the next paragraph. We need not ask if the reader is acquainted with the word "Quantum" as applied to physics. Nowadays, the word "Quantum" is bandied about willy-nilly. Everybody wants to grab that word for his/her glory: quantum healing, quantum touch, quantum leap, quantum mind, quantum anything. In quantum physics proper, there are certain classes of the most mysterious things called probability wave functions. To this day—almost a century after their birth—nobody knows what exactly they are. But they work like hell. They give results accurate to a billionth of a billionth decimal. For all you know, those probability functions could be not even ghosts but shadows of ghosts. But they work like hell. One famous scientist is alleged to have said in frustration, "Even if the creator incarnates on this earth and studies probability-waves, he would beat a hasty retreat vowing never to visit the planet earth again!" That must surely give you a good idea about the world of mathematics.

Let us return to the point in question—shells and JJ Bagden. JJ had a mischievous sense of humor. He constructed elaborate (abstruse, recondite, impenetrable, super complicated) mathematical structures to describe the cosmic shell and its descendants. The mathematics was self-contained, consistent, perfect, and irrefutable. (Sorry for the redundant adjectives, but they are meant to emphasize the great perfection achieved by BB Bagdenborg.) It was a very tough situation for those of his colleagues who had access to his equations. The mathematics was flawless, so they had to accept the Theory of Cosmic Shell. On the other hand, they cringed in horror at such an outrageous (in their opinion, according to their blinkered view) theory. If a crude pun is permitted, it could be said that they were shell-shocked. To sum up, it can be argued that the theory of Cosmic Shell stands within its own rights as a sublime mathematical theorem. If the practical, experiment-oriented physicists are riled, BBB/JJB's answer would be, "Well, it is up to you to discover it. Work hard, gentlemen; keep at it as long as it takes. It is my promise that you are bound to discover it sooner or later." He would encouragingly point out to them that a good many discoveries in science were made after they were theorized first—a couple of them, decades after the birth of the theory. We have no other option but to acquiesce, especially when we think of the "god's particle." It was postulated first and was discovered many decades later, just recently. This is nothing when compared to the theoretical frameworks of recent modern physicists. Furious research has been going on in what is called string theory. (If you are hearing that name for the first time, for God's sake, don't be alarmed. It has got nothing to do with G-strings.) The theory proposes an idea that will propel your brain into super vertigo.

The theory assures us that our mundane world of three dimensions, which humans have been experiencing for thousands and thousands of years, is actually made of TEN (ten, ten, that is correct) dimensions. We know only three dimensions—front, side, up. It is impossible even to imagine what the other six, apart from time, are or where they are. As if that were not enough, "improvements" have been made on that theory. The latest wisdom tells us that ten was wrong. Sorry, it is actually eleven! Even if you inject yourself with psychedelic drugs, we doubt whether you will be able to imagine, let alone understand, what those extra seven dimensions are. Physicists, serious, dedicated men, are working on even far stranger theories. We don't want to further tax your already spinning brain. Let us take up such matters when you are more relaxed. In passing, we just want to mention that no experimental verification has been done about those spooky dimensions as of date. They have been working on the mathematics itself for more than forty years, and still, it is far from being completed. And those brave men are convinced that the universe must be made of eleven dimensions. Because the mathematics demands it.

Now, compared to the foregoing theories, Bagdenborg's theorem of the shells is far simpler, down-to-earth, and homely. His mathematics is complete; it does not need any further additions or alterations. This fact alone weighs heavily on his side.

Proceed to the next arrow tip, fentology gently holding you by the hand; its soft, love-filled touch filling you with assurance.

Milk and cream:

Pour some quantity of milk into a vessel and place it on your hotplate. Watch it grow hotter and hotter. What happens? When the milk reaches a certain temperature, you can see a layer of cream forming on the top surface of the milk. Quite a commonplace phenomenon, isn't it? The thing to note, fentologic asks you gently, is that the layer of cream is not extraneous to the milk. The layer of cream on the top surface of the milk was formed out of the milk itself. That is the point of relevance to us—the internal process occurring in the content itself is responsible for the formation of a layer seemingly different from the content but actually a part of the content itself.

Another analogy may help you further. That cobweb in the ceiling of your house came out of the internal contents of the spider over there. The silk came out of the internally processed contents of the silkworm.

Such analogies will be of use in gaining insight into the formation of the electron's shell. Bagden's laser-like insight arrived at the surprising conclusion ("not all that surprising") that the electron's shell—as in the above analogies—was formed out of the content of the electron itself. It was genius. The rest was easy. Introduce a few (minimally required) parameters into the energy field, the content of the electron itself, and the derivation and characteristics of the enclosing shell will automatically come out of the mathematical equations. Bagdenborg did a thorough job of it. One small step, as it is said, leads to another bigger step. We have already related how Bagden raced forward, formulating the calculations for the shells of all particles and systems, crowning his achievement with the grand theorem of the cosmic shell.

Nailing Entropy

Science does not embrace the concept of God ; its typical stance is that it operates effectively without the need for a divine presence. Yet, within science, there exists a deity of sorts known as entropy. Much like it is challenging to fathom God and His mysterious ways, understanding entropy is equally enigmatic. We don't intend to bewilder the reader with intricate, convoluted explanations. to say that the god of entropy wields a terrifying weapon known as the Second Law of Thermodynamics and ruthlessly penalizes anyone who dares to challenge it.

The official explanation of entropy is that it serves as an indicator of "disorder" in a system—this is the fundamental concept. Volumes have been written on this subject, including an ironclad mathematical formula devised by the renowned scientist Boltzmann. The primary purpose of introducing entropy here is to acquaint the readers with what we might call the eleventh commandment. This commandment states that within the universe, entropy always increases—relentlessly and irrevocably. Don't trouble yourself too much about breaking this law and invoking God's wrath upon you. To simplify, this means that, on a universal scale, the overall level of disorder continuously grows. Here, "disorder" encompasses all the particles and constituents of the universe, along with their physical attributes such as motion, velocity, temperature, position, and so on.

Now, many people hold ambivalent attitudes toward entropy. Some find it fascinating, while others do not. Some grasp its concept, while others remain perplexed. JJB belonged to the former category. While contemplating his shell theory, he found an opportunity to challenge entropy. (We do not know whether God's wrath descended upon him or not.)

Once again, we ask you to go back to the arrows image and have a look at the electron shell from the tip of one more arrow; from entropy's angle of vision.

Recall that we said the content of the electron is energy. Got it? Now, follow this beautiful paradigm ensuing from the fertile womb of fentologic. In passing, it is to be stated that "fentologic" was the great invention of Jestus Jesticus Bagdenborg, a most revolutionary improvement on logic that can be deployed to combat any kind of situation involving hard logical propositions, problems in science, or any problem in general. Let us proceed, now, to the syllogism constructed by Bagden.

The electron, as we have already noted, is energy in a bundle, however small the electron may be (its radius is estimated to be around 2.82X10-15 meters). Don't be fooled by its minuteness. We digress again, but never mind. It is worth to know an electron's power. Have you ever slipped and fallen down from the landing of a staircase? Have you by any chance taken a drop down from the tenth floor of a building? (God forbid!) Imagine the damage done to your body. That is the power of gravity. Gives the shivers, doesn't it? But compared at the subatomic level, size to size, the force of the electron is trillions of times more; much more. (About 1, followed by 40 zeros!) That is the power of the electron.

Now, with such enormous energy inside it, entropy of the entropy guys would play unimaginable havoc. It would have a field day, creating the maximum amount of disorder inside the poor electron. However, the electron, as is well-established, is one of the most prolific constituents of matter in the universe and, more importantly, one of the most stable particles. How can that be? It can only be stable if there is some mechanism that can keep its disorder to stay within itself. In such a scenario, fentologic shows that disorder (inside the electron), having reached a maximum amount of disorder, cannot proceed further and stays put. It reaches a permanent state, which is stability, which is order! It is like nailing entropy, like putting a tether around its neck. This kind of condition can only be obtained if the electron is a closed system. That is what Bagden's electron shell does. QED – Quod erat demonstrandum.

On to the next arrow tip. There are umpteen numbers of arrows like this, all eloquently, frantically spelling out the burden of one song—"shell, shell, shell." We can enumerate all of them, but we feel we have firmly established the point. So, let us look at the shell, the necessity, the inevitability of it for just once more.

Fentologic lovingly guides us along the route of inspired thinking. Begin with the universe. We mean all of it, the entirety of it in one all-encompassing glance. What happens? There will be the whole of the undifferentiated universe, and nothing else. There will be nothing else to speak of—no you, I, he, she, it, they. That is to say, there will be one and only one object. The immediate response is to say, "But the universe contains uncountable objects." Yes, of course.

Yes, take any object, say a galaxy. If we consider it as a separate object, we must be able to recognize it as being apart from (or within) the universe. How are we able to do it? We are able to do it because we are able to discern a boundary for the object. Galaxies, stars, planets, Earth, the billions and billions of objects of the Earth, all have boundaries that set them apart from other objects. Boundary, that is the operating word. Need we say more? Yes, only that the electrons too have boundaries (shells), the protons have, the neutrons have—anything that dares to declare that it is a separate entity has a boundary. "It is all as simple as that," announces fentologic, takes a bow, and exits. Yours to ponder, yours to wonder at the beauty of it.

The shell in action

After firmly installing the shell on its pedestal, Bagderborg proceeded to examine its action.

What does it do? What does it not do? It does nothing, it does everything.

The shell actively serves as a "wall" of demarcation, so that the particle becomes a separate unit from the rest of the universe, but it does not prevent the particle from reacting with or responding to the environment in which it happens to be. Thus, if two electrons meet, they repel each other. Their shells, in no way, interfere with this action. If an electron meets a positively charged particle, both are attracted towards each other. Their shells, in no way, interfere with the mutual attractive force. This is not surprising if we remember the analogy of the milk and cream. The layer of cream is there on the surface of the milk, but it allows the heat from the milk to be radiated.

The point to be underlined is that the shell absorbs the interior energy (of various forms) and radiates the same uniformly in all directions. This is possible because the shell is made of the same content as that of the particle. This phenomenon resolves the "particle versus wave" duality in an elegant manner. (We will elaborate on it in another chapter).

Bagdimedes discovered an interesting feature of this radiation. The shell radiates a very tiny portion of the energy it receives from the content back to the interior while allowing the major portion to propagate outwards – 99.998877665544332211 percent. This aligns with what he found about the cosmic shell too. (Recall that we mentioned earlier that the cosmic shell is radiating a disproportionately huge amount of energy outside of it, as compared to what it was reflecting back into the cosmos). Where does this cosmic radiation go? What happens to it if it is going beyond the universe? These questions appear to be tough to answer. Bagdimedes has the answer – Thus far, and no further. "Such questions are beyond the scope of science," is the direct quote from his notebook. It is the most astonishing, most disliked, hated, derided quote in scientific literature. Bagdenborg was a pragmatist too. He did not discourage or disapprove of technological innovations. But, as regards fundamental scientific research, he drew a firm line. (In the Indian sub-continent, they call such a line, "Lakshman rekha." His attitude remained a mystery even to his most ardent admirers.

Let us leave the man's attitudes and eccentricities for the present. Bagenborg found another surprising property of the shell. More than the contents of the shell, it was the shell itself that represented the uniqueness or the identity of the particle it enclosed. This too is not far surprising. Both the tennis ball and the ping-pong ball, as in our previous analogy, contain the same matter, air. But their physical behaviors such as bounce, spin, speed, resistance to movement, etc., are different because of the difference in the shells that enclose them. The analogy, though rough, holds good for the Bagdenborg shells (to name them as such in his honor).

To be more explicit – the electromagnetic and gravitational properties of a particle, etc., can be represented by equations that are derived from the "structure" of its shell. A further generalization was found. The equations for all the particles are almost similar in form. The differences in the outputs (which identify a particular particle as such) are obtained by varying certain parameters of the "structure" of the shell – we again draw your attention to the "materials" that make up the shell of a tennis ball and a ping-pong ball. So simple, yet so profound.

Three is Enough

Starting from the electron and ending at the universe, the range (of the shells) appears to be enormous – in fact, humongous. But if you ponder for a minute, you will realize that the hugeness of the range is one of size. Apart from that, the other differences in the shells' properties are not much.

So, how do we derive, or describe these seemingly various properties in a manageable form? Here too, the stroke of genius exhibited by Bagdimedes is evident. "Hiding in plain sight" is one of his favorite aphorisms. "Nature has strewn abundant clues all around us. We only have to look," he wrote in his notebooks. "Economy is the key word. Nature loves economy. Nature achieves abundance and infinite variety employing severe economy."

Let us see what he meant. Look at all the flowers and the huge variety of colors they exhibit. Look at the birds and the astonishing range of colors they possess in their feathers and bodies. The illustration can be replicated in almost everything animate and inanimate around us. In fact, your TV brands boast of a "million colors" display.

Did that ring a bell? If you were a computer buff or an artist, you would have immediately caught on. All the colors (millions and millions) that the eye can see are composed of three basic colors, the primary colors: red, yellow, blue, RYB for short. By suitably mixing different amounts of these three primary colors, we can produce any shade of color we desire. In fact, the colors we see on the monitor of the computer are produced by a program that assigns an appropriate color to each 'pixel' by suitably altering the ratios of the red, green, and blue values assigned to it. Thus, an almost infinite variety is achieved by employing just three variable quantities, or parameters in science lingo. That is unbelievable economy on the one hand and the most beautiful paradox on the other hand. "Nothing to beat nature," Bagden wrote.

JJB drew his inspiration from this phenomenon. His fentological reasoning ran like this: The casing, the shell enclosing the variety of particles and systems was the common factor – like color in our previous example. If the shell exhibits different properties, all of them must be derived from a combination of three basic parameters, like the RYBs of color.

A small digression here, in the form of a relevant question: Why three, why not two? Those who object thus may point out that just two variables, zero and one, are enough to construct a great system of mathematics, that 0 and 1 are sufficient tools out of which the whole modern field of computers, programming languages, communication, and almost all modern miraculous gadgets have been invented. To such an objection, Bagden's fentologic offers a fento-intuitive answer. The world we experience is a three-dimensional world. The binary mathematics of 0 and 1 belongs to an abstract field, and that makes all the difference. The most brilliant binary program is in unseen limbo until it is brought upon to act and manipulate a physical object. That is all. (In this context, Bagdenborg wrote a footnote in his book. Fento-intuition was what prompted Fermat to declare his famous last Theorem, to solve which, most gifted men spent more than two hundred years, entangled in webs of more and more complicated calculations. If only they had realized that, as Fermat no doubt did, the world we live in is of three dimensions, that his theorem was based on geometry, whose 'geo' is of three dimensions, they would have smiled in ecstasy at the simplicity of it.) Also, Bagdimedes had a strong mystical streak in him, which was apt to infiltrate at unexpected moments into his scientific studies. In one of his marginal notes, he had written down, "One is pure being, two is for generation, three is for proliferation." The sentence could have been copied from some ancient oriental text. So, three parameters were all that Bagdenborg needed, and three he chose.

He named these three basic ingredients simply as SS1, SS2, and SS3 (SS, for shell stuff). He disliked giving strange, silly names to scientific entities. His admirers have noted that during the course of discussion, if words like quark, gluon, up, down, black hole, etc., cropped up, he would knit his brows in displeasure. Science was a serious subject, and frivolity in employing scientific terms was in bad taste according to him.

One word of caution: These ingredients are not to be thought of as things different from the shell stuff itself – like "quarks" in the previous paragraph. SS1, SS2, and SS3 are the primary shells out of a combination of which all varieties of shells are made. They too are shells only, just as R, Y, and B are colors only. Bagdenborg formulated a series of mathematical expressions describing the outcome of "mixing" the three basic shell stuffs. The equations fill up hundreds of pages. His conclusions were thorough and indisputable.

Can the shell be observed?

The question is, of course, one of pure formality. As almost everyone knows, particles like electrons, protons, and neutrons are extremely tiny. We cannot observe them directly; not with the existing technology, and most probably not in the foreseeable future either. But their properties can be discovered, inferred (and put to good use through technology) by observing the effects they produce on interacting with other particles. To give a crude example, you cannot see photons (the particles of light) directly, but you can learn a good deal about light by passing it through a lens, a prism, when it strikes certain metals (which produce electricity), by its effect on a photographic film, and so on.

But detecting the shell even by such methods poses a problem because of a special reason. We found that the electron's shell – to take an example – represents the electron itself, that is to say, all the characteristics of an electron. So, if we set upon conducting experiments to discover the properties of the shell, we end up summing up the properties of the electron itself! A real tricky situation.

Bagdenborg's imagination is prolific. When confronted with impossible situations, he is ready with a dozen impossible solutions. ("To remove a thorn, use a thorn.") Of the many ways of detecting the electron shell suggested by him, we give here one that is nearest to being called practicable – almost, say. The method is akin to pinging – first developed during WWII for detecting enemy submarines. The ship's equipment sends down a certain range of frequencies through the water, which hit the enemy submarine and return. The echo is analyzed. This is similar to radar; only, radar employs electromagnetic waves. Using a similar idea, but employing different modern techniques, it has become a routine affair nowadays to scan almost every location inside the human body.

Bagdimedes' thought experiment can be described as follows. (Recall what we said earlier – that Bagden never bothered to step inside a laboratory). Isolate a single electron in a vacuumized tank. It is possible to produce single electrons – the technology exists now. Magnetic fields of appropriate strength are to be produced along the X, Y, and Z axes of the electron; three dimensions, in common parlance. The fields are such that they will repel the electron, which has a negative charge. The action is mutual. The electron's charge acts on the magnetic "probes" and alters them. The changes in the magnetic field can be measured and mapped. By incrementally rotating the detectors around the central electron, a 3D map of the electron's shell can be obtained.

Bagden envisaged further refinement too. By using certain techniques, the 'focus' and the depth to which the probing magnetic field penetrates could be controlled. Thus, 3D mapping of the shell at different depths can even give us its thickness. But carrying out the experiments at such small scales is beyond the capability of present day technology. Remember that the radius of an electron itself is of the order of 10^-15 meters. The shell thickness will be around a hundred thousand times smaller than this!

Unfortunately, as of the date, nobody has volunteered to carry out the experiment. Bagdenborg is, of course, divinely unconcerned. His convictions are deep-rooted, as deep as the womb of the subatomic particles he explored.

Endnote: Thinking about light, the readers may be reminded of its properties like reflection, refraction, diffraction, polarization, etc. These properties have been thoroughly studied, and innumerable experiments have been conducted. So, the readers may naturally become anxious if the shell theory of Bagdenborg may come into conflict with the results of the proven experiments. Rest assured, Bagden says, the shell of the light particle, in no way hinders light from behaving as it has been behaving since the beginning of creation. He is not interested in experiments, he insists. According to him, when you truly understand the inner essence of something, it is unnecessary to "indulge in the vicarious pleasure of conducting experiments". Any and all experiments have to bear out the truth of the theoretical insight; otherwise, the experiments are polluted. The last sentence may send a chill down the spines of traditional scientists. But that is Bagus Bagliochus Bagdenborg for you. He gleefully draws your attention to the hectic cerebrations of the String theorists. Nobody has seen or detected a string so far – except the "G" variety, let alone the tenth or eleventh dimension. But that has not stopped these theoreticians from their fierce computations for the last thirty years.

Chapter 2

A MATTER OF WAVES; WAVES MATTER

There is a strange bond between Nature and man. Nature has continuously fascinated man and, at the same time, perplexed him. The more a man delves into its secrets, the more puzzles it throws at him. Nature seems to take a perverse pleasure in teasing man, especially the inquiring man. The funny paradox is that the more you inquire, the more puzzled you get. It is one of the basic tenets of Bagdenborg's fentologic. A whole book could be written on the subject, but we don't want to digress unnecessarily.

For the present, let us focus on two simple topics, such as matter and waves, and see what insights Bagdenborg's fento-science offers us.

In broad classification, the world we live in and experience consists of matter, life, and mind. Let us leave out mind in this context, as we are talking about physical sciences. We can exclude life too for the same reason. Besides, life needs matter to manifest – and most scientists also equate mind with the brain. (Forget ghosts, fairies, and spirits).

Next, ponder this matter of matter. Taking the exclusions we made just now into consideration, the world, or the universe, is made up of matter only. We learn about the existence of matter through sensory inputs; we see matter, feel it by touch, and proceed along the fentological route and discard the last three in the previous sentence. That leaves us with sight and touch.

There was a reason for selecting sight and touch. It is these two faculties that strongly create a sense of "solidness." If you see something, if you feel its touch, you are sure it must be "matter." Permit us to elaborate a wee bit. You see a fifteen-foot stone wall in front of you. You know it is "solid," and you know you cannot walk through it (unless you have imbibed a good quantity of a psychedelic drug). More proof; if you attempt to go through it, you will end up in the nearest hospital with a broken septum. At the mountain resort, you come across a huge boulder. You know you cannot push it aside. At its base lies a smaller piece of rock, weighing about two hundred kgs. You know you cannot lift it. A few feet further, there is a pebble. On your way back, you step on it, and nothing happens to you, except that you could sense that there was something solid under your foot.

The above examples were put forth to illustrate two important properties of matter – size and mass. And, of course, "solidness." This sense of "solidness" is important. It is at the core of all our experiences of the world. It is what gives you the assurance that the world is really out there; that it is made of stuff we call matter. The stuff – matter – can be in three states, as every schoolboy knows. Solids, liquids, and gases are the different forms of matter. They are all "concrete," they exist out there; we have to repeat it.

Even at the earliest stage of his curiosity, man found that big-sized matter (objects) could be broken down by cutting, crushing, grinding, etc. Even though his tools were crude, it was not difficult for the early man to conclude that all matter could be reduced to dust. Later, the Greek thinkers, who had a flair for abstract thinking, speculated on this feature of the reducibility of matter's size. Theoretically, if stone can be ground into powder, the powder could be ground to fine dust, and that dust could be ground to still finer forms of dust…and so on. It was obvious to them that this process of reduction in size cannot be carried on infinitely. It has to stop at some point. There comes a stage when dust/particles cannot be reduced further in size. They named such an irreducible particle as an atom. They concluded that the world of matter was made of such atoms.

Almost fifteen centuries later, the birth of science took place. From there on, science and mathematics progressed rapidly. Within a span of three centuries, the amount of scientific and mathematical knowledge had increased to an unbelievable extent. It was discovered that even though the world consisted of an uncountable number of items – a grain of sand, metals, non-metals, all the daily artifacts and articles man uses; the list is truly endless – they were all actually made of about one hundred and odd "basic" atoms only, called elements. This knowledge is very basic now. But the discovery of this knowledge must be rated as one of the top-most achievements in science. These one hundred and odd elements can exist individually by themselves (very few do), or two or more or more of them combine to form compounds. (Their numbers are vast, too vast to enumerate). Please see the grandeur of the discovery. All the millions and millions of things you see in the world are made out of these elements only – just 118 of them!

As we said, Nature does not give up its secrets easily. But man's curiosity is also not easily satisfied. Science dug deeper and found more surprising discoveries. By the end of the early twentieth century, even these varieties of elements were "broken down." It was found that the atoms of all elements were made of only two essential components: a central "nucleus" and one or more "electrons" orbiting around the nucleus. The nucleus held within it two particles called "protons" and "neutrons."

That is all. All elements are composed of electrons, protons, and neutrons. However, the number of these fundamental particles varies from atom to atom. For example, the atom of hydrogen, the lightest of the elements, contains one electron, while one of the heaviest, the atom of Uranium, contains 253 electrons, and so on for various elements.

Science had stumbled upon another grand vision, even grander than the previous one, which we are not at all sorry to repeat. Think again and behold the unbelievable beauty and simplicity of it all. Everything you see in this world (the million million things) is actually made up of only three particles: electrons, protons, and neutrons!!

This is how Nature plays with man. First, it offers him euphoria and a sense of complete understanding. Then, gradually, more teasers are thrown in, bringing a fresh wave of dissatisfaction and puzzlement. (In those heady days, a famous quotation from a reputed scientist was making the rounds, claiming that all that was to be known was known, and that science could be wrapped up soon!)

Soon, experiments and observations forced the scientists to add more particles to the list in order to explain many subatomic phenomena. The list kept on growing: quarks, muons, mesons, photons, gluons, gravitons—all sorts of strange particles were added to the list. The root of the universe seemed simple, and then it branched off into more complexities.

The foregoing brief synopsis of discoveries was presented to illustrate one aspect of Nature – the "matterness," the solidity of the world. True, we descended from mountains and molehills, delving deeper and deeper into unimaginably small structures like molecules, atoms, and nuclei, and found the tiniest of particles. Yet, they were still particles, as when we say, "A particle of matter." Matter, you see, was still there.

The agony

The seeds of the coming agony were lying dormant for more than two thousand years. A particular kind of ore with a strange property was known in those days. It was named 'loadstone.' It possessed a strange property – it could attract iron pieces or powder from a distance! The word 'magnet' became more popular. The strange power of attracting iron was dubbed 'magnetism.' (The compass was invented utilizing the magnet's other property of pointing its one particular end always towards north when freely suspended.)

The next chapter in our intriguing story was written by the apple. No, not the apple Eve gave Adam so lovingly; the apple that fell on Sir Isaac Newton's head. Thereby the theory of gravity was born. Men were aware of gravity's existence, of course, from time immemorial – when the first man stumbled and fell, when the first baby accidentally slipped from its mother's arms. Since everything unsupported fell back to the earth, people ascribed a strange power to Mother Earth. One ancient philosopher even proclaimed wisely that all things fall back to the earth because everything belonged to Mother Earth. The genius of Newton lay in that, in an unprecedented flash of intuition, he ascribed the power of gravitation not only to earth but to all bodies in the universe – the sun, the moon, the planets, to matter itself. What he did next was, laying once and forever the unshakeable foundation for modern science. Along with physical description and experimentation, he formulated exact mathematical equations describing the laws of gravity and motion of bodies. If we are permitted to use poetic similes, we would say that Newton set off the Big Bang in science, and science has been expanding ever since.

Another chapter in the story was added with the discovery of electricity. In the initial stages, it was what is now called static electricity; that is, static, not moving. It is produced when certain materials rub against each other – like a glass rod against silk cloth. The nylon dress you wear, while you walk, rubs against your body and gets charged with "static" – a familiar phenomenon everybody is aware of. After the static kind, the moving kind, "current," was discovered. It is also one of the discoveries that changed our civilization forever. (In the present age, we simply cannot live without electricity. If there is no electricity, our world will come to a stop.) In the early stages itself, it was found that electricity and magnetism were interlinked. Moving electricity produces magnetism. This phenomenon is behind all the great inventions of the modern world: radio, TV, communication, remote control, cell phone, internet, and so on. With the advent of atomic physics, it was soon found that the electrons, the particles which orbit around the nucleus of the atom, as we said in the beginning, are the source of electricity (and magnetism). The agents that carry the radio, TV, and cellphone signals, etc., were found to behave like waves and were promptly christened as electromagnetic waves. Waves propagate – they travel in space. Almost simultaneously, it was discovered that light too was an electromagnetic wave. Electromagnetic waves come in different shapes – they can vary in frequency and wavelength, and the range of variation, fortunately, is huge. Otherwise, we would not have all those umpteen forms of inventions like radio, TV, satellite communication, etc. We have kept the description of the scientific discoveries as short as possible, with the intention being to focus on a very intriguing aspect, from which the agony began to germinate, after the initial bursts of ecstasy.

Where did the punch come from?

You are engaged in a drunken brawl... oops, sorry, undo/delete that. Tim and Tom are engaged in a drunken brawl. A lightning-fast left hook lands on Tim's jaw, causing him to fall to the ground, seeing stars. He does not know where the jawbreaker came from. However, you, who were watching it, know. You saw Tom's fist moving up in an arc, and you saw it land on Tim's jaw.

The point is that a force was transmitted to a body (Tim's jaw). Another body served as the agency (Tom's fist) that transmitted the force (knockout punch). In the physical world, force is transmitted through an agency, through direct, immediate contact, much like a bullet fired from a pistol. An arrow from a bow, a shock wave from a blast, tsunami waves, and a stone from a sling are further examples of force being transmitted through an agency (medium, as it is termed).

Now, let's replace Tim and Tom with a magnet and an iron piece. When you keep the iron piece at an appropriate distance from the magnet, the iron piece will immediately move and become attracted to the magnet. The magnet and the iron piece are physically apart; there is nothing connecting them. Yet, the iron piece moves – force is transmitted. There is no visible agency. How do we "explain" this? In ordinary language, you can say that the magnet has the power to attract iron, that it "attracted" the iron piece. However, that explanation doesn't align with scientific theories. You see, the universal method of transmitting force is like this: there is a source of power (the stretched string of the bow), and force is transmitted from the source to another body (the arrow). The body, acting as the agent or medium, delivers the force across space (the arrow travels and hits the target). In the case of the magnet (the source), we do not actually see any such agent or medium. This type of action was termed "action-at-a-distance." It was impossible to explain this kind of action-at-a-distance using any known theory at that time.

In passing, we would like to touch on one exquisite paradox; Nature's irony is a better way of putting it. When one discovers something new, there is excitement, pure pleasure in the act – that is ecstasy. Later on, you try to "explain" the phenomenon, tentatively at first, and gradually with assurance. After some years, or even decades, another person re-examines your explanation (theory) and finds some loopholes in it. Or, your explanation does not align with some latest discovery. You have to start theorizing, finding a correct explanation all over again – that is agony. Usually, the ecstasy belongs to the discoverer, while the agony – protracted and never-ending – belongs to the theoretician. The "wow!" part is easy; the "how?" part is tough.

Let us return to the action-at-a-distance puzzle. To explain the phenomenon of a magnet attracting a piece of iron from a distance, new concepts of "lines of force" and "field" were introduced. It was found that a bar of magnet always consisted of two distinct points at its two ends, called poles, one north and the other south. The magnet was supposed to produce a "magnetic field" all around it, and "lines of force" joined its two poles. A similar action occurs when electricity flows through a coil of wire; a magnetic field is produced, with lines of force joining the two ends of the coil. Under controlled conditions, this magnetic field can be transmitted across space (to infinite distance, theoretically). The standard names for these waves and fields are electromagnetic waves and electromagnetic fields. Mathematics is justly called the queen of science. A full-fledged theory of electromagnetic waves was developed using mathematical equations, with Maxwell being the chief architect. An exciting and surprising conclusion awaited at the end of this theory/discovery. Light too was found to exhibit the properties of an electromagnetic wave! Now, light is not treated as something separate, like 'light', but only as an electromagnetic wave. Detailed mathematical treatment has been performed on this (light) electromagnetic wave, and innumerable calculations and experiments have been done.

Earlier, we spoke of apples falling down and of the force of gravity. Well, gravity also exhibits the mysterious "action-at-a-distance" property.

So, a gravitational field was introduced to explain this strange action. As usual, mathematics proved useful in describing the gravitational field and gravitational force. Every science student worldwide is familiar with Newton's laws of motion.

To sum up, we observe the interplay of forces in two ways. One, which we can conveniently label as "mechanical," occurs through perceivable, tangible matter (such as arrows, bullets, air, and water). The other, known as "action-at-a-distance," occurs through relevant fields (such as electromagnetic and gravitational). Light is categorized as an electromagnetic wave.

Just when everything seemed to be going smoothly, a controversy emerged. The source of this controversy was light, specifically its nature. When you light a candle, the room fills with light in all directions, suggesting that light must be a wave. To counter this argument, consider lighting an incense stick, which fills the room with perfume composed of molecules. From this analogy, one could argue that "light" is also made of particles. In fact, the eminent Sir Isaac Newton himself believed that light consists of particles. Huygens developed a wave model of light to explain certain phenomena, such as the refraction of light through a prism. The wave-like nature of light is also evident in cases of diffraction. Light spreads out in waves when passed through a very tiny hole and bends around small obstacles in its path. When a beam of light strikes the surface of a mirror, it is reflected like a particle, behaving as a solid object – with the angle of incidence equal to the angle of reflection. This behavior is characteristic of a particle. The pendulum of opinions continues to sway back and forth. There is a phenomenon known as the photoelectric effect. When light falls on the surface of certain metals, it generates electricity, causing electrons in the metal to be knocked out. Albert Einstein successfully explained this phenomenon, earning him the Nobel Prize. In his explanation, Einstein demonstrated that light behaves like a group of particles. He termed them "photons," and the official name for the light particle is now "photon."

But historically, the most famous experiment on light was Young's double-slit experiment. It could truly be said to have opened Pandora's Box. The "agony" we have been so often referring to reached its climax with the double-slit experiment. Things became so complex and complicated that, as our hero, Bagdenborg put it, "The devil must have been mightily pleased."

Volumes have been written on the double-slit experiment. Innumerable experiments have been conducted. The experiment has taken many avatars since the original one conducted by Young in the early 1800s. The experiment changed the direction and nature of scientific inquiry too. A very brief description only will be given here.

A beam of light was directed at an opaque screen (i.e., it does not allow light to pass through) with two narrow slits, which could be closed or opened as desired. At a suitable distance behind this screen, another screen was placed so that the images formed on it could be seen. It could be a photographic film too, as in the initial experiments.

First, only one slit was opened, so that the beam of light could pass through and fall on the second screen. As expected, as "common sense" tells us, a clearly defined, single rectangular strip of image formed on the screen. That was not surprising. Next, the second slit too was opened. Now light could pass through two slits. In this case, common sense tells us that two strips of images would be formed. But what did actually happen in the experiment? Voila, instead of two separate, distinct images, a band of dark and light images was obtained! The experiment was conducted many times. It was the same result always – a band of successive light and dark strips formed on the observation screen. This kind of effect can only be explained if light behaved like a wave. The pattern of dark and light strips is called an interference pattern. Interference occurs when two waves meet each other. Observe water waves. They have high and low points, crests and troughs. So, when two waves meet head-on, the crest of one "cancels" the trough of the other. That is how the dark band forms on the screen. When the two crests of the waves meet in time, they reinforce each other. That is the bright band of light on the screen. Thus it was conclusively proved that light was wave-like in nature. But then, the photoelectric effect showed that light was corpuscular in nature. Dash it.

The story gets curiouser and curiouser as we proceed through the years, from the time of the original experiment. A doubt (a valid one too) may arise in the reader's mind that the beam consists of an innumerable number of particles of light, so that the huge number of particles as a group may exhibit the property of a wave – like the huge number of water particles in a wave of water, molecules in a wave of air. As technology advanced, in the latest state-of-the-art experiments, physicists have been able to fire single photons, one at a time through the slits. The result is the same – an interference pattern is created! The technical details are too complicated, so they are omitted here. But the conclusion, the formation of an interference pattern, has been proved beyond doubt. Remember they are firing single photons, i.e., particles. And particles are acting like waves! ("They are androgynous," was the tongue-in-cheek note penned by B.B.B on the margin of a textbook he was reading.)

The boffins didn't stop there. Their attention fell on the electron. The electron was a particle and it had a charge too. (It has a negative charge.) Just as with the photon of light, the physicists fired single electrons, one at a time at the (damned) double slits. Surprise, surprise! The electron particles too produced an interference pattern, proving that they too were both particles and waves at the same time. The "agony" had reached unbearable proportions.

Those were the days of intense excitement, frustration, and great intellectual efforts. "They had everything, except patience," was what Bagdenborg wrote in his diary. There was at least a modicum of justifiable reason for that. Because, in their haste to somehow solve the riddle of the particle-cum-wave paradox, the great intellectual community of physicists (some of the greatest in the history of science, no doubt) arrived at very bizarre and awkward (and inelegant too) solutions. It was accepted that at such tiny scales as of the subatomic particles, a particle could be a wave too. The mollifying modifier was that a "particle" was a "packet" of energy – a quantum packet. To explain the wave-like behavior of a particle, they formulated matter waves. Then "probability-waves" were introduced. The concept of the "probability-waves" will make you cry and smile at the same time. You will smile because the equations work like a charm – they give results to unprecedented levels of accuracy. You will cry because when you think of them and ask what exactly those mysterious and mystifying "probability-waves" are, you will not find an answer. A few of the top-most scientists have confessed that nobody knows exactly what the probability-waves are!! Bagdenborg, as usual, made a note, "If ever the aliens visit our planet and come to know of this theory, they will beat a hasty retreat and swear never to come back."

As usual, a good many books have been written on this theory and related topics like quantum theory, et al. We do not want to burden the reader with all that. Our main interest lies in introducing B.B. Bagdenborg's insights in these realms. Let us meet him. Come, and get yourself acquainted with his fascinating insights and charming logic that have broken all barriers.

Left-right jabs on particle theory

At his most brusque and severe form, Bagdenborg was wont to declare that there are no such things as particles. Yes, for that matter, there is no such thing as matter itself, if only you look at it from the true perspective. To dilate upon these ideas will lead us into the age-old dialectics of philosophy and mysticism – a vast and dense forest from which you cannot come out once you enter in. Let us better avoid that route. Let us take a concrete example.

a) The illuminated (but not so illuminating) globe

Imagine that you have a source of light of constant brightness. The source, for the sake of argument, is assumed to be a small globe, say six inches in diameter. It is radiating light uniformly in all directions. There is no obstruction for the passage of light at any conceivable distance, which means that the light is either directly observable by the human eye or can be detected by suitable instruments.

Now, consider the immediate surface of the six-inch globe. At any given moment, a fixed number of light particles will be emerging from its surface since the brightness is constant. Bagdenborg pleads, "Please follow the ensuing line of reasoning with close attention, at each step. And for God's sake, please do not digress or wander off raising objections or blurting out smart answers." We respect his pleading.

Let us say there are a hundred million light particles about to leave the surface of the globe. The exact number does not matter. The point is that the surface of the globe is tightly covered by the particles, and there is no gap. To make it easy for visualizing, consider just ten of these particles, still on the surface of the globe, about to travel outward. They are all packed tightly, and there is no gap in between any of the ten particles. (See Figure 1)

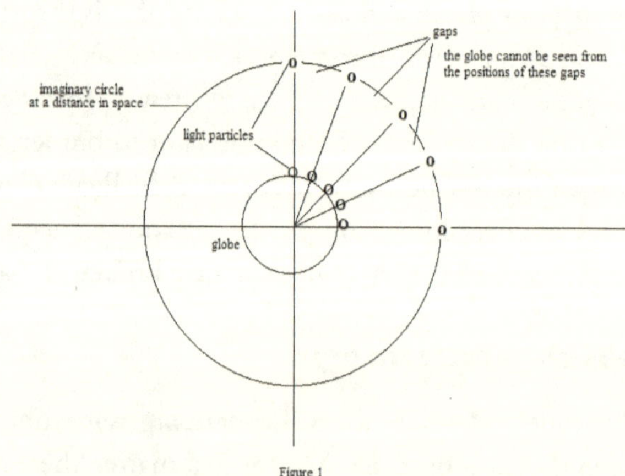

Figure 1

Suppose that the first batch of particles on the surface has now traveled for one second (about 186,273 miles). If you draw an imaginary sphere at that distance, a sphere with a radius of 186,273 miles, and locate our ten particles on that surface, they will be placed as shown in the figure.

Did it strike you? Observe the enormous gaps between each adjacent particle. Follow this. From the surface of the globe, ten particles journeyed outward, and these ten particles are at a distance of one light-second from the surface of the globe. All along the route, there can only be these ten particles and ten particles only. Therefore, there cannot be any particles at the locations indicated by the gaps. What does it mean? If an astronaut is orbiting our globe at that distance, he will not see (or detect) the globe whenever he is at the position of the gaps in his orbit. We considered only ten particles for our convenience. Actually, there will be millions of particles on the surface of the imaginary sphere, and there will be as many gaps. Whenever he comes across the gaps, the astronaut will not see the globe. So, in making one complete orbit, he will see the globe a million times, and he will not see the globe as many million times too! A bewildering situation! Suggestion – if you feel that the astronaut will be frightened by what he sees (and sees not), you may advise him to take a companion with him. Instead of the astronaut, if you deploy a super robot and make it take photos of the globe from all angles, you will get photos of a globe with a million punctures.

If you allow the light particles to journey for one year, the radius of the imaginary orbit of our astronaut (on second thoughts, better deploy a super robot) will be one light-year (186,273 X 60 X 360 X 24 X 365 miles). The corresponding gaps between the particles will be quite huge. Many solar systems could be placed in such gaps. The Earthlings of such solar systems will never be able to see our poor globe. That means you will never be able to communicate with them via signals (from the exact position of your globe, assuming it is fixed, not moving or spinning). This scenario can be expanded in many other ways, leaving you helpless on the floor rolling in laughter.

"I think I have made the point," writes the admirer (of B.B.B). He also further illuminates the MO used by him, "This method of picking holes (ha, ha) in a theory, in the good old days of Euclid, was called Reductio ad absurdum."

Obviously, the above scenario is absurd. Let us try to set it right. One way of doing it is to patch up the gaps, that is, not to allow the gaps to be formed. We need to do this because we intuitively feel that the globe must surely be visible from all angles and from all points at any distance we choose. In the example given, the distance of 186,273 miles was not chosen out of sheer perversity. Bagdenborg had a bee in his bonnet about the speed of light. (We will take it up later). In fact, you can fix the illuminated globe in your lawn and go around it from a reasonable distance. The same arguments we made in the case of the orbiting astronaut will hold good. But you will have to take a bit of precaution not to contaminate the experiment. You should create a perfect vacuum, with no other stray particles in your lawn, because if air is there between you and the globe, the emerging light from the globe will produce a scattering effect, and the experiment will definitely be polluted.

So, back to our suggestion of removing the absurdity of the gaps. ("Normalizing," as the physicist-cum-mathematicians are fond of saying.) Let us recall what we said about the gaps. We found that, at the distance of one light-second, there will be gaps between each of the ten particles we asked you to consider. Please refer to the figure, in case you do not remember. We also mentioned that we feel intuitively (and reasonably confidently) that we will be able to see the globe from all points of the astronaut's orbit.

That means we should be able to see the globe even if we are "standing" at the points where there are gaps.

But there are only ten particles.

There cannot be more than ten particles; it is impossible, it is out of the question. Nature does not allow it.

But we are sure we must be able to see the globe (from the gaps).

But how do you fill the gaps? How? How? How?

Ah, there, we got it! The ten particles will remain as ten particles only; we guarantee that. But the particles have grown in size (bloated, expanded, you see), so that in their expanded state, they touch one another, shoulder to shoulder, so that there are no gaps left!

That must be the logical explanation. As a corollary, we deduce that as the (light) particles travel further and further away from the globe, they have to keep on expanding in size. Since the energy of a given particle cannot increase, as the particle grows in size, the same amount of energy is distributed in a greater volume. That means it becomes dimmer, and that fits well with what actually happens – an object appears dimmer and dimmer as it moves further and further away from us.

"But the idea of light particles expanding in size is blatantly absurd," you will exclaim indignantly.

"Sorry," says the admirer (of BBB), "we just tried to neutralize the first absurdity – that of the gaps."

"In trying to remove one absurdity, you have given rise to a greater absurdity."

"That is one up on reductio ad absurdum."

Okay, we admit that both ideas are absurd. But then, go back and think about how the absurdities arose. They arose by assuming light to be made of particles.

Do we need to say more? The particle theory of light is hereby smashed forever – in spite of the billion-dollar equipment they have at CERN!

b) Particle disembodied

Fentologic respects humor. Normally, humor is frowned upon by knit-browed, lucubrating Science. But fentologic gently tickles your funny bone and assures you that humor often hides in its laughing folds "many a gem of purest ray serene," to borrow from the famous poet. So let us look at the plight of the poor light particle again from another angle.

No experiments this time. We just fire a salvo of logically armed sentences at the light particle, adopting the highly-revered Hellenic way of arriving at insights using the reasoning process alone.

Obviously, our first duty lies in understanding what we (sorry, we mean, they – the boffins) mean by a "particle." The word is well-established in scientific circles. We have "particle physics," "particle accelerators," and so on.

The general idea we have of a particle is that it is solid, it is matter, it is palpable, it is observable, and so on. However small it may be, it must have a definite size – otherwise, it is not a particle at all. It must have a marked boundary to identify it as being a separate entity from the rest of all else in the universe – this has been already said. Now, let us begin our thought experiment with the light source. We don't need a globe. Just imagine one single photon in empty space, standing still. You may object that a photon's nature is to move; that it cannot be standing still. Check out the latest news. They have been able to keep a photon still for almost three minutes.

A particle must be visible from all 360 degrees of angles. That is axiomatic. If the particle is not self-luminous, like that of carbon, it can be seen by illuminating it with light. If it is a self-luminous particle, like a photon, it must send light in all directions: up, down, left, right, front, and back. By light, we mean energy; electromagnetic signals/messages. If it is radiating energy, that energy, signal, message, whatever, cannot be from another particle because we are already considering a single, further indivisible, particle. Thus, if the single particle is emitting energy, there must be a source of energy within the particle! If you say that the particle itself is energy, then there is no particle as such; it has become disembodied, no shape, no place to stay. Permit us to repeat the subtlety of this argument. A glass globe will emit light (energy) if it is illuminated from within. A piece of coal cannot emit light by itself; it has to be heated. The heating coil of your room heater will emit energy only if it is heated by passing current through it. It is that energy – electromagnetic wave – that can radiate/move in all directions; not your inert piece of heating coil or the dead lump of coal.

"So, pray, tell us from where that energy is being supplied to the (light) particle?" asks Bagdimedes desperately.

"If you say the particle itself is energy, then, I am sorry for you. You are repeating the already repeated argument ad nauseam."

We are not repeating the same argument out of perversity. We want to induce a flash of intuition in the keen reader (that is you). If there has been a delay, here it is. The above arguments are eloquently shouting:

"There is only one way out of this dilemma – the shell theory of JJ Bagden!"

The photon has a shell, as we conclusively proved in the previous chapter. The shell behaves both like a particle and a wave, as has been clarified there. Truly, Bagden's insights are wonderful. The photoelectric effect can now go on working in peace. So may all the particle accelerators in the world.

Chapter 3

PARTICLE IN MOTION (A MOVING EXPERIENCE)

Have you ever watched snooker or billiards? The cueist strikes the ball on the baize table. The ball moves leisurely, hits another ball, is deflected, and touches another ball.

How about cricket? The bowler delivers a fast and furious delivery, and to his dismay, sees the ball soar into the sky and cross the boundary, while the thunderous roar of applause from the sea of spectators heaps insult over injury.

The common point we want to draw your attention to is that you, as a spectator, can see the object in motion. If the batsmen only were able to see the ball, then the game of cricket will quickly go out of business. You are able to see the ball and follow its path of motion. As said before, you are able to see it because light is being reflected off it; we said that earlier.

Let us bring back our favorite, the self-illuminated (that is, the energy-emitting) particle into the arena. We examined it earlier in its static state. You might have already demurred at least once or twice, that in nature, free particles of this size cannot be in a state of rest. So, let us consider our particle in motion – a truly moving experience.

Before we start moving

Bagdimedes (JJ Bagdenborg) is a holy terror when his intuitions are firing on all cylinders. He does not mind toppling a few established idols from their pedestals. He cannot hold back from thumbing his big, but well-sculpted nose at the great men of science. Truth is all he cares for. One of his admirers overdid it when he said that, for Bagdenborg, "The search, the search, the inspiration was the most important thing – the act, the process. Truth is secondary, a minor outcome of the process." Be that as it may, let us get acquainted with Bagden's notion of motion.

One of Newton's Laws of Motion states that an object in motion will keep on moving unless an external force opposes it. That is truly a beautiful and awe-inspiring insight. In everyday experience, we always see objects coming to a halt. However hard you may throw the stone, it always comes to rest. It is because an external force, gravity of the earth, opposes the stone's motion. Secondly, the frictional force, the friction from air, will eventually bring the stone to rest. But in outer space, where there is no friction, an object, once put into motion, keeps on moving. That is why we are able to send mission vehicles to the moon and Mars and put artificial satellites orbiting around the earth. Thus, your arrow, once shot in outer space, will keep on moving forever – unless it is gobbled up by the gravitational pull of a star or planet on its journey to eternity. A moving body keeps on moving – a truly fantastic insight. Pause.

Here, Jestus Jesticus Bagdenborg raises his royal nose (at whom, we do not want to say. You guess, and you will be correct.), and thumbs it, declaring cryptically, but firmly, "Insight, gentlemen, insight is the operative word. Has anybody ever shot an arrow into outer space AND TRACKED IT TILL ETERNITY?"

That accusation appears to be startling. It may seem silly or outright mad to some, but let us be honest and examine his question without prejudice. The plain answer will be that nobody has carried out the experiment suggested by him.

A very subtle point here: You may object that it is not necessary to test and track the motion of the particle/object forever. A reasonable time will suffice. More importantly, all the artificial satellites, all the space vehicles launched so far, point to the correctness of Newton's theory. To irrevocably clinch your argument, you will point out the mathematical formulas that describe the dynamics of an object.

Bagdenborg puts forth his side of the argument

a) What is "a reasonable time"? Compared to the age of the universe, the period of time from the Great Man2 up to now is ridiculously small. (Note: Jestus Jesticus Bagdenborg considered three men as the Greats: Archimedes, Newton, and Einstein.)

b) The mathematics of the dynamics of a particle (that is, objects in various states of motion) may be working fine. It's all a question of accuracy. Until

Einstein proposed his theory about gravity, Newton's calculations were doing fine. But Einstein's equations give you greater accuracy.

c) There is nothing like infinity in this world – as simple as that. A moving particle cannot keep on moving for an infinity of time.

Apart from the above points, Bagdenborg had other reasons to be convinced that a moving particle has to come to rest finally.

Physicists have been working diligently to comprehend the nature of mass and motion. At the most fundamental level, the universe, as we see it, reduces to these two properties.

To understand how a particle acquires mass, the physicist Peter Higgs proposed what is now called the Higgs field, which uniformly permeates the whole of space. The resistance that this field offers to motion "creates" mass in a particle. Sir Higgs was recently awarded the Nobel Prize. His theory was formulated almost fifty years ago, so Bagden was aware of the Higgs field concept. He turned the concept around 180 degrees to prove his point.

"Whether the particle acquires mass by moving through the ocean of the Higgs field is of secondary importance to me. What is important is that this very resistance that the Higgs field offers to movement will cause the movement to cease at some point in time," he wrote in bold letters in his notebook.

"That is a startling insight," his admirer remembers to have said to JJB.

"Not much," JJB had replied, "it gives me a bit of pleasure as I hoist them with their own petard."

That aside, the concept of the Higgs field takes us back to the good old days of Michelson and Morley. At that time, in order to explain the propagation of electromagnetic waves, it was necessary to postulate the presence of an all-pervading medium because "waves" require a medium to propagate. That medium was called ether. After the famous Michelson and Morley experiment to detect the existence of ether, the idea of ether as a medium was silently dropped. But the Higgs field revives the idea in a new avatar.

It seems as if Nature is still holding back a few dark secrets inside the already mysterious entity called space. Space seems to be incapable of being completely "empty."

Returning to the concept of the Higgs field and resistance to motion, let us see why Bagdimedes used the phrase, "hoist them with their own petard."

He had an altogether different and revolutionary insight as to why a moving particle in empty space has to come to a stop.

Even disregarding the reason discussed above, there is one dominating factor, which alone is enough to force a moving particle to come to rest. It is space itself. "Space," as a dimension, is a different matter, he claims. That kind of space belongs to the neither here nor there type of mathematically manipulatable domain of symbols. You can split space into three dimensions for mathematical convenience. But space as an all-pervading entity exists, he claims, by itself. Therefore, when a particle is moving in space (free space, empty space, vacuum, whatever you wish to call it), space itself offers resistance to the movement. This is logical, cogent, self-evident, and inevitable, as it should be. (JJB has added two dozen qualifiers. His admirer has edited them lest the readers be overwhelmed.) This single fact alone is enough to modify the law of motion of the Great Man2, as per JJB's contention. (Edt. – We feel B's use of "topple" is too strong. "Modify" is more appropriate.)

We said BBB was firing on all cylinders. Here is one more argumentary arrow from his quiver:-

What ensues now is a beautiful example of the felicity of his fentologic. The rungs in the ladder of his logic are built like this. By now, it must have become quite clear to the intelligent reader (and undoubtedly, you are one) that the so-called particle is only energy contained in a shell of its own making. The shell-particle is radiating energy into the world outside. This is its way, or rather, Nature's way of giving a separate ID to the shell-particle – of proclaiming its existence, to use a cutting-edge fentological expression.

Now, consider your particle moving dutifully in empty space without obstruction from any kind of interstellar objects. What is actually taking place? As the shell-particle is traveling, it is writing its signature all along its track. That is to say, it is radiating energy. That is all, and that is enough. There is nothing more to say, actually. But the kinetic momentum of the previous sentences compels us to carry on a bit further (ha, ha, LOL). On its long solitary journey, the particle is radiating energy, isn't it? Pray, ponder how long it can keep up the show. Its energy is finite. The energy is leaking away all the time. The leakage may be extremely minute. Yet, the shell-particle has to run out of its content, and your particle has to stop moving someday because on that day, there will be nothing left that can be called a particle.

It was a long journey for the particle. It has been a long journey for us too. See, from where we started our fentological quest and to what a fantastic end it has brought us!

This discovery of the death of the particle is one of the major insights of Bagus Bagliochus Bagdenborg. We will expound it again with its mind-boggling conclusion in the final chapter as a fitting end to the great man's contribution to science. The hasty reader is likely to identify this phenomenon incorrectly with radioactive decay. Radioactive decay is quite different from what we have described. That type of decay happens inside the nuclei of unstable elements like uranium, etc. Usually, alpha, beta, and gamma particles are emitted by the atoms of such elements. The reason for the decay is ascribed to the number of neutrons in the nuclei predominating the number of protons. What Bagdenborg has discovered pertains to individual particles, not the nucleus. Please note also the nomenclature used by him; it is 'death,' not 'decay.' This is a mind-boggling concept, to say the least.

Lemma

"Standing on the shoulders of giants" may be a familiar, trite phrase, but it is often true. A few, very few of Bagdenborg's admirers dared to attempt that act; dared, because the view from the shoulders of such a giant is apt to induce severe bouts of vertigo. One such modern-day Adeimantus to Socrates had a view from those shoulders. He was inspired by JJB's view of the particle in motion. He drew his conclusions and derived a lemma. Let us examine it now.

Visualize this scenario, and the lemma will become obvious to you too. The shell-particle is moving in space. It is radiating energy as it moves – that means energy in the form of waves. "Wave" is the operative word here.

Just hold it for a minute. We want to remind you of a more familiar picture. There is a pond full of clear, undisturbed water. Throw a pebble at the center of the pond. Circular waves of water begin to travel outwards from the center. Observe the progress of the waves. When a wave touches the edge of the pond, its shape is altered.

Now, please come back to our shell-particle, moving in space, emitting waves all around. According to JJB's theory, space is offering resistance. Repeat that. So, what happens? What else? The shape of the shell-particle's waves gets altered! When Adeimantus realized this, it was such a tremendous shock to him that he screamed. For minutes, his body could not stop shivering. He had to run to Bagdenborg's study for solace. Bagden heard him out, delivered an appreciative thump on his shoulder, and said in clipped sentences, "Nice work. Don't be frightened. Keep up the show. Go back," and promptly shut the door, pushing his acolyte out. The poor man was frightened, but he was thrilled too at his discovery. The thrill won over the fright. Soon he was back, perched on the shoulder of the giant. He saw more and promptly set about recording what he saw.

The waves being emitted by the shell-particle will get altered due to the friction offered to its movement by space. Could that be the cause for the famous red-shift effect occurring in the light reaching us from distant galaxies? On second thoughts, he realized it could not be. The waves of the moving particle (photons, in this example) will be undergoing a compression effect. So, their frequency must increase slightly. The effect will be opposite to that of a red-shift. He named it the V-shift; the V standing for violet.

Lemma to a lemma – shock waves

When his admirer had barged in with the exciting news of the shell-particle in motion, Bagdenborg was actually immersed in deep thoughts about gravitation. But that did not prevent him from deducing a second conclusion from what he heard from the mouth of his admirer. As soon as he shut the door behind his admirer, he rushed to his study and steadily wrote down, filling up many pages on one more interesting phenomenon produced by the particle in motion. As usual, his insight was remarkable. Let us consider, again, the extraordinary journey of the particle moving in space.

Here, we have to introduce Bagden's magic wand. It is a very powerful tool, and one of his favorites. Lift an ordinary, everyday occurrence and place it in new surroundings. Apply a familiar concept to a new/unfamiliar phenomenon. More often than not, you will get very surprising insights and easy solutions to difficult problems. This, in short, is Bagden's Magic Wand. Its application to situations is unlimited; your zeal and willingness are the only limiting factors. Let us now weave his Magic Wand and see what we get.

Familiar scene one: Throw a voluminous object in the air. As it moves, it pushes the air in front of it. If the speed of the object is high enough, you will hear the sound of the object moving. The sound is due to the air waves created by the object. The nature of the sound depends on the size, shape, and speed of the object; hiss, whoosh, whistle, boom, and so on.

"Boom," makes you recall another scene very familiar to us, modern men – it is the sonic boom. (Blessed be, Mach.) Sound, as you know, travels at a speed of 340.29 meters per second. An aircraft, while speeding in the air, produces airwaves in front of it as it pushes through. When the speed of the aircraft overtakes the speed of the sound waves it is producing (that is 340.29 meters per second), you hear an ear-shattering boom – the sonic boom as it is called. The boom is frightening when you hear it for the first time. Okay?

Now, lift this concept and place it in the new scenario – our by-now-familiar sight of the shell-particle moving at the speed of light. Not your paltry 340 and odd meters, allow us to point out, but at 186,273 miles per second. Recall that our object is moving against resistance; not of air but of space itself. Keep in mind the tremendous speed at which it is moving. Here comes the little subtlety. The shell-particle is radiating energy/waves. Space is offering resistance. So, the speed of the waves gets reduced, as Bagden has proved. But the object, the shell-particle is moving at its original speed of light, got it? So, what happens? The object, the particle overtakes the waves it is producing. This is analogous to the supersonic aircraft overtaking the speed of sound. Therefore, a VIDEO-BOOM IS created! This is the fantastic deduction that the admirer, Adeimantus, had missed, but which Bagdenborg instinctively obtained on the spot.

"Always go one more step further," is another one of JJB's many alluring aphorisms. He went – along the path of our moving light particle. He found out that a video-boom is created when the shell of the light particle overtakes the energy waves it creates. All this is the action taking place at one instant of time as we are examining the particle's journey. The space-drag effect affects the shell of the shell-particle too. So, the very next moment, (bear in mind that the time intervals we are considering are extremely small) as the shell slows down infinitesimally, its wave front catches up and goes ahead of the shell, establishing the original, normal configuration of the energy/wave front enveloping the shell, slightly ahead of it (naturally). But then, it is again subjected to the resistance from space.

Its speed decreases ever so slightly. The shell, moving at the speed of light, overtakes it again. There is one more video-boom! This cycle goes on repeating as long as the light particle keeps on moving. The net result is that when the light particle is moving, bursts of video-booms are produced continuously.

Mystery rays

The natural question that the intelligent reader (you) will ask is, "Why have the video-booms not been detected or recorded until now?"

Good question, as the TV show's anchor man would say. What is BBB'S answer, then? BBB leaves it to his acolyte to answer such minor questions. The admirer, now perched on the giant's shoulder, will reply thus.

His master's sense of humor has rubbed off on him. "But of course, naturellement, the Bagdenborg video-booms have been observed and recorded long ago. Some observatories have been studying the phenomenon for a long time. Only, they have not recognized the thing they have been studying!"

Still puzzled? Fret not. Ponder this, and you will recognize the wolf in sheep's clothing - pardon the archaic and somewhat misplaced idiom. It was pointed out that when the wave front of the moving shell-particle meets with resistance from space, the wavefront gets compressed ever so slightly, was it not? What does it mean? It means that the frequency of the light waves increases. (Again, fret not; we said frequency, not speed. The constancy of the speed of light is sacrosanct to all of you. Somewhere else, we will see what JJB has to say about that.)

So, if the frequency of the light waves has increased, what happens to them? What are they? There are, dear readers, many kinds of waves that have frequencies greater than that of light - THEY ARE THE COSMIC RAYS!! Physicists have been studying cosmic rays for decades, unable to fathom their origin. If only they had known of Bagdenborg's discovery of video-booms! The video-boom is the wolf in sheep's clothing that we alluded to. The scientific community can now heave a sigh of relief.

The final word – particle's last breath

We have been studying the exciting journey of the (light) particle for some time, discovering surprises at every stage. Let us take a look at its last lap. No, not a lap exactly. It is one hell of a straight line marathon, the mother of all marathons. (Remember what happened to Phidippides? Brush up on your Herodotus.)

We started this topic by highlighting the extraordinary discovery of JJB, that space itself offers resistance to the moving light particle, and that as a consequence, the particle has to come to a stop – like a train that has run out of steam, to use a whimsical analogy.

The analogy is not so whimsical at all. It was deliberately introduced to provide you with an innocent clue. Let us proceed now with Bagdenborg's analysis of the situation.

We beg your indulgence to bear with a final analogy. Analogies do offer us interesting perceptions. Recall Bagden's Magic Wand. Some time back, the manufacturers of a particular brand of ball-point pen claimed that you can draw a straight line one kilometer long using their pen. Imagine a black, thin straight line running that long. Apply Bagden's Magic Wand and see what happens at the end. The ball-pen was using up its ink all along, and then it gave up.

Now, replace the ball-pen's tip with our dear old light particle. Like the pen, it has been marking a straight line in space, not one kilometer, of course, but a good billion light-years. There are two acts in this drama. The first act, of course, is that the shell-particle comes to the end of its long journey. It stops. It is not an ordinary stop; it is a full stop with special significance. That is what the second act is about, and the specialty of the drama is that the second act is being enacted simultaneously, along with the first act.

Actually, it is very simple and logical. The shell-particle, as explained, has been emitting high-energy cosmic rays all along, the video-booms. Therefore, it is losing its energy. Right? The shell-particle started its journey with a definite, fixed amount of energy. That energy is getting depleted as it is moving. So, at the end of the journey, no energy is left.

So, in the end, only the particle shell remains, with no content inside. The poor shell now has nothing to guard itself against, nothing to protect – like the bare walls of an abandoned fort. In the final throes of its existence, the shell implodes violently and immediately explodes into one final burst of video-boom, singing its own requiem, and then there is no light anymore.

It is a tragic drama, fit to have been penned by the great Greek Bard. Truly, nothing lasts forever.

Whenever a new theory is put forward, it is natural that a slew of questions and doubts should arise. The most vociferous objection will rise from the camp of JJB's opponents. The immediate reaction will be to throw – rather, shoot – the law of conservation of energy at Bagdenborg. It is The Law, the most sacred law in science. As you all know, energy can neither be created nor destroyed. The universe, as science knows it, obeys that law under all circumstances. The lighted candle burns itself out. But the original content of matter is converted into light, heat, and gas (smoke), etc. The total energy of these products will tally with the original contents of the candle; energy is only converted, not destroyed. The tiny, planted seed grows into a huge tree bearing so many fruits, flowers, leaves, and branches. It is because the tree gathers energy from the earth and the sun and so on; energy is only gathered and processed, not created. This is how the physical universe runs – without exception.

So, if our dear light's shell-particle deletes itself in the end, how is it possible? The admirer's mischievous answer will be, to point at the products of video-boom – the cosmic rays. (We put in the adjective 'mischievous' deliberately. You will know why shortly.) Yes, of course, the energy of the light particle has been converted into the form of cosmic rays, even though the light particle has managed to delete itself out of existence. The opposition may breathe a sigh of relief.

Not for long! The admirer patiently explains thus. The story of the demise of the light particle is not a story of one particle alone. The same methodology of Bagden's fentologic-impregnated ratiocination applies to the by-product of the video-boom, the cosmic rays.

The cosmic rays too, if left alone and moving in empty space (like those that do not hit the Earth's atmosphere), will perform similar journeys like our dear light's shell-particle and will end up deleting themselves out of existence. From there, it is one more step to show that all energy-carrying particles will eventually fade into non-existence. Tell us, which particles do not carry energy? Coming to the nitty-gritty of it, Bagdimedes has proved that there are no such things as particles. All "particles" are energy systems enclosed in a shell. Thus, generalizing the case, it may be stated that all "particles" will eventually fade out.

By this time, (the admirer says) we can visualize the knit brows, the swollen red eyes, and the fast-beating veins on the temples of our brethren on the opposite camp. "All that energy gone! What happened? Where did it go? Where is the audit?" they will scream.

The answer gets very, very subtle. So we have to refer to J.J. Bag's original and unique exposition on this matter.

Bagdimedes' left brain whirred like a well-oiled machine in the Himalayan peaks of science. At the same time, his right brain was steeped deep in mysticism. His first preference would be to answer the question of an energy audit from his right brain – "That which came into existence has to go back to non-existence, eventually," or even, "Existence and energy are a play of the Grand Illusion."

But science and mysticism are poles apart. Mysticism may be willing to touch science, but science will not touch mysticism even with a barge pole. So, back to science, then; to Bagden's left brain in action.

Go back to the scenario of our shell-particle moving in space (smile). Recall, please, that we discovered that space itself is offering resistance to the particle's motion. There lies the key to your energy audit. It is simple, see. A rephrasing of our discovery will help you understand what happens. We showed that all particles will rub themselves out of existence against the friction of space. Therefore, gentlemen, it does not need Sherlock Holmes' assistance to see that the energy of all particles will be absorbed by space. So simple. Your audit is safe, once again.

The idea may seem outrageous to many – especially to the scientific brethren. Their naturally understandable and anxiety-laden questions will be, "Even assuming the preposterous idea, what happens to space? What does space do with all that energy? Where does it hide the energy?"

A calm and benign (not supercilious) answer from Bagdimedes is as follows:-

Oh, that? Smile again, please. All the energy that space has taken back into itself (sorry, if you do not like that phrase), is there in the open, but you do not see it! Three things...

1. Using an extremely minute part of that energy, space keeps itself a bit, a teeny-weeny bit warmer above the absolute zero.
2. Half of the remaining portion of energy covers itself with an invisible shield and masquerades as dark energy. You have all been speculating about dark energy for decades. Here it is.
3. The remaining energy is anti-matter.

It is all so simple, you see. You only have to apply your imagination; fentologic will take care of the rest.

What we have read thus far is the story of the particle in motion. What about the particle at rest (assuming that such a state is possible)? Such a particle too suffers a similar fate as that of the moving one. Only, there will not be such a fanfare as video-booms, cosmic rays, and all that. All this has an important implication in cosmology. We will refer to it when we take up Bagdenborg's perceptions on cosmology. To sum up what we studied thus far in this chapter: we saw how Bagdenborg analyzed the Great Man2's proposition that a moving body keeps on moving and came up with a startling conclusion. The moving body keeps on moving, but only for a limited time. Don't worry; the time limit extends up to a few billion years – plenty of time to ponder.

Young's old experiment

We cannot close this subject without referring to the famous Double-slit Experiment of Thomas Young. We have already mentioned it, but we will look into it from Bagdenborg's perspective. The original experiment was conducted nearly two hundred years ago, in the early 1800s. The experiment was conducted to demonstrate the wave-like nature of light, as opposed to the corpuscle-like nature proposed by Sir Isaac Newton. Over time, the experiment underwent many changes and variations. A century later, the study of this experiment gave rise to the most revolutionary and abstruse theories in science imaginable. As mentioned earlier, this remarkable experiment continues to mystify the greatest minds in science.

The original experiment in its basic form was very simple. Only the necessary outlines are given here. Please refer to figure 2.

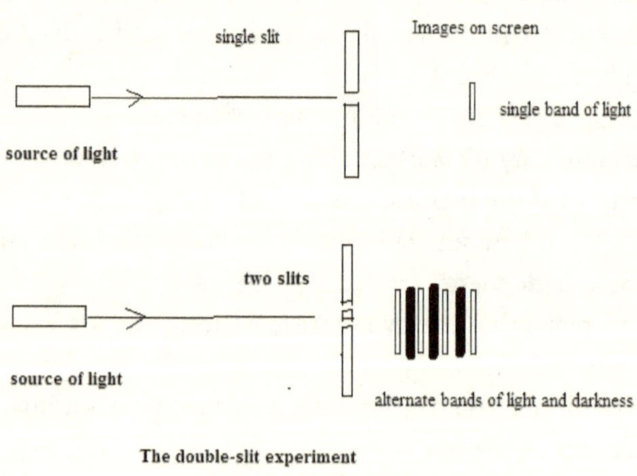

The double-slit experiment

Figure 2

A beam of light was shot at a screen with two small slits placed side by side. An observing screen was positioned behind the first screen to observe the formed images. The slits could be closed or opened as desired. First, one slit was closed so that the beam of light could pass through only that slit. A vertical band of light formed on the screen, as expected. Next, both the slits were kept open. The natural expectation was to see two distinct images on the observation screen. However, to his surprise, Young found that a band of light and shadows was formed. Many controlled experiments repeated again and again yielded the same result. Whenever only one slit was open, he obtained a single distinct image. Whenever both the slits were kept open, the band of light and darkness was created due to the phenomenon of interference, which is a characteristic of waves (like those of air and water). Thus, it was concluded that light was wave-like in nature, a conclusion that remains undisputed to this day.

As previously mentioned, refinements to the experiment have been conducted in recent times, involving electrons and photons. These experiments have required the most advanced technological skills, enabling the shooting of one single electron or proton at a time at the target screen. The result has remained unchanged—a persistent interference pattern that seems to mock the strenuous efforts of physicists. This mockery arises from the implications of the experiment when single photons are shot at the screen—implications that are profoundly serious, extraordinarily puzzling, and tremendously challenging to explain.

You see, a single electron or photon is being shot at the screen, and there are two slits. The "particle" can go through only one slit at a time. But if the interference pattern occurs, it implies that the particle has gone through both slits! Furthermore, the particle must have interfered with itself (requiring a minimum of two to "interfere"). Or, even more surprisingly, half of the particle must have gone through one slit, and the other half must have gone through the other slit for interference to occur. And yet, the interference pattern persists. This lies at the heart of the experiment, conducted using the latest technologically advanced instruments of unbelievable precision. There are other peculiar aspects as well, such as the observation of the particle. The particle seems to somehow "know" when it is being observed (detected) and changes its behavior. When it is not directly observed during its journey, its behavior is one way, and when it is observed in its path, its behavior changes. It's reminiscent of human behavior, isn't it? Let's set aside these stranger-than-fiction aspects for now and focus on the wave-particle riddle.

*Prima facie: - While discussing the above experiment with Bagdenborg's admirer, Bagdenborg's very first question was, "Tell me, has this experiment been conducted in a vacuum? The minimal requirement would be that the space covering the starting point of the particle's motion and the culminating point of the viewing screen should be completely vacuumed. Were the experimental rooms entirely shielded from electromagnetic waves, cosmic rays, neutrons, and so on? If not, the experiments fail to meet my standards. They are polluted." The admirer confessed that he did not know the answer. We leave it to the ardent scientists among you to check with the internet god, Google.

The central point of debate in all this commotion spanning over two centuries is this: Is light a particle or a wave? The prevailing wisdom suggests that it is both, depending on whether it is being observed or not. This solution is highly unsatisfactory, according to Bagden's evaluation, which he describes as "hastily drawn," "desperate," "unrealistic," and "uncalled for." His proposed solution to the problem is elegantly simple. His shell theory provides a beautiful explanation for the double-slit phenomenon. (If you have forgotten, please revisit the section titled "Shell in a Nutshell"). Examine the accompanying figure, and everything will become self-evident and clear.

Double slit experiment as seen from Bagden's Shell concept

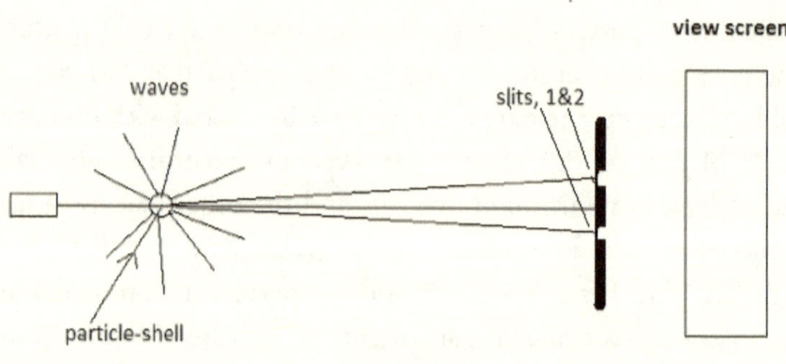

Figure 3

We have used a single photon/electron to shed light on this mystery. Consider the "particle" at a very short distance after it has departed from the source (often referred to as "The shooter"). The crucial point to remember, as Bagden has conclusively demonstrated, is that this "particle" is not truly a particle at all. It is an enclosed energy system confined within a shell. As we have clarified repeatedly, this shell itself consists of energy and acts like a fence or compound surrounding the energy system. This characteristic makes the system distinguishable as a distinct and unique unit, which, in common terms, we refer to as a "particle." The key to understanding this is to recognize that the shell continuously emits energy waves/signals as long as it exists.

Now, please take another look at the figure representing the "shell-particle." The shell emits (sends out) energy waves in all directions. This means that these signals, these waves, are passing through both slits throughout the shell's journey path. Is it any wonder that the interference pattern forms on the view-screen? In fact, it is the most natural outcome. Similarly, when one slit is closed, only one slit remains, and a single strip of an image forms on the screen. It's remarkably straightforward, isn't it?

"This explanation for the results of the double-slit experiment is the clearest I have ever encountered," adds Adeimantus, an admirer, in his commentary. We wholeheartedly concur with him.

Thus, as far as Bagdenborg is concerned, the problem is settled once and for all. There is no need to probe further into the experiment. Even if, in the future, somebody discovers some extra nuance or twist in the experiment, all that can be comfortably explained by his shell theory. However, we furnish forthwith a few tidbits that may be of interest to those who want to know more.

1) It has been noted that the act of observation of the particle alters its behavior. This has been touted as a very mystifying, puzzling phenomenon. In fact, an atmosphere akin to hysteria has been generated, harping on it. "Making a mountain out of a molehill," was the pithy comment of JJB. The act of observing an object does change it. Even in cricket, when the bowler is delivering his best superfast yorker, the flashlights from the cameras, or the stadium lights, impinge on the ball in its course. The effect of the impinging light is there, but it is so minuscule as to be negligible – it is like the effect your sneeze has on the Rockies. But it is altogether a different thing when microscopic, subatomic particles are considered. They are so tiny, so delicate that it will be a miracle if the act of observing them does not affect them.

2) Bagdenborg once got so irritated (a rarest of the rare occasions) that he asked Adeimantus, "If they are so obsessed with observation, tell me, have they conducted the experiment using Wilson's cloud-chamber or the bubble

chamber to track the path of the electron?" The flushed admirer had to admit he did not know.

3) À propos of the same remark, recall that Bagden asked if the experiment was conducted in a vacuum. The obvious inference is that, in the absence of a vacuum, the surrounding air, dust, and other particles will have an obvious and considerable effect on the photon/electron colliding with them on its way to the slits. That is what Bagliochus calls polluting the experiment.

4) This is a stunner, and we don't know how to respond to it. But it is Bagdenborg's idea, and his admirer has faithfully reported it. So, we have to throw this question at you:

They have carried out the double-slit experiment using one screen with two slits (and another serving as a view-screen). Well, has anybody thought of placing one more double-slit screen in alignment with the first one, behind it? Or three double-slit screens, one behind another? Four? Six? How about three slits, four slits? Multiple slits arranged like geometrical figures such as triangles, circles, polygons? We are terrified of reproducing more of his suggestions – which are in legion. We stop here. The admirer too has clammed up on the issue. He refuses to talk about it, for reasons unknown.

5) Along a similar line as 4) above, JJB throws another challenge to the experimentally-enthusiastic group. Forget about all these modern variations like semi-reflecting mirrors, detectors, and all that jazz. Conduct the experiment with one slit! Do we hear right? Yes, it is a one slit experiment. In case you still have doubt, he means that the first passing through shall have one and only one slit; no double-slit stuff.

Then, you may ask, "What is the fun of having a single slit? The purpose of having a double-slit is to demonstrate the wave-like property of light/electron."

The extraordinary proposition, coming from such a genius as Bagdidmedes, must mean something. Yes, there is a catch. Bagdimedes specifies that the single slit shall be of a size, at least one-fourth (1/4) that of a single photon! Actually, one-hundredth (1/100) will be ideal, he suggests. It is the trademark of Bagden's propositions that at every stage, his ideas impel us to go on asking questions, and more questions.

The first basic question is, "What the heck is the idea of providing a hole that is far smaller than the size of a single photon?" The second one is, "Is it possible to make a hole of such an inconceivably microscopic dimension? Can it be practically achieved?" Frankly, the admirer does not know the answer to the second set of questions. Modern technology has advanced incredibly. If they (the boffins) have not yet made such a tiny hole, they may try now, taking up Bagden's challenge. Alternatively, they may surmount the problem (if it is impractical, literally) by setting up surrogate experiments that will simulate the existence of a 1/100th-photon-size hole – modern technology is capable of such ingenious feats.

Okay, come back to the first question. We feel instinctively that if the hole (no longer a slit, poor thing) is smaller than a single photon, the photon cannot pass through the hole! Exactly, says old foxy JJB. If the photon/electron cannot pass through the hole, it means that the photon (or electron) is really a particle! If it manages to pass through the hole and leave a mark on the view-screen, it proves that the photon is a wave. Quite simple, see. "All my money is on the second possibility," he adds. Even though the suggestion put forth by JJB appears to be outlandish, a few moments of unbiased thinking will convince us that his suggestion is worth testing. After all, those who believed in a flat earth must have suffered similar hysteria when a mad man suggested – and proved – that the earth was a sphere.

6) Questions, questions again? The natural question from the Doubting Thomas will be, "Well, Bagden's model is that of a shell. If the light particle cannot pass through the micro-Fermi-sized hole, how can Bagden's shell pass through it, as he so confidently asserts? And he is betting, oh God." Here is the magical answer; not to worry.

Have you ever seen a blob of mercury? Place it in a sieve with one small hole, the size of the hole being far less than that of the blob. Dear Thomas, collect the blob of mercury, as it drops down, in that cupped palm of your hand. Wonder! There is your blob of mercury winking merrily at you. Thus, likewise, similarly, in the same manner, Bagdenborg's light-shell shall and will pass through the micro-Fermi hole, constricting itself at the mouth of the hole and regaining its original shape as it emerges! It is all so simple, you see. Any more questions? Don't feel shy. That is how science progresses.

JJB's shell is unique. Its properties are unique. If the hole in the above example is closed, if there is no passage to pass through, then the light-shell will either be absorbed by the surface of the screen or be reflected, depending on the nature and texture of the screen's surface – the way light behaves normally. There is no conflict. As we said, Bagdimedes has thoroughly worked out all the necessary mathematical calculations. Recall that all this is possible because of the unique three primary essences of the shell – sp1, sp2, and sp3 – which can combine in infinite ways, each combination conferring a unique property on the shell. The shell can be elastic, resilient, and rigid – depending upon the property of the objects it is pitted against.

We began this chapter by examining the particle versus wave debate and the duality. We concentrated mostly on the experimental and behavioral aspects of the particle. But Bagdenborg's forte is theory. We would like to dwell a little more on his fentological insights. Take a breather before we hop on to the next chapter.

Chapter 4

THE ILLUSION AND THE ADDICTION

"The greatest addiction in science is the addiction to measurement." – Professor Jestus Jesticus Bagdenborg.

"Illusion enjoys most, playing the game of Reality." – Bagus Bagliochus Badgimedes

A. Presentation; qualitative

The radius of the sun is given as 695,500 kilometers. That of the earth is about 6,371 kilometers. The distance between the earth and the sun is about 149,600,000 kilometers (it varies during the year). If you look at the earth from the surface of the sun, you may probably not be able to spot the earth with the naked eye. Standing on the moon, you can see the earth, which appears bigger in size than the moon as seen from earth. Approaching the earth nearer, you can see the outlines of the continents. Come nearer yet, land on the top of a small hill. You can see more details, like outlines of individual trees, buildings, roads, etc. Climb down the hill. At a distance of ten feet, you can clearly see a small piece of rock, well-defined; with the sun shining on it and its shadow on the ground. Pick it up and place it in your open palm. You can see further details. Take it to your home and crush it with the hammer you have stowed away somewhere in the basement tool-box. You now have the powder of the rock, still rough yet. Grind it into fine powder in your kitchen grinder (you were going to buy a new one, anyway). Marvel at the fine dust you have now. If you blow hard on the dust, the particles will scatter (you are a five-mile jogger; your lung power is good). Now, collect one particle, throwing away the rest of the powder (not on the kitchen floor; be careful. Missus will most probably make you lick it away). Carefully examine the single particle you have managed to manufacture. Can you break it into still finer particles? Maybe, if you approach your neighbor mechanic who works in that sophisticated nano-factory downtown...

The elaborate exercise above was not an idle fancy. We want to bring home a point or two. So please follow us further along the route of Bagdenesque discourse, even though you have guessed the rest of the story. Your helpful neighbor brings you back from his factory a micro-particle of the rock, wrapped up in thin, smooth tin foil. At this stage, you are not able to see the particle with your physical eyes. You have to trust your friend's word that the particle is there. ("Without being aware of it, you have started your journey into the land of faith.") Your innate curiosity propels you to take the micro-particle to another contact who has access to a hi-tech microscope. When you look at your invisible speck under the gizmo, by God, you see a big ball – perhaps one-foot in diameter (your faith is reinforced). Looking at your dazed eyes, your contact smugly assures you that there are hundreds of thousands of atoms, all abuzz with activity in that ghost-like ball. If not a ghost, what else is it? One minute back, it was not there; you could not see it with your own God-given eyes, however long you stared at it. Now it is staring back at you like a mammoth owl. And your man there, operating the super-duper gizmo, tells you there are still a million smaller things inside it. ("Have faith, take my word for it.")

You are dazed, but your curiosity is stronger. You make further and further inquiries along the list of the contact's contacts. You come to know that even one single particle among those darned millions – atoms, he said – was really quite big when you look at it in proper perspective. That invisible ghost of a particle, they all assure you, holds three more micro-particles inside it. ("You have to have faith; no other way.") If you are really a sensitive man – like those poet guys, etc. – your head should start reeling when you try to visualize that atom thing holding/hiding still smaller things inside its belly. To make you further dizzy, they assure you that those micro things inside the atom are thousands of times smaller than the (already invisible) atom; small, like, say, the way golf balls appear when you look at the golf field as a whole! Those teeny-weeny things are, they tell you, electrons, protons, and neutrons.

Wait. Those tiny things hold inside them still tinier things called 'quarks' (a very strange breed – divided into up, down, and bottom varieties). That about sums it up. That is the end of the string, so to say.

Oh, it was a slip (deliberate), the use of that word, "string". You see, we came to the end of the line, but the string remains! Yes, because recent feverish activity in hypothetical science (that is what Bagdenborg calls it) is busy with incomparably complex (hopeless) mathematical treatment of some darned entities called (ha-ha) "strings". The strings, they claim, are really the end of the line. They claim that the "strings" are the basic units out of which all the fundamental, teeny-weeny particles are made. The strings are unimaginably small – smaller than all those microscopic particles we listed out earlier. And they (the string men) have the final say; there is nothing smaller than strings. They are not made up of anything else. They are themselves – the chapter is closed.

Let us accept all that jazz for the present and proceed to the next presentation.

Presentation – B, quantitative

This paragraph is redundant, but it serves as a brief introduction to latecomers. Light travels at a speed of 186,276 miles per second. Actually, that is an enormous speed. With all our super-hyper technology, we have not yet been able to manufacture a vehicle that can travel at 186,276 miles per hour, even. To repeat, light travels at a fantastic speed. And, as for them (them being the opposite camp to that of Bagdenborg), no object in the universe can travel faster than light. Light is the fastest thing ever and forever.

Imagine the speed of light, please – 186,276 miles per second. The repetition is necessary to show you some mind-boggling facts. Multiply it by 360, and you will get the distance that light can travel in one hour. Multiply that number by 24 (for hours) x 365 (for days). The resulting distance is so huge that it is already impossible to visualize physically. That distance is called a light-year – 5,878,499,810,000 miles!

Just as you took a dizzying dive into the depth of some things, you are now ready to take another dizzying journey outwards. The distance of one light-year is the standard measuring stick employed for measuring distances in space, the universe. Try imagining in your mind's eye how much distance light can travel in one year – the light-year, that is, in so many miles. Allow the light to travel for 100 years... no, 1000 years... a million? ...a billion?(!) Just make it about 30 billion light-years. That is the farthest distance of the universe we have been able to measure at present! Go back to the light-year distance we gave just now, multiply it by thirty, and add nine more zeroes at the end. The human brain cannot conceive such a distance. In this case, there is no end of the line; not as things stand now. Nobody has yet seen the end of the universe.

Inside this humongous space, the universe contains untold numbers of galaxies, nebulae, supernovae, black holes, stars, and planets, apart from individual particles like helium and hydrogen, and so on and so on. The numbers for the galaxies, etc., run into billions. Likewise with the planets, etc. To provide a comparison, the present population of the Earth is 7 billion. And, the spans of the galaxies are measured in light-years.

Just to give you a panoramic view of the scale of quantitative measurements (distance/length), we provide below a small list for you to pore over and ponder:

The longest distance (the farthest point in the universe), as we know now... 30 billion light-years

Size of the milky way in one corner of which our solar system stands) 100,000 light-years.

Distance from earth to the pole star: 433.8 light-years

Distance from earth to the sun: 149,600,000 km

(From light-years, we have come down to miles per km.)

Size of the sun: 864,938 miles; diameter: 384,400 km; distance from earth to moon: 384,400 km.

The size of the moon is 3475 km.

The size of the earth is 12,742 km.

The height of the highest peak, Everest, is 8,848 meters.

The height of the tallest building was 830 meters.

Thickness of flaxen hair: 1/1500 of an inch.

From here on, direct visibility through the human eye ends. We depend on instruments.

Size of some of the largest molecules: 1000 A (100nm; nm = nanometer).

Size of the hydrogen atom: 0.74A (A; Armstrong = 0.1 nanometer).

Size of the electron... 2.82 x 10–15 meters, radius

The size of the nucleus is 1.75 x 1015 meters in diameter.

The size of the proton is 10–15 meters in radius.

The size of the neutron is almost the same as the proton's.

The size of the quark is less than 10–18 m.

Size of the string—roughly about Planck length.

Finally, the Planck length is 1.61619926x10–35 meters.

Science got tired of measuring (!) and declared that the Planck length is the end of measurement of all things small. Please go through the data given above. Please don't nitpick about the exactness of the measurements. Chew on it, ruminate on it leisurely. Then you will be ready to receive Bagdenborg's insights.

The two presentations, A and B, are closely interlinked. To use the good old, overused simile, they are the two faces of the same coin. Let us forget the laboratories, the equipment, and experiments for the present and take a comprehensive outlook. It often helps us to see where we are going and what we are doing.

Begin with appearances. Big is small and small is big, fentologic says. The Earth as seen from the sun is a speck. It will be invisible when observed from many distant galaxies. If you lie flat on the Earth and look, your eyes are not enough to take in the whole of the Earth. (For that matter, it is so even if you stand erect. But Badgen's admirer often tends to become overenthusiastic to drive home a point). The same analogy holds good for a dust particle, which appears immensely big when viewed through a microscope. Thus appearances are relative, changing according to your point of view and your capacity for viewing. This is fairly obvious and does not need much elaboration. (For an entertaining insight into this matter, see Bagden's "Juvenilia" in the second part of the book.)

Generally, there are two sides to any topic of argument. (There can be many too if you bring in politics and TV soap opera serials.) The standard argument against the relativeness of appearances is this. We choose a common factor and take it as a reference. In all our mundane activities, we stay on the surface of the Earth, and more importantly, the physical action of measuring the size of an object invariably starts or occurs at the place where we physically stand – this is the most basic and most common act of measurement; the yardstick comes to birth in this manner. The next step is to use mathematics. Geometry ("geo" – earth, its measurement) and trigonometry help us to measure things we cannot reach. Again, this too is fairly simple, but here is where Bagden's ideas diverge.

Examine this whole shebang – sorry, that word is in Bagden's original notes. We wanted to retain it – called knowledge at the most basic, fundamental level. There is the immeasurably vast universe. In the midst of that, there is this entity called a human being. The human being becomes aware of the universe. Everything would have been fine if man were just aware. Unfortunately, man begins to react to that awareness. Everything would have been still fine if the reaction were purely and only physical, biological – like that of other forms of life. Man is in possession of a thing called a mind, and the human mind begins to size up the universe ("environment," if you want to use a bland term), to explore it, to speculate about it. The exploration and speculation never cease. This is where "The agony and the ecstasy," the eternal theme of man's existence, originates. If you look at this propensity of the human mind, you will realize that there is actually nothing special about it. It is only one side of the mind's activities. Opinions are bound to differ on this – that is the nature of the human mind, again! We touched on the above sentiments in passing only. The irony is that, to proceed further, we too have to adopt that same route – exploration and speculation! Let us get on with it.

The next important point to note is the nature of viewing. This is so very subtle, intriguing, and actually awe-inspiring if you ponder that. We may have to repeat it – sort of bring back your attention to it – often. What is so awe-inspiring about what? Here it is, the original golden egg.

One. You cannot view the whole of the universe at once, in one single, whole glance. You can do nothing about it. It looks like an obvious, almost juvenile statement, you think. How about this? You cannot view the whole of the galaxy and do anything about it. Same category, you feel. Lastly, you cannot view the whole of the moon and do anything about it. Coming down-to-earth, you cannot view the whole of a building and do anything about it. Patience, patience, we are not playing a silly game here. There is a catch, as they say. The catch is the word 'whole'. Please see the word in a new perspective, and you will follow what we are trying to convey. When we said 'whole,' we meant the whole of it, all of it in one single glance, warts and all, as one unit. If you look at the house as one single, complete unit, it is just a house and nothing else. No further statements arise. Same with the moon, same with the galaxy, same with the universe – no further statements arise apart from saying that they are they.

Further statements arise when you visually break down the whole into parts. You break down the house into different parts like the door, the windows, the wall, the floor, and then it is possible to build a cornucopia of knowledge, filling up volumes and volumes of books. Similarly, you break down the universe into many parts like galaxies, stars, planets, etc., and then it is possible to fill up volumes and volumes of books, to go on expanding your "knowledge," as long as you (human beings) live. This differentiation is the root cause of all knowledge – repeat.

Your immediate response will be to exclaim, "But differences are there everywhere. It is an undeniable fact. If there were no differences, then life would be so boring, so meaningless!

Hold on there, please; you brought in two new words, "life" and "boring." We are not concerned with them – not in such a serious study of science as this (of matter that fills the whole universe). You also employed the word "meaningless." We agree with that – that is what we too were talking about. You see, "meaning" is also a mental construct, and that mental construct is sustained due to the mental activity of dwelling on the differences as elaborately as possible and as long as possible. (Fortunately for man, the scope for both seems to exist forever).

Now, a wee bit of elaboration on differences – we are gradually zooming in on Bagden's central idea. Take a system. Let us say it contains ten differences in a broad way. There are 1x2x3x4x5x6x7x8x9x10 ways the differences can be shuffled. That is, your scope for studying the differences is so huge. Imagine how many "differences" the universe, or for that matter, our Earth contains. The shuffling of such huge numbers gives rise to a scope of study that is beyond human imagination. That is why Bagdimedes said somewhat sarcastically, that there are enough differences in the universe to satiate man's lust (that was his word), to keep feeding his curiosity till doomsday.

This too is a side issue. Let us zoom in further along Bagden's fentological path. The shrewd reader (you) will allege that Bagden's reasoning as delineated in the previous paragraph is misleading. There may be innumerable differences in the universe, but modern science is gradually filtering down all of it to a manageable few items. That is what science is trying to discover; a unifying, common base that can be applied to all those differences. We are back to what has been repeated many times; the fundamental particles like protons, electrons, neutrons, and so on. There are roughly less than a dozen such particles. It is quite a great feat of the human mind to have reduced the trillion trillion trillion (unlimited) things of the universe to such a small number. Science is still more gung-ho on the quest of finding still more fundamental particles so that even those dozen particles could be decocted into possibly a single unique something.

Neither technology nor Badgen has any quarrel with that argument. In fact, you can even imagine hearing the gleeful applause of Bagdenborg's clapping hands at the valiant mega-mega marathon race of science. (The comment is from the admirer). We are zooming in; we are almost there.

All right, great, says Bagdenborg. We will go along with your arguments. In fact, we will go further and anticipate the glorious day when those dozen particle fundas (that is a word Badgen has literally used) have been distilled into a single funda. The quark of all quarks, say, the zuark. (Z is the last letter of the alphabet). You have the zuark in the palm of your hand – metaphorically speaking, and you're inspecting it with a beating heart.

Then what? Nothing! ("The agony starts, the ecstasy ends.") The agony has two prongs.

The first prong is the age-old conundrum of infinite regression. Beginning with the universe, you go on confirming, "This is made of this and that." You come down to the atom. The atom is made up of electrons and protons. The protons are made up of quarks. You have come to the final, tiniest of them all, the Zuarks. What is it made up of? You cannot help asking that question once you start breaking down matter into finer and finer sizes. Like the string people say, you may reply, "Well, that is the final stage, a Zuark is a Zuark." Oh? Then what exactly is it? What is that stuff? If you say it is matter, then matter, by its very definition, is something that can be broken down into further finer sizes because matter has form and boundary. If you say that the Zuark is a bundle (tiniest) of energy, then it is either a gaffe or a big bold bluff. Because, as fentologic points out, energy is a property of matter. It is a concept. Get it clear again. Energy is a property of matter. It is a concept. Get it clear again. Energy is a beautiful, almost perfect concept most ideally suited to explain the behaviors of matter, such as its motion and change in state. Energy is a concept; repeat, repeat, repeat. It is a fantastic mathematical symbol, which by being used in millions of equations, has hypnotized us into believing that it is a real entity. (The admirer admits that when he read that sentence in Bagdenborg's notes, a shiver ran down his spine.

The second prong of the agony is more subtle. When asked what your ultimate particle, the zuark is, you may sidetrack the issue by describing its properties. To do that, you have to bring in parameters, that is, measurable quantities like mass, charge, etc. ("whatever"). This gets more subtle; please follow patiently. These measurable quantities are attributes of things already known, like your electron and proton ("whatever"). Then, you are forced to compare the Zuark's parameters with those of existing, known particles. In essence, without being specifically aware of it, you are trying to define the new in terms of the old. Thus, the new is nothing but a conveniently distorted (his word, that) form of the old. If the Zuark is to be really the most fundamental particle ("Whatever"), then you have no way of describing it! Repeat, repeat, and repeat that. You can only keep on staring at it – and not opening your mouth. This kind of fentologically inspired way of reasoning may seem very strange or even suspiciously lunatic at first glance. But keep on; you will see the justification in the coming paragraphs.

The other side of the coin, as we said, is measurement. We cannot do justice to the insights of Bagdimedes here by indirect, edited reports. Many parts of his notes were of the nature of soliloquy. Let us have a peek.

"Measurement has become an addiction to the inquiring mind, especially for science. At the deep subconscious levels, the act of measuring something gives you a comfortable illusion of 'knowing' the thing. It was natural in the infancy period of mankind, but now it has turned into an indispensable crutch. Without recording measurements, science is lost; so is mathematics. It is an irony too. Yes.

"Measurements can never be exact. I have often labored on this insight, but my colleagues (and even friends) do not pay heed. Look at the thousands and thousands of experiments they carry out. The results are always 'accurate up to so many decimal places.' 'Up to so many decimal places,' see! I am talking from the standpoint of the ultimate purity. The decimals may sustain up to ten, twenty, or even a hundred. That is not the point. The best one can say is that they are impressive approximations only. Ultimate purity, I repeat, is essential.

I am in a querulous mood. I want to nitpick. Take your standard of measurement of length, the meter, as an example. As an ideal international standard, they (you know who) have prepared a bar of chocolate, designating its length as one-meter. So that it should not melt or bend or expand, they have put it in a safe place in some museum, somewhere in Bastille or Timbuctu or Kabrustan. That bar of chocolate (The admirer confessed that he winced here) is the true meter. All others, the millions and billions of meter tapes in the world, are replicas only; not the real meter. They are all impressive approximations only. You know how? This is why, this is how. First of all, tell me how many atoms does your standard bar have? Tell me exactly, not losing count of one single atom. You can't. While such is the case, how can you prepare other measuring rods, tapes, or chains ("whatever") replicating the original exactly? Seen from this angle, the whole of the experimental part of science is impure. (Admirer winced again.) When the data are polluted, naturally all the dependent conclusions must be imperfect. (Admirer felt dizzy on reading this line). I am not being unnecessarily sadistic in communicating these perceptions. I merely want to set the highest standard for science. This is one of the reasons why I do not conduct experimental research.

(Admirer's note: Sorry about that "Chocolate bar." But that is Bagliochus for you. The length of the meter has been redefined many times. It was originally defined as one ten-millionth of the distance between the North Pole and the equator at the longitude of Paris. (Can you believe such crudeness?) Later, in 1999, a platinum bar was constructed and housed in Paris. (This is our Bagden's chocolate bar). The meter was redefined in 1889 using a bar of platinum and iridium. In 1960, the meter was again redefined as 1,650,763.3 times the wavelength of radiation by the krypton-86 isotope. Once more, in 1983, the meter was redefined as the length of the path traveled by light in a vacuum in 1/29,792,498 of a second! Now, we hope you understand Bagden's grouse better.)

All right, let me drop the matter and proceed to my next point of contention. I am greatly chagrined that they have arbitrarily set a limit to measurement in one direction only, conveniently ignoring the other end. Let me clarify. Figuratively, call one direction as the "up" direction. Starting from where we stand on Earth, they go on measuring distances in the "up" direction. That is to say, they measure the distances from Earth to the moon, from Earth to the sun, from Earth to other stars, in terms of light-years. As of now, they have been able to measure the current stretch of the universe as being about 30 billion light-years. My point is that they have not given up searching for yet more distant objects in the universe. To make it more ticklish, they say the universe is expanding. The upper limit for the measurement of distance (length) has not been fixed. No upper limit unless it is infinity. And infinity has no limit. Okay? Now start the process of measurement in the "downward" direction. Start from the standard length of the chocolate bar I introduced earlier, the meter. They have been able to measure smaller and smaller distances like the size of an atom and further and further down to the size of an electron, etc. You are familiar with all those fancy names; decimeter, centimeter, millimeter, Angstrom, Fermi length, etc. Finally, what did they do when they were unable to go to still smaller and smaller distances? They declared that the Planck length (1.61619926 x 10^-35 meter) is the smallest distance measurable. Distances, intervals less than that have no "meaning" as per them. This is where my chagrin wells up. I ask of you, why there should be a limit down under when up above there is no limit? It is illogical. But who will listen to me? Mine is a cry in the wilderness of the Antarctic...

Bagdenborg has made many references to this paradoxical nature of measurement, scattered throughout his notebook. His philosophical and mystical inclination shows up in his view. In a highly condensed form, it can be explained as follows. Imagine a huge "X," or the multiplication symbol of mathematics. The upper half—the cone—can expand upwards without limit, as can the lower half, downwards. We, as human beings, stand at the point where the two cones meet, at the point where the two straight lines cross. That point represents (of course, symbolically and metaphorically) the position of man's everyday experience. His capacity for experience is limited to a certain area covering the up and down regions, by the very nature of his senses, which in Bagdenborg's definition includes the mind as well. The mind tries to overcome the limitations of the senses by inventing numbers and mathematics. The main point of relevance to our topic of measurement is symmetry, he stresses. Thus, if there is no limit to the upper half (as in the size of the expanding universe), there cannot be a limit to the lower half too. There is no limit to the measurement of smallness either. As long as you posit something called infinity in the higher order (∞), you must have one divided by infinity (1/∞) in the lower order too. It is not zero; it is a process, a never-ending process downwards; the never-ending process exists both downwards and upwards.

This is the crux of the problem. Yet, the brain is tempted, no, propelled to ask the illogical questions. "If it is never-ending, where will it end? How will it end?" The answer from Bagdimedes is only a smile, bitter and sorrowful in equal measure. The whole issue, he points out, hinges on the human mind, or brain, as you prefer to call it. You see, the QUEST originated in the human mind/body system. The sensitivity, the range of human perception, is limited. No doubt about that.

The eye (to take one example of the sensory devices man is endowed with) can see the smallest speck; it can't see anything smaller than that. Man, clever that he is, can invent a magnifying glass, a microscope, or a mega-superscope to "see" things smaller than the speck, but that leads us back into the same paradox discussed before. If he (human) can see the "smallest," then there could be, and should be still smaller "specks," and so on. Thus, a little thought will show that out of an infinite range of perceptions, only a spectrum (granted, it is broad) can be available for experience. ("That is what makes us humans. That is the matrix of human existence.") We can only speculate about what lies beyond in all manner of ways – all that will only be a surrogate experience.

In this context, it is relevant to mention that during this phase of his researches, Bagdenborg was deeply immersed in Sankhya, propounded by the sage Kapila. His admirer's commentaries too bear witness to that. The core of the ideas, as applied to the present paradox of the subject that we are discussing can be summed up as below.

The whole range of the "stuff" of the universe can be broadly classified into five categories. The first one in the category is what is called the "earth principle." The "Earth" here stands for all things that are solid, hard, compactly tied together. In other words, the earth principle is the "grossest," densest form of matter. Starting from this base, as we go higher up the ladder, "matter" becomes more and more "subtle," "refined," and unbound (freer). Actually, the word "base" is a misnomer. Creation starts the other way around, according to that ancient philosophical system. Starting from the subtlest, more and more gross forms are created. For the sake of our understanding, it is clearer to start from the grossest form, the "Earth principle."

The next "refined" form of the "earth" is the "water" principle. All liquids, fluids belong to this category – water, honey, oil, and so on. There is a greater degree of freedom in this stage; there is no rigidity of form, no bound structure. The third category is the "gas" principle. It is even further "refined" than the liquid. Already, at this stage, it becomes inaccessible to one of the human sensory systems, the eye. The degree of freedom is also enhanced. The change in the fourth state or stage is striking. Heat, fire, electromagnetic radiation, etc., represent this category of matter. At this stage, matter loses its salient property of looking/behaving like what we ordinarily accept as "matter." "Matter" has almost reached the ultimate state of being refined. "That is why," Bagdenton wrote, "experiments in particle physics confuse and tantalize us, outputting results that could be interpreted either way, as belonging to matter or belonging to waves." He has a good point there, the admirer notes. The final state is that of the "akasha" principle, as the oriental texts say; that is, space. In this ultimate stage, the "physicalness" of nature seems to come to an end. It becomes almost impossible to define it, except in terms of what it contains. The ancient philosophy propounded that as things attain more and more "subtleness," their realm (read, volume or size) increases manyfold.

Indeed, the realm of ultimate subtle form, space, is so vast that it is beyond measurement.

Bagdenborg had scribbled a very amusing, but nevertheless a telling analogy about this concept of "refinement" or subtleness – taking a dig at homeopathy on the way. The readers are, of course, familiar with it. Take a bottle of concentrated sulfuric acid containing a liter of it. Remove one c.c. of the acid and dilute it by adding it to one liter of water. (Recall your old textbook warning – do not add water to concentrated acid; add acid to water). Next, take one c.c. of this diluted acid and mix it again with one liter of pure water. Again, take out one c.c. out of the mixture and add one liter of water... Repeat this process a billion times, and you will gain an idea of what kind of "dilution" matter undergoes when it turns into space! The analogy, of course, is not to be taken literally. It is given to illustrate the range of subtleness or dilution from the state of "matter" to the state of "space."

There is a finer point here. From general descriptions and also from our ordinary experience, we are automatically made to believe that these elements are "separate." They are not. According to the ancient system, all the different elements (the earth, water, gas, fire elements) arise from the subtlest, the "space" principle. Each lower principle in the hierarchy contains some proportion of all the elements above it, being "derived" from it. The "space" element is the origin of all that is seen and experienced.

The natural questions that arise now are whether something more subtle than "space" is there, and how space originated. The answers are there, but they go beyond the scope of the accepted boundaries of science. Terminologies like consciousness and The Source are to be used, which cannot be quantified or put into mathematical formats. So, that is the final frontier for science, asserts Bagdenborg. Anyhow, to satisfy the curiosity of the reader, we will indicate how the ancient system described the origin of space (and thus all creation). There was a "disturbance" or "churning" in the original, solely existing "consciousness," and thus were born "space" and three properties.

Strangely, those words, "disturbance" and "churning," invoke a familiar image. They remind us of the string theory, touted as the latest advancement in science! Don't they? String theory, to put it in a very condensed form, proposes that the most fundamental constituents of all matter-cum-waves-cum-forces are "strings" of unimaginably small size, vibrating in extra dimensions of ten or eleven, including the regular four dimensions of space and time. Note the stress on the word "vibrating." The details are more involved, and the mathematics of the whole shebang are beyond the comprehension of most of us. The mathematics is so complicated that they have been working on it for more than thirty years, and nothing is settled yet. The fundamental-most ingredient, according to this theory, is the string, and if you ask what exactly it is, or it is made up of, you get a poker-faced reply that a string is just that – a string. Full stop. ("It is an artificial full stop intellectually forced down all our throats," groans Bagdensky.)

The bottom line is that even these extremely tiny strings can be quantified in terms of measurement, and so, mathematics can spread its tentacles (Bagden's words) around them. (Even then, it (mathematics) is engaged in its toughest battles in the three thousand years of its history). Imagine then the fate of mathematics if it has to face the non-measurable! Bagdimedes concludes, "A whole new kind of non-mathematical science is required to tackle the ultimate problem. As far as I see, nobody dares to come forward. In my unprejudiced view, science too is a form of recreation, although of highly exacting standards. I say this with a heavy heart and a deep sigh.

"I think the secret of Mona Lisa's smile relates to this topic of mine. Da Vinci too must have intuited the existence of an unbreakable wall between Creation and Recreation."

In his later stage of scientific research, Bagdenisky was tormented by similar thoughts. His admirer conjectures that such sentiments must have compelled Bagdenborg to renounce everything and withdraw from public life.

Chapter 5

FORCEFUL MOTION, PUMPED WITH MEMORIES

Bagdenborg admired the ancient Greek philosophers and thinkers. In his opinion, they were more perceptive in their analysis of nature and more faithful to their subjects of research. The basic reason for this, according to Bagdimedes, was that they were not tempted by technological inventions and progress. Moreover, Big Business was not as substantial in those days, and concepts like careers and specializations were absent. (The admirer notes that Bagdenborg used to repeat the famous witticism on specialists – "A specialist is one who knows more and more about less and less until he knows almost everything about almost nothing.")

When we observe the vast panorama of the objective world, one remarkable phenomenon stands out – that of motion. Objects and living things are always in motion. We take motion for granted. It is so ubiquitous and incessant in our lives that almost all of us never pause to think about it. But when you come to think of it, science in its essence can be distilled down to the barest things: matter, motion, force, and time.

Among the ancient Greeks, Zeno was well-known for his study of motion. It is said he came up with forty paradoxes in analyzing it. The most famous of Zeno's paradoxes are those of the arrow and Achilles and the tortoise. By employing ingenious logic, he proved that the arrow shot from the bow does not move, and that Achilles, the great warrior, can never overtake the tortoise in a running race! Most people are familiar with this paradox. For the benefit of latecomers on the scene, a brief summary is given here.

Achilles, the great hero of the Trojan War, was not only an unbeatable warrior but also a superb runner. In a race with a tortoise, if the tortoise is given a sympathetic lead (of say, ten meters), Achilles will never be able to overtake the tortoise! The proposition is blatantly ridiculous. In an actual race, even the dimmest moron will not place his bet on the tortoise to win. Let us see how Zeno argues his case.

At the start, the tortoise is placed, as said earlier, ten meters ahead of Achilles. Let us say it is at point A. When the race starts, Achilles has to reach point A if he has any hope of overtaking the tortoise; that is quite obvious. But, mark the beginning of the clever reasoning here, by the time Achilles reaches the tortoise's starting point A, the tortoise, not being idle, has managed to move ahead, let's say, to point B. Therefore, Achilles, on his ambitious run to overtake the tortoise, must reach point B if he has to win the race. But again, the zealous tortoise has moved further, to point C, by the time Achilles manages to reach B! This part of the argument too is valid and cannot be rejected as false. By the time the determined Achilles reaches C, the equally determined tortoise will have moved ahead to another point D. The pivotal point of this argument is that this process can go on indefinitely. Thus, Achilles cannot overtake the tortoise!

The case of the arrow in flight is equally interesting. Stripped of philosophical jargon, the argument runs thus. The first thing to note is that the arrow, like any object, occupies space; a space in which it fits exactly. This point cannot be denied. Then the next line, as they say, is a beauty, and a subtle one at that. Read it again and again to convince yourself. If the arrow is in a place (in space) that exactly fits its size, and if you focus your attention on that space, the arrow will be at rest within the confines of that space. Please do not be offended if we ask you to read it again. To give you a convincing analogy, let us take a matchstick inside a matchbox. If the stick fits exactly inside the matchbox, the stick cannot move! Go out into your lawn, take lungfuls of fresh air, and contemplate this beautiful syllogism. Come back and contemplate the flight path of the arrow. At any moment you care to consider, the arrow will always be in a space that fits it exactly. Undeniable. That must mean, then, that at any moment the arrow is in a state of rest because it is lying snugly in a tight space that fits its size (like that matchstick inside the matchbox)! Therefore, the arrow is always at rest!

Even after more than two thousand years, Zeno's paradoxes continue to fascinate modern thinkers. Hundreds of books have been written on the theme. The syllogism style generates both pros and cons. In fact, even quantum physicists have delved into it and come up with their own variations and theories. (The phrase "Zeno effect" has been coined too.) Naturally, Bagdenborg was also fascinated by the logic of Zeno and discovered a startling theory, which we will take up in later paragraphs.

The intriguing point of interest to Badenborg was the alluring process of logic employed to arrive at a conclusion that is absurd and exactly opposite to our practical experience. Even if you are intellectually convinced to your heart's content that the arrow is always at rest, you will not go and stand in its path, baring your brave chest against it.

Then, what exactly is happening here? It is a very troublesome question to answer. It all lies in the way logic (and, by extension, mathematics) hypnotizes us.

Logic, in its essential form, is a process of reasoning. We develop reasoning initially by observing the physical world in action. Things change. There is a change in position. There is a change in shape. Almost all things that can be perceived and measured change. By observing all this and collecting an enormous amount of data, the mind sees certain patterns of relations among the bits of data, and thus, the reasoning process evolves. The human mind is an eminently competent instrument. It is able to form generalizations and draw conclusions after observing cause-and-effect relations among the bits of data. It is also an efficient mechanism because it is endowed with the gifts of feedback and a self-corrective process. So, it hones its skill of reasoning and invents logic, trying to make it more and more rigorous. It proceeds to make abstractions. It is also inventive; it invents mathematics. Simple arithmetic is born. Abstracting and generalizing it, basic algebra is invented, geometry is invented. From these simple steps, mathematics has now grown into such a vast and complex branch of knowledge today that only a select few can understand what happens at the highest levels.

The point to be noted is that as mathematics advanced, it has become a separate study, meaning that it need not necessarily relate to the day-to-day experiences of the mundane world. Expressed in simple words, it can be said that thinking can be directly related to the events of the "real" objective world on the one hand, and on the other hand, it can create its own world with its own laws.

A simple comic or absurd example would be as follows: In the office of Births and Deaths in a small town, they diligently maintain records. In a particular week, it is noticed that there have been 22 deaths and 22 births. The clerks there are keen on statistics too, and they post it on their notice board for public enlightenment. The notice states that the average rate of births per day for that week has been 22/7. The same goes for deaths. If you ever wonder how 3.14 babies could be born, ask the statistician. He will reply, with a deprecatory look at you, that the mathematics is correct and has been double-checked. To put you down further, he will add, "Computers don't lie."

On a slightly higher level, consider obtaining square roots of numbers. The square root of 4 is 2 – or minus two. If you multiply the square root by itself, that is, square it, you get the original number, 4. You can obtain square roots for positive numbers only in the normal course of things, that is, for a number bearing the + sign because either plus into plus or minus into minus is always plus (+). But in math, they have a square root for –1 (minus one)!! (It is denoted by the symbol √–). The square root of –1 does not exist. But by using such a symbol, mathematics has built up a whole branch of discipline (complex algebra) which is a very powerful tool for solving a great many problems!

To sum up, what we want to point out is that reasoning, logic, mathematics can relate to things of the actual physical world of ours or can be formulated as independent disciplines not necessarily related to the objective world.

That is how the paradox of Zeno ("dichotomy," as it is fondly called) has taken birth. That the arrow seems to be at rest when exactly occupying a space of the same size as its own is true. That at every point of its flight, it is occupying a space of its own size is also true. But in actual life, you do not ask the arrow to stop at an infinite number of places so that you can verify the truth of the proposition! It is because of these and such considerations that Bagdenborg developed what we have already introduced in these pages – his fentologic. (When a colleague of his asked him if his theories were really "true," Bagdimedes quipped, mimicking the famous lines of the Great Man3, "The good Lord better take notice of them.")

Similar is the case with Achilles when he is running after the tortoise. When he has reached the point A previously occupied by the tortoise, you have to tell him, "Please stop there! I have to see how far the tortoise is from you; wait a sec. I have to measure the gap between you and the point B, where the tortoise is now. I will be fair to you; I will ask the tortoise too to stop – no cheating. Well, there, off you go now, sir." How does that scenario strike? Only, you have to go on repeating it an infinite number of times.

The point to note is that time and motion, which are smooth, continuous operations, have been arbitrarily frozen. The second point involves observation. Observation too takes time; it is not instantaneous. We can confidently assume that Zeno was unaware that light has a fixed limit to its speed. By the time you observe that Achilles has reached point A, he would have already moved a bit further ahead! That is how and why we conclude that an object is moving.

That automatically draws our attention to a brief, though relevant, diversion. If you ask a painter to paint the race of Achilles, he will most probably draw a simple scene depicting Achilles and the tortoise at different positions on the canvas. He will do his best to convey motion through the various anatomical parts of Achilles placed in appropriate relation to one another. The sense of motion is skillfully invoked in your mind, but if you look at the painting with a stone heart and devoid of imagination, you will see that both the competitors in the race are at rest at the instant of painting. If the painter has to show you the entire race, he has to paint an infinite number of such paintings! (Bagdenborg's note – I personally have an intuition that sly, old Zeno must have got his paradoxical inspiration from a painting of some such scene.")

That, again, draws our attention to modern-day inventions – the camera and Edison's great invention, the movie. In parallel to the painter's depiction of Achilles, you can now capture a 'snapshot' of the race. The developed photograph will provide you with a presentation of the race at a particular moment, much like the painting. Applying the same previous principle, if you want to view the entire race of Achilles, you would theoretically need to take an infinite number of snapshots. (Now, we are arriving at a significant point.) However, as even kids know today, we do not need to take an infinite number of snapshots. We have video cameras, TVs, and cinemas.

The human eye has the ability known as retention, meaning that the image of an object seen by the eyes remains on its retina for a brief period of one-sixteenth of a second. The cinema projector (and the recording camera) takes advantage of this natural ability of the eye to produce an effect of continuous motion. It is sufficient to capture photos of a moving object every one-sixteenth of a second and then project the sequence at the same rate on the theater screen. The human eyes will "see" continuous motion.

Let us pause here for a moment (one-sixteenth?!) and inspect the significance of this extraordinary invention. By suitably controlling the number of 'frames' that are projected on the screen, the effect of motion can be altered! As is commonplace now, especially in sports and in cinemas, the speed of action "seen" on the screen can be slowed, sped up, or even frozen! What does it all mean? It means that an illusion is being created on the screen. Only frozen 'frames' are being presented before the beholding eye (at controlled rates), and the eye (mind/brain) is conjuring up an image of motion. It (motion) is an illusion when you look at it objectively!

Here, Mister Clever Objector will shoot back, "That may be an illusion. But that is a description of what has been happening inside a theater, on the silver screen. Surely, what happens in the world outside is a different ballgame." To which Bagliochus will reply with a smile, "Not much of a difference, my friend. Let us take the help of fentologic. Hold fast to its gentle, assuring hand. It will take you to new insights."

So, with fentologic guiding us unerringly, let us go back to witness Achilles racing his heart away against the tortoise, or the poor arrow struggling to pierce the target, all the while being persuaded by the insinuating voice of Zeno, that it is actually taking rest while making/faking movement.

Recall that the projector in the theater is projecting sixteen frames per second. In other words, snapshots (frames) of a moving object taken at every one-sixteenth of an interval are enough to recreate a sense of motion. Well, in the actual field, while the arrow is moving, the human eye is doing a similar thing. As we said, it takes some time for the light (from the arrow) to travel up to the human eye, however minute that time may be. It takes some more time for the information recorded on the retina to travel along the neural paths, through the optic nerves to the brain. Again, it takes some time for the brain to decode the signals and recognize the picture – essentially a "snapshot," a frame. The whole process may take a very tiny amount of time, say, t. In that interval of time t, the arrow would have definitely moved some distance! So, the brain, through the eyes, receives the next snapshot of the arrow after that interval of t only. It is essential to stress this point. Thus, the brain, even in the actual world, processes a series of snapshots (stress, still frames) and re-creates the image of the moving object. A fentological shock is warranted at this stage. We said the brain "re-creates" the image of the moving object. The phrasing of the sentence is misleading. The brain does not "recreate." It creates! Strictly speaking, fentologic insists, even the words "of the moving object" are unwarranted. "Of a sense of movement of the object" would be more apt.

This kind of reasoning will lead us to the age-old, familiar fight of 'matter versus mind.' Let us avoid it for the moment and see what fentologic has to say – as a tailpiece, sort of. Let us consider the physiological aspects: the brain, the eyes, and the physical aspects – of light needing time to reach the eyes, etc., from a different angle.

On to the favorite pastime of Bagdenborg – the thought experiment. Imagine that the value of time, t, is zero. That is, we are assuming that light travels from the arrow to the retina instantly, that the neural signals reach the brain instantly, that the brain decodes the signals instantly. All these are happening instantly, along each imagined infinitesimal point of its flight. You know what will happen? We are back to good old Zeno. Since the eye-mind is 'seeing' the arrow (its length and the exact space it is occupying) every damn micro-microsecond, the arrow appears to be stationary! Don't believe it? Fentologic calmly assures you that the arrow must appear stationary. How Zeno would have loved to hear this! Pause a while, take a breather. (Fentological assertions are like that – they do funny things to your breathing mechanism).

The thoughtful reader (you) will be stimulated and excited by the foregoing explanation. You will be naturally spurred to add your flash of insight. So, you might argue, going along with fentologic, "Ok, but, there seems to be a small defect in the above argument. As you said, the eye is 'seeing' the arrow all the time. So, it is seeing the arrow at all points along the path of flight fifty miles, you said somewhere. Therefore, mark this, if this process is happening instantaneously, the brain/mind should actually see an arrow fifty miles long or it must see a long stretch of fifty miles tightly packed, head-to-tail, with arrows, their number being equal to fifty miles divided by the length of a single arrow!!"

(Did we hear claps of applause reverberating in the air all around us?)

Excellent, Bagdenborg would say approvingly. Our argument is steadily zeroing in on the crux of the problem. Can you guess what it is? You (being a thoughtful reader) have just half a second to respond.

Okay, let's go back to the beginning of Zeno's reasoning. Please do not think we are unnecessarily repeating the same lines. Have patience; there is a purpose here. The old fox was correct as far as the scope of his investigation is concerned. If viewed at each point in its flight, the arrow appears to be stationary ("at rest," as he claims). But he forgot something, which is most vital, at least as far as human beings are concerned, as far as the very functioning of the brain is concerned. It is MEMORY! We'll continue with the next lines of the argument for the sake of formality, since you are already illuminated. The brain sees the arrow at, say, point A initially – and records it in its memory bank. The next instant, when it sees the arrow (even if at rest) at point B, the brain automatically records that fact too and compares the positions A and B automatically. This act of recording (MEMORY) and comparing can happen in two ways. In everyday surroundings, the positions of fixed objects in the background are recorded, so that the comparisons in the shift/displacement of the arrow are computed automatically and more easily. If there is no discernible background object (as in a clear sky), the changes in the movements of the eyeballs and the muscles of the neck, etc., are unconsciously recorded. Thus, memory is the essential factor that imparts the knowledge of motion of an object being viewed.

Even mathematically, memory is essential. The terminology is different, of course. You fix or denote the initial position of the arrow by a symbol – it is a record, memory. You do the same for the next point in flight, B – it is a record, memory. Then you manipulate the symbols so that a mathematical description (interpretation) of the motion of the arrow can be formulated. This is the basic foundation on which that great genius, Descartes, built his coordinate geometry and heralded a new era in mathematics.

À propos the illusion and re-creation of motion discussed earlier, another interesting and relevant observation is in order here. Suppose a fast-moving object, like an airplane, passes before you, across your line of vision at roughly a hundred feet away from you. You will feel the tremendous speed of the airplane, and the brain too registers it as moving fast. If you see the same plane crossing the sky at a distance of a few kilometers, the apparent speed (speed as actually "seen") appears to have reduced considerably. If the distance increases even more, you will see just a small dot lazily inching forward, against the blue background. A person who has never seen an airplane flying will judge that the object is moving very slowly. This phenomenon is, of course, intimately connected with the "cone of vision," which, centuries ago, Leonardo Da Vinci had studied and recorded in his notebooks at great length. (The distance between two points appears to shrink as we move further and further away from those two points). The most familiar instance is that of the sun moving across the sky during the day. (That is, the earth spinning on its axis, sweeping enormous arcs across the sky.)

The earth is sweeping an enormous circle of about 6.28 X 149,600,000 kilometers of circumference (with respect to the sun) every twenty-four hours. (A truly huge speed.) Yet, we see the sun lazily – almost reluctantly, it seems – inching millimeter by millimeter. The earth also covers, roughly, the same distance, physically, traveling around the sun in a year. We do not even feel it, except as changes in the seasons or the apparent movement of the sun northwards and southwards from the equator.

These and similar examples are apt to raise pertinent doubts about the nature of motion. Is motion, then, an illusion, or does the motion of an object really occur? Is motion "true"? These are sticky questions.

When the question of true motion is mentioned (or absolute motion, to give it a scientific look), everybody in this world (yes, everybody) will immediately remember the name of the Great Man3 as Bagdenborg termed him – Albert Einstein. With his Theory of Relativity, he shattered all our previous notions about motion and showed that motion is relative. Imagine that you are shut inside that speeding airplane. There is no communication of any sort between you and the external world. There is no reference point external to the airplane. The airplane is moving at a steady speed. Einstein has shown that under such circumstances (a closed system), you will not "feel" the motion neither of the airplane nor of yourself. The object, as far as it is concerned, is not at all moving!

The funny (and somewhat perplexing) thing is that an observer standing on the ground below will actually see the airplane moving at a fast rate! No doubt about that. He will even take a legal oath, testifying that the airplane is moving. The next funny thing is that if the same observer gets into another plane and travels along, parallel to your plane, at the same speed, he will now say that your plane is at a standstill! A second observer on the ground who sees both of you will swear that both of you are traveling! Of course, these examples are very old and familiar, from the days of the Theory of Relativity; a century old. Peace be unto Relativity; let us move from its tight and somber mathematical structure into the more free regions of fentologic. Incidentally, and ironically, the old fox Zeno can be said to have been justified in a way. Replace the airplane in the above example with Zeno's arrow – big enough to ensconce you safely and comfortably inside its innards. In such a case, you will agree with Zeno that neither you nor the arrow is moving!

Our opinion about the nature of motion seems to be swaying – swinging this way once, that way again. It moves, it moves not. The situation is funny. It could be funnier still if we could spin funnier yarns out of it. Why not, when fentologic is on our side? Follow this scenario.

This time there are two airplanes. You are in one, and your friend, Ben, is in the other. Both the planes are moving at a steady speed of a thousand miles per hour. As said before, you do not feel the motion of your plane, and neither does Ben, of his. You are just able to see Ben's plane about a hundred feet in front of you. You have been watching it for an hour, and you see his plane at the same position all the time – as if it is hanging in front of you, held by invisible ropes. The damned thing isn't moving. Suddenly, (something snaps somewhere in the universe) and Ben's aircraft loses all its motion. Its speed becomes zero at once. (Forget all about inertia, momentum, and such sundry things. This is a thought experiment, remember?) You have never seen an airplane reversing. You are filled with wonder and excitement at receiving this piece of knowledge. Unfortunately, you are unable to communicate your newly discovered knowledge to the world at large because it is all over by the time your thrill turns into horror. The world at large is beset with more urgent concerns – it is busy searching and picking up pieces of metal and flesh scattered over a wide area on the ground.

In your disembodied state, you still insist that you were at rest, that your plane was not in motion…really. Ben, by your side, and looking down ruefully at the mess below, would insist that it was the other way round.

Proceed to scenario number two. This time Ben's vehicle slows down very cautiously. It loses speed just by a fraction of a foot per second. Now you (who are not at all moving) see his plane reversing leisurely but determinedly. After a couple of minutes, you see the tail of his plane gently kissing your plane's proboscis. You feel a tiny jolt; not much damage done.

If you examine the above two scenarios and if you really have a sense of humor too, you cannot help being bemused. In both the cases, you are at rest. In one case, you get a gentle kiss on your schnozzle, and in another case, you are blown to pieces; all for no fault of yours.

A bit more drama before we plunge into more esoteric theories. As before, you are at rest; and the observers on the ground measure your speed at 1000 miles per hour. You see a mountain cliff. As time moves, the cliff seems to grow larger and larger, until you can see the grain structure on the face of the rock. You realize that the cliff is approaching you at a very fast rate. Soon, it is all over. After that:

1. The disembodied you swear that since the cliff moved at a terrific rate, and since it smashed your plane into smithereens, it must have had a huge amount of energy.
2. The observers on the ground, on the contrary, testify that since you moved at a terrific rate, and since your plane blew itself into pieces, the plane must have had a huge amount of energy.

If the Sphinx were present at the scene, it would have asked, "Who, or what had had that huge amount of energy? You, or the cliff?" Your grandson, brought up on a rich diet of relativity, may say that both you and the ground observers are correct. Forget Relativity for the moment. How about sharing the guilt fifty-fifty? Or, how about this variation on quantum theory? The energy was hovering around in mid-limbo, and also was probabilistically present here, there, and everywhere. The moment you, as an observer, open your mouth, it jumps on the cliff. The moment the ground observers open their mouths, the energy shifts on the belly of your excellent airplane. That is called ultra-wisdom. It is also called the most sophisticated and unbeatable strategy for explaining anything; Quantum is the mother of all theories.

Let us quit this mad scenario of the twentieth century and go back a couple of centuries, to the calm, peaceful, ordered days of Newton (Great man2). Our arrow is there, flying through space, having been discharged from a mighty bow. Let us keep it simple and agree that the arrow is moving. The Great man2 has derived beautiful equations for describing moving bodies. Now, a moving body is endowed with a special form of energy called kinetic energy – the energy it acquires due to its motion. The equation, Ke = ½ mv2, stipulates the quantity of that energy. The greater the speed of the same body, the more kinetic energy it possesses. The mystery, Bagdenborg muses, is that the object is the same in both cases, ("It is it. An arrow is an arrow.") and yet has less energy in one state and vastly more in another state.

Apart from that, his more puzzling question is this. If the object (the moving arrow) is storing energy, where is it storing it? How is it storing it? What is that mechanism? We need a place to store something. You store your old bric-a-brac in the basement cellar. You store your favorite Swiss-rolls in the kitchen refrigerator. You store your old photos of your old flames in your secret album.

The objector may sneer and give a facile reply, "Of course, the kinetic energy is in the body of the arrow itself."

In its body? Ah, that means in the molecules, and the atoms, you mean? That really means, in the electrons and protons and neutrons, the constituents, does it not? Fine. Then, discard everything else and confront that one single electron. Think for a moment that that single electron represents the arrow. Just as you asked of the arrow where it stores its energy, in which secret compartment it is safeguarding that energy, ask of the electron now where it is keeping watch (and accounting for) over that mysterious kinetic energy, so that in the event of an immovable object meeting it on its flight, it may check the accounts and give back all that energy to the demanding immovable object, either making a small dent on it, or piercing it deeply as the case may be, depending on its own speed.

The questions are asked neither casually nor with intransigence. Bagdenborg has an ulterior motive in asking them. He is leading us there in his own inimitable style.

Recall here that the amount of this kinetic energy varies with the speed of the object. That means motion is involved, which is invariably linked with time and space. The second point to note is that the object remains itself, as it is, but only acts as an agent, an exchanging medium, receiving "energy" (or "force") and passing it on under certain circumstances to another object.

Now, let us, for the last time, go back to our movie theatre and recall how "motion" was detected. This directly leads us to Bagdimedes' ultra-quantum jump in understanding the hidden secret of space.

The Great Record Keeper

We said that when sixteen frames per second of the moving object are projected on the screen, the brain keeps track of the successive frames, compares them, and thus "re-creates" the sense of motion of the original object – even though neither the screen nor each of the snapshot frames is moving. Memory – record – is the crucial thing.

This is a purely biological, a physiological phenomenon, it seems. Or, if you want to view it from a stark physical point, you can compare it to the way a programmed software runs, the brain being considered as a super-super electronic processor.

Bagdimedes took this concept as the springboard to make his astonishing leap into the depths of intuition.

HE CLAIMED THAT THE MOVING OBJECT, AND SPACE, TOO, MAINTAIN A RECORD – NAMELY, THAT THEY TOO HAVE MEMORY!! He claimed that every object makes an impression on the space it occupies. This, he called, the memory of space.

1. An object, as it moves, leaves its mark on space. The mark or impression is maintained as long as the object keeps moving or until it interacts with another object.

2. Even when the object is stationary, it leaves an impression on space; on the space it occupies.
3. Surprisingly, the object too retains the "memory" it creates on space. This memory is retained in the space inside the object. But this is not really all that surprising. You see, the object reacts with the space on which it sits, and so, that space reacts on the object. This is in consonance with the Great Man2's law, which proclaims that action and reaction are equal and opposite.

Bagdenborg's admirer's further clarifications are adduced now—in case there are any lingering doubts on this issue. The foregoing concepts may appear bizarre at first, but a patient perusal of the commentary will convince the reader about the inevitability of Bagdenborg's deductions. In an exegesis of this kind, repetitions of certain key points are unavoidable, especially since they deal with unfamiliar Bagdenborgesque concepts. We solicit the indulgence of the gentle reader (you).

First, we showed how motion on a screen is conveyed to us, leveraging the property of "retention" of the human eye. Then, we demonstrated how a similar process occurs outside of the theater, in the real world of objects too—with a slight variation. A study of this process inspired Bagdimedes to assert that just as memory was necessary for humans to experience or observe the motion of objects, so too, objects and the space they are in have their memories. Questions will naturally arise at this juncture. Why should space and the objects have memory at all? More seriously, are they sentient beings like us? Exactly what does this Bagdenborg's memory thing mean? What part does it play in the drama of force, motion, and energy?

Now, when Bagdenborg said that space has the capacity to memorize, it does not sound far-fetched or impossible. Just think of Einstein's (The Great Man3) revolutionary insights about gravity, which he proposed in his General Theory of relativity; Bagden's idea will appear to be a natural progression to that. According to the General Theory of Relativity, gravity is defined in a different way. When matter is said to possess gravity, the theory proposes that matter distorts the space around it, creating a "curvature" in space. This concept was quite revolutionary when it was introduced; many were shocked. But the General Theory of Relativity incorporated a thorough mathematical treatise based on this concept. It was so successful, and the accuracy of its equations was so outstanding that the theory was able to make minor corrections to the calculations based on the hitherto respected and well-established Newtonian formulas. The theory also made some predictions that were later confirmed experimentally. It had predicted that light rays would be bent when passing near an object possessing enormous mass—like the sun. It was experimentally verified. And so on. Even after a hundred years, the fundamental concepts of the theory have withstood rigorous experimental/observational tests. A seemingly strange concept of yesterday is the most revered theory today.

Thus, Bagdenborg's insight that matter leaves its mark on space (and vice versa) should not surprise us. It is only a matter of terminology; he used the word "memory" freely in his copious notes. But his admirers have come to the conclusion—after a thorough study of his notes—that Bagden actually meant "mark" when he wrote "memory." As we said, it is all a matter of terminology. (Besides, when we say "matter leaves a mark on space," it sounds more acceptable in scientific circles than when we say "Space has memory." Strange, but true!)

Bagdenborg must certainly have had his reasons when he preferred the word "memory." It becomes clearer as we proceed further. As an additional note, it will be stressed here that Bagdenborg did not believe that gravity—as an attribute to matter—distorts or creates curvature of space. Making a mark is far more insightful and elegant. He was firm on that point. Then, what exactly is that 'mark'?

Here, you may recall Bagden's immense fondness for analogies. The analogy of the human brain or a data storage device is very illuminating in this context. Seen from the outside, when the brain stores additional information, there is no change as we see it. But internally, changes happen in its electrical state, just as in an electronic device. A similar action happens to space when matter (an object) moves. Space, according to Bagdimedes, has many attributes—which have not been explored thus far, but which alone, he insists can provide us with a truer understanding of the universe. By extension, it means the entire phenomenon we observe in the universe.

So, an object leaves a mark on space. A corresponding memory point—or mark—is also created in the object, which too, now has memory. This memory is created in the space that is within the object (obviously, an object, if it is really an object, or even if it appears to be so, must have some size, however small, and that implies that there is space "trapped" in it.) Bagden's man assures us that there is no need to be puzzled by the two kinds of space—space on which the object sits or rides, and space which is inside the object.

Both are space, not to worry. He quotes Bagdimedes, "It is space inside, space outside, and space everywhere."

Now, let us proceed and place the final piece in position, of this jigsaw puzzle of objects, motion, space, and force.

Bagdenborg's astonishing insight.

To truly appreciate Bagden's insight, we have to hark back to the drama of the moving object. Let us put the video of the Moving Object on rewind and watch it accompanied by new commentaries.

The object is moving, and you are inside it. The ground observer is watching it. At a certain point, your object meets an immovable obstacle/object. Your object is shattered, and you descend to the ground. The old quarrel continues. You argue that you were stationary, that you never had any force with you. It is a mystery that your object is blown to pieces. The ground observer insists that you were moving, that you and your object had kinetic energy, and that energy/force was the cause of your object being blown. ("Action and reaction are equal and opposite.") Yak, yak, it goes on.

A diplomat arrives. He is an expert arbitrator and shrewd too. He makes an important observation, which both of you have missed in the heat of the argument. He says that "force" comes into play when two objects interact. This remark is thrown especially at you since you were insisting that your object did not carry any force with it, as it was stationary. The diplomat's explanation is very brilliant—force is indeed an interaction between two (or more) objects. Even if you want to determine whether a single, isolated object is carrying force, you have to measure or detect it by using another object (a measuring device).

In the background, we can hear Bagdenborg laughing. The diplomat's explanation is not only brilliant but also more clever.

Because, keeping in tune with Bagdenborg's background barking, your mind has started growling suspiciously. Your mind is wandering along some such path of thinking as follows: The interaction took place, no doubt. My object was blown, no doubt. The mathematical equation for the kinetic energy of my object might have been correct, too. But how did my object know that it had kinetic energy? You see, if your immovable object did not come in the way of my object's path, my object would still have been intact and moving merrily.

Bagdenborg takes the stage at this point. He begins with terse, clipped sentences. Space is not a passive object. They have all got it wrong. Space is ever active; sensitive, receptive. No object is passive. Space inside it too. Nothing is passive. If passive, no creation, no universe. (Then, he unfolds).

Space, being endowed with memory, keeps track of the moving object. (Who are we to say, "endowed"? We are also part of nature). While the object is in motion, its parameters like speed, mass, and position, etc., are being continuously monitored and stored in its memory. It automatically calculates—sizes up, would be a better description—what the Great Man2 described as the kinetic energy of the body. When your moving object meets the immovable object, space records it too; and acts according to the situation, taking into account the parameters of both the objects. A new pattern of the constituents of your object may form—like your object being disintegrated. That is a secondary issue. There is a redistribution of energy. That is also a secondary issue, in my opinion. According to me, the most beautiful aspect is that space has memory. I feel almost ecstatic about it. I again urge you to see the beauty of it. See, if your object, with the given velocity, is traveling unhindered for one year, or ten years or a million, nothing happens. If it meets another object after one million years, instantaneous action takes place. If this is not memory, what else is?

Further commentaries by Bagdenborg's admirers are added here.

Bagdimedes was tremendously fascinated by the mnemonic nature of space. That is okay. But there are some subtle points that are equally exciting in this drama of motion. Bagdenborg may term them all as secondary issues and leave it at that. It is his unique way of speaking. He throws a stone into the pond and moves away. It is for the likes of us to observe, analyze, and record the ripples that are created. His nature is like that. He almost literally did it once.

A follower of his once came to him seeking an answer to a tough problem on electronic orbits. Bagden literally punched the man on the forehead, on a spot between the eyebrows. The man immediately fell into a trance! He woke up two hours later, mysteriously laden with a complete solution to his problem. This is an authentic anecdote, witnessed by two of his admirers who were present at the scene.

Now, when one reads his theory of memory, the first instinct of the reader is to feel that space is behaving like a sentient being. Having memory and keeping track of things! Especially after that one-million-year journey! Apart from the memory aspect, the statement about space making instantaneous calculations of all parameters like force, mass, speed, energy, and so on is mind-boggling. It is as if a superhuman brain is in operation.

If you let the excitement cool down, you will see the phenomenon from a different angle. We used the phrase "human brain" as a hint. The calculations made by space may be more akin to those of a supercomputer!

The idea appears to be more probable once we tone down the phraseology. The skeptical reader may still feel that it is far-fetched. Ponder the ensuing reasoning at a slow pace. (Yes, again, go outside to that lawn of yours, take deep breaths, have your favorite cuppa, and resume the invigorating cogitation.)

Don't be frightened by the word "memory." Essentially, memory is a recognizable pattern—permanent, temporary, modifiable, etc. The pattern can be anything. You of the electronic generation might not have seen it, but ask your grandpa about an abacus. (His eyes will light up with nostalgia.) He will tell you how they used the abacus in his days to perform simple calculations using colored beads. Come forward a bit more in time. Ask your dad, who has now retired from service. (No offense meant). He will tell you of those wonderful, innovative machines of IBM, which used punched cards. You, of course, may remember eyeing with wonder those small electronic calculators that could be carried in your pocket. (Your prodigy son, who has not touched his teens yet but who is right now texting on his cell phone, will hoot in derision if you dare to talk about those days). Now, you can purchase at any road-shop a pint-sized memory card that can store the contents of thousands of books. What a great wonder!

But after all, that wonder employs the simplest of tricks for registering memory—what is called the binary state. The uninitiated can think of it as an electronic switch that can be either on or off, with these states representing a zero or one; as simple as that. Employing such simple patterns, the most sophisticated instruments and machines have been built. That is all there is to memory! So, one need not be frightened if Bagdenborg suggests that space has memory.

Probably you are still adamant and want to argue further. Having memory (or a mark) is one thing, but manipulating it to perform calculations is quite a different matter, you might argue. Hold on.

Inside a computer or cellphone, there is what is called a "processor"—truly a marvel of the twentieth century. Once the processor receives inputs, it swiftly performs all necessary calculations and manipulations specific to its internal architecture. It does these unerringly and millions and millions of times—all accomplished, basically, employing the movement or state (charge, etc.) of electrons. Memory, calculations, manipulations, electrons → inanimate "matter"; see the link? Are you still left with a residue of doubt, simmering uncomfortably at the back of your mind? You are probably eager to object that the processor or chip was manufactured by a human being, aren't you? Your doubts are uncalled for. Come this way.

Visualize a human being. From the moment of its conception in the womb to the time of its full growth many years later, how much changes it (the human body/system) undergoes! Taken item by item, it is a huge list. How is this enormous, most wonderful task accomplished? By an entity so small that you cannot see it with your naked eye. You got it—DNA!

Two thin invisible entwined strands control the growth and development of the human (and other bodies) body in all its stages of growth: shapes and sizes of various parts like nose, ears, lips, hair color, color of the eyes, skin, at what stage certain glands begin to work—a long list of innumerable characteristics. The DNA can teach a thing or two to the best of management gurus. A fat volume can be written on what the DNA can do and control. As said, all these stupendous tasks are accomplished by a pair of ultramicroscopic strands. Repeat that, stress on that. To bring you back to the link in our thesis: - Fingerprints are memory (unique patterns). DNA is memory; unique patterns. Thus, when Bagdenborg proposes that space has memory, there is no need to feel surprised, none at all. In fact, by appreciating the analogies of fingerprints, DNA, memory chips, and processors, we see that his theory is almost self-evident.

A last vestige of doubt may still linger in the minds of the naïve (very rare, these days, surely) readers. Even granted that space has memory, how can it perform complicated calculations? Just like the programmed processor, is space programmed? Or, is it a sentient being like human beings or other life-forms? At the moment the moving object strikes the immovable obstacle, how can space compute all those complicated mathematical calculations involving force, mass, momentum, speed, and so on? Bagdenborg is making tall claims.

Those are formidable questions indeed. However, the answer is simplicity itself. The questions arise from misconception, are misdirected, and are uncalled for. To dispel this misconception, it is helpful to consider a simple example.

Imagine that an object, weighing, say, one kg, falls to the ground from a height of ten feet. At the beginning of its descent, its speed (velocity, as they say) is zero. It takes a certain time to reach the ground. Starting from time zero, its speed continues to increase (referred to as acceleration) until the moment it touches the ground. All the while, the gravitational force of the earth is acting on the object. When the object reaches the ground, it creates an impact that depends on its mass and final speed. If the same object falls from a greater height (let's say 1000 feet), it takes a bit more time than before to reach the ground, gains more speed, and creates a greater impact. Now, the variable quantities involved here, such as the final speed of the object and the time taken to cover the distance, can be calculated using mathematical formulas. Everything is clear and straightforward so far – use formula A to calculate this, use formula B to compute that.

The subtle point eludes us innocently in this discussion. The object is not bound by any law or formula laid down by us. Many textbooks and popular science books implant a wrong (or distorted) notion in the minds of students by employing unnecessary terminology:

"Obeying Newton's (such and such) law, the object gains so much energy during that time."

"According to this equation, the final velocity of the object must be so much."

"As determined by this formula, the object will take so much time to reach the ground."

Please notice the words in italics. They give the impression that the object is obeying someone's laws. It appears as though scientific laws are being imposed on objects – similar to how constitutional laws are imposed on citizens! When we encounter such descriptions, we are being subtly influenced and conditioned.

The formulas, the equations, the "theories" are not dictating the behavior of any object in the universe. No way. The "theories" are our mental constructions by which we are trying to understand the behavior of objects in the universe. The formulae are convenient instruments for making predictions about the behavior of the objects out there. The object's falling down and hitting the ground with a thud is a phenomenon by itself – independent of our way of describing it. It is also indifferent towards what we theorize about it. This is a very powerful and equally disturbing statement. So, it is safer to leave it at that for the present. To sum up, when the moving object meets the immovable obstacle, what happens as described by Bagdenborg is a natural phenomenon (a phenomenon occurring in Nature), and no additional implication needs to be imposed on that.

Bagdenborg wrote, "An event can be viewed and described at various levels. The ancient Hellenic philosophers, perhaps were satisfied with describing the moving object from a certain angle. The great Man2 (and Galileo) went deeper. The Great man3 delved still deeper and came up with his famous theory. I saw that there was scope in diving into yet deeper depths, and have done so; that is all. Without false modesty, I say that we have reached the rock bottom. I am not being arrogant either."

As the admirer remarked, space is the ultimate frontier. We cannot go beyond that. True, attempts can be made. But all such attempts will only take us outside the boundaries of science.

In the course of reaching this ultimate stage, Bagdenborg spent innumerable hours wondering about the fascinating aspects of force, mass, and motion. We give below a gist of his random thoughts to throw additional light on the subject.

Force at a distance, mechanical force

During the course of our lives, we accumulate chunks of knowledge which are common to all of us. That kind of knowledge can be classified as common knowledge, or common sense, or even as being self-evident, not needing further explanation. ("Everybody knows that." "If you don't know that, you must be a moron.") This is good in one way because it offers us a sense of stability, or contentment, so that we may carry on with the more serious business called living. But knowledge is really a very funny thing. The moment you start probing it, it changes its color! It changes its face. It begins to play hide-and-seek with you. The more curious you get about it, the more dissatisfied and frustrated you become. But man too is a funny animal. He cannot help getting curious about things...So, let us get a little bit curious and see where it leads us.

Take the word "force." If you exclude the scientific jargon, there is no need to explain what force is; the meaning is self-evident and woven into every moment of our daily experience. The force of the wind, the force of a punch on your body, the force you need to push a heavy object – the list is endless. A common factor in all these cases is the physical contact between two objects.

"They" classify this as mechanical force. (The term "they" was the usual way in which Bagdenborg referred to his colleagues.)

At a certain stage in history, humans discovered a strange object called the magnet. The magnet attracts metallic objects like iron and steel. (Apologies for this, but we must explain what a magnet does since we are engaging in serious scientific study here.) The magnet attracts an iron piece that is not in direct contact with it. This type of force, known as magnetic force, is described as "action-at-a-distance." The fact that a body could act on another body without physically touching it was indeed quite mysterious.

Somewhat later, another mysterious force was discovered – gravitational force. The phenomenon of bodies falling down-to-Earth was, of course, the most well known manifestation of it, with its effects deeply ingrained in the memories of all living beings. It fell to the great Man2 to intuit that this attractive force was a property not only of the Earth but of all bodies in the universe. More than a century later, with the discovery of the electron (and subsequently, subatomic particles), one more type of force emerged – that of charged particles. The electron is attributed a "negative" charge, and the proton, a "positive" charge. Like-charged particles repel one another, while opposite-charged particles attract one another. This type of force, too, falls under the category of action-at-a-distance. Setting aside further developments in this field, let us focus on the fundamental puzzle – the transmission of force without physical contact.

To "explain" this mysterious behavior, the concept of 'fields' was introduced. A natural magnet carries a magnetic field around it. An electric coil, through which current passes, produces an electromagnetic field. Isolated charged particles are surrounded by static fields, and so on (electromagnetic waves can travel too – indefinitely across space). The introduction of the concept of fields/waves was a brilliant one; it offered scope for exhaustive mathematical analyses, paving the way for the inventions of a zillion gadgets. The boon came along with a headache too because a wave needs a medium to express (transmit) itself, the way water and wind form the basic material for producing the respective waves. To solve the problem, a hypothetical medium called ether was introduced, but nobody was able to find it or prove its existence!! The idea was abandoned reluctantly.

Once again, let us discard the details, leaving it to the experts to cure the headache they brought on themselves quite merrily. Let us see the funny part of it. The operative word is "action-at-a-distance." As opposed to it, we have what may be termed physical or mechanical transmission of force—the way you push an object, as we said. That is, force acting through physical contact, OK? Hold it right there. Take a breather in that lawn of yours and come back. (This is becoming quite a habit, what?)

The myth of physical contact

We will just compare numbers now and leave the rest to your imagination. (Don't blame us if you are overcome with epileptic seizures).

Take two bar magnets, each approximately three centimeters in length and of medium power. As you know, a magnet possesses two poles: north and south. Like electric charges, like poles repel each other, and opposite poles attract each other. Place the two magnets side by side with both north poles facing each other and both south poles likewise, maintaining a significant distance between them. Now, slowly bring one of them closer to the other. When the gap between them narrows down to about 1 cm, the other magnet will be repelled, preventing the gap from decreasing further. The magnetic force at this distance is sufficiently strong to push the free magnet away. Observe this experiment with the wonder-filled eyes of your childhood days. This clearly demonstrates action-at-a-distance, as the magnets are not in physical contact. Reiterate this fact: the distance between them is merely one centimeter. Yet, a force is actively influencing the objects. Do not be concerned if the following words seem like the ramblings of a drunken person – one centimeter, no contact, such force, one centimeter... no contact... force, force... no contact... whatsoever... no contact... one centimeter, my god... We want the enormity of the distance between the objects (the surprising explanation will follow shortly) to impress upon your mind, along with their size.

Now, come back to your home. Go and push that door of your bedroom, placing your fully stretched palm on the door panel so that there is full contact between your palm and the panel. The door swings open. Note it down, repeat it – there is full physical contact between two objects in this little uneventful drama, the objects being your palm, which transmitted a force, and the door on which the force acted. This is a clear example of mechanical or direct force. So far, so good.

You may even sneer, "It is quite a common experience, so self-evident."

Let us give a little more thought to what happened between you and the bedroom door. Let us look at it, not with the physical eyes of a nine-to-five householder but with the enhanced and empowered eyes of a scientist.

The hand is on the door. Freeze that shot. Zoom, zoom, and zoom.

The skin of your palm is composed of innumerable cells, and the wood on which the palm just pushed is made up of an enormous number of molecules. Zoom, zoom, zoom.

The cells of your skin are chemical substances; they consist of molecules, which in turn are combinations of atoms. Similarly, the molecules in the wood are also combinations of atoms.

So, ultimately, atoms were pushing atoms. The "mechanical," physical force was directly transmitted through atoms. This is quite apparent and requires no further explanation.

Do you think so? Proceed, but tread cautiously. Examine the figure below. Out of the millions and millions of atoms on your palm and the door, two have been represented, one from your palm and the other from the door. One atom is pushing the other.

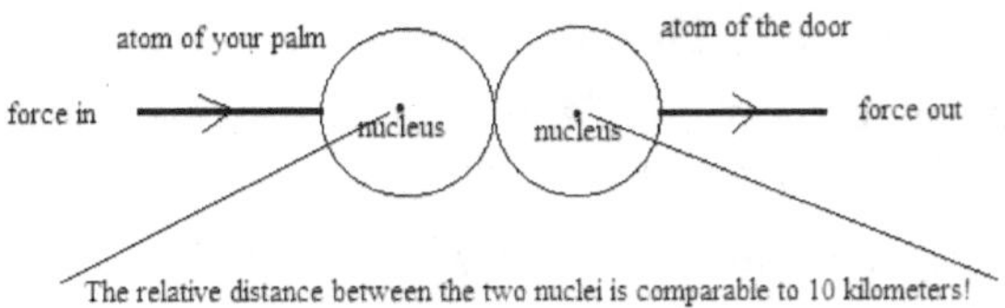

Figure 4

This is old hat, but refreshing one's memory can do no harm. On the left is the atom of your hand. In its center is the glorious nucleus, zealously guarding protons and neutrons in its fort. Electrons orbit around the nucleus. The same description applies to the atom of the door, except for the difference in the number of electrons and protons. Now, consider the statistics, the numbers. The (average) diameter of an atom is on the order of 10-8 cm. The size of the nucleus is on the order of 10-12. The minus signs on the superscripts do not immediately convey the recognizable scale of the distances involved. Visualize it as follows: If the nucleus of one atom were one-meter in diameter, the other nucleus would be 10,000 meters away (equivalent to 10 kilometers).

In the "action at distance" scene of the magnets, the distance was one centimeter. In comparison, it would be even less, considering the bar magnets were three inches in size. So, what is one centimeter compared to ten kilometers? It would be on the order of 100x10,000 = 1,000,000, a million!

THUS, THE SO-CALLED PHYSICAL FORCE IS ACTING AT A COMPARATIVELY DISTANT RANGE, ONE MILLION TIMES GREATER THAN THAT IN THE CASE OF THE ACTION-AT-A-DISTANCE.

You once believed there was firm, solid contact, and now you realize that there exists a comparative gap of a million units. Can there be a greater illusion than this? Or perhaps irony? Bagdenborg thinks it's comedy because he sees Nature laughing at us, playing its exquisite game of hide-and-seek.

After spending many frustrating hours contemplating the mystery above, you must force yourself to conclude that there is no difference between "physical" force and that of the action-at-a-distance. Ironically, it implies that there is nothing "physical" about a physical force!

Your doubting Thomas, the eternal skeptic from the previous pages, may raise an objection. His arguments and the replies to them will follow a somewhat ridiculous path. He might point out that the atom contains electrons orbiting the nucleus. The "force" from your palm is transmitted to the electron (the left one in our figure). Since this electron is orbiting, it will transmit the force to the door's electron while reaching the other side of its orbit. This, he will argue, is the physical transmission of force.

The reply: - Alright. That electron that "received" the force is also orbiting. So, it will dislodge the electron in its neighboring atom, assuming a new position. The dislodged electron will, in turn, dislodge its neighboring electron... and so on. Do you know what this activity is called? It's called the flow of electricity! So, merely by pushing the door, you are generating electricity. Remarkable, isn't it? But dear chap, the door panel is made of wood, which does not conduct electricity. (Certain materials, when subjected to pressure, produce electricity. This phenomenon is known as the Piezoelectric effect. Not all materials exhibit this property.)

Second reply: The force from your "push," if transmitted to the electron, need not necessarily be conveyed to its neighboring atom's electron. The extra force from your push might merely alter the state of the electron, such as changing its orbital path.

Third reply: If your force travels from electron to electron all the way, the nuclei of the atoms would remain in their original positions! That implies there is no physical motion at all! (Ha, ha, ha, isn't that the ultimate absurdity?) Therefore, it's evident that the "force" must act not only on the electrons, the outermost citizens of the atomic region but also on the nucleus (the capital) and its constituents. However, as we mentioned earlier, there is an enormous gap of half a million units between the outermost electrons and the inner nucleus, which means your "physical" force isn't a physical force at all!

Tailpiece to the third reply: This is the appropriate place to remind the reader of Bagden's shell theory! Recall that Bagden's shell encloses and maintains the individuality of the atom, thereby making the atom with all its innards an individual unit. So now, the objecting Thomas can reasonably argue that since Bagden's shells are in contact with one another, the force (from the palm on the door) was transmitted physically, through contact. Doubting Thomas has been vindicated after all.

Taking the wind out of his sails: Bravo, Thomas, but wait. Look at what happens to the door. It moves. That means our atom of the door under consideration moves. Understand? Now, if the atom, carrying its Bagden shell, moves, it implies that the inner nucleus also moves. If the shell moves along with its contacts, the "force" has surely been shared by its contents (electrons, nucleus, protons, neutrons). But, circling back, we must emphasize that there is a gap of half a million units between the shell and the nucleonic contents! Therefore, once again, there is only action-at-a-distance, not a physical or mechanical force. Gosh! What a flip-flop!

The kinds of arguments introduced above represent only a select few among the countless arguments and counter-arguments that can be generated. (If you doubt this, simply share these pages in any internet "group" and observe the ensuing discussion.)

This is why we must embrace Bagdenborg's theory that space possesses memory! The drama appears to unfold above the surface, but the script is being written beneath, beyond what meets the eye. As Bagdenborg states, "The master plan for the visible architecture of the universe is concealed within the deep recesses of space."

It all hinges on the existing depending on the non-existent.

Navigating his ship with the assistance of his fentologic-powered rudder, Bagdolumbus often arrived at unfamiliar shores. His research on force, energy, motion, and mass led him to a profoundly startling conclusion. To fully appreciate the beauty (and rigorous precision) of his insights, it is advisable to accompany him on his journey with an open mind. In reality, it's all remarkably straightforward, rational, and logical. As usual, let us commence with the most common level of our experience.

Who harbors any doubts concerning energy and force? (In physics, they are interconnected. Force, when applied over time, gives rise to energy. For instance, in electricity, "watt," the wattage of a device, is synonymous with force or power. If you utilize that device for a certain number of hours, the energy consumed is referred to as a "watt-hour.") None of us questions what these terms signify. You don't need to consult a marathon runner to comprehend the concept of energy. The tennis player who has played for five grueling hours, the Everest climber, the heavyweight champion who has endured fifteen rounds; they all grasp it. The force required to clear a one-foot-high hurdle differs significantly from that needed to clear a seven-foot-high bar in high jump. To reiterate, the meaning of energy is self-evident.

Yet, the most obvious knowledge has the strange characteristic of becoming obscure when examined closely or seen from an unusual perspective.

In grammar, there is a certain classification of words as "abstract nouns." For example, take the word "beauty." You look at a flower and admire its beauty. You gaze at the snow-capped peaks of the distant mountain, and you are enthralled by the beauty of the scenery. You behold the beauty of a face and lose all sense of time – apart from losing your heart to the possessor of that beauty. Now, study the above examples carefully, and with rigorous objectivity. Where is the "beauty" that we spoke of so gloriously? It is nowhere. The flower is there, the mountain is there, and the face is there. They exist as objects in the world. But "beauty" does not exist the way those objects do! It exists only in the dictionary. We are not indulging in linguistic acrobatics here. Take your time to analyze the previous sentences; no hurry, no worry. When you get acclimatized to the pure logic of it, proceed to ponder our by-now-familiar moving objects.

The moving arrow strikes the tree and pierces it with a sharp twang. The huge cannonball, screaming through the air, strikes the (poor) mud wall of the enemy's fort and smashes it. A big chunk of a meteor zooms down through the atmosphere and impinges on the earth, blowing up a huge crater.

In the above examples, we automatically speak of the force, the energy of the moving objects – and may even compare the relative amounts of destruction caused by the moving objects. The cannonball must have a great amount of force to make the fort's wall fall tumbling down. The meteor must have surely had a far greater amount of energy to have created a crater on solid earth. The words "force" and "energy" automatically stand out in describing the above scenes. Force, energy, see?

Now, perform the same intellectual exercise we did with beauty. Consider, reconsider, and carefully go through the images again and again. With a calm, dispassionate mind, ask yourself, "Where is energy in the above scenarios? Dear reader, dear friend, my dear sir, there is no force anywhere!! They (energy, force) do not exist. (Repeat it at least a hundred times, like a mantra, and you will be convinced about the truth of it.) Please don't fall prey to the wiles of automatic, reactionary reflexes. Look at the scenes with the eyes of a robotic camera.

You see the cannon. You see the cannon firing. The cannonball moves. You see the mud wall. You see the ball hitting the wall. You see the wall crumbling, accompanied by sound and flying debris. That is all. That is all that you see and hear (or feel if a piece of the flying debris hits you). This process can be described as the pure and first stage of perception – "the input" as Bagden says, "The input" alone can claim to exist out there, excluding other philosophical considerations. Everything else connected with that input is inference, which could be a vast amount, often enormously complicated. In spite of heated debates, the ticklish truth is that all inferences need not be correct or true. A more ticklish (and subtle) truth, according to Bagden's fentologic, is that even if an inference is correct, it need not necessarily have an objective existence. ("One of his veiled barbs at mathematics," comments the admirer.)

The notebook of Bagdimedes contains many pages of more abstruse arguments along these lines. His final conclusion is firm: Force and energy do not exist; they are only concepts. This is a stunning proposition that is sure to raise howls of protests. The strongest protest will be, "Then what about those grand formulas and equations? They are perfect and unshakeable. They not only describe what has happened but predict what will happen in different circumstances. They are infallible and exact."

As for the infallibility and exactness, Bagdecartes has already tackled the issue with rigor and purity – please see the chapter on addiction to measurement. The infallibility, when seen in the proper perspective, does not really belong to the equations but to the actions and events of Nature. Full credit goes to nature. Having doubts? Then, ponder this gem of a fentological poser. If the fired cannonball, after the end of its journey, does not touch the wall but comes back and falls at the feet of the artillery man with an apologetic grin, what will be the consequence? If nine apples fall down to the ground but the tenth one flies off whimsically and attaches itself to the branch of another tree, what will happen? All the scientists will have to scratch off all their equations and hurry, worry-faced, to their blackboards. Savvy? That is only one chapter of the story. Move on to the next page.

"What is this, lad? Lass, this is that only.

What is that, then? Lass, that is this only." (Gist of lines from a movie song.)

Before we capture the quintessence of the formulas, let us throw a lasso around them and capture them – the lasso made out of flexible but strong and sturdy fentological strands. We begin with the most universal statement: All knowledge boils down to the act of description. Description involves using words in various meaningful combinations. Description can be long – like the great epics. (The famous Indian epic, Mahabharata, is said to contain more than one hundred thousand couplets; not words.) It can be brief and succinct, like poems, sonnets, haikus, etc. Science too is a branch of knowledge, with the exception being that it has two branches – qualitative and quantitative. The former type is useful in studies like anatomy, botany, biology, and so on. The quantitative mode is useful – and unavoidable – when studying the purely physical world of matter and its behavior, where generalization, abstraction, and quantities (numbers) are the dominating features. Thus were the seeds of mathematics sown; which has grown into a vast forest, some areas of which are impenetrable except to those equipped with special talents.

So, in essence, mathematics too is descriptive. Only, it has invented its own exclusive alphabet of symbols (inevitable and necessary, as we said). Just a basic, simple example will illustrate the point. Descriptively, the famous Pythagoras Theorem states, "In a right-angled triangle, the square of the length of the hypotenuse is equal to the sum of the squares of the lengths of the other two sides." It (the statement) is quite cumbersome, especially if you are going to refer to it often. The same theorem can be described symbolically thus – $a^2=b^2+c^2$. Not only is the formula convenient, but also, it is extremely useful in performing calculations, and more than that, amenable to further manipulations – derivations as they are called. In many cases, the derivations can be huge.

This is the crux of the matter – equations and theorems too are descriptive only. ("They do not override Nature," – Bagden.) The observation is apt to raise many questions, to kindle elaborate debates, but space does not permit us here to go into all that. We are just underlining the bottom line. Because, as the admirer says, all that serious discussion has to come to a funny termination, condensed into the dainty ditty at the head of this section. (Please read it again and savor it to appreciate the following disquisition.)

There is a famous witticism in semantics that says if you start defining one word, you have to define all the words in the dictionary. For example, if you want to define what "hair" is, you will say something like, "It is a thin, inert strand-like growth on the skins of human beings and animals." (The exactness of the words does not matter here). Consequently, you have to define the words you have employed, like skin, humans, animals, etc., let alone the adjectives and verbs. To define skin and the other words, you have to bring in other sets of words. The chain is obviously endless. Look at the alternative to avoid the mess. You have to assume that the word "hair," with which we began, is the only unknown word, and that all the other words are known or familiar. What does it import? It means that, to define or "know" the unknown, you have to take the help of that which is already known. And that means that when you feel you "understand" the unknown, you are in essence manipulating that which is already known. Nothing new has been actually known! So, to repeat, the new is only a modified or altered form of the old. The unknown is just that – unknown; forever. The conclusion seems to be heavily tinged with philosophy. As Bagdenborg was fond of saying, "They are the two sides of one coin." Let us flip over the coin and look at the "science" side.

Let us leave the poor harassed hair alone and take up a well known formula dealing with our subject properly – force, mass, and motion. The formula, F = m x a, is quite basic but fundamental. Let us examine it using everyday language and see where it leads.

The symbols, F, m, and a, stand for force, mass, and acceleration, respectively. The equation defines the relationship among these three quantities – variables, or parameters as they are called. Let us assume that our Simple Simon is unfamiliar with these three parameters. So, he asks Teacher1. Teacher1 explains in a pitying, pedantic way.

"Simple, Simon. Force (F) is that entity required to produce an acceleration, a, on an object of mass, m. Multiplying the value of m with that of the acceleration, a, will give you the value of the force, F."

Simon is bewildered. He does not yet know what mass and acceleration are. Afraid of being made fun of, he approaches Teacher2 and asks what mass, m, is.

Teacher2 says, "Simple, Simon. Mass is that quantity which acquires an acceleration, a, when a force F is applied to it. You divide the numerical quantity of F by the numerical quantity of 'a,' and you will get the numerical quantity of 'm,' the mass of the object."

Again, Simon is frustrated. He does not know what acceleration is. Afraid of being criticized, he goes to Teacher3 and asks what acceleration 'a' is.

Teacher3 explains, "Simple, Simon. Consider the above equation. When a force F is applied to an object of mass, m, the object acquires an acceleration, 'a.' You divide the numerical quantity of F by the numerical quantity of m, and you will get the numerical quantity of 'a.' It's simple, see."

Simple Simon is stunned into silence and numbness – both. He realizes that he has traveled a full circle and is back where he started. Somewhere in his childhood, his grandfather used to amuse him by singing the dainty ditty quoted before, and the lines begin their tintinnabulation in his ears. "What is this? This is that, see! What is that? That is this only, simple." During the same period of his childhood, his kid-brother used to amuse himself by tying a strip of cloth to the tail of a cat and clapping with joy as the cat fiercely chased its own tail, whirling in frenzied circles. That image too now comes back on the mental screen of Simple Simon. In despair, he wonders whether he will ever be able to understand physics.

The above illustration may appear hilarious, but there is a good deal of truth lurking behind it.

Let us take the place of Simple Simon – and cogitate, instead of despairing, whether it is possible to break out of the deuced circle he is trapped in. An elementary strategy would be to stick to what is observable. It may not carry an intellectual appeal, but it promises results. The directly observable entities in the deuced formula which perplexed Simon are: mass and acceleration. (Mass, in the loose sense of "an object.")

A moment of reflection tells us that mass, force, and acceleration are the properties attributed to the visual object.

So, we begin with the object and its mass. "Mass is a mass of mess," Bagdenborg once declared, tongue firmly held in check. There is a reason for his dry humor. A very common (and understandable) impression is that if an object is big in size, it must have a big mass too. Recall the common phrases, "a massive structure," "a massive object," and so on. But mass, as defined in physics, is not connected with the size of an object. In basic textbooks, it was customary to define mass as the "quantity of matter" and proceed to the next lessons. To make the concept a bit more understandable, we may use the word "weight." Using "weight," the idea of the real mass, as opposed to its apparent size, becomes more manageable. For example, a bale of cotton having a size of one cubic meter will definitely appear to be bigger in size than a gold bar of one-foot length by one-foot breadth by one-foot height. But when you put them on the pans of a weighing machine, the pan containing gold will come down; meaning that gold has more weight than cotton (of the same size). In physics, instead of saying "weight," we say "mass." This is fairly simple. But, as we said, if you go on digging deeper, simple things tend to get complicated.

Why do we—not exactly we, but they, the boffins—prefer to use the term "mass" instead of "weight"? It becomes obvious when, instead of using the weighing balance, you try to lift the gold bar. It will be so heavy! What does it mean? It means that the force of Earth's gravity is pulling down the gold bar when you try to lift it. That is what is meant by weight—the influence of the force of gravity. For example, the same gold bar would "weigh" about 1/6th of what it "weighs" on Earth when it is on the moon; you could lift it more easily there because the moon's gravitational force is less than that of Earth.

Incidentally, it is worth mentioning an intriguing fact, while we have touched on the topic of weight and gravity. It is customary, while writing a book on popular science, to tell the readers that often the discoveries in science dramatically fly against common sense.

Let us follow suit, at the same time utilizing the examples to examine the old F, m, and a. In the course of normal experience, we see different objects falling down to the ground. A dry leaf detaches itself from the branch of a tree and leisurely flutters its way down, gently kissing the earth (if you are gifted with rare poetic propensity, you may say the ecstatic experience lasted an hour). On the contrary, a brick, if let fall from the same height as that of the leaf, appears to zoom down and crash on the ground with a heavy thud. To make it more persuasive, consider it personally. You do not mind a leaf or a flower falling on your head—not at all. But you would rather be farther away when the brick falls down, even though from the same height. The obvious conclusion is that heavy objects fall down with a greater impact than lighter objects. There is no doubt about it at all.

To truly appreciate the next idea (or rather, discovery), you have to travel back in time by about four hundred years. You see, the contrast between the lazy descent of the leaf and the sudden drop of the brick automatically leads us to a conclusion. The conclusion is reinforced again by the striking contrast between the impact of the leaf on the ground and that of the brick. The weight of the brick is hugely greater than that of the leaf. So, automatically, almost instinctively, we surmise that a heavy object falls down with greater speed than a lighter object. It is "common sense." Before the great Galileo arrived on the scene, people thought the conclusion was self-evident. (You too would have agreed with it if you were there.) To the amazement of all, the (blasphemous) Galileo proved that both the heavy and the lighter objects attain the same speed; they reach the ground at the same time when let fall from the same height! Even in the present day, if you temporarily set aside your school studies, the idea appears amazing. All objects, irrespective of their 'weight,' fall down to the earth with the same speed when falling down from the same height. (By speed, we mean the final, terminal speed, at the moment when they touch the ground.) Just a bit more amusing but interesting jugglery here. If the same object, of course, falls down from a greater height, its final speed will be more. If it falls down from a still greater height, its speed will be so enormous that, owing to the friction of the air (at such speeds), the heat generated will be enough to burn the object! (That is what happens to most of the meteors we see streaking across the sky.) In fact, this too is a bit mysterious. Come to think of it, if an object falls down from either ten feet height or a thousand feet height, why should its speed increase? The speed should be constant, no?

But the actual fact is that, under the influence of Earth's gravity, the speed of a falling object keeps on increasing every second. This kind of continuous increase in speed is called acceleration (The term 'a' in the equation F = m x a). That the speed of an object should continuously increase is not really so obvious; it's a bit puzzling, in fact. Here is where the term 'F,' force, comes into play. A force, as long as it is acting on an object, induces acceleration in the object, not constant speed. Only an uncommon genius like Newton could envision such a fantastic yet simple relation between force, mass, and acceleration.

We will sum up this discussion. The acceleration, that is, the continuous increase in speed of an object, is the same for all objects under the influence of a common gravitational force like that of the Earth or any other object like the Sun. For Earth's gravitational force, the acceleration is 32 feet per second per second. (Note the repetition of 'per second'; that is the way to denote acceleration). On the surface of the Moon, the acceleration will be considerably less since the mass of the Moon is less than that of the Earth. The Sun, being tens of thousands of times bigger than the Earth, has a far greater gravitational force.

A second property to remember in connection with gravitational force (or the electromagnetic force too) is that the force becomes weaker and weaker as one moves away from the object. In fact, the force diminishes as the square of the distance from the object. (It was child's play for the great man to deduce it.) The force spreads equally in all directions from the object. So, the further it "moves," the volume of space covered by it increases naturally, like the volumes of bigger and bigger globes. The surface areas of such bigger and bigger globes increase in proportion to the square of the distances from the center.

And finally, the strength of the gravitational force of an object is in direct relation to its mass (not size, remember). The greater the mass of an object, the greater its gravitational force. Here is the clincher – all objects, whether huge, big, small, or microscopic, possess gravity. It is a fantastic insight of incomparable depth, which only men of Newton's stature are privileged to have. A speck of floating dust too possesses gravitational force, but its mass is so small that the force is infinitesimally weak, almost to the point of being non-existent. Refer again to the table of fundamental forces and notice that the gravitational force is billions of times weaker than the electromagnetic force. To cap off the discussion, the bottom line is that "mass," of any kind, possesses gravity. At the subatomic level, it is fashionable to use the term "particle." So, throughout these discussions, the words "object," "particle," and "mass" are used synonymously. As pictured earlier in the Table of Fundamental Forces, the "particles" are supposed to possess (or exhibit) one or more of the fundamental forces found to exist so far. But all "particles" (mass) exhibit gravitational force. Now, doesn't that seem curious? That fact should put us on instant alert. According to the admirer, Bagdimedes is reported to have told them often, "That is where you have to start if you want to build your TOE" (TOE, for the uninitiated, stands for Theory of Everything). We have strayed a bit from poor Simple Simon's determined pursuit of F, m, and 'a.' Let us go back and walk along with him, following his simple and straightforward ways of reasoning. If he appears to get stuck, there is always Bagdenborg's Fentological force to spur him into acceleration.

Simon started his inquiry with what was "directly" observable – the object and its motion. We found ourselves in a kind of cul-de-sac while considering a property of the object, defined as "mass." If you look through Simon's eyes, you will see that an object and its mass are two different things. Mass is only an attribute of the object, one of its properties, like size, force, etc. Surely, the object must be something other than its properties, mustn't it? (Whiteness is the property of milk, but "milk" is surely different from "whiteness.") On the other hand, it can also be argued that an object is the sum of all its properties. For example, a triangle is the sum (is composite) of all the properties it exhibits, like the lengths of its individual sides, the internal angles, and so on. This kind of quest again takes us deep into the inextricable depths of verbal quagmires—not exactly the standards set by science. So, for the present, let us accept the word "particle" as standard currency and move along, accepting Bagden's proposition that mass is only an abstract property of that which we see or feel as an object. If Simon, still intrepidly goes in search of the "object" in its real essence, he will be sorely disappointed and perplexed too, as we have already described in the light of Bagdenborg's exegesis on the spectrum of human perception. That is why, as the best practical solution, Bagdimedes put forward his Theory of Shells, which too, we have described sufficiently well in the initial chapters of this book.

Thus, the next alternative left for Simple Simon, in his examination of the "directly observables," is the motion of the object, defined by the terms acceleration and speed. Take speed, the simpler one. In plain terms, (uniform) speed is the distance traveled by an object in a given time interval. If an object moves by a distance of 10 meters in a span of one second, we say its velocity is 10 meters/second. We have already demonstrated, in the light of Bagdenborg's insight, that "motion" too is a kind of illusion, or a software program being executed in space itself. That insight of his culminated in the startling theory that space has memory.

Now, if that theory appears quaint, you can define the motion of an object as a change or rate of change of its position. The operative word here is change. That leads us to the final, silent actor in our drama of F = m x a – time! Change is the very essence of time. One can even take it as the definition of time. At last, we seem to have come across the real manipulator who is pulling the strings.

Try to go and grab him; he too will begin to play hide-and-seek, like the other participants in the drama do. Let us have a go at it.

Dealing with and manipulating things in the practical world is far easier than defining them—a superb irony. Ideally, defining a word should be simple and succinct. It is so only in a dictionary. Funnily, if you want to really grasp what the word or concept actually stands for, you usually get dragged—willingly or unwillingly—into the treacherous quicksand of more and more words. How do you define time? Let us leave aside philosophical and mystical considerations and concentrate on proper science.

Essentially, the act of measurement consists of comparison. We create or invent a universally accepted yardstick. Then we compare the magnitude of whatever is to be measured with that yardstick. Intrinsically, there are no big or small objects or things in this world. 'Big' and 'small' arise when we compare, that is when we try to measure. (See the chapter "Addiction to measurement" and read what Bagden called "The Chocolate Bar.") Just like distance, time too is one enormous stretch of infinity that we cannot grasp as a whole. So, we attempt to 'measure' it by breaking it up into small, manageable units, which we invent using repetitive action (cyclical) – like the to-and-fro swing of a pendulum. (Sand, shadows, and water were other means used once upon a time. Digital, electronic timers are ubiquitous nowadays.)

Apart from this, there are theories and speculations about time in modern science. It is not necessary to go into all that since we are mainly concerned with the unique ideas of Bagdenborg. A couple of sentences broadly touching on these concepts will do. For example, the Great Man3 propounded that even the 'time' as we have been accustomed to measuring is liable to change, either to run slow or to run fast depending on the speed of the object. Thus, there seems to be no "absolute time" as per the General Theory of Relativity. Still, many scientists have speculated about what is called "The Arrow of Time." Another word, called 'entropy,' is much bandied about when discussing time. Entropy is venerated as if it is God's Law. (But the word "entropy" itself is as thoroughly vague as can be humanly possible – "A feat only men of great intellect can achieve," as Bagden wryly noted.) Let us leave all such intricate high-brow theories and explanations for them to brood narcissistically in their snug corners. Let us roam freely in the vast Bagdenborgian area, uninfluenced by them, thus being untroubled or unhindered by them.

Time, as we said, is change. Change comes in many forms, but here we are sticking to change in position (motion in particular) since we saw that in the physical world, everything boils down to space and motion in the final analysis. Stating more explicitly, an object is in motion when it occupies position x at a certain time and then position y later. Notice how the change is intimately bound with both "time" and "motion." To define time, you bring in motion, and motion itself connotes time. Both these things appear to arise because of the change in position. Now, focus on the important word, "change."

How do you know a change has occurred? You are in New York now. Sometime later, you find yourself in Washington. How do you know you are in Washington, and not in New York? You know because Washington is different from New York, for one thing. But, more importantly, you remember you were in New York. That is MEMORY in operation. Memory, as pointed out earlier, is a kind of record, a mark. See, again, we have zoomed in on this interesting, unique phenomenon – memory or record.

The creation of a unit of time (for purposes of measurement) is made possible because of the unique property of recordability (memory) in a cyclical fashion (identical repetition). The tip of the pendulum swings left and right, with the extreme points being the "record." The cyclical repetition of this process allows us to use it as a means to measure time; that is change. (The same repetitious movement happens even when measuring distance – like using the same "one-meter" rod/tape again and again to measure a kilometer). This is the ultimate end that Simple Simon will come to in his search – memory, memory, always memory. And memory is a form of impression! (We have already explored all that). Only, the unique discovery of Bagdenborg is that the ultimate substance on which impressions are created is space itself, not amber, shellac, magnetic tape, or your Blu-ray disc. What a thrilling journey we have made, and what an enormous discovery awaited us at the end!

We will recapitulate, adding the extra bit of information we have discovered. To begin with, Bagdenborg showed that the "mass" of the object is stored in the memory of space. In addition to that, the memory of successive positions is also automatically stored in space. From these two types of data, space computes the speed of the object, taking into account the time taken for the successive transitions of the object. (A small amendment – "computes" is a better word than "calculates.") Along his incessant leaps from insights to insights, Bagdenborg discovered that the above two types of data are not the only ones that space keeps track of. As a matter of fact, space records and keeps track of all the events that occur in it!! (We will take it up later so as not to get distracted from the present line of investigation.) This act of computation, we repeat, is not to be confused with that of any agency; it is a phenomenon of nature itself.

The Great Grandfather Clock

When we mentioned in the previous paragraph that space computes the time taken for the object to move along successive positions, the perspicacious reader (you) is sure to be intrigued. In our external, objective world, a separate instrument is required to measure and keep track of time – a clock employing a mechanism. Even if you accept the breathtaking idea that space keeps a record of the positions of objects, you are bound to wonder, "Heck, where the heck does space hide its clock?"

To Bagdimedes, this is not a tough riddle at all. Incidentally, his insight puts to rest the debate on the existence of an absolute, universal standard of time. "They are unnecessarily confusing and complicating the issue," he wrote. (By now, you must be familiar with whom "they" alludes to.) "We have to use the pure and rigorous form of Socratic reasoning to decipher some types of riddles."… The prevailing wisdom says that time is a variant. The time of a moving object is different from the time of another object at rest (relative to it). If a third object is moving at some other speed, its time is different from the other two. See, it goes on and on. Even distances (lengths, measuring rods) are different relative to different moving objects. Everything is relative.

Pounce on that word, 'relative,' and pin it down like a sumo wrestler advises Bagden! Concentrate on that word for a while, and the word will reveal the hidden background against which (and with the help, only with the help, of which) your word is performing its impish antics. The fundamental perception – in fact, the root of any perception – is that any kind of change can be perceived as a change against a background of the unchanging.

In the Eastern tradition, there is a wise saying which goes, "Even elixir ingested in excess acts as a poison." The same can be said of logic or ratiocination. "Logic is a double-edged instrument," wrote Bagdenborg. "It can clarify. It can also confuse. It even has the capacity to delude." Consider all those innumerable 'relatives' – and try to protect yourself from vertigo if you can. Object A is moving relative to object B, which it considers as being at rest. At the same time, object B is moving relative to A, which it "sees" as being at rest. Who is at rest? Who is moving here, actually? Both claim they are correct! If there is a third object C, you will get three contrary opinions, which are also correct. In the universe, there must be quadrillions of objects, and more. Go, and ask all of them! This is where Bagden applies his sumo-hold. Don't focus (wildly) on the objects. Focus on the common thread – motion, a variant, a change. Change can only be perceived against a background of the changeless, an invariant. There may be your quadrillion-drillion of "relative times" in the universe. All those can be said to exist only in comparison with an invariant. "That is the universal clock, the clock of space," he declared – "The Primordial Clock," as he termed it. For a clock to work, some kind of repetitive (cyclical) mechanism is necessary, like a wheel spinning, like the Earth turning on its axis, or going round the sun, etc. Imagining such a kind of movement of space leads to terrible complications. But there is another kind of, a far simpler – and elegant – cyclical movement. It is vibration. Bagdenborg found that space does exactly that, at an unimaginably high frequency. You may be familiar with frequencies, like those of processors of computers and cell phones; 1.6 gigahertz, 2 gigahertz, the user manuals, and the ads explain. The frequencies of cosmic rays that originate in outer space are in the range of 2.4 x 10^23 hertz. Those are really very high frequencies indeed. Yet, when compared to the frequency at which space vibrates, they appear to be extremely sluggish; phlegmatic, if one can be permitted to bring in that word in a scientific context.

Though Bagdenborg disliked mathematical analysis, he had to employ it to satisfy his own curiosity. His mathematics showed that space was vibrating at a frequency of 10^80 cycles per second! That magnitude is breathtaking – compare it with the most powerful gamma rays discovered thus far, which have frequencies of the order of 10^27 hertz.

Two intriguing doubts arise immediately. As a rule, electromagnetic waves possess two properties. You see, frequency and wavelength are interrelated. The higher the frequency of an electromagnetic wave, the smaller its wavelength will be. For example, radio waves have frequencies that are millions of times less than those of gamma rays. Their wavelengths can exist in the range of meters, whereas the wavelengths of gamma rays are so small that they are fractions of the size of an atom! Thus, if we consider Bagden's space frequency of 10^80, the wavelength will be so small that it poses a problem. You see, as per the prevailing understanding of nuclear physics, there is a limit to the measurement of length called the Planck length (we touched on this aspect earlier). Bagden's wavelengths fall far below the Planck length – and there lies the rub. Secondly, as the frequency of electromagnetic waves increases, they are found to be more and more energetic. For example, ultraviolet rays, which have a higher frequency than that of ordinary visible light, carry more energy. X-rays are far more energetic; they pass through the human body. Gamma rays are immensely more energetic. They interact with matter and shatter it. So, if (as Bagdimedes claims) the space frequency is billions of billions times higher, then the effect of such frequencies on matter is unimaginable – all matter should shatter, with our earth being the most important casualty in the list! From this point of view, it can be argued that Bagden's proposition is untenable. (His opponents have not hesitated to use the term "lunatic"). What Bagden has to say on this deserves a separate chapter, and we will do justice to it there. If your worry graph is rising sharply, it can be quelled for now with this tidbit in a capsule.

What was said about the relationship between frequencies and wavelengths and energy levels is okay as far as the electromagnetic waves are concerned. But Bagden's space frequencies are not electromagnetic in their nature. They are vibrations. They do not propagate – travel – like waves. Such waves are called standing waves. Bagdenborg's waves are unique, producing most exciting effects. As promised, the details will be taken up in another chapter. One last point. As regards the statement that the vibrational frequency is so high, doubts may arise about the disruptive and destructive effects of such implausible energy levels on the surrounding matter. Here it may be pointed out that the energy levels of waves depend on the amplitude of the waveform to a great extent. An analogy will bring home the point better. A very tightly wound (metallic) string may produce a high pitch. But the volume can be as low as one can control, by the plucking of the string.

A summary

The salient points of Jestenborg's astonishing research into the nature of the motion of objects can be summed up as follows:

*Force is an illusion. At best, it is only a notion.

The same thing goes for mass and motion.

*Mass is a property only, but it leaves its mark on space.

*Space has memory and stores up the properties of an object in motion, like its position, rate of change of position, etc.

*Space is intelligent in the sense that we talk of intelligent appliances and gadgets. All relevant computations on the properties of matter are done automatically.

*Space is the absolute clock. It is the fundamental-most timer in which the original time is born, the original time that keeps track of all types of changes occurring in space and its contents.

Things do not exist. They can only be described by virtue of their properties. All descriptions are circular.

Chapter – 6

THE WOMB OF CREATION I *(TABULA RASA)*

First, a few words about Bagdenborg's methodology before we step into the main field, the minefield, of his researches. As he grew more and more mature, he tended towards avoiding mathematical treatment of his copious conjectures, postulations, and theories. "I am losing faith in mathematics. My colleagues will rightfully dub me a science atheist!" he once confessed to his admirer.

According to him, scientific analysis can be of two kinds: qualitative and quantitative. The quantitative method, by necessity, uses mathematics. There is, of course, no doubt that mathematics is a brilliant, highly useful tool. But it is very selfish, taking delight in misleading or even befuddling its user. "It is like heroin. Once it gets into your system and you get used to it, you become a slave for life," Bagdimedes warns. Those are strong words indeed, and most of us may not agree with Bagden's sentiments. But that is Bagdenborg's Bagdenesque style of talking. In his view, the qualitative approach is tougher (and more beautiful). It yields quality science, as he put it. Because of these convictions, we find in his later works more and more descriptive science. Be that as it may, we may rest assured of one thing – his ideas are always off the beaten track and startling.

Baglileo jotted down ideas in his notebooks as and when they struck him. His notebooks were not, thus, written with a view to publishing in the form of books. We are collating ideas on classifiable topics here, adding minimal editorial touches where warranted, but certainly in no way interfering with the stream of his thoughts. Scattered randomly across the vast spread of his notes, we find abundant insights related to space, matter, and creation. It was natural for a man of his temperament. Similar to the broad classification of human beings as extrovert and introvert, science too can be classified as running in two modes – extravert and introvert. The extrovert science exuberantly races along the path of more and more experiments, newer and newer discoveries, and flashier gadgets. Introvert science, though in touch with the activities of the extrovert, is more interested in going deeper beneath the glamorous phenomena to crack open the riddles of fundamental mysteries: the origin of the universe, space, time, etc. The exquisite irony is that in spite of our astonishing leap in material progress, matter by itself is still an unsolved riddle. So is the creation or origin of the universe. Man cannot help wondering about this puzzle, the only puzzle worth cracking either from a philosophical point of view or from a scientific one.

Roots – The fatal attraction

When we observe the universe, our curiosity can be broadly classified as being two-fold. One is how the universe works. The other is the creation of the universe, or to put it in other words, "When did creation begin?"

This is the proper place to introduce Bagden's paradigm of "fatal attraction." Its origin is very subtle, deep, and almost always hidden. To understand this, go back to your idyllic school days. You were intelligent and keen to learn. Your mathematics teacher gave you "homework" – assignments – to solve certain problems given in your textbook. You got the answers; you earned the teacher's kudos. You were gung-ho. You wanted more problems to solve. So you went to the library and brought home more books. The problems were tougher. You solved almost all of them. You approached the teacher regarding the few unsolved ones. He provided you with clues, showed you different ways of tackling the problems. In the end, you got all the answers correctly.

You know what was happening, unawares, in the deeper layers of your mind? Pause and think it over. One, your mind was fully trained to tackle any problem, to dig out the answer, however deeply it might be lurking, whatever effort it might require to unravel. That is good, appreciable. Two, your mind has become convinced by now that there is an answer to every problem. Note it carefully. Your mind was trained, but in the process, it was also conditioned – it was conditioned to expect an answer to every problem. There may not necessarily be an answer to certain problems, but the mind refuses to accept such a possibility. That is what Bagdenstotle calls Fatal Attraction. (Not for nothing was the myth of the Sphinx created.)

Fatal attraction – that is exactly what the problem (puzzle, riddle, myth, call it whatever you like) of the origin of the universe can be called. From the dimmest past, man has been trying to solve it. The philosophers and mystics had a go at it. Lucky men! They had an easy time. They "solved" the problems and shelved it. But not so, the men of science. They have been working hard for the last three hundred years, but still there is no irrefutable, unshakeable theory coming forth. The best candidate is the much-touted Big Bang theory. But even there, there is no consensus among the scientific community. Many brilliant and eminent scientists espouse the Steady State theory, in direct contrast to the Big Bang.

An enormous amount of literature has accumulated over the Big Bang theory. As usual, much of the mathematics involved is beyond the pale of the common-man, or even the fairly educated, for that matter. (It is said that the scientist who coined the phrase, Big Bang, did so in a self-deprecatory manner, diffident about the soundness of the theory). To explain in plain common language, the Big Bang may be described as an enormous explosion. The magnitude of the explosion was unimaginable. The mind cannot visualize or conceive such a magnitude. Incidentally, this is invariably the case when we deal with the things and properties of the universe. (The best that the mind can visualize with great effort is up to the edge of the solar system.) Coming back to the Big Bang, the great "explosion" has been estimated to have occurred about 14 billion years ago. The universe, as we know it now, did not exist then. (There was nothing.) The universe evolved out of that big bang – all these planets, stars, galaxies, nebulae, supernovas, black holes, the whole shebang. A whole generation of scientists has been painstakingly building the grand story of this creation page by page, going back in time, tracing each stage of the evolution of the universe, performing gargantuan mathematical calculations. But the irony is that they have not touched ground zero, meaning to say, the exact zero point in time. They (the researchers) are mum about exactly how the big bang occurred. Tracing back the evolution of the universe, they have been able to calculate the process almost up to a few microseconds after the Bang occurred. Those microseconds may appear to be insignificant compared to the 14 billion years of time afterward, but in terms of calculations, they make a big difference. It is a long story...

Lay readers must surely become curious about how the boffins are able to assert that the Big Bang took place precisely fourteen billion years ago. And, was there any compelling evidence to support the conclusion that a mighty bang had occurred? That, too, is a lengthy story, but we will attempt to condense it into as few words as possible. The original seed of the theory was not directly linked to the Big Bang. The Doppler Effect, as it was termed, was named for the way sound waves behave when the source of sound is either rapidly approaching us or receding away. When the object producing the sound approaches us (the observers), the pitch of the sound waves increases, and if the object moves away from us, the pitch decreases. (That is, the frequency of the original sound waves increases or decreases.) The effect was discovered by Doppler long ago. Many years later, another scientist, Hubble, discovered that the frequency of light emanating from distant galaxies (in outer space, naturally) and reaching us was lower than what it should have been under normal circumstances. When the frequency of light decreases, its color tends toward the red end of the spectrum. (VIBGYOR represents the spectrum of light, with R for red having the lowest frequency.) This effect is called the famous Red-Shift. Drawing an analogy from the Doppler effect, scientists concluded that the galaxies were moving away from us! Over the years, a substantial amount of observational data was compiled. The results were initially quite shocking. It was found that the more distant the galaxies were, the greater their speed of recession. Finally, after many heated arguments, the scientific community arrived at an inescapable conclusion – that the universe is expanding. That is the long and short of it; it's Hubble's law.

Once the idea caught on, the next guess is inevitable. If the universe has been expanding, it must have all (all the contents of the universe) been together in one place at some stage in the past. Calculations were promptly performed, taking in the observed data. It was found that the expansion must have started 14 billion years ago. That was the easy part. The tough part was working out the state of the contents of the universe. According to their calculations, all this mind-boggling matter—the billions and billions of galaxies, stars, etc.—must have been cramped into a very tiny space! Just try to imagine it! That is where and how the Big Bang must have started. The best brains of the twentieth century have worked it all out.

We have left out all the intricate details—mainly of use to those who either want to pursue the theory further or to dispute it. Bagdenborg is interested in neither. His focus is on the central fallacy—what he calls the fatal attraction. Still, he could not resist throwing a few irreverent stones at an idea accepted by the majority.

The major hurdle in tackling any theory of creation is one of time. The human brain is thoroughly soaked in time. Standing in the middle of an immeasurable field, we look forward and call it the future. We cast our glance backward and call it the past. The frustrating and fantastic thing is that both ideas are justified in our daily lives—billions of times. It is exactly this experience that invariably propels us to ask what there was in the beginning, or to put it in a rather jocular vein, how the Beginning did begin. This is the same kind of conditioning that, as we pointed out, has made us accept that there should be an answer to every question, a solution to every problem. The Big Bang theory is no exception—an irresistible conditioning urges us to go back and further back in time. This is a most ridiculous attempt according to Bagzenborg. You see, the question, "What was there before that?" can be rightfully thrown at every answer suggesting any event in the distant-most imaginable past. Similarly, regarding the future. The irreverent stone that Bagdenborg throws at the Big Bang House is in this form.

Fortunately or unfortunately (preferably the latter), someone discovered a pattern in the skies called the expansion of space. The pattern was temptingly convenient to fix a point of convergence. That point of convergence—however pregnant with meaning it may be—is just that. It is just a point in the infinite field of time!

But that is not all. The Big Bang hypothesis depends on the supposition of the expanding universe as observed now. The supposition of the expansion of the universe depends on the phenomenon of red-shift, which has been explained earlier. The red-shift bears a very close analogy to the Doppler effect. ("Therein lies murder," Bagdenborg strongly wrote.) The observed red-shift effect may not necessarily mean that the galaxies are receding from us. There could be other explanations. "If you are really in earnest and imaginative, you can invent a dozen causes," Bagdimedes says. Yielding to his peculiar sense of humor, he even points out, "At least you can be humble enough to accept that there could be other causes, which you have not discovered yet." And, "Who knows? In the not-distant future, they may discover something new in the womb of space, which will throw a completely new light on the red-shift."

There is an obvious alternative explanation for the red-shift—gravitational effect. The Great Man3 has conclusively proved that a gravitational field affects light. When you take in the vast distances of the spread out galaxies, it is impossible to enumerate, let alone compute the composite effect of the number of gravitational fields that seethe and abound in space. It is highly reasonable to assume that these gravitational fields must have a considerable effect on the light from the other galaxies passing through them. Many eminent scientists have suggested this alternate explanation, though the credit must go to young Bagdenborg who had speculated on this in his juvenile scrapbooks. Later, in the full bloom of his inspirational years, Bagenstein propounded a more authoritative and surprising answer, which we will see in the ensuing chapters.

To hark back to Bagdenborg's theme, he mercilessly categorized all speculation about the Grand Beginning of the universe as a fatal attraction. ("It demands unparalleled mental discipline to accept this. I am being terribly practical here.") According to him, there is nothing in it for Science. On the contrary, creation as it is now, as we see and observe now, contains enough and more than enough food for all that science can chew and ruminate on. One can sense a peculiar undercurrent in the phraseology he has employed above. It seems to imply that knowledge through science is one rung below knowledge of some other kind. Better leave it at that; different folks, different strokes, as they say.

Having briefly touched on a sore point, let us proceed to more interesting issues. The most interesting thing, in Bagden's view, is space itself, though space is crammed with billions and billions of masses of matter in every "nook and corner," as the old expression puts it. Matter is the stuff of which our universe is made. Matter is the most "solid" ("real") entity that confronts our senses, relentlessly intruding into and interacting with our lives every moment. In fact, without matter, there would be no human beings to tell the tale! Yet, Bagwolfgang set his sights on space, which, to our ordinary senses, personifies emptiness. The reason is not much difficult to understand if we remember Baglileo's propinquity – that of traveling off the beaten track (riding in his 1000 HP jalopy of fentologic). He chose to adopt the Eastern philosophical insight as his main paradigm of scientific exploration. We had a glimpse of it earlier. The "world" extends over a huge spectrum of manifestation, starting at the top with the most "crude" (i.e., solid, dense, tangible, etc.) form at the top and descending into more and more "refined" forms. To use a "template" kind of terminology, these generic forms are Earth, Water, Air, Fire, and Space. Even traditional science, digging deeper and deeper into "crude" matter, has ended up with forces and force-carrying particles – refinement as far down the line as is possible, corresponding up to the "Fire" element (force, radiation, spreading out). The most natural jump in the series would be that into "space" itself – the ultimate refinement. Here we have to recall a mysterious or ungraspable statement; that the cruder, denser forms are born out of the more refined ones down the line. The most "refined" element, space, is at the very bottom. That was why Bagplato called space utero creationis, "The womb of creation."

Prevailing scientific wisdom may scoff at the use of non-scientific description given above, but yet the core idea is worth some consideration.

Modern science too (read: quantitative) is slowly, hesitatingly inching its way towards the Bagdenborgian (read: qualitative) path. It too has come up to the last frontier of "refinement," space, but is dithering to take a bold dive into the very womb of space. Their (the boffins') way of refinement is to move along the route in search of the famous TOE (Theory of Everything). TOE does not need an explanation since every science buff is supposed to be aware of it. Science has been able to distill down the whole of the universe to its most fundamental level. But even at that fundamental level, there exist distinct phenomena – like the four forces we have talked about many times, and the different 'particles'. (Just to refresh your memory, the list of these distinct entities goes something like this: electromagnetic force, gravitational force, weak force, strong force, electrons, quarks, gravitons, and so on.) The world of science now stands on the two giant shoulders – The theory of Relativity and Quantum theory. Efforts have been going on for more than half a century to "merge" the two theories and formulate one all-comprehensive theory that can explain all the known phenomena in the universe. Such a theory has been christened TOE (in advance of its birth). So far, they (the quantitative science men) have not been able to construct the TOE.

At present, the attention-grabbing candidate for a complete theory is the much-hyped string theory. String theory has crawled up to the very shores of space but is afraid of diving in, preferring to stroll on the surface. For one, the theory envisions what are called "strings" that "vibrate" in space. Note that "strings" and space here are two different entities. Secondly, the theory introduces unnecessary complications by bringing up extra dimensions, up to eleven dimensions in the latest count. The most challenging aspect is that these extra dimensions, in which strings vibrate, are supposed to have millions and millions of shapes. It is purported that different types of vibrations of the strings (in different 'shapes' of space) give rise to all the known properties of the universe! The concept of the extra seven dimensions itself is complicated, and the mathematics involved is a million times more complex. (It is rumored that some top scientists have estimated that working out the mathematics itself may take a hundred years!! Moreover—and this is very important—there is no way to test the theory through experiments! As they say, the existing technology is not enough. It may need another hundred to two hundred years of technological development in order to devise experiments capable of testing string theory. Hordes of scientists all over the world have been hectically working on the theory for the past thirty years—you can imagine how complicated the theory must be. The latest candidate in the development is what is called the M-string theory. (Bagdenborg was reported to have quipped while he was in a vile mood, "G-strings are far less complicated, more attractive, and easier to unravel.")

In the above theory, we have to note that there are two parameters: strings and the space in which they vibrate. Bagdenborg's vital question is, "Why have two?" If we examine it deeply, we can dispose of the strings. He quipped, "By using strings, they have tied themselves up into inextricable knots." Space, all by itself, is vast and potent enough to create anything imaginable, he proposes. In his opinion, if the mathematicians had applied only a thousandth part of their efforts on space alone, space per se, they would have long ago succeeded in their search for the Golden Fleece of Science. Bagdenborg rightfully called space the womb of creation!! So, let us have a look at the various insights he has to offer on space.

***

At the very outset, it should be pointed out that Bagdenborg's concept of space is quite different from the prevailing ones. From the beginning of classical science, there have been opposing views on space. The Great Man2 (Newton, if you have forgotten) believed in the existence of what is called absolute space. Another contemporary of his, from the continent, argued otherwise. He argued that space was only a useful "construct" in describing the properties of two or more objects. Space, thus, is only an inferred property when considering objects; it does not have a separate existence. Bagdenborg's concept of space tends to agree with that of the Great Man2, but with essential differences. As we said, space is a form of "matter" at its most "refined" state. (You may even say "diluted," if it affords you a better idea of space). And more importantly, *space is also the origin of matter.*

Gravity and expansion

Bagneitz brought off a beautiful indirect deduction. It started from the "observed expansion of space," though he did not like the Big Bang tailpiece of it. Let us, just for the moment, assume that the expansion of space is a real phenomenon irrespective of the red-shift. Forget the big bang too. Then what else could be the reason for the galaxies receding from one another at such a truly amazing speed? To the fertile fentological mind of Bagernicus, the answer is simplicity itself – and most obvious. The answer, the sublimely simple answer goes back to the old, famous exposition of Newton's bucket of spinning water! The good old faithful centrifugal force; nothing less, nothing more, nothing else! Though the astute readers (you) have caught on, there is no harm in confirming the readers' smart deduction. Where there is a centrifugal force, there must be a spinning object/mass behind it. We are no longer able to hold back the stunning answer. The universe is spinning, the universe is spinning! Oh, what a grand sight! ("It is impossible to surpass the breadth of Professor Bagdenborg's vision," the admirer exclaims.) It (the vision) is ecstatic. Hold on there for a few moments, admiring the beauty and grandeur of that vision. After those rare moments, we, of course, descend down the cosmic stairs and stand steadily on terra firma, and then proceed to evaluate the vision in terms of calm scientific reasoning (aided by liberal doses of Bagdenborg's fentologic).

We have discussed the centrifugal force countless times in these pages. If an object or mass is spinning, it generates a centrifugal force—a force acting outward from the center—that tends to "push" everything away radially. The universe is spinning, creating a centrifugal force of unimaginable magnitude, which "pushes" everything it contains away from one another. This explains why all the matter (including galaxies or any other entities you may consider) is receding and being pushed outwards. This also clarifies why distant galaxies are moving away at an accelerated rate.

Of course, Bagdenborg did not delve into the mathematics of it; he did not see the need. His stance was simply, "Let them work it out. It's a fairly straightforward task."

Now, let's take a moment to contemplate a subtler aspect. This requires just a bit of basic physics and the formula that must be familiar to you by now: F = m x a, with 'F,' 'm,' and 'a' representing the trio of force, mass, and acceleration. The third element in this list requires some clarification. Acceleration is not merely an increase in speed; it implies that speed continually increases with each passing second (or any fraction thereof). If a body experiences acceleration and has a speed of ten km per hour now, its speed will continue to increase: 15...30...60...100 km per hour, and so on, as long as the acceleration persists. In essence, the body or object will remain in an acceleration mode as long as the force continues to act upon it. Therefore, if a force acts continuously on a body, the speed it attains, even in a short span of time, will become substantial. Two straightforward examples illustrate this concept clearly.

a. You kick the football, and it flies into the air, eventually landing. The ball descends because the gravitational force of the Earth pulls it down, and the resistance of the air reduces its speed. If you were to kick the ball in empty space, far from Earth's gravitational influence, the ball would continue to move – theoretically, forever. The crucial point here is that the final speed of the ball has a definite magnitude, determined by the force of your kick. There is no acceleration after it reaches a certain speed because your kick – the applied force – was very brief in terms of time, lasting for only a fraction of a second. If the force were to act continuously, then it would be a different situation, pun aside.

b. Consider the gravitational force of the Earth. It is a force that acts continuously on any object within its field. When a meteor enters Earth's gravitational field, its initial velocity might be small. However, once it enters Earth's gravitational influence, the force acts on the meteor incessantly. The meteor experiences acceleration until it reaches Earth's dense atmosphere. During this relatively short period, the meteor's speed increases second by second. By the time it encounters Earth's atmosphere, its speed is enormous – sufficiently so to cause the meteor to ablate due to the heat generated from air friction.

Thus, the crucial point to remember is that as long as the force is acting, the object's speed continues to increase continuously. Theoretically, the object's speed can reach infinity (and beyond, if you dare to envision it!).

We purposefully elaborated on this aspect of force and acceleration so that you may appreciate the significance of Bagdenborg's discovery. Let us go back to the expanding universe and how Bagopernicus deduced that the universe is spinning. "Universum est valde," he declared. This spinning is not to be confused with the spinning of the objects contained in the universe. For example, the Earth is spinning, and the Sun is spinning. There are neutron stars whose rate of spinning will make you dizzy just by mentioning them. This is not the kind of spinning that we mean. We mean that the universe as a whole, like a single object, is spinning. In other words, it means that space itself, in its entirety, is spinning. We arrived at this simple, straightforward (and beautiful) deductive conclusion because the universe is expanding. Bagdenborg put it the other, more natural way: Because the universe is spinning, the universe is expanding.

Now, consider the time element and work out what should have happened. It will leave you breathless. The universe has been spinning for about 14 billion years, more or less. That means the centrifugal force has been acting continuously for 14 billion years on the receding galaxies. Recall now what our formula showed us. If a force acts on a body even for a short period of time, the speed attained by the body at the end of acceleration will be enormous (see the meteor example again). So, if the force, our centrifugal force, has been in existence for fourteen billion years, the effect of that force on all the bodies of the universe should be impossible to imagine. All the billions and billions of objects in the universe would have been scattered so far away (infinitely, no doubt) that there would have been practically nothing left for us to observe in the skies! Why, then, has not such a (horrible) thing happened?

Simple, once more (This sort of simplicity is referred to as Bagden's Simplicity by his admirers). Take a small piece of rope and attach a reasonably heavy object to one end of it. Now, spin it rapidly. What happens? Your spinning generates a centrifugal force on the object, causing it to attempt to "fly away" from you (similar to the receding galaxies). You can even feel the tug of the object on your arms. Clearly, what prevents the object from flying away is the rope. This type of force that restrains the object is known as the centripetal force.

The centripetal force opposes the centrifugal force produced by the spin. Do you have the concept in mind?

Bagdenborg suggests that this is akin to what occurs in the spinning universe. Some force is preventing the receding galaxies from disappearing from view by now, holding in check the tremendous centrifugal force of the spinning universe. What is this mysterious force? What kind of tether is keeping the galaxies in check? Simple, once more – Bagden's Simplicity.

SPACE ITSELF IS THAT TETHER! Take a moment to catch your breath. Revisit the breathing exercises we recommended in the previous chapters, and then return.

"Space is that rope," quoth Professor Bagdenborg. Only, that rope is not like the nylon rope you used in the previous example. It is like a rope woven out of rubber strands. And, the rope, of course, is invisible. Space is elastic.

That is how, even as the galaxies are receding, it is holding them back from zooming out into infinity. And, of course, space is not like an elastic linear rope, obviously; it extends in all three dimensions. The simile of the elastic rope was used to illustrate the idea of elasticity. OK? Tarry there. Take a leap into the next obvious insight, after mentally imagining the cosmic sight.

The billions of galaxies (and all kinds of objects) are furiously trying to run away. At the same time, billions and billions of (the invisible) elastic strands are holding them in check while at the same time allowing them the freedom to move too. The next step consists of just rephrasing. Instead of the "elastic strands," you think of "lines of force"! Doesn't that ring a bell?

It should. The "lines of force" belong to the old familiar 'field' of physics! Here, in particular, our lines of force belong to the gravitational field; only, we do not use those terms; that is all. We say, with a nod of approval from Bagdenborg, that space is elastic. (And, that elasticity is but one of its many strange properties). To put it another way, it can be stated that the universal gravitational force is an attribute of space. What does this mean? It means that all particles, if left free, tend to attract one another. A small correction; that statement is secondary. The primary one is that all particles "rush" to meet at one central point! This point, of course, has a direct relevance to the misguided Big Bang theory – misguided, as per the assertion of Bagdenborg.

A curious question arises at this juncture. Let us leave aside, for the moment, the idea of all particles (matter) rushing to converge at some central point. What about the other observed and almost indisputable proposition of the Great Man2, that matter possesses gravity and matter attracts matter? No problem there. Only a subtle (and elegant) differentiation is needed, spiced with just enough of Bagdenborgian fentologic and a willingness to take imaginative leaps.

In the previous pages, a unique property of space and "matter" was mentioned. It is explained in the following manner, exemplified by two famous statements. The first one is that matter (objects) exists in space. The other and more familiar one is that objects occupy space. Remember the famous axiom which states that, "Two things cannot occupy the same space at the same time"? Collate these axioms with the insights we obtained in earlier discussions about the wave-particle duality and Bagden's theory of shells. There, we saw that particles – the ultimate smallest denomination of matter – would be indistinguishable from the rest of the universe except for the defensive/protective shells around them. A careful consideration of all the above data will lead us to the beautiful dual nature of space. (In fact, there is no duality).

Objects exist in space, and space exists inside objects. How wonderful! It is space, space all the way. If there is any vestige of confusion in the minds of the readers, we clarify further, thus. There is what can be called the universal space – the space when we consider the universe as a whole. Then there is the individual or local space. It is the space that exists inside a particle. Bagden's particle shell will provide you a better picture. Space is holographic. By that, we mean that the individual "space" of a particle possesses the same properties as that of the universal space. One property of the universal space that we just discovered is "elasticity," or gravitational force. Similarly, the individual, local space inside a particle too possesses the same, identical gravitational force. OK? Now, to the Great Man2's gravitational theory.

Consider two objects, A and B. There is space A, so to say, inside object A and space B, inside B. Both spaces possess gravitational properties as we described in the previous paragraph. So, what happens? Space A and Space B attract each other. In other words, particles A and B tend to move towards each other. This is just our old familiar Newton's gravity at work; that is all!

The only difference, in the new view of Bagdenborg, is that "gravity" is acting in two ways. Two objects, while attracting each other obeying the law of the Great Man2, are at the same time rushing to meet (once again?!) radially at another central point – which is the case with all other particles that reside in space. The only thing that is preventing the particles from meeting at that universal center is the centrifugal force generated by the spinning of the universe. (The admirer could not help but comment, "I am dumbstruck at the grandeur of this vision." Amen, we say.)

At this point, the astute reader (you, who else?) will begin to wonder where exactly the axis of the spinning universe lies, if Professor Bagdenborg claims that the universe is spinning. It is a tough question to ask. We mean, it is tough to ask such a question! You know why? Because the answer is simple in Bagdenborg's fentological way, but is tough on the mindsets of those still stuck with the traditional hard-line scientific way of thinking. The explanation is as follows. Bagden would say that there is no particular axis of spin to be physically pinpointed. Choose any axis you like, he would say. The universe is so infinitely vast that any arbitrary axis you choose would serve! In that sense, there are countless numbers of axes of spin. If you find it hard to visualize, then ponder about the eleven odd extra dimensions propounded by string theory. Compared to that, our spinning universe must be far simpler, surely. Bagdenborg would like to make it a bit easier for you. You see, normally, a spinning object, with respect to the axis, spins on a single plane. The spin of space, he claims, is on multiple planes! This idea too, gels with that of multiple axes of spin – hanging on the same argument that the universe is infinitely vast.

The dissenter in you would still grumble (or growl?). What about a mathematical treatment of the spinning universe, you would ask. Surely, there must be mathematical formulae to predict the magnitudes of the centrifugal force and the speeds of the receding objects. There must be equations showing the relationship between the centrifugal force and the "elastic" gravitational force of space. Well, there must be – Bagdenborg had worked out the whole, shed-loads of equations. Child's play, he had claimed. But he tore up all the papers and fed them to the oven, eccentric genius that he was. He had an inexplicable love-hate relationship with mathematics, mathematricks as he called it. As said earlier, he distinguished two types of science; the qualitative and the quantitative. He preferred to work in the former field, which he insisted, had greater freedom and offered more scintillating insights, not to speak of the aesthetic pleasure. ("Knowledge is pleasure," was one of his bon mots.) That aside, a few of his admirers indeed tried their hands at providing mathematical support to Bagdenborg's theory. It is beyond the scope of this book since – as usual – the mathematics is very complicated, and our modest aim is to present a "popular" picture of Bagdenborg's adventures in science, with an equally modest intention to incite the readers to blaze their own Bagdenborgian trails in the exciting fields. Now that we have sufficiently ignited your inspiration, let us consider a few exotic ideas.

Expanding universe; virtual, illusive?

We have dwelt at length on the expansion of the universe (or space, as they claim). Scientists have extrapolated the scenario backward in time and deduced that the whole of the present universe was crunched at some point in time – 20 billion years ago or so – into an infinitesimally small space, and that there was a Big Bang, and then the universe began to expand, and the universe has been expanding ever since, and so on. Incidentally, that densely packed region before the Bang could have been as small as the size of a pinhead. So, honestly, that tiny dot cannot be called a universe! Let it pass. The important thing to notice here is that if things are moving away from one another as we see them now, they must have been grouped together at some time in the past. That time in the past can be calculated by observing the speed at which the objects are moving away now, and the distances between nearer and further objects, and so on. This is where Bagdenborg takes off at a different angle. To be fair to his opponents, we have to agree that what they infer is logical – if objects are seen flying apart now, they must have been together in the past.

But Bagdimedes makes very strange statements: "Beware of logic. It can brainwash you." "Logic is a kind of mental conditioning." "Logic is addictive," he has written in his notebooks. (And more acerbic aphorisms on logic, which we do not wish to print here.) So, what does he have to say about the expanding universe? It is this:-

"If the universe is seen to be expanding now, (a very big if there) it does not mean there was a Big Bang. More explicitly, if objects are seen to be moving away from one another, they need not necessarily have been together in one place in the past."

That is a very strange remark. What does Bagdemusplato mean by it? Come this way, take a tour.

Many views, many scripts

Script 1

You have been driving along a long stretch of road in the Sahara desert, say. You do not know how long you have been driving, but the script starts at this point. You notice a prominent milestone by the roadside with the number '4' written in big bold letters on it. You keep on driving, and after a long time, you see another milestone with the number '5' painted on it unmistakably. Still, after another stretch of driving and a long time, you see '6'. Your curiosity is roused. You keep looking out. You come across numbers 7 and 8. Unfortunately, the script ends here. Your journey has been terminated. (No reasons given.)

But you are a very curious and intelligent person. (You know that, we know that.) Pondering the significance of the numbers, you conclude that back along the road (which, unfortunately, you had not the privilege to watch) there must have been milestones with numbers 3, 2, and 1 on them. You are reasonably sure of that. You are not sure if there could be a zero milestone or what lies there, but you are willing to bet on the existence of numbers 3, 2, and 1.

The point is that you will physically never again go back on the road you have traveled. Still, the sequence of the observed numbers 4, 5, 6, 7, and 8 feeds fuel to your logical prowess, and logic screams at you that there must be 3, 2, and 1 somewhere, there back along the road. Now, be reasonable and scan your logic more rigorously. The sequence containing 4, 5, 6, 7, and 8 need not necessarily mean it began with 1. It is hard on your faith, but it is a fact.

Script 2

You are all familiar with those ubiquitous illuminated ads displayed on all marquees and billboards, public service vehicles, and so on. We are, of course, referring to the moving text ads:

"See you later, overtaker, I am your undertaker."

"Pampering pizzas. Heavy in taste, light on your purse."

The texts continuously move across the screen and vanish on the other side, only to reappear from the opposite side. The text actually appears to be moving, does it not? In railway stations and airports, you see those big display boards continuously showing the progress of time second by second, as if an invisible hand is wiping out and rewriting the numbers:

"12:34:56."

You know, too, of course, that the texts do not physically move; it is all an optical illusion created by electronic software. But, all the same, you accept in your normal day-to-day experience that the text is moving.

What Bagdenborg suggests is that the phenomenon of the receding galaxies could possibly be an illusion along the lines of the moving texts on the marquees! Naturally, nobody has physically seen the galaxies moving away, despite their deduced enormous speeds, since their distance from our point of observation is immense. Go back to the previous pages and look up how much distance one light-year represents. And those distances across galaxies range from hundreds to thousands to millions of light-years, with the farthest presumably being more than 20 billion light-years!

We have to note that the speeds of those receding objects are calculated indirectly, using the red-shift phenomenon as an interpreter. To put it simply, light coming from different galaxies is analyzed by appropriate instruments like spectroscopes and such. They have developed methods for calculating the distances of the galaxies from us. (Call it ironic, frustrating, or plain funny, but the light that reaches us now has taken quite a lot of time to make its journey across space; therefore, even though we see it "now," what we see "now" is actually "then"! For all we know, the object might not be really there now; what we see of it now is the image of what it was a hundred, thousand, or million years ago. The same goes for its distance.) When the "red-shifts" of the different galaxies are compared, it is seen that the red-shift varies. From this, it is inferred that the galaxies are moving away from us (and from one another). The farther a galaxy is from us, the greater its red-shift. That implies that the more distant galaxies are moving away at greater speeds. This is the simple overall picture of the expanding universe, developed by scientists.

You see, in this high drama, everything hinges on the most important data: the innumerable records of the measured red-shifts of the various galaxies. Let us say that these various values are represented by values a, b, c, d, etc. In direct physical terms, instead of the values, we actually observe the light on our laboratory display screen. Then we analyze the light through spectroscopes and instruments. After all those activities, we infer that the objects, the sources of light, are moving away from us.

The subtle idea that Bagdenborg introduces into this script is that the variation in values such as a, b, c, d, etc., is in a way similar to the variation in illumination of the individual cells of the light matrix from which the moving text of the ads (described in the beginning of this section) has been constructed. This is a very subtle Bagdenborgian idea, and we have to take it in the spirit in which it is offered; otherwise, we will be missing his point. Note that there could be some other reason for the red-shift phenomenon, and we are not speaking of that. It is the pattern in the observed data that he (Bagden) is focusing on. Bagdenborg had, in fact, published an article on this hypothesis, but there was only a lukewarm response to it. That, of course, did not deter him from pursuing his high adventures in descriptive science. He had his own ideas about the red-shift data. The salient point about the data is that the amount of the red-shift increases as we observe light from more distant objects. That means that light from more distant galaxies has to travel proportionately longer distances. We refer you to the earlier chapters where Bagdimedes has shown that light gets "tired" in traveling through space. That is, light loses a minute part of its initial energy. This loss of energy naturally pushes the light waves towards the red end of the spectrum. This is why distant galaxies (objects) exhibit the red-shift. The idea is simple and elegant. The idea also leads us to a somewhat hilarious flip-flop.

If Bagdentotl's explanation is accepted, then it means that the galaxies (objects) in the universe are not moving away from us! It will be a great disappointment to those who staunchly believe that the universe is expanding. On the other hand, Bagdaedaulus offers to wipe their tears. Consider his revolutionary (pun, accidental) theory of the spinning universe, with its concomitant centrifugal force, pushing objects in space further and further apart, and you have the expanding universe back in the saddle! (Safer than it was under the reign – again, pun accidental – of the red-shift). If anything can be dubbed as an adventure in ideas, Bagden's theory of the spinning universe is just that.

Script 3 – From cymatics to cybermatics

It appears that Bagdenborg was fascinated by the red-shift even in his younger days. What follows strictly belongs to his juvenilia, but we have included it here, en passant, since the idea is both romantic and brilliant. Who knows, it may spark further new ideas in the minds of the readers?

Cymatics, in general terms, may be described as the study of the patterns created by sound waves on different materials. Take a thin metallic sheet (or consider any vibrating membrane). Spread fine dust or powder on it uniformly. Now, if you induce audio vibrations in the metal sheet, the powder on the surface will gradually settle into a fascinating visual pattern. Different kinds of vibrations on different materials will induce a rich variety of patterns. You can even use vocal sounds (songs, music, anything), and each audio vibration will produce its own individual pattern. One is reminded of the infinite variety of patterns in snowflakes when looking at photographs of these sound patterns. Just log onto the Internet and search for the image in the Google search page for 'cymatics' – you will find innumerable pictures.

Of course, there was no World Wide Web (w.w.w.) in Bagdenborg's juvenile days, but he was familiar with cymatics, which already had a good deal of literature published about it.

Young Bagdenborg's imagination jumped from material membranes to space itself. His reasoning ran along the following lines.

Forget about the drums, membranes, and plates of the previous example. They are small fry in comparison with the magnitude of space. The same goes for the sound waves. Just think about the electromagnetic waves, their propagation, and the activity going on incessantly in space. The situation is simply impossible to conceive. To begin with, space is uniformly filled with what they call the "Cosmic background radiation," which incidentally affects your TV screen too when it is switched off (for a very brief second). Consider the havoc created by solar flares on Earth. There are billions of such suns in the universe. Can you even begin to imagine the combined magnitude of such activity? And then there are supernovae, countless nebulae that constantly send out all types of electromagnetic waves. Add to this the mysterious bursts of powerful cosmic rays (whose origin has not yet been solved). The innumerable black holes are emitting their own signature radiations. Add to this natural activity the equal contribution being made by us, the Earthlings. The range of communication and other types of signals that we are broadcasting, 24x7, taxes imagination. (In a way, it can be said that we are polluting space with our radio, TV, and communication signals).

Now, replace the vibrating membrane of the earlier example with space itself and the sound waves with the infinite variety of electromagnetic waves. Instead of cymatics, we now have cybermatics, coining a new word. In the previous scenario, sound waves acted on the material membrane, and the membrane responded by creating distinctive patterns. In this new and far grander scenario, the seething electromagnetic activities we described affect space itself. And space responds by producing corresponding, distinctive patterns. Bagdimedes argued that the red-shift is one such pattern! The idea is actually tempting. It is not far-fetched, nor is it illogical. This is the essence of his methodology of "descriptive science" – salted, remember, with just enough of fentologic. The red-shift could very well be the offshoot of the cybermatics effect.

Then, if such is the case, can we conduct a simple experiment, just as we did with the metal sheet and sound waves? The answer is, "Alas, no; we cannot!" The answer may seem pessimistic to some, or even a sly way of defending oneself. It is natural to get such impressions at first sight. But a more patient consideration of what is involved in conducting such an experiment in cybermatics will yield a more realistic perception. What do we mean by that? It is obvious in a way, but we will be glad to state the obvious anyway. Look back at your metallic sheet and observe its size. Was it six inches by six inches? Twelve by twelve? Whew! Gentle reader, compare it to the size of space, the pure, the absolutely unlimited-in-size outer space. Even the question of comparison is ridiculous. In order to conduct a cybermatics experiment on space, you would have to encompass all of it as a whole. And that may not be possible for the next thousand years, at the least. You may say you will select a representational, manageable region of space for an experiment. That will not do, obviously, because even in the case of your metal sheets, the patterns developed by a small piece will be different from those by a larger piece of sheet. While such is the case with small sizes, it is impossible to predict what will happen in the case of infinite dimensions like that of space.

The problem could possibly (probably only) be solved using mathematics. The proponents of mathematics are welcome to make an attempt. (Bagden has his usual dig at the tribe. He quips, "By employing appropriate mathematricks, the red-shift pattern can be derived.") They will surely succeed. After all, they have been able to establish that the first burst of a cracker occurred 14.7 billion years ago. You may ask if anybody has seen it or if there is any record of it. The answer is presented to you on a UBR platter (Universal Background Radiation). Yes, we are seeing it even now. What we are seeing is the aftermath of that first-ever spurt from a cracker. Thousands and thousands of scientific papers have been published on that theory. In the light of all this enterprise, it would not be difficult at all to prove that the red-shift is the outcome of cybermatics.

Space: mammoth salmagundi, ultra-miraculous memory, super human algorithms.

In India, there is a well known saying about the legendary Swan. In Sanskrit, it is called "Hamsaksheera nyaaya." Mix water and milk thoroughly and place it before that Swan. The Swan, it is said, has the ability to extract milk out of the mixture. It will drink the milk alone and leave the water as residue in the container. This may be a legend, but we will show you a practical, living miracle that will put to shame the legendary Swan. First, we ask you to do these simple things.

Exercise A

Take a sheet of writing paper and draw a rectangle of about 2" by 3" in size, or even smaller. Use a thick-tipped pen and draw four horizontal lines and four vertical lines across the rectangle. (The lines need not be evenly spaced.) You will naturally see a grid now. More importantly, you will be able to distinguish the four horizontal and vertical lines that you have drawn. Next, draw four more horizontal and vertical lines, as before, across the visible white spaces. You get more grids. Repeat the process of drawing the lines, keeping count of the number of lines you draw. Ah, repeat, persevere—go on drawing lines across the white spaces. What happens in the end? It is a silly question, but we are not sorry to ask. Naturally, after a certain stage, there won't be any more white space left inside the rectangle; it has all been inked-over. You see a black rectangle now (or whatever colored ink your pen contains). The important thing is to keep count of the number of horizontal and vertical lines that you have managed to draw till the end.

Now, go to your friend and show him the colored rectangle. Ask him what he sees. He will say he sees a colored rectangular plane. But you know better. He will not believe you until you explain to him exactly what you did. Then he may laugh in a good-humored way. Then you ask him to retrieve the original lines you had drawn. You have not told him the exact number of lines you had scratched across the empty rectangle; you insist that he should retrieve your original lines. He may possibly calculate, by simple arithmetic, the number of lines, but for that, he should know the thickness of the original lines. If he does not know that information, he is stumped. Here, invoke the reincarnation of our legendary Swan. It will easily "drink" your ink and spit back the original, exact number of lines you had drawn. This is not a fatuous tale; you will see its significance by and by.

Exercise B

Go to a countryside pond. Or, if you own your own indoor swimming pool, go there. We are assuming that there is no atmospheric disturbance, and that the surface of the water is smooth. Throw a pebble in the center of the pool. Observe the simple pattern of ripples – circular, concentric waves are produced, traveling to the edges of the pool. Next, throw two pebbles in, separated by some distance. Two rings of waves are created now. The purely circular pattern changes as well, wherever the two waves meet each other. Throw a handful of pebbles and watch the pattern of waves. If you get tired of throwing the pebbles, imagine that there has been a sudden downpour of raindrops in the pool. The pattern created now is so complicated that it is impossible to retrieve the individual patterns created by each of the raindrops if you are confronted with a photograph of the surface of the pool. Once again, invoke our legendary Swan, and it will easily...

Exercise C

You are in your house, having a pleasant conversation with your wife. You can hear her because of the air surrounding both of you. Yes, of course, when she talks, she produces audio waves in the air, which travel up to your ears and beyond. The waves are similar in nature to the waves produced in water in the previous exercise, with one noticeable difference. The patterns – the waveforms – are much more complicated. The waves are created in the air, instead of water (and travel faster too). The point of interest here is that the surrounding air is filled with waves from one source.

Sometime later, you are at a café, sipping your favorite cup of coffee. Two persons are engaged in conversation at table A, and two more at table B – simultaneously. Waveforms (of sound) are being produced from two sources: table A and table B. Obviously, the patterns of waves from the two sources differ. The point of interest (and it is really interesting) is that the air inside the café is the same, and it is responding to both sources of sound. In other words, the sound waves from A and B are getting mixed, and an altogether different pattern (C) is being continuously created. Pattern C is more complex and is completely different from either A or B.

After finishing your coffee, you go out and enter the street. Stand on the sidewalk for a few minutes and observe the sounds. The sounds you hear are far more varied: the casual conversations of the passersby, the various noises created by the vehicles on the road, the chirping of a solitary bird on yonder tree, and so on and so forth. The air in the street is responding to all those sounds. The hundreds of individual sound sources are producing their individual patterns of waveforms. At the same time, all those waveforms are interacting – they are getting mixed. The resulting waveforms in the surrounding air are unbelievably complex. To make a comparison, the "disturbance" created by all these sounds in the air is thousands of times more complex than the one you witnessed in your swimming pool.

The thing gets curiouser and curiouser here (and, in fact, highly mystifying if you look at it properly), but we have been so accustomed to it from birth that we never bother to notice it or give it a thought. Recall the colored rectangle from the first exercise and how it was impossible to retrieve the original lines. The air in the street can be compared to that colored rectangle—it is so thoroughly "saturated" with those hundreds of waveforms, you see. Remember too that we talked about the legendary Swan that could retrieve the lines from the patch of colored rectangle. Here comes the "curiouser" part. You need not invoke the Swan; you are the Swan (!), because you are able to hear (that is, retrieve) all those hundreds of sounds effortlessly. It seems so natural to us that we are able to distinguish individual sounds out of the melee, the Babel of noise. We would like to draw your attention to the fact that the vibrating air in the street is a composite, a thorough mixture of a hundred sounds. Yet, you are able to distinguish the individual sounds: their frequencies, their loudness, the locations of their sources, etc. It is really marvelous. (Nay, more than that; it is a grand miracle of Nature). You—equipped with your ear—are that legendary Swan, as we assured you.

Exercise D: This is more of an exercise in visualizing. In the previous scenario of the street, we said that the "disturbance" in the air was thousands of times more complex. That disturbance is like somnolent stupor in comparison to what we are going to show you now.

As before, go into the street and stand on the sidewalk. Instead of concentrating on the sounds, try your best to visualize. Look at the empty space all around you. Leaving aside the concrete objects, the space by itself seems to be so calm and peaceful, doesn't it? Well, you have another thing coming, as they say. Go back to the earlier pages and recall what we said about the electromagnetic waves oscillating in space 24/7, the solar flares, the cosmic rays, the Universal Background Radiation, the radiations from supernovae, the black holes, and all that and much more. Consider the stupendous ranges in the frequencies, the wavelengths, and waveforms (especially man-made). The "disturbance" created by all this in space exceeds those in the previous examples by billions and billions of times. Quite obviously, all these billions of waves are propagating in one common medium, like the water in exercise B and the air in exercise C. (Space is that medium, as Bagdenborg insists). The resulting "mixture" of all those billions of signals should be so thorough that, using the imagery of the inked-over rectangle from exercise A, we should obtain a rectangle of the size of the universe completely and uniformly "inked-over" with electromagnetic signals.

Yet, the greatest miracle in creation is taking place every second before our very eyes. You see, in spite of such a stupendous disturbance or mixing as discussed above, we are able to retrieve and distinguish every individual signal! It is the mightiest miracle—no less. Every individual who owns a cellphone is able to communicate with everybody else. Every individual who owns a TV is able to view any broadcast channel. This is made possible because of technology, which utilizes special "tuners" or receivers to filter the desired signals individually. That is similar to the process of retrieving milk out of water, which we mentioned in the beginning. It seems that the legendary Swan has reincarnated into a second species—the electronic gadgets! Don't envy it, because you too are another reincarnation of that Swan. Even without the gadgets, if there are ten (a million, for that matter) different sources of light emanating lights of different wavelengths (recall VIBGYOR) and different intensities, you (equipped with your bare eyes) will be able to retrieve all those individual signals separately. The legend of the Swan is not a fairy tale at all. It tells the tale of a fundamental mystery in nature. (Miracle is a more befitting word.)

There is, of course, a third incarnation of the swan. It can be called a virtual incarnation because it belongs strictly to the species of mathematics. In mathematics, there is what is called Fourier Analysis. It can be explained in broad terms as follows for the layperson. In general, a wave shape, as you know, is like a kind of curve (or squiggles) that goes up and down—like those cardiographs your friends tend to show off after being discharged from the hospital. There are some waveforms that are either rectangular or square in shape. Fourier Analysis proves that such shapes can be equivalent to a composite waveform made out of several individual curves (squiggles), waves. To give a plainer imagery, the colored rectangle we introduced can be shown to be due to the overlapping of several curved (egg-shaped, say) blotches of paint. We mention this in passing as a curiosity since we were discussing the act of retrieving different shapes out of a single composite one.

The miracle consists of two parts. The first part is what we have described thus far—the ability to retrieve desired individual signals from the thoroughly jumbled mixture. The second part is where Bagdenborg's insight takes over. Consider a very simple analogy, and you will understand what Bagden is trying to say.

Take a plate and throw in it a handful each of two different types of grains; say wheat and rice. Mix the grains thoroughly. This mixture is, as a composite, an entity in its own right. If you are asked to separate the grains into two heaps of wheat and rice, you will be able to do so quite easily, though the task may be tedious. The point to note is this—you are able to retrieve the original two types of grains because, in spite of being thoroughly jumbled, the individual grains of wheat and rice have preserved their identity. We suggested grains of comparatively thicker size so that the task can be easy.

This kind of mixture is what is called a physical mixture—the constituents do not interact. In chemistry, the constituents interact, and the resulting mixture is termed a compound. Common salt is a "mixture" of two elements: sodium and chlorine. Water is a "mixture" of two elements, hydrogen and oxygen. The separation (retrieval) of the original elements from these compounds is not as easy as that of the mixture of wheat and rice. But the separation can be accomplished using suitable processes. For example, water can be broken down into hydrogen and oxygen by passing electrical current through it along different electrodes.

Again, the point of interest is that even though the "mixtures," salt and water, appear completely different from their individual constituents (like sodium, chlorine, hydrogen, and oxygen), the original elements are still there inside them. The fact that you are able to separate them proves it.

The foregoing two analogies are sufficient for us to enter the portals of Bagdenborg's intuition. However, the temptation is too strong to resist carrying the analogies further. For example, even elements like sodium, chlorine, etc., can be seen as another type of "mixtures." (For that matter, all elements in nature can be called "mixtures.") An element is a grouping together of three kinds of constituents called electrons, neutrons, and protons. There are more than a hundred elements with a wide range of properties, which appear to be very different from one another. Yet, the individual constituents—electrons, protons, and neutrons—always preserve their identities. Enough with the temptation to proceed further with the analogy.

The essence of the argument is that in a mixture or a composite, the identity of the individual constituents is always preserved.

Apply this insight to the phenomenon of the propagation of electromagnetic waves, which we explained a couple of pages before. Let's revisit the topic and see what intriguing ideas will surface.

If we proceed along the traditional route, we will be forced to tread a frustrating path once more. We previously discussed wave patterns in the exercise where we threw pebbles into the swimming pool. Physically, it was water that was moving up and down and forward. The force of the pebbles thrown was transmitted to the particles of water immediately surrounding the points of impact. These particles transmitted their force to their adjoining particles and so on. A similar process occurred when you were chatting with your spouse. We discussed sound waves and their patterns. Physically, it was air that was moving. The force from the vocal cords of your dear spouse was transmitted to the particles (molecules) of air immediately surrounding her mouth. They, in turn, transmitted their forces to the adjoining particles, with the last set of such particles entering your ear and striking the tympanum. In both cases, a physical entity, like a water particle or an air molecule, was necessary for the creation and propagation of waves. In physics, such an entity is called a medium. For the transmission of waves, a medium is necessary. We have already discussed this under the topic of mechanical action and action-at-a-distance. We return to the old million-dollar question: What is the medium through which electromagnetic waves (say, your radio and TV signals) propagate? Mathematically, these waves have been analyzed and treated in the most thorough manner possible, and all that jells—every electronic gizmo, among the millions and millions in use throughout the world, is built on those mathematical principles.

But the funny and persistently recurring bottom line is this: When you talk about a wave, a wave is an abstraction; it refers to or describes a form. And, a form must belong to a physical entity. We are once again faced with the age-old question of a medium—through what medium do electromagnetic waves propagate? As mentioned earlier, an imaginary medium, ether, was proposed, and later the idea was dropped, thanks to the Michelson-Morley experiment. There were other considerations, such as the speed of the waves and the calculated "density" of the medium needed to account for it, and so on.

This is where Bagdenborg comes to our aid. Why worry and rack our brains trying to invent an imaginary medium? Space itself is that medium. Bagdimedes offers us another enlightening perspective. You see, when calculating the properties of space, we automatically employ the same methods as we do for ordinary matter. "This is where they all stumble unwittingly," Bagdimedes remarked. We cannot use the regular mathematical models when dealing with space, he warns. Space is, of course, matter, but it is matter refined to the utmost possible level, allowing intuition to take precedence over mathematics and common sense when dealing with it. Here comes one of his intriguing propositions.

We can draw an analogy with water and air. Waves propagate through these two mediums by means of their respective particles. Presto! The same must be the case with space! The idea is simplicity itself, even though the traditional scientific attitude may recoil at such a suggestion. But let us persist and delve further into the matter, setting aside our prejudices. This means we have to understand (intuit, to use a better word) that space too has its own 'particles'! Bagdimedes named these space 'particles' as 'spaceniks'. He also provided a reason for the existence of such particles; the spaceniks. Actually, it is intuition working at its finest level. Many times, the birth of an insight depends on where and how you focus your mental laser.

Let's focus on the speed at which waves travel. For example, sound waves travel at a definite speed, as you are aware. This is because of the discrete nature of the medium, that is, air. When sound travels through air, even though air may appear to be continuous and uniform along the route of travel, the wave is physically transmitted through the "particles" of air. This quality of discreteness-in-continuity is a crucial factor in the propagation of waves. Even in something completely "solid," like a metal bar, the discreteness of the individual atoms (molecules) is ever-present. Please underline the following sentence – it is a great piece of intuition by Bagden: IT IS THE DISCRETE NATURE OF THE MEDIUM THAT IMPARTS A SPECIFIC SPEED TO THE WAVE. Does it appear to be a bit curious? Not at all. Just for the sake of argument, indulge in a fantasy-cum-thought experiment, à la Bagdimedes. Imagine you are in a room filled with air. (Don't laugh. You will see what we mean.) If you stand at one end of the room and shout, your voice will be carried to the other end, taking its specified time. (Divide the length of the room by the speed of sound, and you will get the value of that time.) Note, we said, specific time. Note also, that the room contains a huge number of air molecules. If you are still smiling in a tolerantly amused way, then, imagine that the room is now filled with one molecule of air! Yes, it is a single molecule, and it is gigantic, filling the room from end to end. Now, take a breather, and shout. You know what should happen? YOUR VOICE SHOULD REACH THE OTHER END OF THE ROOM INSTANTANEOUSLY. We will repeat it, in case you are in a state of shock. If the room is filled with one single (giant) molecule from end to end, the sound should travel to the other end instantaneously. That is to say that the speed of sound should be infinite! And THAT is pure blasphemy! No object, as the Great Man3 has shown, can move at a speed greater than that of light, let alone that infinity thing. Please go through this paragraph again to truly appreciate the beauty of Bagdenborgian logic—it is intuitive and logical at the same time, and in equal proportions.

Once you have digested this, the next step is quite easy. Instead of the room, think of the space between the Earth and the Moon. Instead of 'shouting,' you shoot an electromagnetic signal at the Moon. In place of the single gigantic (freakish) molecule of air, imagine space as a single, UNDIFFERENTIATED LUMP touching the Earth at one end and the Moon at the other end. Just as we said that the sound should reach the other end of the room instantaneously, so, here too, by analogy, the electromagnetic signal shot from the Earth should reach the Moon (and back, too) instantaneously. That, again, means that the signals should travel at an infinite speed, far, far faster than light – which again is anathema to science. See the beauty of the logic, and you have to accept Bagdenborg's solution that space too is discrete in nature. Space is not a single undifferentiated lump. It is textured. The discreet elements are the spaceniks. It is because of this discrete nature that the speed of light is of a definite value.

A point of interest here for the connoisseurs. In Maxwell's study of the electromagnetic waves, the speed of the waves is derived by the mathematical equations. In the Bagdenborgian revelation, the speed becomes definite because of the nature – the texture of the medium. The former conclusion is theoretical. If you are a real 'practical' scientist, you must agree with Bagdenborg's deep intuition.

Following Bagdenborg's methodology of descriptive science, we can have some glimpses of information on the "spaceniks," which can be summed up in a couple of sentences:-

1. Spaceniks do not move like the discrete particles of air or water. It is because they are infinitesimally small and packed unimaginably densely.
2. They cannot be detected as far as the state of the present technology is concerned. Size-wise, they are a million times smaller than Planck's length. Recall here, that Planck's length is the bottom-most limit for the measurement of length. Anything less than that has no significance in science. But that is quantitative science for you. Bagdenborg's is descriptive science. Space is the ultimate state of refinement. In that region of refinement all rules of measurement and mathematics break down. (If you insist on having mathematics, you have to invent a totally new kind of logic which has not existed so far.)
3. If you still are keen on knowing the properties of the spaceniks, you can manage to get an inkling about their indirect properties, by skillfully using the known constants. An indirect property, as per Bagdimedes, is a property derived from the known behavior of objects which interact with that of which you want to discover. Direct properties are the "essence" of the object of study – space, specifically in this case. ("Better leave it alone,"

was Bagden's strange remark. "They cannot be exploited practically.") The most famous known constant is the speed of light. By leveraging it mathematically, one may extract the "indirect" property of the spacenik. "Set the mathematical whiz kids on that," Bagdenplato is reported to have said, "They will surely wring out some equations on spaceniks." The 'fact' that light (usually) travels at a speed of 1,86,273 miles per second – in space – offers a clue to the nature of the spaceniks.

4. However, Bagdenborg's fento-science has quite a different view on spaceniks. The speed of light is only a minor clue. The most significant aspect of space is that it contains (holds) in its delicate folds (to say, rhetorically), the jumbled mixture of billions and billions of electromagnetic signals and yet, is able to preserve the identity of the bits and bytes of every (damned) individual signal. What it signifies is obvious. It means that space has memory. We have already seen that in a different context – while studying force and motion. We have arrived at the same conclusion by different routes (which augurs well for Bagden's theory of the memory of space). There is also a third clue, pointing at memory. Recall that Bagdimedes intuited that space is "elastic". Even at the mundane "coarser" level of matter, elasticity implies memory! A stretched rubber band, when released, goes back to its original length, or shape.
5. All the physical laws of nature are directly related to this – memory of space. The laws are analogous to the computer's pre-installed software/programs. That is why Bagdenborg called space, "The womb of creation".
6. In the section, "Shell in a nutshell", it was shown that everything that can be considered as discrete or a system, from the microscopic to the macroscopic level, had a shell. The spacenick is no exception to that rule – it too has a "shell" that defines its discreteness. Size-wise, the shell of the spacenik is the smallest in nature. Considered from the fentological level, the adjective "small" is a misnomer; its (spacenik's) length is a million times less than the Planck length. Because of this, Bagden declared that the spacenik is the origin of all dimensions and directions. Truly – and marvelously too – as Bagdusplato suggested, a wholly new kind of mathematics is to be invented if we are to deal with spaceniks.
7. One word of caution about the nature of spaceniks. In the analogies of water and air, we mentioned their respective particles. These particles, while transmitting their waves, are in motion. (In fact, they are in motion

even when not transmitting waves, as when they are sealed in containers. For example, the molecules of water in a container are in constant random motion called the Brownian movement, named after the discoverer. So, is the case with the molecules of a gas, on which Avogadro has derived some beautiful equations.) Even the still smaller, subatomic, fundamental particles are in constant motion.

Spaceniks are not to be imagined along the above analogies. Even though they are described as being discrete and "particle-like," they do not move about like gas molecules, electrons, photons, etc. Spaceniks are more like the texture of space. If they are thought of as moving, it will be like begging the question. Where or wherein can they move? In space? They are the very essence of space itself. That is why Bagdenborg concluded that they act like memory software when they transmit signals and forces.

Tailpiece: We have journeyed thus far through strange and existing ideas, ideas which nevertheless are cogent and compelling. We have seen how Bagdenborg has laid firm foundations for a new kind of science. Stop at every stage of the journey and mull over it. You will have glimpses of many sidelights. (Descriptive science is a fertile land). For example, a few pages back, we saw that space—the universe—is spinning. A corollary to this insight offers us information about the shape of the universe. Due to the centrifugal force generated by the spin, the universe develops a disproportionate bulge. Thus, the universe must be a spheroid—like our Earth. This is just one example placed before the reader as an appetizer—to whip up his hunger for further research. We are sanguine that the intelligent readers (you, who else?) will be able to discover many cookies on his own, along the above lines, so long as they have by their side the infallible vade mecum of Bagdenborgian fentologic.

Chapter 7

THE WOMB OF CREATION – II

There are two aspects to the mystery of creation: the origin of the universe. One pertains to time. This is the most alluring route to follow. Yet, at the same time, it is also frustrating. In the non-scientific mode of thinking, we go back to yesterday, the day before yesterday, and so on. A problem immediately arises. How many yesterdays do we have to go back? A billion? A trillion? One more yesterday peeps out behind that trillionth yesterday. Finally, we have to give up the exercise and arbitrarily assume the existence of a certain point in time as the beginning of creation. Nevertheless, the frustrating question rises up stubbornly – what was there before creation? Some systems of thought try to side-step the problem by positing cycles of creation and destruction, running on forever. But that is no solution to the problem. Science too attempts to travel back in time in its way. Science got a major fillip in this direction when the phenomenon of the red-shift was discovered, from which it was inferred that the universe was expanding, the inference leading further to the postulation of the Big Bang. (We have had plenty of occasions to mention that name – almost ad nauseam. Please grin and bear it.) The Big Bang is the official origin of creation, calculated to have taken place fourteen billion years ago. To be honest, even the Big Bang theory does not stop us from asking the uncurbable question – "What was there before the Bang?" Besides, time-wise, if a definite figure like 14 billion years is presented, the mind immediately wants to peep back behind that figure. As an aside to that 'besides', Bagden would like to point out that the figure, 14 billion years, is pretty small when compared to the kind of huge numbers science itself delights in throwing at us. ("Even a billion-billion-billion years will not satisfy my appetite," BagdenChaldes). Curiously, the Big Bang votaries hint at a future Big Crunch, meaning that the present expanding universe will one day stop expanding and start contracting, eventually leading to the same state of affairs conducive to another Big Bang. We are back to the "non-scientific" concept of cycles of creation and destruction. Time mockingly continues to flow on!

The second aspect that we mention is, again, equally tough, if not tougher, to crack. Discard the notion of time for a while. Just think of the act of creation itself; of matter or wave or energy; whatsoever you want to call it. Here too, science follows a similar method to the one it took regarding time. That is, it proceeds from big lumps of matter and goes in search of smaller and smaller lumps: molecules, atoms, subatomic particles, quarks, and so on. The latest candidates on the list are the strings – the ultimate in smallness. They are supposed to be the stuff of creation. They are not made of anything else. If you ask what strings are made of, they (you know, who) will answer, "nothing." Strings are strings. (Were they alive now, the old Greek philosophers would have laughed their hearts out.)

What we have sketched in the previous paragraphs is just the barest of bare outlines. Thousands and thousands of tomes have been written on the subject. Suffice it to say that there is no one single universally and unanimously accepted theory. Bagdenborg's opinion is that it is safer and saner to stay on this side of creation. He has a very valid reason for saying so. You can study creation as an object after it is created, not before. The subtle irony that most people miss is that you, who wish to study creation, are also a part of creation. He (Bagdenborg) once quipped thus, in response to a question from his follower, "If you seriously want to study the universe as an object, you have to stand outside of it, ideally. As far as I know, no scientist has done that." Further on the subject, he once clarified, "It is futile to attempt understanding what creation is. Consider creation – after it is done and put in your lap – as a recreation, a toy to play with, and you will have plenty of fun." That is what he meant by staying on this side of creation. The bottom line, as the trite phrase goes, is that we have a fabulous machine in our backyard guaranteed to keep us intrigued forever. Get going. Explore it, play with it until you are satiated, or frustrated, or exhausted. Don't worry your pretty head about how it came to be there. Bagdenborg writes a second bottom line in fine print below that. Carry your exploration in a spirit of recreation. Science too is recreation, albeit being far more sophisticated. (If you are stuck on the way, Bagdenborg's fento-science is there to help you.) Many intellectually oriented scholars may be horrified at Bagden's stance, but, "That is how it is."

With this brief introduction, let us explore what fresh insights Bagdimedes has to offer. Let us try to see the working of the universe through his wonder-filled eyes.

Even if we designate the universe out there as the objective universe, a peculiar situation exists, even in terms of its objective assessments. The first of such assessments is of size, naturally. The peculiarity of the situation is that our assessment is limited and shaped by our capacity of perception. As an obvious example, think of how men looked at and perceived the universe before the first avatars of the microscope and telescope were invented. Man invented instruments that extended the range of his bare perceptions by enormous ranges. As a consequence, his view and understanding of the world changed. We have to add instruments of detection too to that list now since such detectors help us in determining the existence of submicroscopic particles which cannot be perceived directly with advanced instruments too. Before the advent of modern science, a fine speck of dust floating across a beam of light was the lowest limit of smallness of matter. In those days, though they guessed that the sky was vast, all that they dared to estimate was that it was crammed with a million stars. We, of the present day, will be amused at their audacity (as they felt) in guessing. Now we talk, not of millions, but billions, not of stars but galaxies! We can see sizes less than a millionth of their "speck."

But Bagdenborg admonishes us that there is no cause for us to feel superior. The common underlying thread, he points out, is that our knowledge is an extract of what we are capable of perceiving. In the days of yore, they had a certain range of perception, and in our day, the range is greater. When we recognize this, an intriguing question arises. Will the future generation be able to see, perceive, and detect more than we are capable of doing now? The answer would most probably be yes. If it is yes, it is a trap, for it invites the same question to be asked of the next generation! (Comparison is odious, it is said. We can slightly modify that statement and say that the comparative degree is dreadful.) How far can we extend our range of perception? Keep in mind that we are using the word "range" specifically with regard to sizes and distances. That question too gives birth to interesting paradoxes – the kind of paradoxes that the ancient Greek philosophers loved. If we assert that there is no limit, theoretically, to the range of perception we are capable of, then it essentially means that there is no limit to scientific discovery. That is good news. That is good news that invites dour bad news. If there is no limit to discovery, then it means we will never be able to understand all that is to be known, forever. Our knowledge will always be incomplete! What can be more sour to hear than that? On the other hand, if we accept that our perceptions are limited, that will be far sourer to hear! (Bagdimedes – "I think it is ruminations along these lines that made Plato describe the famous picture of the cave.")

Bagdenborg sides with the second alternative, with a slight modifier. We have already described his concept of the spectrum of perception. To recap it briefly: The existence of the universe is infinite in its modes. The range of perception of human beings is limited to a band of the spectrum. Whether the spectrum has a small band or a wide one is of secondary importance. As said earlier, the word "perception" includes both the direct perception through our senses and the extended perception obtained through instruments. Most people ("Incorrigible optimists") would protest and say that the sensitivity and range of instruments can go on improving indefinitely. Bagdenborg's tense and highly cryptic remark on that score is that the usefulness of all the instruments in the world hangs on human senses of perception. That statement, though true, is a bit puzzling. Bagdenborg's admirers have interpreted it at many levels, to go into which will be a vast digression. We will look into one interpretation.

Fundamental particles like electrons and photons are not directly perceptible through human senses. For that matter, we cannot see even larger entities like atoms and molecules. Imagine, for the sake of argument, that they have invented an instrument – a kind of ultra-ultra-microscope – that can project the image of an electron on a screen. The funny part is that even though you are "seeing" the electron, you are able to do so because you are able to see the screen.

This is not at all a perverse argument; it is fully valid. Set aside the visual "seeing" of the electron. Even if you want to just detect it, utilizing its property like electric fields, ultimately, the detector has to translate it into a channel that can be fed to your senses. If you want to discard visual input, the detector has to produce a sound, an alarm, a ringtone, etc. You are able to "hear" the electron because you are able to detect the sound from the loudspeaker of the instrument. It is in this sense that all the instruments of measurement or detection hang on the existence of our senses of perception. To repeat, the argument may not have the appeal of high-brow stuff, but it is based on undeniable facts.

The example in the previous paragraph was chosen to introduce Bagdenborg's favorite concept of the spectrum, which we have examined earlier in another context. The universe – call it creation or whatever – exists, or manifests in an infinite range of gradations. Recall that we talked of the five states of "solidness" toning down in refinement, finally ending at the most refined state; that of space. In an analogous way, there is the human range of perception; a spectrum. Whereas the range of creation is infinite, the bandwidth of human perception (including the mind) is limited. So, in the infinite ocean of creation, the human bandwidth is able to perceive (to gain knowledge of) only a fraction of the manifestation. That is the gist of the Bagdenborgian philosophy. The statement naturally invites logical paradoxes. ("Cannot be helped. Logic is like that only. Any statement may be cunningly dissected, mauled, and bastardized, employing logic appropriate to the purpose." – Bagdenborg) A little demonstration follows, to show (just to satisfy the curiosity of the readers), how "obvious" arguments can be put forward left and right, any which way you like.

"If human perception is limited, that is all there is to it. What it perceives is the only reality that can be."

"Whatever exists outside of human perception has no relevance – no meaning."

"Why?"

"It is because we, as human beings, are experiencing the universe and examining it."

"But that is anthropomorphism. Your philosophy is human-oriented, homocentric."

"Thank God you did not say 'eccentric.' But seriously, whatever knowledge there is, including your science, can only be the endeavor of us, as humans. If you think otherwise, go and tell it to the birds."

"Who said human perception is limited? For the past three thousand years, we have been continuously discovering one thing after another."

"If a tree falls in a forest, and nobody has either seen it fall or heard it fall, has it really fallen?"

"As they say, if a microscopic ant is living on a two-dimensional line, poor thing, it can never know what a three-dimensional world is."

"What does the ant care? The line of two dimensions is its world. That is all there is to it, as far as it is concerned."

"There is a three-dimensional world. We know it."

"Then, do you mean to say there is a four-dimensional world in which different entities, like aliens, live?"

"Gentlemen, we are in a four-dimensional world. You seem to have forgotten your Einstein."

"Okay, make it the five dimensions, whatever. Then the ETs are living there?"

"Why are you miffed about the fifth dimension? String theory proposes ten dimensions. No, the latest buzzword is eleven."

These, and such, will be comments you will receive on your blog page. The comments can run into pages and pages. Enough of it. Let us get going and tag along with Professor Bagdenborg. In his theory of the spectrum, he does not go as far as the aliens and ETs. But he emphatically insists on the existence of "matter" of vastly refined ranges.

The ultra-refined states exist but are not perceivable. More to the point, Bagdenborg assures us that they are not even detectable, let alone perceivable. To posit the existence of something that cannot be detected is hard to digest on an initial take. But once we get familiarized with the concept by repeated reading and rumination, it does not seem to be so far-fetched. You see, the kind of refinement that Bagdenborg contemplates belongs to the outermost fringes of creation; almost on the other side, as he would like to put it.

Is there a rational necessity for postulating such kinds of particles? (They are so far refined that the descriptive word, "particle," usually accepted in traditional science, does not apply. That is why Bagden used the suffix "nik," such as in his spaceniks.) Yes, they are necessary because the bubbles of creation rise from those depths. An imagery may help here. Imagine that bubbles are rising from the bottom of the sea. You are on the surface and unable to go down. You see the bubbles breaking up on the surface. That is the stage at which your range of perception begins.

Thus, Bagdenborg posits that there are many exotic "particleniks" in creation, which we will never be able to detect, but whose effects manifest at the level of detection. At this stage (state) of detection and perception, their properties are different! It is not surprising. Look at an analogy. You cannot see infrared waves, but they are also electromagnetic waves. At just the level of reaching visibility, their frequency differs enormously.

Bagdenborg's spaceniks are at the farthest edge—or deepest depth, if you prefer—of creation, lying just this side of it. The scientific game of re-creation of Creation can be pursued from there on. We have already furnished a sufficient description of the spaceniks. Bagdenborg says that from there on, we can undertake hidden journeys (his phrase) until we arrive at the more comfortable and manageable level of the fundamental particles. The best way to perform such a journey—to navigate through those "hidden" territories—is to take the help of his descriptive technique.

The Fountain of Creation

Bagdimedes favors the "cycles of creation" view, with a slightly altered stance. He is not interested in knowing how many cycles of creation there have been, or how many more there are going to be. That is a futile exercise. According to him, studying one cycle is enough because that one cycle represents all other cycles in its essence, even if the other cycles differ in details. Creation has to end at some time or other. The end, in the present context, means dissolution. "Dissolution" is a better word because the word "destruction" may wrongly remind the readers of apocalyptic floods and fire and things of that sort. We will presently examine what exactly is the nature of dissolution or even whether it is warranted, and so on.

Creation and Dissolution

Necessarily, we have to talk at the most abstract and fundamental level when we examine the meaning and implication of Creation. The best way is to use simple but expressive analogies. Imagine you are staring at a very large white sheet of paper, so large that it completely fills up your field of vision. In fact, it is so large that you do not even see its edges. The "whiteness" of the sheet is absolutely uniform throughout. In such a situation, you cannot make any statement at all. Anything you say can be mercilessly cut down with the secateurs of somber logic. For example, you cannot even use the word "white" because whiteness needs a contrast to be differentiated. Further, you cannot say "paper" because here, paper is introduced only to highlight the uniformity of a property, like whiteness. You may replace it with any uniform background. The stern logician immediately says, "Hold on, right there. You cannot use the word 'background' because, alas, a background is recognized only when there is a foreground!" The situation is truly indescribable. (And we hope you will stay there for a few moments to appreciate the wonder of it.)

Now, as Socrates of yore would be delighted to say, a second object, something other than whiteness, is required to proceed. That means the one, by itself, is not enough to be described or perceived. Two is the starting point, the origin of everything. Ah, wait a minute, to appreciate the nuance here. That "two" need not be something separate, something apart from the "oneness"! The statement may smack of mystical abracadabra, but no, we are talking plain science here. You know how? Just replace the "whiteness" with water – a vast uniform surface of water, and we are back to the age-old metaphor. In that primordial calmness, a small ripple arises. (Don't ask how or why.) Ah, now you immediately recognize it as a ripple, a series of waves. That is to say, a separate, recognizable entity, which can be given a name, which can be described, is "born," even though water is water, even though a wave too is water.

Or, it need not necessarily be a ripple. Even the slightest of protuberance – a kind of wart, a kind of knot – is enough. In a vast sheet of uniform ice, a small protuberance on its surface is enough to get itself distinguished, to be given a name, to claim a separate existence.

This, then, is the distilled essence of the primordial act of creation—the original seed, if such an expression is permitted. First, there is absolute uniformity, which is an indescribable state beyond analysis. Then (somehow), non-uniformity occurs, giving birth to the primordial "seed of creation." The amazing thing is that this one single act of separation is enough to pave a royal way to infinite expressions of creation. When the one becomes two, that very act has created a potential for two to become four, four to become eight... proceed in that direction until the mind gets dizzy and gets seized—the way an overheated engine does. The relevant factor to recognize in this is that, after one has become two, there is full scope—almost inexhaustible—to observe, analyze, compare, dissect, synthesize, wonder, puzzle over, despair; the whole field of Nature is at your disposal.

Before we delve further into multiplicity, let us briefly consider the other face of creation—dissolution. Earlier, we wondered whether dissolution should necessarily follow creation. Bagdencarte's fentologic asserts that it is so. Common-sense-led logic seems to think that if something is created, there seems to be no reason for it to be destroyed, that the thing should go on existing forever. Destruction, as we said, is not a fully correct word in this context. The usual image one gets when the word is mentioned is that of buildings and constructions getting destroyed (bombings, tornadoes, hurricanes, earthquakes, meteor impacts, and so on). Even hills and mountains get eroded ("destroyed") in the long run. We are not talking about that kind of destruction. That kind of destruction is only a change of state. What was solid, when it crumbles, may turn into fine powder. Under the proper temperature, the powder may melt. Under still higher temperatures, the molten liquid may turn into individual molecules—gas. The progression may lead to—molecules, atoms, subatomic particles. At that level, as science has found out, the distinction between matter and waves becomes blurred.

Okay, take that fundamental particle, say an electron. Whether it is matter, wave, or energy (or ghost) is secondary to our discussion. The primary point of interest to focus on is that whatever-ghost thing behaves like an individual unit. In fentological parlance, that particle is declaring itself as being separate from the rest of the universe. (Would the verb 'asserting' pacify you?) In the above description, leave out the specific name of the particle-wave-ghost-whatever and replace 'universe' with the phrase 'uniform background.' You are describing the act of creation that was defined earlier. That is the level from which Bagdenzeno wants us to witness the grand spectacle of dissolution. Come this way, please.

There are two formal approaches as defined by Bagdenborg: a) the naked, and b) the clad.

A Brief History of the Naked

Don't be alarmed. We are not going to describe the physical state of the primordial Homo sapiens. We are going to examine the primordial particle—a particle as conceived in the discipline of modern physics. Only, we want to remind you that whatever is going to be presented is a reflection of Bagdenborgian thoughts—like everything else in this compendium. The only guilt we confess to is that we have toned down, here and there, his strong/brusque, impatient language.

Why did Bagdenborg designate the fundamental particles as naked? Because, in his view, they are defenseless—left entirely naked amidst the surrounding universe. If a human being is thrown into the cold wilderness of the Arctic, how long can he survive? Not long; short is the word. How short will his period of survival be? This is not an attempt at sensational digression. We want you to get the picture of a naked human being, shivering in the unimaginable coldness of the Arctic. We want you to clearly see that there is absolutely no chance of his survival. His dissolution is a foregone conclusion. Replace the word "dissolution" with "destruction," and we are on the way. The plight of the primordial particle is just like that of your man in the Arctic.

Bagdenborg had a quaint sense of humor. When he called the particle a naked one, he was having a dig at his adversaries who opposed his theory of shells. Remember the "shells"? Please go back to the chapter, "Shells in a Nutshell," and refresh your memory; you will immediately understand Bagden's wry reference to nudity. (There, Bagdenborg has shown how every particle, or even a separate system has—must have—a protective shell surrounding it.)

Back to our basic "particle" now. It has been stressed umpteen numbers of times in these pages that at the subatomic levels, the usage of the word "particle" is notional. The fundamental particle is not a particle of "matter" in the ordinary sense. Let us pay homage to the Quantum Theory; let us borrow from the jargon of the Quantumists for a moment. (Oops! Was that a typo? Stet!) The basic particle, therefore, would be either a packet of energy or a wave. That dainty packet, as you are well aware, is so tiny that it honestly can't be dubbed as a packet. Besides, a packet, we need not tell you, implies a container and its content. ("Neatly packed and bound.") Do you notice the irony of it? "Bound," gentlemen, "bound." That word itself reveals that the Quantumists (oops! again) have unconsciously accepted Bagden's shell theory! If the content of their packet is not put in a packet, the content evaporates—escapes like the jinn in the bottle—in a jiffy. So much for packets.

Let us, then, think of our basic particle-as-a-wave, thus gladdening the hearts of the wave theorists. Accepting it, we have to revisit that swimming pool of yours wherein you dropped a pebble. You proudly remember that, back there, when you dropped a single pebble, a ripple of waves was created. The point to focus on is that the waves travel outward until they reach the edge of the swimming pool. Right? Now, a similar phenomenon happens with our basic particle.

Somebody threw a pebble in the vast pond that is the universe. The funny (or, the anxiety-inducing) thing is that we do not know who threw the pebble or why Professor Bagdenborg does not care and advises you to do likewise. (Never mind if your anxiety level rose up by another notch). The funnier thing is that we do not know the nature of the surface of this other swimming pool—our universe. (Did your anxiety level rise by one more notch?) Naturally, when funny turns to be funnier, it has to end up being funniest. So, the funniest thing is that in spite of our double ignorance, we recognize the final outcome of the swimming pool mystery—we recognize the waves! So, let it be; amen.

Enough said. Let us read the story of the waves. To see the beauty of the story, you have to logically take just a single wave to start with. From the moment the wave is created, it begins to spread out uniformly in all directions. Here, the famous inverse square law of the Great Man 2 comes into play. The strength of the wave decreases in proportion to the square of the distance it travels. It is not a geometric progression like – 2, 4, 8, 16, etc. It is far more severe, like – 2, 4, 16, 256…and so on. Only, remember that the strength decreases; that is, 256 becomes 16, 16 becomes 4, 4 becomes 2…etc. That is an extremely rapid rate of decrease indeed. Thus, after a certain distance, the wave becomes so weak as to be almost non-existent—especially if you consider the vast distances across the universe. To offer a familiar example, you can see a candle brightly from a distance of one-foot. At a distance of a hundred feet, it will be so dim as to be barely visible. If it is burning on the moon, forget about it. If it is burning on some other galaxy than ours, it is practically non-existent as far as you are concerned. The point to note is that the wave gradually thins out—spreads itself out into non-existence. It is the dissolution of the wave for all practical purposes because, in its journey, there comes a stage when it is no longer possible to detect the wave using even the most advanced instruments. To use Bagden's terminology, the wave has descended below our spectrum; that is the end; the dissolution in short.

There was an intention behind choosing a single wave for the study of dissolution. For one, it offers a vivid picture of the process of dissolution. ("You saw a brief flash in the dark sky and then there was nothing.") Secondly, it invites a peculiar attitude in the reader—a mixture of preposterousness and self-deprecatory humor tinged with a spray of curiosity. At the same time, you will have to appreciate the beauty of Bagdenborg's chain of logic. Perpend.

In the beginning, there was the basic "particle" in the form of a wave. The wave "flashed" for a brief second and was no more. (Even if it traveled to the outermost edge of our "visible" universe, and took 14 billion years as estimated by the esteemed cognoscenti, it is only a "flash" in our metaphorical language.) To write a terse tale, there was creation, and then there was dissolution. Next, what happens to one particle obviously happens to all particles everywhere. It is the same terse tale but in capital letters—universal creation immediately followed by universal dissolution. Next, to the preposterous part.

The preposterousness consists of envisaging a single wave. Our basic particle—and many other particles too—last for a longer time; some, like the proton, seem to live forever. It is said that the decay of a proton has not been observed so far. All that is beside the point—mere bagatelle, as they say. Let us stick to the ideal, our original basic particle, and proceed along the chain of logic. First, we see the particle. It exists, it is created. We see it after some time. It is still there, what does it mean? Simple. More and more waves are being created, and they strike our detectors continuously, and so the particle existed and continues to exist. Right? Here come the preposterousness and the beauty.

Imagine the scenario (as vividly and sincerely as possible, please). A wave was created, touched your sensor/detector, and went away; literally passed away. Another wave followed in its wake, touched your sensor/detector, assured you of the existence of the particle, and went away; passed away. A third, a fourth...Did you catch the beauty of it? EVERY SECOND THERE IS CREATION AND DESTRUCTION! And wonder of wonders, the particle, as far as you and your detectors are concerned, continues to exist! What can be more paradoxical, more wonderful than this? Not for nothing did Bagdimedes say that creation implies destruction.

Bagdenborg has furnished an exciting commentary on this enthralling dance of continuous creation and destruction. Before we take it up, it is worth casting a second glance at the "destruction" of the particle. Yielding to poetical fancy, call destruction as death. You will see that our particle undergoes two kinds of death! This is not a clever puzzle made up to tease you. We are stating a wonderful phenomenon of nature.

Up to this point, we have seen how the particle is destroyed continuously; it dies innumerable deaths in a fraction of a second (yet, maintaining its life all the while). This kind of death is a temporary death! You can call it an inside story. The particle has an outside story—a second one it presents to us, in the external, temporal world. In this second story, the particle lives for some time and then dies permanently; the second kind of death. See the fine nuance here. The particle first puts up an act of continuous birth and death—billions and billions of times. Then it ends its act; the show is over.

Why should there be a permanent death of the particle? To answer that, we have to go back to the old physics of the twentieth century. Bagdimedes rues the fact that the brightest minds of that century missed a great insight by a whisker. Two items of those bygone days are relevant to our present study. One is mass, and the other is radioactivity. Take mass first. The Great Man2 showed that every object has mass. Agreed. Then came the Great Man3 and showed that mass and energy are equivalent. Agreed. So, every particle, including our basic particle under study, has a certain amount of mass. That is logical. That amount of mass M is equivalent to a certain amount of energy, say E. That is logical. In fact, you can even put it the other way round and say that the energy E is equivalent to the mass M. Now shift the logic into the next gear. We began this exercise on being and nothingness by accepting that our particle is a "packet" of energy. (Remember?) Again step up the logic to the next gear. The particle is continuously emitting waves, one after another. Each wave is dying out. No need to shift gears now. You have a water pot, (big or small, it does not matter) and one drop at a time is leaking out of it. Need we tell you that the pot, eventually has to become empty? So simple, yet pregnant with profound significance. Just like the pot, our particle eventually dies out. That is dissolution.

In fact, in the olden days of the twentieth century, they (you know who) had many analogies at their disposal. Yet they shrank away from drawing the one supreme conclusion. We mentioned the phenomenon of radioactivity just a while ago. As all of you know, there are certain elements that are radioactive. They emit "radioactive" rays spontaneously and continuously. Sans the details, the relevant point is that the radioactive element starts its life with a particular mass, say, at present. Since it is continuously emitting radiation (energy), it loses its initial mass after a certain time. In the parlance of physics, they use the term "half-life." Half-life of an element (radioactive) is that period in which it loses half of its initial mass by way of radiation. Half-life may range over thousands of years for certain elements, while some have half-life as short as a trillionth of a second. But the element loses its mass because of radiation. In a kindred analogy, you may liken this to the way a candle burns itself out; only the life of the candle is very brief compared mass to mass. Take another analogy; that of the stars. Stars, like our sun, radiate stupendous amounts of light (energy) at a steady rate. They too lose their mass gradually. (The period of loss is usually in terms of millions of years.) The astrophysicists have done plenty of calculations in this regard. What happens to the star eventually—all that jazz—is a different story with which we are not concerned here. What we want to point out is that stars (and many objects) lose their mass since they are radiating out their energy—they are slowly dying. In fact, "death of a star" is a familiar phrase in astrophysics.

This is the platform from which Bagdenborg took the breathtaking leap. He carried the analogy to its farthest border. Not only the radioactive elements and stars, but every object in the universe is "erasing" itself out. Sure, the mechanisms of a radioactive element and of stars divulging out their energies are different in nature. But, if you are perceptive, if you cut to the quick, you notice a common factor. Replace the word "radiating out" with 'leakage'. Next, notice that those systems (elements and stars) are open. (Open. Every single object in the world is open to the environment around it;

hence the word leakage. This observation naturally leads us to the inevitable conclusion—if energy is not enclosed (protected, sealed in), then it leaks out into the environment, it spreads itself out into more and more thinness until the thinness ends in nothingness. This is the fate of all objects since all objects are made of fundamental particles, which are ultimately products of the "basic particle". The basic particle dies, the fundamental particles die, all objects die. That is the grand dissolution that Bagdenborg Der Bagdimedes envisaged. That is the end.

But not quite the end. Interesting stories raise interesting questions. Answers to questions raise further questions—you know how it is. Dissolution, no doubt was a high drama on the seas of space as we just saw. But on ruminating, one disturbing question raises its anxious head. The essential process of dissolution, we saw, involved the spreading out of the energy/wave, thinning out until it sank below the spectrum of observation or detection. (You can even add "speculation" if you are in the mood!)

If you stand alone in the midst of that immense, empty, silent graveyard of the particle and meditate, sooner or later the voice of the ghost will be heard. That ghost is the famous law of conservation of energy—the most sacrosanct, inviolable law of physics. What happened to all those billions and billions of waves that rose and sailed out of our basic particle? If, as Bagdenborg claims, the particle is dead, if it is no more, then surely the energy originally represented by the particle must be somewhere. "Energy cannot be destroyed," all the textbooks on science across the world go on screaming. Even if the waves die out, the original energy representing the sum of all those waves cannot be destroyed. Where is it? What happened? What has Herr Bagdenborg Der Bagdimedes to say? Bagdenborg's answer is a Sphinx-like smile. Do the textbooks scream? Let them. They are vigilant; that is fine.

Tarry. Tarry a while before we examine a few odds and bits, tying up the topic in a proper manner. Just a bit of patience. There is a famous Indian saying, "The fruits of patience are sweet indeed." We promise that the answer you get will be sweet indeed – sweet and elegant. Now, to the odds and bits.

If you go back to the beginning of this particular chain of thought we walked through until now, you will notice that the original, the first link, was what Bagdenborg delectably described as the nakedness of the particle. We also want to remind you that what Bagdenborg meant by the "nakedness" was that the particle had no border, no shell (container) either to protect it or to define its separateness. Suppose we accept Bagden's theory that the basic particle has a shell to protect it; what then? Does the particle still die?

It makes no difference, he says (and as an aside), vehemently protesting against the usage of the word "theory," for, to him, it is a fact that the particles are enclosed by shells; not a theory. In the chapter dealing with the shells, it has been clearly stated that the shell does in no way interfere with the behavior of its contents. It serves primarily to demarcate the individual particle from the rest of the universe. So, while the particle sends out its waves to spread, the shell does not interfere. At the time of dissolution, the particle goes, the shell goes.

Another aspect, another objection. ("Objections are good. They testify to the strength, the solidarity of a theory." – admirer.) In our brief history of dissolution, we accepted the basic particle as being wave-like in nature. There is another kind of expression of energy – charge, which is supposed to be static. That is, the charge does not move like the waves. (For example, an electron is supposed to possess a negative charge.) Even in such a scenario, the Bagdeonborgian script does not change. For the sake of formality, we will review it as briefly as possible.

A field is essentially a gradient of energy. Visually in terms of a graph, it can be represented by a slope. The top of the slope represents the highest point of energy, and (ideally), the bottom, the lowest point – say zero. A pyramid with its sloping sides provides a visual picture. If you are at the apex, you have maximum energy (for that pyramid). Just imagine what will happen to you if you roll down from there. As you descend down the sloping sides, your energy ("potential") decreases proportionately. Finally, at the base where the slope ends, you do not have energy – you can roll down no further. What this means is that, as you move further and further away from the "basic particle," its field strength diminishes rapidly. Observe the parallel with the previous wave phenomena. Finally, there is a certain point at which it becomes impossible to observe/detect the field. The essential point to note is that though the charge (the field) does not travel like a wave, it too certainly leaks out – diluting itself into non-existence. (One more visual analogy may be of help here. Imagine that a thick, viscous fluid is being poured on a level surface. At the point the fluid touches the surface, there is a mound-like formation, and as the distance from the center of the mound increases, the fluid levels out). In terms of actual physics, "leveling out" means reaching a ground state – which is zero. That zero, that ground state is Bagdenborg's state of dissolution.

In the case of the field scenario too, a similarity to that of the particle-as-a-wave can be observed.

There, we saw that to sustain the "existence" of the particle (either briefly or for a long time), the waves are produced continuously. The same thing happens with the field too. Imagine again the viscous fluid being poured on the level surface. If only a single drop falls down, the "mound" (read highest field strength) is formed for the briefest of time and vanishes. That is, the field is created and gone. But in practice, the field persists for a considerable time. That means the viscous fluid is being poured continuously to sustain the mound – the point of highest potential, like the apex of your pyramid – to keep it in existence. The "existence" could be for a fraction of a second or a thousand years; that is secondary to our probing analysis. As Bagdenborg tersely says, "Dissolution is dissolution." To sum up, whether the particle is a wave or a field, it dies. Dissolution is the ultimate fate of creation. (Bagdenborg cheerfully admits that even if the particle is a ghost, he can prove that the ghost too dissolves in the end.)

Having covered the ground thus far, we are now back to the last tantalizing question, "What happens to the energy?" You can again hear the textbooks screaming, "Energy audit, energy audit!" We promised you to reveal the answer, the great insight of Bagdimedes. The time has come. It has been some time since you took that last breather in your lawn. Go, refresh yourself, and come back to the next paragraph. You may need that breather when you read Bagden's explanation.

The Fountain

Many of you must be familiar with the famous fountain at Trafalgar Square. It is an enchanting sight. Beautiful spouts of water rise high into the sky. It is an exhilarating spectacle, and if you are in the proper mood, you may go on watching it against the backdrop of the Nelson Column, forgetting the rest of the world, including your cares and worries.

But we urge you not to forget one point. Do this simple exercise. Watch the water – the spout, the spray, the individual droplets as they rise in the air. Watch the trajectories, watch the force of the spout; watch it all as the water rises up, up, and up eighty feet in the air. Don't bring down your eyes. No, we are not being facetious. This is not an attempt at a burlesque joke. Please watch the force of the water jets, try to estimate the amount of all that water spewing up majestically. Imagine the force, the energy that is at play there.

Next, imagine that there is a momentary failure of power. The pumps shut down. What happens? Watch. The jets of water rise up to their maximum height, carrying great power, and fall down silently. What happened to all that water? For a moment, there was a powerful spurt of energy, which spent itself out – and then everything is silent. Well, what happened to the water? It fell down and settled back into the pond. That is the clou, as they say. Luckily, the power supply is restored, and the spouts of water are back at their merry play.

The above analogy is exactly what Bagdenborg Der Bagdimedes has in mind as a reply to that agonizing question we asked twice; a soothing, assuring reply to the screams from all those textbooks. ("Conservation of energy, conservation of energy. What happened to all that energy of the basic particle?") Whew! You cannot beat the elegance – the concinnity – of the analogy. Further explanation is actually not necessary, but since formality demands it, we will go through the paces.

Back to our basic particle of creation one more time. We saw that the particle was essentially an act of creation. We saw that it was energy in action, be it a wave or field (or ghost). We saw that energy played itself out, like the water spout, and went into dissolution. Then we asked what happened to the energy. The answer lies at the base of the pond of Trafalgar Square! Just as the water collects back at the base of the pond, the energy of the basic particle, after dissolution/dissipation, collects back at the base of a pond – only, this pond is universal. It is everywhere in the universe. In technical parlance, when energy at a higher potential settles down to its lowest level, such a collecting point is called a "sink." Professor Bagdenborg opines that "sink" is a very undignified, lowly term for the grand phenomena occurring at the level of creation. He prefers to use the term ocean-bed or space-bed.

To paraphrase, energy expands out, plays its role in the act of creation, and then returns to the space-bed.

Additional comments

*Though it is obvious, we would like to point out that there is a difference between the water falling down to the bottom of the pond and the energy of our particle of creation going back to the space-bed. In the former case, gravity is the cause for the water coming back to the pond. In the case of the space-bed, such is not the case. As Professor Bagdenborg says, the energy returns to the space-bed because it has nowhere else to go.

*You can visualize the space-bed by another analogy. Space is like the solid sheet of ice on a frozen lake. Whatever happens in the act of creation is perceivable/detectable only above the surface. What happens below the surface cannot be seen or detected because, as we have already said, space is the borderland between creation and non-creation. It is the horizon from where creation heralds its emergence. Everything else beyond that, as Bagden says, belongs to the other side of creation. Space-bed lies in that region.

*In the analogy of the water fountain, the pumps, of course, pump back the water from the pond into the air. But in the case of our basic particle (particle of creation), there is no such agency pumping back energy from the bottom of the space-bed so as to make it break up on the surface of space. To repeat, the other half of creation cannot be seen, nor be speculated upon. It is (the other half) like a mysterious coin that presents only one side of its face to the viewer. ("Why not? The moon does it to us, earthlings, thereby indirectly pointing at Bagdenborg's Theory!" – the admirer.) As has become our habit, we will present a very nice ("elegant") analogy to you whereby you can appreciate Bagden's insight. You are in a room where a pendulum is swinging. The pendulum is swinging from left to right (sorry, gentlemen; that is Bagden's quote, and he insists it not be edited), swinging to the extreme end on one side, coming back to the central point, and swinging the other way, to the extreme. You are witnessing the scene from a distance, and there is a ceiling-high screen fixed in front of you such that you can see only one-half-swing of the pendulum. You are in no position to go behind the screen. What do you see in such a case? You see the pendulum shoot up from the level of the vertical edge of the screen. It (the pendulum) swings to one side, to the extreme, and returns to the vertical position. Then it vanishes from your sight. (Very puzzling). After a bit of time, the pendulum again emerges into your sight – apparently starting from a vertical position – repeating its previous maneuver. (Mysterious). If you are not acquainted with a pendulum, ("Abject apologies again." – Bagden's quote. Herr Professor insists on not bowdlerizing) the phenomenon will be most mysterious indeed... Whatever is happening behind the screen is analogous to what happens in the "unfathomable depths" of the space-bed.

*Admirer comments: We need not go for the Big Bang speculation. Professor Bagdenborg's theory is more elegant and satisfying. Indeed, creation and dissolution are the two sides of the same phenomenon. Unfortunately, as the professor has shown, we can know only one side of the coin. Perhaps it is better that way. Just by studying creation, man (especially Science) has invented horrendous instruments of destruction. (What an irony!) If he were to know more about dissolution, God alone knows what unimaginable inventions and instruments of annihilation man would invent. Truly, ignorance is a blessing in this case. These thoughts naturally lead us to the topic of the Big Bang and even enable us to see it in a new light.

Trillion trillion big bangs

"Here is there, and there is here."

"The whole contains the part and the part contains the whole."

The above may sound like sentiments reflected off some ancient mystical texts – at first glance. It may appear to be so for the man-in-the-street, completely unacquainted with the advanced regions of science. Scientific and relentless logic often have a way of carrying us away to distant boundaries of thought rarely visible to the common eye. Enough said.

Just take the logical route – simple, not even abstract.

We saw how the bundle or packet of energy spreads out and dies. All the while, we were talking of a single particle. It was to demonstrate an idea. As a matter of fact, if you count the number of such particles in the universe… ah, forget it; it is an impossible task. They are everywhere in the universe. So, naturally, logically what is happening to one particle is happening to all of them, everywhere. (That is how, dear readers, here is there, and there is here.) Thus, if you take in the whole of the universe in one glance, creation and destruction are happening everywhere in it – in every nook and corner, as the dear old idiom says. What a grand sight to behold! Remember too, the two kinds of death of the particle that we witnessed. One kind was of the million deaths in an instant, and the other was of the long-drawn-out kind.

"After understanding this, the second quotation becomes almost self-evident; it is a corollary to the first. The Big Bang theory is correct in a way it is unaware of. All bangs, big or small, come to an end; they expend themselves. See the beauty of it. A trillion trillion silent bangs are occurring everywhere, unobserved, unheralded (as Professor Bagdenborg proudly explains). At the same time – to use a jocular phrase – the mother of all bangs, The Big Bang, is supposed to have occurred once, fourteen billion years ago (according to them). Bagden would like to remind us that, strictly speaking, the Big Bang (if ever there was one such) is not over because whatever we see of the universe now is an aftermath, the fallout of that bang. Obviously, we and the universe are still merrily cruising along, and that means the bang is still going on – one heck of a long bang. The second line of the introductory quotation smoothly dovetails here. Whatever is happening at the universal level is also happening at the local level. The whole is distilled in the parts, and the parts are mirroring the whole. This is as far as the physical process is concerned. There is a second, beautiful parallel concerning time. Time-wise, the Big Bang began 14 billion years ago and may probably last another fourteen. At the same time, we saw that inside the basic particle, the process of creation and destruction occurs a million times an instant! The vision is beautiful, breathtaking, and awesome – and more."

While we are admiring the grand concept, Professor Bagnimarcus Bagnaurelius has one last trick with a card lying on the table (carrying the picture of the Big Bang). He just flips it over, and lo! It is a joker. It is a joker innocuously introduced by him while discussing the million micro-deaths of the particle. What does the dissolution of the particle imply? You see, it is happening to all the particles, everywhere in the universe. Therefore, it is not necessary to speculate about the Big Bang! Bagnimarchus magnanimously adds, "If the Big Bang gang is bent on retaining it, they better get busy reinterpreting it. The mathematics is not difficult." An irreverent aside – Bagden is indulging in his favorite pastime, that of taking a perverse dig at mathematics.

Now, is there some significance in this continuous act of creation and destruction? What is nature up to? There are quite interesting significances, both scientific and philosophical. Before we pursue those deeper perceptions, let us have a glance at another curious tidbit, since we were examining the Big Bang.

The Big Bang is closely related to the age of the universe, as estimated by them, the fourteen billion years of which everybody is familiar. Add another fourteen (billion), and rounding off, we can make an assumption that from birth to extinction, the life span of the present universe is roughly thirty billion years. Thirty billion years is indeed quite a long period if you ponder it. For most of the human beings, even the ideal lifespan of a hundred years seems to be interminably tedious. The ancient Indian texts have speculated on the age of the universe (creation). They too favor the concept of cycles of creation and destruction. We give below a small table detailing the span of creation. The data may not be strictly scientific or verifiable, but is sure to astonish the reader if he is not already familiar with it. Here we go:-

Brahma is supposed to be the creator of the universe. Actually, they posit something else which is beyond the creator, which, it is impossible to define. Brahma, as the creator, is a kind of agent of THE IMPONDERABLE. The lifespan of Brahma is taken as 100 years – his "years" which, we are going to compute now.

There are four Ages, which go on repeating cyclically. They are the four yugas (Sanskrit): Krita, Treta, Dwapara, and Kali. Kali is the yuga (Age) in which we are all living now. Their duration in terms of human years is given below.

1. Krita Yuga 1728000 years
2. Treta Yuga 1296000 years
3. Dwapara Yuga 864000 years
4. Kaliyuga 432000 years

Total of one cycle of four *yugas* = 4320000 years.
One thousand such cycles make Brahma's one day-time = 4320000000 years
One day of Brahma (day+night) = 8640000000 years
One year of Brahma = 3110400000000 years
Life span of Brahma = 311040000000000 years!

Even if it is all imagination, you have to salute the daring of the people who conceived of such durations in those ancient times. (That is 31,104 billion years!) And there is no end to it.

Brahmas come and Brahmas go, eternally engaged in creation and dissolution. There must be a moral in this. We think the moral is that it is useless to speculate about time – and for that matter, even about creation and destruction. That is why Bagdenborg advised us to think of creation as a recreation and not to take it too seriously (a view unpalatable to dedicated scientists). Of course, Herr Professor has a more serious reason to say what he says, which we will consider now.

The stuff of experience

"Astonishing is the illusion of reality, whereas jaw-dropping is the reality of illusion."

It is inevitable that at some point in an inquiry into the enigma of the universe, science has to meet the boundary of philosophy. It is not a clear-cut boundary, and as scientific inquirers, we will have to hover over the hazy boundary. After all, if we are after knowledge with a capital K, we cannot afford to seal ourselves in watertight compartments – mostly self-made. In contrast with psychological and biological sciences, theoretical physics seems to be strictly objective.

But think about it this way. Even if that knowledge is supposed to be objective, it is an undeniable fact that it is we, human beings, who are pursuing the knowledge. Our knowledge is based on experience. Experiencing is the act of perceiving and reacting to whatever is out there in the universe, all around us. In physics, we are specifically interested in objects, their properties, and behavior. At the most fundamental level, perceiving an object involves the mysterious phenomenon of awareness. (This is where science hovers on the border of philosophy.) The hard-boiled die-hard physicist may say that awareness is also a consequence or function of the electrical activity (such as "neuron firings" or whatever) inside the brain. But that is a very vapid answer; dull to the point of boredom. "We can as well wind up all scientific research and sit stupidly staring at one another, and all around us forever," says Bagdenborg. "Occasionally swatting a transgressing fly that perches on the nose," he adds wryly. There are some ticklish questions that cannot be answered using words only. Let us steer clear of such problems and come back to this side of the boundary. We will take the meaning of the word "experience" in the general sense that is universally accepted at a certain level. Experience, in that sense, can be fairly described as the summation of the inputs we receive through the senses of sight, hearing, touch, etc. Thus, when we see an object, either moving or immobile, we experience it – the object is "real" for us.

That qualifying word, "moving," reminds us of the discussion we had about motion and its reality (See chapter, "Forceful motion..."). There, it was shown that motion itself was a variety of illusion – a story constructed by the brain out of a series of images, recorded at intervals of 1/16th of a second. We will recapitulate briefly to see if immobility – an object at rest, as they say – is much different from motion. Examine the figure given below (Figure 5).

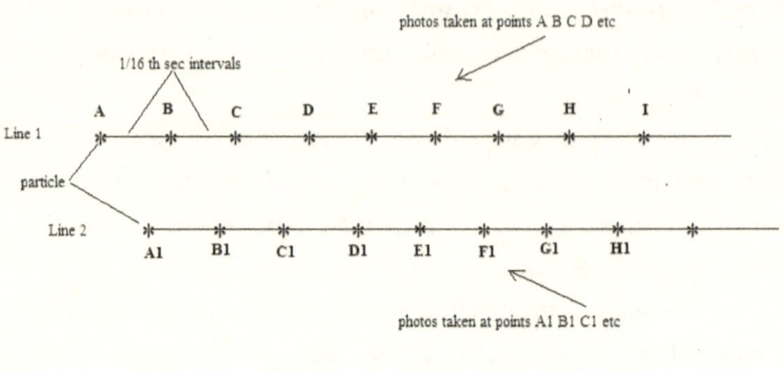

Figure 5

A heretic view: hidden journeys

We are going to present a totally revolutionary view – Bagdenborg's hallmark – here. It may seem unorthodox, or even heretic, but there is a lot of sense in what he says. In the figure above, the various positions occupied by a moving object are marked as A, B, C, D, etc. Snapshots are taken of the object at these positions at equal intervals of 1/16th of a second. If this recorded movie is projected on the screen at the same speed ratio, we will see the object in motion. This corresponds to the actual, real-life experience of seeing an object in motion. To stress the point – we actually "see" the object as moving continuously, smoothly, without a break in its journey. This is where our blaspheming professor enters, shouting, "Halt, stop there!" What do those dramatic imperatives mean? Well, you have to literally halt and reroute your thinking process to appreciate the wizardry (witchcraft?) of Bagdenborg's insight.

You see, if the object is at A in the beginning and at B after 1/16th of a second, and at C after the next 1/16th of a second, and so on, that information is enough for you to assume (and experience) that the object is in motion. Now, if the object, instead of going straight from A to B during that (crucial) interval of 1/16th of a second, meanders along a different path but is back at B exactly after the expiry of that 1/16th of a second, the snapshot represents the object as being at B only. Similarly with the other points C, D, E, etc. The snapshots will be officially correct, and you will officially "see" the object moving along its expected/calculated trajectory – that is a straight line in this particular example. See the beauty, the wizardry of it! The object is being naughty and actually traveling in a zigzag way, while it is hoodwinking you into believing that it is traveling honestly in a straight line! It is performing hidden journeys, and you are unaware of it. Imagine a parallel line some distance away from the apparent line of travel of the object (Line 2 in the figure). Notice the points A1, B1, C1, etc., which are also spaced at the 1/16th-second interval. Imagine also that the object is traveling in this fashion: from A to A1, to B to B1, to C to C1, and so on. If you take snapshots of the object at positions A1, B1, C1, etc., at 1/16th-second intervals and replay them on the projector of another person, he will swear that the object is traveling along Line 2, whereas you know that it is traveling along Line 1 only! You will smile tolerantly at his ignorance or the blatant error in his instruments, whereas he will be responding in kind. We can cut the comedy. The object, instead of moving to A or B, etc., may go all the way to hell and be back at B at the correct interval of time. Your projector will be showing you an object moving along Line 1; you are satisfied. ("Where ignorance is assurance." – Bagdenborg)

Talking seriously, let us assume that the object is, in fact, moving in a zigzag fashion, from A to A1 to B to B1, etc. Unfortunately, you have no way of knowing where the object has been in that interval of the 1/16th of a second. You know only that at the specified time, the object is at A, B, C, and so on. On your screen, you watch the object moving along line1. That is all, as far as you are concerned. Now, here comes the paradox. The object's travel in a straight line is an illusion, but it is your experience, and it is real to you. Thus, experience is real as long as it lasts – even if it is an illusion! It is real as long as the experience lasts consistently. (This is a stock syllogism for philosophers who declaim that life is a dream, that a dream is "real" as long as it lasts, that everything is an illusion, that, no, everything is real, since everything is an experience and therefore real as long as it lasts...so on and so on. Let us get back on track.)

The above analysis of the motion of the object branches off into many directions. It is even connected to the double-slit/multiple-slit experiments that we discussed in the initial chapters, if you just replace the object with an electron or a photon. If you ask whether the object (or particle) really makes its jay-walking journey outside of its honest trajectory, Professor Bagdenborg will wink at you, executing a sly gesture towards the proponents of the probability-waves, uncertainty principle, and hidden dimensions. The subject is interesting, and we can dwell at length on it, but it is all familiar territory, though our route will be different from the well-trodden tracks. What is of relevance to us is that the very process of experience is itself fraught with alternative (and alternating) implications. What Bagdenborg is more interested in is to show that the above analysis can be adopted to examine the state of a static ("non-moving," "at rest") object. Such an analysis will lead us to jaw-dropping (nay, jaw-shattering) perceptions.

So, let us take a look at an object by itself – as if we have placed it on a laboratory table and are examining it. Let us play the ostrich game. The ostrich, it is said, buries its head in the sand at the sight of a dangerous enemy. The idea behind it, they say, is that if you don't see the enemy, the enemy does not exist! The behavior may appear to be dumb, but if seen from a different level, we can learn something from the ostrich. Let us start the game of the ostrich.

Place the object on the table and begin recording a video. The room is pitch-dark. Your camera does not have a flashbulb. A separate source of light is flashing light on the object at our familiar 1/16th of a second interval. Make a recording, say, for a duration of three minutes. If you play back the recorded video, you will see nothing special. On the video screen, you will see the object (unmoving) continuously for three minutes. Fine. Next, you record the video, keeping the flashlight on for ten seconds and switching it off for ten seconds – alternately. Remember, the room is pitch-dark. If you play back the second video on a screen, the object will be seen for ten seconds, and it will vanish for the next ten seconds, and so on, repeatedly.

We are assuming, for the purposes of this experiment, that the only way of knowing about the object is through visual input (to our senses). Let us indulge in playing games – both physical and intellectual. Take the first experiment. There is a flash of light this instant, and everything is dark for a duration of the next 1/16th of a second. Now, some mischievous elf has entered the room. It removes the object during that period when there is darkness and quickly replaces it just in time when the flash is on. Your video recording will still show the object to be firmly placed (unmoving) on the table. If you inform the elf that the object was on the table continuously all the time, the elf will be laughing in its sleeves. This experiment was described in simple terms to give a graspable picture of what is involved.

The underlying idea is that, just as with the body in motion, the experience of continuity is also an illusion. We can make the case a bit more rigorous, though it is not necessary. We do not know about the experimental room, and we do not know about the elf too. We are simply asked to observe the video only and are asked to give our opinion. So we will naturally say that the object was lying on the table continuously. Our experience is obviously an illusion since the elf was taking out the object regularly. (In fact, the elf was introduced to add a bit of drama. A third, human party, unknown to us, could replace the elf). To repeat, continuity is an illusion. Bagdenborg stresses that there is no such thing as continuity at all! In fact, according to his deepest insight, continuity is an impossibility if creation and thus experience are to occur at all.

The second experiment with the flashlight being kept on and off illustrates another principle. In a way, it is the reverse side of the same coin of creation-cum-experience. It is meant to show that if you cannot observe or detect an object, it does not "exist" as far as "experiencing" is concerned. (And experiencing is all that we, as human beings, have).

There is another alternative to the experiment, which the discerning reader would have already noticed. We assumed that our object was "inert," "dead," as we were flashing light on it to observe it. What if the object were alive, in the sense that it is self-illuminating? That is an interesting question, but it does not thwart our chain of reasoning. We need to add a few more details; that is all. If the object is self-illuminating, it means that it is emitting light (electromagnetic waves, to use a grandiose expression). In our experiment, we used a flashlight at intervals of 1/16th of a second. That is indescribably tardy in comparison with the frequency of light, which is millions of cycles per second. What does that description, "cycles per second," mean? Just a minor clarification is needed; or a reminder. As you know, a wave starts building up from scratch (zero), reaches its greatest height ("crest"), and symmetrically subsides down to a value of zero, to begin the process of building up again in the opposite direction ("trough"). That is to say, that the light waves are virtually acting as flashlights but working at enormous rates. That is all – we are back on track. Only, an extremely ticklish technical detail remains to be accomplished. We do not need a separate flashlight to video-record the object, of course, but what we need to do is to "snap" the object exactly whenever its wave strength is at the point zero. Technically, this sort of synchronization is an immensely tough task; we better conduct the task as a thought experiment. Now, if we do the video recording as prescribed, the playback will show an empty screen. That is, we have to conclude that there is no object "there." Also, as we did before with flashlights, if we record the crests of the light waves for a few seconds, followed by the record of the "dark," zero points, we will see on our screens that the object will be there for a few seconds and will vanish for a few seconds.

But apart from this line of analysis, (and more importantly), we see that if the object is self-illuminated, it is a packet/bundle of energy. And we have already examined what happens to an object/particle that is a bundle of energy – it dies a million transitory deaths per second and also dies a permanent death eventually (dissolution). Thus, through the foregoing paragraphs, we have neatly tied up the theory of creation and dissolution.

The distilled essence of all these elaborate arguments can be summed up as follows: There cannot be an unbroken continuity of anything because the very essential nature of experience is one of change. Without experience, there are neither you nor me, nor knowledge of anything. In our mundane life, we observe objects to be existing continuously because the change at the deepest levels is happening at such an enormous rate that we are unable to perceive it.

Lastly, there was a good reason for giving the example of the movie projector. Forget about the technicalities of the experiments and explanations. The essential point to underline is that the motion of the object on the screen was an effect, the "existence" of the object too was an effect. The same thing is happening in the vast theatre of the outside world, only more magnificently. When we see the external objects, their existence too is an 'effect' – that is what Bagdenborg is driving at. It is not necessary, on that score, to label the phenomena as an illusion. The world and its objects are an effect – an effect of change. It is that simple and that fundamental. In fact, if we come to think of it, there is no necessity of bringing in label-words like reality and illusion. The single, simple word, "effect," subsumes both and much more. We truly feel that Bagdenborg has the last say on this topic, that he has elegantly wrapped up creation, destruction, and experience. Any further venture beyond this boundary of thought will inexorably land us in the quagmire of unresolvable speculations and fantasies. Besides, as Bagdenborg maintains, all such speculation pertains to the "other side of creation," to deal with which is futile. On the other hand, this side of creation (where we stand) is wide open to limitless amounts of inquiry, an inquiry which too, Bagden advises us to take in a spirit of recreation and joy. So, let us turn our faces toward this side and play with joy in our hearts, as he said.

The play of numbers – Grand Recreation

Once we turn our face toward this side of creation, the most striking observation that confronts us is the bewildering multitude and multiplicity of objects in the world. Let alone studying, even just enumerating all the objects (animate and inanimate) of the world is itself a daunting task. (We are leaving aside all the man-made artifacts). But the human mind has a wonderful capacity for classification and unification. Thanks to the brilliant studies in physics and chemistry, it was seen that all the millions of objects in nature (everything) are really made of about a hundred and odd elements. Then, how are the multiplicities of objects formed? They are formed by a combination of two or more elements – apart from the stand alone single elements. The combined forms for the elements are called compounds. That means, all the objects in the world are either elements or compounds. This knowledge was truly a great step in understanding the mystery of nature and its workings.

With the discovery of the structure of the atom, another era of deeper penetration was ushered in. Electrons, protons, and neutrons were discovered one by one. It was found that they were the constituents of the atoms of all elements whatsoever. Only, the numbers of those particles varied from element to element. Thus, the fundamental constituents of all matter could be said to have been identified. This is no small achievement. Surely, this can be described as one of the greatest triumphs of scientific investigation. We will not go here into further and deeper details on these particles, since much of this knowledge is familiar to the readers. We would just like to draw the readers' attention to a particular aspect that is pertinent to our line of appreciation – that of the formation of multiplicity.

Note that we said, "formation," not "creation" of multiplicity. In our assessment, creation is a unique act, and the "formation" of multiplicity (of objects) is only re-creation, a kind of recreation for Nature. That is not a cryptic or clever remark because if you delve deep into the matter, you will see that the original, the true act of creation is that of one becoming two, or one begetting two; not even begetting, but becoming two. That primordial act of one becoming two is all that matters, is all that is needed. See the beauty of it. When one becomes two, it has already sown the seeds of two becoming four, four becoming eight…ad infinitum. That is why – repeat – we said that after two (creation), everything is recreation, a grand play on an infinite scale.

Numbers count: effects mount

Numbers do count, and how! (We are not abashed about the pun.) Numbers and "effects" are the two magic wands with which Nature takes delight in exhibiting its wonderful, indescribable wizardry. We are holding back the upwelling of strong poetical urges here. However, we would like to recount a fable.

"Long, long ago, nobody knows how long ago," is how the fables start. That is very apt for our tale. So, long, long ago, nobody knows how long ago, there lived an old king who held sway over a vast empire. The king had 127 sons. Now it came to pass that the king desired to distribute his empire among his sons, who had come of age. The king and his empire were unique. Doubtlessly, his empire was vast, but all that the empire consisted of was steel balls; like small round ball bearings. He was unique, you see. Wherefore, the king called his sons, and he opened his mouth, and he spoke to his sons his desire to distribute his empire among them. The sons were glad to hear the tidings, but they were unique, even each one of them, having inherited that propinquity from their venerable father. If the empire was shared among them, each one of them would be in possession of the same item – ball bearings, ball bearings every one of them. So, pray, where lay their uniqueness? Each one of them wanted to maintain his uniqueness. So they put forth their demand before the king, and they were adamant on that score.

The king was puzzled and then deeply perturbed as he was unable to solve the problem. All he had were ball bearings, an immeasurable quantity of them. He could only give ball bearings to his sons. Now, the king had an old venerable minister whose wisdom had saved the king in many a difficulty. At last, the king called the wise minister and threw the problem into his lap. Isn't that what ministers are meant for? The old man slept over it because his intuition told him that he would get the answer in his sleep. And, sure enough, he had a dream that night, and his dream gave him a beautiful solution to the problem. The solution was, at the same time, childishly simple, dream-like, prophetic, playful, and magical. He explained his dream to the king the next day morning. The king heard him out, smiled, and then laughed heartily. Immediately, he issued instructions to his officers on how his wealth (the ball bearings) was to be distributed among his sons. This is the scheme of how the king's property was allotted to his sons:

To the first son, one ball bearing will be sealed in a container, and plenty of such containers will be prepared. Note again that the container contains only one ball bearing. All the containers containing one ball bearing will belong to the first son. In a similar fashion, the second son will receive containers holding two bearings, the fourth son will have containers holding four bearings in each, and so on. The king's sons, though initially reluctant, had to agree to the proposal. They took their share of the containers and stamped their heraldic insignias on them. This precaution was necessary because the containers could not be geographically segregated, and the heraldic emblems would easily identify each container as belonging to a specific son. Besides, they had further cause for satisfaction. Each container was distinct from the others in various ways – apart from the number of bearings it contained. The weights of the containers differed, and their sizes varied too. When moved or thrown, each container behaved in a unique manner. Even when rattled, each one produced a distinctive sound. Some containers floated on water, while others sank. All in all, the sons were satisfied. They went to the king and expressed their satisfaction. The king thanked the minister, then turned to his sons, blessed them, and said, "Go forth and multiply. May your progeny increase as the grains of sand on the seashores." And the sons went forth everywhere, and their progeny increased as abundantly as the grains of sand on the seashores.

That fable is indeed quite ancient. However, fables have a unique way of remaining relevant in every era. A contemporary adaptation of that fable – yes, even a scientific one – can be effortlessly crafted by substituting specific keywords. Readers have likely discerned this, so we will keep it as concise as possible.

A modern fable in a nutshell

Yes, in a nutshell. [Hyperlink it to the chapter with the suggestive title.] Replace the king with Nature. The sons are no different from the containers they possess – they possess them and are possessed by them. The containers represent the periodic elements of our modern-day. So, naturally, the ball bearings are the fundamental subatomic particles: the electrons (and their related cousins, the neutrons and protons). Now the fable is complete and updated. The king asked his sons to go forth and multiply. Mother Nature asked her sons, the elements, to go forth and multiply. They did. They gave birth to innumerable hordes of compounds. As we mentioned earlier, don't attempt to catalog the number of (chemical) compounds; you will be exhausted by the time the list becomes exhaustive.

The moral: Nature is exceptionally clever and inventive. By manipulating just three particles, it has managed to create over a hundred elements. By manipulating those hundred and odd elements, it has successfully generated thousands upon thousands of objects, each differing in their properties.

This is the play of numbers. Compare a shard of charcoal with a bar of gold. What a difference! Yet, when you peer into an atom of charcoal and an atom of gold, you will find the same ingredients – electrons, protons, and neutrons. The only difference in the atoms lies in the numbers of those three particles contained in each of them. This point has already been reiterated throughout the pages of this book. Nevertheless, no amount of repetition can truly capture the remarkable wizardry of nature. We are going to emphasize this idea once more, so please bear with us. The topic is worth revisiting repeatedly from different perspectives.

Group behavior; another effect

The behavior of individual entities (of some kind) when considered in isolation is identical for each entity in terms of its properties and physical behavior. However, when two or more of them are closely put together, such as in an enclosed system, they lose their individuality. They behave as a single unit, displaying quite different – and sometimes astonishing – properties. The wonder (we may even say, the greatest wonder) is that the system/unit is, in fact, not a "new" entity at all! It is composed of nothing but the old individual units. Nature employs this simple tactic to deceive and astound all of us. This method adopted by Nature (creation) is so simple and at the same time so ingenious that all the praise and appreciation heaped on it will not be enough. The best way to study the process is through analogies and examples. Intricate explanations are unnecessary, even uncalled for. Ceaseless wonder is the only explanation for this great Cosmic Recreation. We will start with visual analogies and gradually build up the picture.

Draw a straight line on a piece of paper. When you look at it, you see just a straight line; that is all (one straight line). Next, draw a second line somewhere else on the paper at a sufficient distance from the first line. Now there are two lines; that is all. Two lines, we repeat. Take a second sheet of paper and, this time, try to bring the two lines together. You can do so in various ways as shown below (Figure 6).

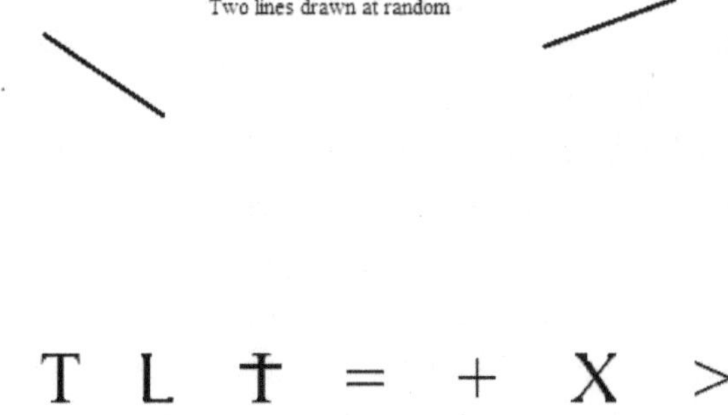

b) The same two lines when brought together in various configurations, now remind you of different letters and symbols

Figure 6

Now, what do you see? What is your visual experience? You will see the letter T, a right angle, a cross, the mathematical symbols "equals," "plus," "times," and "greater than." All the seven figures are, in essence, two lines only, and yet, by virtue of their union and configuration, they mean different things to us now. This is what Bagdenborg calls the experience, the experience itself being the outcome of "the effect." Two numbers of the same item stick together to produce an effect, inducing a new experience. The example just given is that of a diagram or picture and may not mean much. So, let us talk in terms of physical objects.

Take two rods of equal length. Prepare the T, the cross, the plus sign, and the arrow tip, which we saw in the figure above. The physical behavior of each of the objects you have prepared changes drastically. The centers of gravity (balancing point) of the objects change. Throw them in the air, and each one of them moves differently. Do you see the point? Each new object is still made out of two rods only, and yet some of their physical properties have changed; they move differently. At first glance, this phenomenon may not appear to be so strange or striking because it is so commonplace and so ingrained in our everyday experience that we fail to notice the wonder lying beneath numbers – the grouping together of a number of identical items seems to produce new objects. Even this second example too may not mean much ("not so earth-shaking") to many people. It is because we have been so thoroughly conditioned by mundane, commonplace experiences. But we don't intend to give up our exercise in persuasion. (Yes, we are trying to push you into a deep sense of wonder, a wonder of a fundamental, primordial kind!) Actually,

"The Grand Illusion" is the proper phrase to describe this play of Nature, but philosophers, mystics, and religious men have monopolized that word, and besides, science frowns upon that phrase. So we are using the word "effects." Illusion is not such a bad word at all, but... Okay, let us move on further.

The previous example of rods was a bit crude. We will go deeper. Consider a simple (the simplest) element, like hydrogen. If you peer deep "into" it, you will see that it is made of one electron and one proton. It has its own unique properties. It is a gas, lighter than air. Imagine that you are actually inside an atom of hydrogen. All you see is – an electron and a proton. That is all there is to it. Comparing with our previous analogy, say that there are two rods of different types. Two rods, two particles – that is the actuality. Now, come outside of the atom and look at it. You will see a hydrogen atom which has its own unique property, and we have to call it by a separate name! All this happens because the electron and the proton are staying together, knit into a unit. If this is not a real play of numbers, what else is? Effects, effects, effects, Bagdenborg is shouting at the top of his voice, and Nature is silently laughing at us!

Consider another atom, say that of gold. Go inside it as before, and you will see 79 electrons, 79 protons, and 118 neutrons. The three particles are yet the same; only their numbers have increased. Just by sticking together, the particles behave so differently. They are now called "gold" and behave like gold. (One is reminded of social psychology here – group behavior, as being quite different from individual behavior.)

The same is the case with all the hundred and odd elements found in nature. The same actors – electrons, protons, and neutrons – just by grouping themselves in different numbers play different dramas. They are all individuals in their own rights, but when grouped, they lose their individuality and become strangers.

Modern science too has understood this strange play in an intuitive manner (though not explicitly in terms of the words used here) and is trying to search for still more fundamental particles lurking inside the electrons, protons, and neutrons. In that effort, they have posited what are called "quarks," out of a combination of which, the three particles could be derived. Theoretical and mathematical models have been ("cleverly," says Bagden) built up using quarks. But the joke (played by Nature) is that quarks too come in different varieties; like up-quark, down-quark, and so on. They have strangeness; they have color and whatnot. An actual, real quark has not yet been caught in the experimental nets – that is the bottom line.

Return of the spaceniks

This is where Bagdenborg differs drastically. This is where he insists we must look up to fentologic to deliver us from the insidious trap of infinite regression. ("It is a Gaderene slope down which science is tumbling headlong in its search for a single fundamental particle," wrote Herr Professor.) See the irresistible pull of logic. We observed billions and billions of objects in the world. We searched and experimented and brought down the multiplicity to compounds, though still the multiplicity was big. We then distilled the huge number of compounds into a very small number of 118 or so elements. We wanted to go still deeper and posited quarks. Ironically, it is not one quark of one kind, as said just above. So, we are forced to posit some other entity – a spark, a dark, a nark – out of which quarks are made. But then, again, you have to posit a stark to explain that nark… See, it goes on and on; you can't stop. (That is why Herr Professor used strong words like 'Gaderene slope').

The fundamental problem underlying the infinite regression is that, in the search for a basic particle, we always need at least two particles, out of a combination of which, the properties of the first particle are being derived. This problem can be resolved by leveraging the phenomenon of the play of numbers (Bagden's Effects) in an elegant manner. We just need one entity – like our straight line, which we introduced at the beginning of this topic.

We have already met that one entity earlier in a different context; we just need to recall it from the backstage. It is the spacenick. One enormous advantage in dealing with spaceniks is that we do not need elaborate (and most strenuous) mathematics. ("Simplicity, simplicity, Nature admonishes us." – Bagdenborg. Bagdenborg is especially referring to the hordes of string theories reeling under the unbearable weight of mathematics.) The basic explanation for Bagden's theory was laid out in a few paragraphs above in the second figure involving straight lines.

The trick of geometry

We saw that two straight lines, when brought together, can produce a variety of effects. Nature uses the same tactics to "create" matter. Two or more spaceniks are enough to produce all the subatomic, microscopic, fundamental particles discovered so far. (Forget quarks and narks, gentlemen, including their strangeness.) When two spaceniks join together in a particular configuration, they "produce" an electron. When three or more spaceniks are welded together, they become a proton, and so on and so on. One minor detail – how do they stay together? No problem there, assures Bagdenborg. Just as atoms have their shells, just as the nucleus of an atom manufactures its own shell, the spaceniks too weave their own shells. The stuff of the shells is the same as that of spaceniks. Recall that we gave the simile of milk and the layer of cream on it. (Chapter, Shells in a nutshell.)

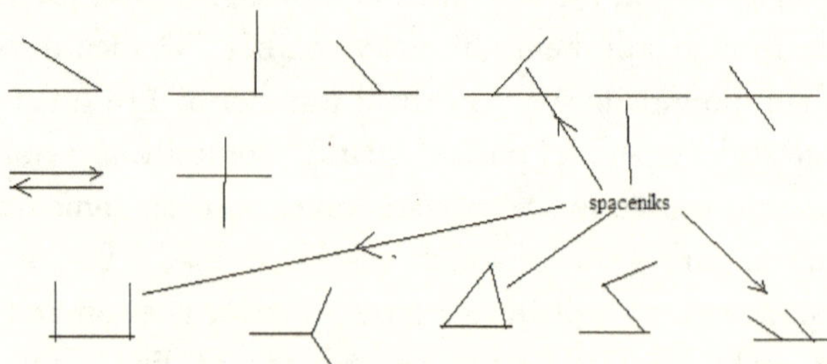

Various possible combinations and configurations of spaceniks

Figure 6A

So, the essence of Bagdenborg's theory is that there are only spaceniks at the most fundamental levels. We cannot go beyond that, and there is no need to. If this appears to be an arbitrary declaration, may we remind you of a far more oppressive diktat in science, which sets a limit to the meaningful length of distance – the Planck's length? Professor Bagdenborg Von Bagdemedes has dared to cross that line and gone far deeper, touching the bottom-most point. There he found his spaceniks. This he was able to achieve solely because of the power of what he terms the descriptive technique. Well, to come back to the point; the spaceniks combine into different configurations. Those configurations are enough to create (or, to produce "effects" of) all the fundamental particles observed by science so far. Even if new particles are discovered in the future, the configurations are a handy guide to explain the properties of such particles.

As a matter of fact, the startling effects produced by configurations are not new to science. Molecular chemistry is replete with such instances. At the level of molecules, structure and combination produce astonishing diversities.

Carbon affords the best example. Charcoal is black and soft. Diamond is transparent, and one of the hardest substances. Yet, chemically, both are made of carbon atoms. What can be more contrasting? The structure of the atoms makes all the difference. When combinations of atoms (molecules) are considered, we can see a zillion examples. Hydrogen is a gas. So is oxygen. But when two atoms of hydrogen combine with one atom of oxygen, they form water! Again, when two atoms of hydrogen combine with two atoms of oxygen, they become hydrogen peroxide, a solid! Just by being grouped together, the properties of the combined atoms change drastically. Carbon, hydrogen, and nitrogen are by themselves innocuous (in limited quantities). But if they group together (as molecules), they become hydrogen cyanide, a deadly poison. Such "combination" of atoms is called a compound, and as said, there are countless numbers of compounds (or molecules). In fact, there are certain groups of molecules called proteins which come in many shapes. Proteins, as all of us know, are essential to the body, but there are some forms of protein which are deadly poisonous! (Snake venom, for example). Recall the fable of the king and his sons, told earlier. The king blessed the sons and said, "Go forth and multiply." The molecules, the compounds are the method by which the sons multiplied. How they flourished!

All the examples cited in the previous paragraph clearly illustrate the play of numbers and the effects, to use Bagdenborg's expression again. Kindly forbear our reiteration one more time.

Consider a few hundred thousand electrons floating freely in space. The exact number does not matter, as this is for illustrative purposes only; it will not be a matter of much concern. We may choose to gaze at them with idle curiosity. Throw in an equal number of protons and roughly double that number of neutrons. Note that these particles travel almost at the speed of light. Our gaze of idle curiosity still stands true – assuming we are able to see those particles, of course.

Imagine now that in that soup, one electron and one proton choose to bind together; they turn into an atom of hydrogen. Similarly, a prescribed number of electrons, protons, and neutrons gather together, forming atoms of carbon and nitrogen. Soon, the air around us is buzzing with atoms of hydrogen, carbon, and nitrogen. Note that, strangely, the speed of these atoms has reduced quite drastically. Now our curiosity may be roused, for sure, but still there may not be much concern (in terms of personal safety).

Very soon atoms of hydrogen, carbon, and nitrogen choose to combine, bonding themselves into separate units (note the word "bond"). The new formation is, as we know, hydrogen cyanide. Now, that is a matter of real concern; in fact, it is an emergency. It is one of the deadliest poisons. Time to scarper from the scene! Formation and combination – what mighty changes they bring about! That is what we have been stressing and reiterating all along. And we are not at all sorry for the repetitious litany.

"Effects" are a natural consequence of formation and combination, as we saw above. The term "effect," as used by Bagdenborg, is imbued with strange shades of meaning. In one sense, "effects" act as if they are real, but when looked at from a different focal length, they appear as if they are an illusion. This concept was developed while we discussed motion at length. In that discussion, we saw that the motion of an object was not "really" real, but only an induced effect. That was a visual example, and so it may not upset many readers. The other side of "reality," in terms of common experience, is the property of an object. But even this knowledge receives a shattering blow if you come to ponder it from the unconventional angle of Bagden. You see, when hydrogen, carbon, and nitrogen bond together, they form hydrogen cyanide. Right? No, not quite, not absolutely. Look again with clearer focus; there is no such thing as hydrogen cyanide, a new product! You look and look, and you will see only the constituent elements: H, C, and N. Hydrogen cyanide is a myth, a fictitious name – or at best, it could only be a collective noun! From that standpoint, even the "property" of cyanide – its deadliness, as one example – is an 'effect.' Disband the three elements H, C, and N from their tight alliance, and the property of the cyanide vanishes, as if it never existed. If we are permitted to rave poetically, we would say that the "properties" of objects are like shadows – effects created by the play of lights. Throw five light beams of different intensities on a pole from different angles; you will see as many shadows of varying depths. Remove the lights, and there will be no shadows. The shadows are real as long as the lights are there. In one sense, the "effects" of Bagdenborg are akin to that. Generalizing this thought, the whole world of external phenomena can be termed as a recreation being indulged in by Nature. Even such a deep thinker as Plato employed the metaphor of shadows – not for nothing did he do it. The above thoughts may imply as if we are flying away from science. But if we perceive objectively, these "flights of fancy" in no way contradict technology – the invention and use of machinery and instruments.

He would like to add one last detail to this mind-tickling manifestation of "effects" vis-à-vis properties. At the bottom of the list of properties of objects (matter) lies the plinth of what are called the fundamental forces (which we have come across earlier). All observed properties of matter can ultimately be shown to arise from these fundamental forces ascribed to the respective fundamental particles. To recapitulate, four kinds of forces have been posited by traditional science, namely: the gravitation force, the electromagnetic force, the strong force, and the weak force. Of these, the first two are universal, while the last two can be said to be local in the sense that their ranges are limited to the areas within the nucleus of the atom. Bagdenborg, in his own way, has straightaway rejected the last two forces; he recognizes only the gravitational and electromagnetic forces. The strong force was posited by regular science because inside the nucleus, the positively charged protons naturally repel one another and therefore cannot stay clubbed inside the nucleus. To resolve this problem, gluons were posited, holding the protons and neutrons inside the nucleus, with gluons being responsible for the "strong force." Bagdenborg did not see the necessity of such a hypothesis because, as described in the initial chapters, the nucleus itself has a shell, the Bagdenborgian shell. This shell keeps the protons, as well as the neutrons, from flying apart or flying away.

They too are effects

In the Bagdenborgian version, the spaceinks are the ultimate building blocks of creation. Two or more spaceniks align and bond themselves in distinct geometrical configurations. This, in itself, is sufficient to induce properties in the combination. The electromagnetic property is just that; an "effect" produced by the combination and configuration of spaceniks. For example, one specific configuration, say CNF1, produces an "effect" of an electron along with the electrostatic/electromagnetic forces. A different configuration, CNF2, produces the "effect" of a proton with its concomitant properties like heavy mass and positive charge. A third, CNF3, gives us the "effect" of a neutron with its low mass and neutral charge. Following the same methods, it can be shown that all types of particles discovered so far are the outcome of configurations like CNF4, CNF5, and so on, and so forth.

A note from the admirer: The admirer remembers a particular incident relevant to the above topic. The admirer had met Bagdenborg at his house, about a month before the professor went out of sight, becoming untraceable.

Bagdenborg was busy scribbling furiously on a sheet of paper, while a bundle of written notes lay on its side. The admirer had a chance, later, to glance at those papers. Bagdenborg had worked out elaborate diagrams, delineating many configurations that represented the "effects" of about two dozen micro-particles, including electrons, protons, and neutrons. Even though Bagdenborg was allergic to mathematical treatises at that stage in his life, he had managed to write about a hundred pages filled with mathematical equations, descriptions, and explanations. The admirer had naturally assumed that the professor was going to publish his thesis. About a fortnight later, he had an occasion to meet Bagdenborg again and excitedly asked him when he was going to publish his papers. "Oh, I tore them up," the professor had nonchalantly replied. The admirer was aghast. He knew all too well that it was of no use asking the professor why he did what he did. He could only muster enough courage to mumble, "The papers could have been of much use to the scientific community." The impossible man had replied, "Don't worry much about that. Sooner or later, the others are bound to stumble upon my discoveries. As for mathematics, there is going to be a glut." That was the end. The admirer confesses bashfully that when he had a look at the papers, he was so excited that he forgot to note down (mentally) the diagrams, and also that regarding the mathematical part, he was not up to the task. He fervently hopes that, with the hints given in these pages, somebody, in the near future, will provide a complete mathematical analysis of the exciting concepts of Professor Bagdenborg.

With that said, let us return to the "properties" aspect, to have another glance – from the Bagdenborgian angle. The most striking thing, when the electromagnetic and gravitational forces are compared, is the enormous differences in their "strengths." In a "strength-wise" comparison, the electromagnetic force is billions of billions of times "stronger" than that of gravitation. Bagden unceremoniously pushes aside the question of comparison. There is no point in unnecessarily concentrating on that aspect at all. Apart from that, to explain the gravitational force, a particle, graviton, has been posited, and the photon, for the electromagnetic force – as being carriers of those forces. With the advent of the spaceniks, there is no necessity to imagine two different particles exhibiting two different properties (force). Spaceniks, by themselves, are enough to exhibit (read, effects) all the properties one can imagine. Even the enormous discrepancy in the two forces can be easily resolved in an elegant manner. An example can be given here. Suppose there are two vectors of equal strength. If they are aligned in the same direction, their forces will add, and the result will be double the strength of one vector. If they are aligned in exactly opposite directions, the resultant will be zero. In this second case, if their angles are changed by an infinitesimally small amount, the resultant will not be zero, but infinitely small. This is exactly how spaceniks align and configure themselves in different ways to produce "effects" of forces that seem to range from very minute strength to stupendous power. In fact, Bagdenborg has a different insight into the gravitational force, and so we can preclude that "force" from the above previews. Bagdenborg states that space itself is elastic (as explained earlier) and that is the property which exhibits its effect as gravitation. That leaves us with the electromagnetic force only, as a second valid force. The strength of such a force belonging to any kind of particle can be easily explained by using the vector alignment technique. The detailed mathematics of it is waiting to be rediscovered by a future Nobel Laureate.

Bonds and bombs

"Actually, the content of this section is highly classified. The category should be, 'For my eyes only' (pardon the parody), or 'Destroy before reading.' Only our sense of staunch loyalty to Science compels us to publish the content. In the course of making such a decision, we offer our apologies to Professor Bagdenborg." – The Admirer.

Just a little while ago, we mentioned the anecdote of Bagdenborg's tearing up his research papers. Apart from being whimsical, the man had another strong reason for destroying his papers. Most probably, the motive force behind his seemingly irrational action could be one of the reasons that propelled him to abandon science and vanish into seclusion. Even while he was halfway into his research on spaceniks and their configurations, he had leaped to a conclusion. It was a spine-chilling conclusion burdened with terrifying consequences, before whose might the favorite games of Doomsday and Armageddon writers would look like harmless kid-games. We are not deliberately building up a mystery to tease the readers. We are going to reveal the secret in a fairly straightforward manner. First, we warn you; tighten your seat belts. And those with queasy stomachs better have a washbasin conveniently nearby. Perform the by-now-familiar exercise of taking a breather on yon lawn and come back.

We will proceed step by step along our familiar path of analogies. Consider the bonding of materials; that is, objects. A very simple and old example is that of stamp glue. Glue is applied to the reverse surface of the stamp. If you want to stick it on an envelope, just lick it (if in a hurry) and press it on the envelope. A bond is created between two objects. The bond, though appearing to be permanent, is not really strong. By wetting the stamp, you can peel it off, thus breaking the bond.

An example of a stronger bond would be that created by cement mortar between two bricks; the bond could be broken, but the force needed to do so is far greater. These are, of course, man-made bonds. Nature adopts a far subtler bond – the molecular bonds. This is how nature builds up a myriad variety of objects of all sizes and shapes – from gigantic rocks, ores, to minute crystals. And the thousands and thousands of chemical compounds too are examples of molecular bonds. Incidentally, without such bonding, our world would have been quite drab indeed. There would have been no life-forms, to begin with, let alone human beings to survey such a scene.

These molecular bonds can be extraordinarily strong indeed. Try to break a piece of steel, and you will know. Even then, these bonds too can be broken, unloosened, and regrouped by treating objects with suitable chemicals. (Somewhat akin to using a thorn to remove a thorn.) This form of interaction is called a chemical reaction. Indeed, life itself can be described as a non-stop movement of chemical reactions.

Already, we have moved to matter at extremely small sizes. Atoms make the next smaller units. Here, the bonds are far stronger and more difficult to break. No amount of physical force can break or smash an atom. The outer regions of the atoms are amenable to being "chipped" off. The electrons orbiting the nucleus can be knocked off, for example, by using the photoelectric effect in some metals. A magnetic field can move (or align) electrons across a chain of atoms, like in a metallic wire, and so on. But breaking apart the inner core of the atom, the nucleus, is a different proposition altogether. As we saw in the table of fundamental forces, the inter-nuclear "bond" is called the strong force and is far stronger than the electromagnetic force. Nevertheless, it was discovered in the early twentieth century that even the nucleus could be split apart. This process is called nuclear fission – every student of science around the world is familiar with this word. A more familiar word is the "atomic bomb," which is essentially a process of nuclear fission (that is, the splitting up of the nucleus of a uranium atom or of plutonium into two pieces). The consequences of the atomic bomb's explosion need no mention at all – everyone is familiar with the immense destructive power unleashed by a nuclear bomb. The further we go down in the microscopic scale of matter, the greater is the power unleashed when the bond that holds the particles is broken.

The next progression down this line belongs to the sci-fi category, as of now. Yet, the conjecture cannot be ruled out. After the splitting of the atomic nucleus, we naturally think of the splitting of the next smaller units: the electrons, protons, and neutrons. According to the standard theory, these particles too are analogous in structure to that of an atom since they are also made up of quarks. So, just as an atom can be split, each of the elementary particles (electrons, protons, neutrons) can be imagined to be amenable to being "split" open. If such a thing does happen, we can hazard a guess (by the analogy of atomic fission) that the power released could be a million times stronger than that in a nuclear fission. Such an ultra-nuclear fission has not been achieved yet – thank God.

Pursuing analogies can be dangerous too, especially when motivated by morbid curiosity (and we know what curiosity did to the cat). That is why Bagdenborg tore up his papers. You see, descending down the scale of smallness, we arrived at the ultimate limit – the speceniks. Just like the nuclear particles, the spaceniks are also held together by bonds. Since spaceniks are the final frontier in smallness, the bonds that hold them together are unimaginably stronger than the binding forces inside the nucleus. The destroyed papers of Bagdenborg contained formulae that assessed the strength of such forces. By extrapolating the analogy of nuclear fission, we can fairly arrive at the immensity of the devastating force that can erupt if inter-spacenik bonds are broken. We made a guess before that the explosive power following the splitting of elementary particles could be a million times stronger than that of nuclear fission. Multiply that figure by a billion, and you could be approximating the cataclysmic eruption of the spacenik fission! The immensity of that power is mind-boggling. And there is no guarantee at all that such an immense power can be controlled – the way they are able to control nuclear power to produce electricity, to run submarines, and ships, etc. Extreme optimists may imagine (daydream) that such power could be harnessed someday in the future. Bagdenborg's terse reply to such optimists can best be summed up in the expressive slang, "You have got another think coming."

The reason for raising an alarm in the previous paragraph will not be apparent immediately. This is because, when we hear about fission, we are accustomed to thinking of the splitting of individual units, like atoms. If one single atom splits, that is of no consequence at all – the energy released is very,

very minute. Nuclear explosions occur because of the famous "chain reaction" effect. The splitting of one nucleus also releases neutrons, which enter the adjacent nucleus, priming it for its split, and in turn, primes the next nucleus by the same process. All this happens extremely fast, and more importantly, the number of atoms in a prepared (critical mass) lump of uranium is extremely large so that the energies released add up almost instantaneously. That is what causes the explosion. (In a nuclear power plant, the chain reaction is controlled by using what are called moderators, so that the rate of energy release is under tight control.) To sum up, in a nuclear explosion, millions and millions of atoms take part.

Professor Bagdenborg warns that the scenario in the case of splitting apart the spacenik bonds is entirely different. This statement needs a bit of explanation. There is a major difference between the nature of inter-nuclear bonds and spacenik bonds. First of all, space is not only all-pervasive, but it is one single unit – from here to eternity. True, things exist and move in space independently, but that is the peculiar nature of space. In traditional "modern" science, space is treated as a dimension – like the space-time dimension in relativity. But, in the Bagdenborgian discovery, space too is an element – an element of the ultimate refinement. It is an element that does not exist as a separate, independent "wayward" particle, like the way other elements and objects exist. It is one whole, unbroken unit of infinite size. This has to be firmly borne in mind if one has to understand what comes next.

Spaceniks apparently seem to be separate units, bonding themselves to create various particles, with these particles able to move about freely in space. However (this is a big "however," a very big one), the relationship between the original space and the spaceniks is a unique one. In terms of non-scientific language, the spaceniks are the offspring of space, but their umbilical cords have not been cut. The invisible umbilical cords of space hold on to the spaceniks at all times and under all circumstances, so that what happens to the spaceniks affects space as well – the entirety of it.

The U- cord

The concept of the umbilical cord may seem strange to readers. That is because of the terminology employed by Bagdimedes. In fact, science has been treading on this invisible path without realizing it. Can you guess what we are talking about? It's entanglement, "quantum entanglement" as they call it.

This mysterious phenomenon has baffled scientists for a long time and has been a rather painful thorn in the side of theoretical physics, defying a proper science-based explanation. Quantum entanglement can be briefly described as follows: Suppose there is a source from which two particles (say, electrons) emerge, each continuing along its own path. In other words, the electrons are physically separated, without any apparent connecting mechanism, as far as science has been able to detect. Now, the most mystifying occurrence is that if you alter the "state" of one of the electrons, the other electron responds and suitably changes its own state! The electrons (particles) can be a few meters apart from each other or thousands of miles away! Yet, if you change the state of one among the pair, that action spontaneously induces a change in the state of the other particle! So far, no connecting mechanism that mysteriously seems to link the particles has been found. But the phenomenon is real and has been tested and confirmed in laboratories worldwide. Recently, scientists have even been able to utilize this phenomenon to carry out a kind of teleportation. In their experiments, they were able to "create" an exact replica of one electron in a laboratory thousands of miles away from the source. To sum up, what happens to one electron (or particle) affects another electron (particle) originating from a common source. To stress again, no common connecting mechanism (or medium or whatever) has been found as yet. We hope we have painted the picture vividly enough. This invisible connecting mechanism must surely be what Bagdemedes called "the umbilical cord." He hopes that this broad hint will spur further research in the field of quantum entanglement. The U-cord of quantum entanglement is, so to say, a once-removed cousin of the space U-cord. The space U-cord is far subtler, stronger, and more flexible. So is the corresponding "space entanglement" effect. Now that we have provided the requisite background, we would like to delve into the spine-chilling scenario of Holy Terror.

Holy Terror

We will try to stick to a bland technical description as far as possible, leaving it to you to visualize the chills, thrills, and terrors. The primary participants in this possible process are the spaceniks and space. The spaceniks are bonded together in some particular configuration, creating the "effect" of a fundamental particle. Each of the spaceniks is, as we said, tied to the original space by an umbilical cord. Now, if the bond between the spaceniks is broken – by employing a super-technological method not yet discovered – a tremendous shattering effect is created. This shattering effect is not limited to the spaceniks. Through the umbilical cords, the tremendous force is transmitted to the original, the mother space. Bagdenborg pointed out that the energy released due to the fission of spaceniks is billions and billions of times higher than that of nuclear fission. But that is nothing compared to what happens at the base, the origin of spaceniks. The force transmitted through the umbilical cords will shatter space itself. And remember that space is one single, whole entity. That means THE WHOLE OF SPACE WILL CRACK OPEN from one end to the other end! In the study of fractures occurring in materials, they use a term, "conchoidal fracture." You must have seen many pictures of fractured glass of the front windows of cars. Such fractures are termed conchoidal fractures. You can even visualize the terrible pieces of broken glass scattered on the road. Bagliochus Bagdimedes was not sure how space will shatter in the above scenario just described. One possibility is that the whole of space may break open along a single fracture-line. In this case, the universe as we know it will break into two pieces. The earth, of course, would have been blown apart into dust by the power of the explosion. Just as two separate nuclei are created in nuclear fission, in this doomsday explosion, two universes will be created. If, on the other hand, space shatters in the "conchoidal fracture" mode, the universe will fly apart into many pieces of various sizes. We will then have multiple universes. The only disappointing factor in this mammoth drama is that there won't be any humans left either to observe or to record it. "Holy Terror" is a very mild word to describe it. Now you can understand why Bagdibus Der Bagdenborg tore open his research papers. (There is no doubt that he must have incinerated the shredded pieces as a further precaution).

You must have noticed that all these terrible consequences hinge upon the possibility of breaking apart the bonds between spaceniks. You may wonder that all this is highly theoretical, or even speculative. We urge you not to feel smug, not to lull yourself into a sense of false security. There are valid reasons for our concern. For one thing, what one person discovers, another is sure to rediscover sooner or later. If the first person has kept their discovery as a secret, the second person will not. Bagdenborg had envisaged a way of dislodging the tightly bound spacenicks. Another person is sure to stumble upon it, or they may even find an alternate technique. Human nature is such that it cannot hold down a titillating piece of knowledge in secret, especially in this age. Once such dangerous knowledge is made public, then it is goodbye time to planet Earth. For another thing, Bagdimedes was keenly aware of the many particle accelerators, particle-smashing programs that have been going on for decades. The particle-smashing programs are heady stuff, and there is no telling when a most unexpected result will crop up. Serendipity has played a major role in scientific research. Playing with nature, apart from being an exciting adventure, could be deadly too. (Remember the famous legend of the person who discovered cyanide?) We close the topic with these grim forebodings. We even hope against hope that nobody, in the future, will be able to unravel the structure and configurations of the spaceniks. It is better to remain as an unsolved puzzle forever.

Summary

We had the good opportunity to study quite a few of Bagdenborg's insights and perceptions. The various aspects can be brought together and condensed into a tight, convenient summary as follows:

* Bagdimedes favors the philosophical, Eastern line of thought as far as the primordial act of creation is concerned. It is impossible to know it since even the attempt to "know" is also a part of what has been created.
* Everything else on this side of creation is one gigantic field of "recreation," and that can be studied. The study is limited only by humanity's capacity for recreation, which, as we know, has been quite active from as far back as human history runs.
* "Duality" is the act of one becoming two; from where creation begins. We can trace it to spaceniks growing out of space, like bubbles; we cannot go further back. In essence, spaceniks are not different from mother space.
* Spaceniks bond together into different configurations, which action produces an "effect" of fundamental particles possessing various properties. The properties too are "effects," as particles are not separate from their properties.
* Space is an element in its own right; the most refined form of "matter."
* Even force(s) and motion are effects only, and so is time too. Thus, there is no point in trying to trace the origin of creation via the time route. ("We do not need Big Bangs." – Bagdenborg)

Concluding Remarks by the Admirer

Professor Bagdenborg's insights are remarkable. Nature's "recreation" is immeasurably clever. Look at the modern invention of binary mathematics.

Just by using zero and one, you can represent a zillion numbers. The computer goes even further; it can represent anything—objects, graphs, videos, music, language; anything. All this, just by using a zero and a one—just a matter of sequencing and grouping. Ah, look again at the wonderful DNA—again a matter of sequencing. There can be no doubt that, as Bagdimedes insists, Nature has adopted the same technique at the bottom-most level (the level of spaceniks) to "create" all the astonishing verisimilitudes that we are able to observe. Software, software, everything is software. Hats off to the great man. May his tribe increase. No, that is not necessary. One such man in a millennium is enough!

Chapter 8

FURTHER EXPLORATIONS

Bagdenborg's primary interest lay in studying the most fundamental aspects of the world, like the origin and creation of the universe, as we have seen in the previous chapters. It is natural that in the search for such a subject, he had to explore a wide range of phenomena, if not extensively, at least in essence as directly related to his main subject. His notebooks are filled with hundreds and hundreds of brief notes on a variety of topics (which we hope to bring out in separate volumes). However, we would like to present a few of such assorted ideas that are relevant to what we have studied so far.

1. The quick and the inert

It is inevitable that when we study the act of the creation of matter, we have to think of an important aspect – at least as far as we, as human beings, are concerned – that of life. Matter naturally reminds us of life. Though our study is purportedly focused on "inert" matter, we will briefly touch on life. Bagdenborg did and came upon some exciting perceptions.

Again and again, the mysterious play of group behavior stands out to capture our attention at whatever level we examine nature. While studying the so-called "inert" matter, we saw that the fundamental particles were an "effect," a play of group behavior. That is, spaceniks grouped themselves into different configurations, and what we had were particles of various denominations. Life-forms—humans, animals, multicellular organisms—demonstrate the same phenomena in the biological field. At the grosser level, cells group themselves in different ways, and we have organisms adorned with extraordinary structures like limbs of all sorts and sizes and internal organs of great complexity. The idea that group behavior ("play of numbers") is the cosmic template at all levels can be clearly appreciated when we delve deeper into life-forms too.

Look at DNA. It is all a matter of sequencing four basic protein forms. Observe the parallel, the analogy. The grouping of spacenicks in different configurations "produces" different forms of matter, fundamental particles, and so on. The grouping of four basic protein forms controls the growth and properties of cells. In this sense, "life" too is an "effect" just as matter and its properties are "effects". Since we mentioned DNA, the reader may connect to the natural link and think of chemical reactions as being the essential property of life – apart from that of reproduction. That observation is still at a "grosser" level. Greater insights, as Bagdenborg used to say, are obtained by receding into more and more abstract levels of thinking. Seen from that plateau, there is a telling difference between inert matter and a living organism.

To analogies, once more. Consider a simple engine, which runs, say, on petrol. You can use such an engine, incorporating it into complex machines, to do many kinds of jobs. As the technical jargon says, the machine does "work" – you can get an output from it. Leave aside that matter of extracting work out of the machine. You can even keep it "on idle." The point is that the engine can run only for a period of time, long or short, and then it stops. It is because the petrol tank (fuel) is empty, and you need to fill up the tank with fuel – even a moron knows that. The fact is so obvious that it may seem ridiculous to state that machines need an external source of energy (fuel) to keep operating. The fact is obvious, sure; it may induce boredom to hear it stated again.

But then, in the above analogy, replace the engine with a living organism. If you are really sensitive, you will sit up straight and ponder the matter with wonder, though the fact is still obvious and as old as creation. Life – all living organisms – needs an external source of energy; it takes in energy from the environment and processes it. (With due admiration, we would like to quote – the gist of – Canon Doyle's observation. He said that life is full of obvious things, but that nobody ever sits up and notices them). This is the basic difference. The simplest living cell takes in energy from outside of it, like a machine. The process of living (growing, multiplying, etc.) can be seen in terms of continuous chains of chemical reactions. What does that mean? Seen from a purely scientific perspective, it is also a software; a software of a higher order, if you prefer to call it so.

On the flip side, look at lifeless, inert pieces of matter, like fundamental particles. Bagden has shown us earlier that the particle gives out energy to the environment. And also, we have seen thus far that the particle is also an "effect" only. The effect is the outcome of the play of the spaceniks, which the particle contains. That "play" – the configuration, too is a software, as we have seen already. Now, we have completed a grand overview of Nature and its recreation – and seen that everything, from alpha to omega – is a huge software of cosmic proportions. In fact, the cosmos itself is a software with a capital S. At this point, a subtle paradox seems to arise. In truth, it is not a paradox. Still, a doubt may arise after reading the above statement on software. In a computer and other electronic gadgets, energy is required to run the software – like the tiny nickel-cadmium button, a wall power socket, etc. Considering this, readers may ask where the energy to run the (Bagdenborgian) cosmic software comes from. It is a good question and deserves a good answer. Better still, we will give Bagdenborg's profound answer. The answer may sound like a Zen kōan, but rest assured that it is final and perfect: "Energy itself is a software, and software is energy in action." That settles it. Meditate deeply on that. (A picture of the uroborus might help.)

2. Minor details

The notebooks of Bagdimedes are dotted with innumerable marginalia, many of them being liberally provided with cross-references — forward and backward. We produce a few such notes as pertaining to what we have discussed thus far. The notes shed additional light on one or two knotty puzzles.

In the Bagdenborgian version of Genesis, we saw that spaceniks are born out of space — the original mother space. The original space is like a cosmic ocean. You can think of spaceniks as bubbles rising out of the ocean, free to move but still being a part of the ocean. There is another intriguing solution to the question of how the spacenik "bubbles" are formed. Recall here that space itself is elastic. That is to say that the gravitational force is inherent in space. What happens in such a situation?

Imagine a spherical water-filled balloon with tiny holes. The balloon, of course, is in outer space, far from the gravitational forces of either the Earth or any other object. The water will stay put inside the balloon. Now imagine that the balloon is compressing itself; nobody is doing it. The water will naturally escape through the tiny holes. This analogy can help you understand what happens if space is constantly trying to compress itself. That is the action of the gravitational force inherent in space itself. So, just as water droplets escape through the tiny holes of our balloon, spaceniks (droplets of space) escape through tiny holes in space. The analogy ends there because there are no holes in space in the literal sense. The concept of "holes" can be described in a more refined way. In physics, there is a term called a gradient, used to denote the strength of fields (like magnetic or electric) from point to point. Graphically, the gradient is represented as a sloping line, a curve, etc. In other words, if a field is spread out in space — as it usually does — its strength will vary from one point to another point. Likewise, due to the constant compression in the original mother space, steep energy gradients are created at certain points. You may call them hot spots, which are analogous to the holes in our balloon. Spaceniks are emitted through such hot spots in space. Remember that spaceniks too are essentially of the nature of space and, thus, are endowed with the primordial attribute of space, namely, gravitational force. You know the rest of the story from there on. "Spaceniks combine and configure into more complex systems, creating "effects" of all kinds of fundamental and microscopic particles and so on.

Thus, from this scenario, Bagdenborg intuited that gravitation is the only original force. The electromagnetic force is an offshoot of it, showing itself as an "effect" due to the configuration of spaceniks. The positive charge, the negative charge, the neutral charge, the magnetic field, all these are manifested owing to particular configurations of the spaceniks. Bagden's spaceniks encompass all the discovered and hypothetical particles to come. Even the latest discovery of the so-called "god's particle" is no exception. So also is the case with the much-hyped superstrings. The superstringers (as Bagdimedes called them) almost stumbled upon the truth, but then, they caught the wrong train at the crucial junction, driven by an overpowering fascination with brainy mathematics. Their theory requires strings that vibrate in complicated fashions in more complicated shapes and dimensions of space. But they missed a most vital point at the start itself. The theory, you see, posits two entities — strings and space.

Wise intuition gently points out that everything must proceed from one. After all, while searching for unity in diversity, why should they stop at two and be satisfied with that? That "one," which has eluded the scientific community so far, must be space and space only. ("Axiomatic" — Bagdenborg) Space itself splits into spaceniks (at the high-gradient hot spots). "If they concentrate on this region," Bagdimedes wrote, "they can obtain their TOE with one-hundredth part of the efforts they have ineffectually put forth till now."

Bagdenborg's theory has another advantage. With it, we do not need a Big Bang, which, of necessity, propels us to journey back in time. It is a journey that can neither succeed nor stop. This year "they" will announce that they know what happened a thousandth of a second after the Big Bang. Fifty years later, after performing laborious calculations, they will announce (triumphantly) that they know what happened a millionth of a second after the BB. A hundred years later, their descendants (if they are not tired yet), after performing more elaborate and more cunning calculations, will announce that they know what happened a trillionth of a second after the BB... It can go on and on forever. This powerful argument itself is sufficient to reject the BB. As Horace observed, "parturient montes, nascetur ridiculus mus."

Along with the rejection of the Big Bang, Bagdenborg boldly swept aside the conjecture of the expanding space. ("Conjecture," that is what he calls it.) Elsewhere in these pages, we have discussed how it is not necessary to deduce the expanding universe from the red-shift phenomenon. This naturally leads us to think that space was as it is now from the very beginning. The word "beginning" should be qualified here. It is a virtual beginning. ("A beginning that has no starting point and therefore, no ending." – Bagdimedes.) Thus, the creation of "matter" in Bagden's scenario takes place at all suitable points in space — the hot spots. In fact, creation is happening right now too.

*Dark matter – the dark secret

Dark matter has been one of the darkest secrets of the universe. The story, in short, runs like this. Scientists (astronomers, cosmologists) became interested in calculating the amount of matter contained in the universe. The misgivings began somewhere around 1982. Astronomers discovered that galaxies were moving as a whole in certain ways — the spiral galaxies, for example. When they made calculations that included the effects of gravitational fields, they were baffled to find that the total matter, as observed and detected, was not sufficient to explain the behaviors of those objects. Then came the study of gravitational lensing. Gravity acts as a kind of lens, affecting light and other electromagnetic rays that pass through its fields. While studying this phenomenon too, they found that the amount of (known) matter which produces the 'lens' effect was not sufficient to account for the disproportionately stronger field exhibited.

There is then the famous universal microwave background radiation. As far as is observable and in all directions of the universe, uniform microwave radiation permeates space. While studying this phenomenon too, astronomers found that a large quantity of invisible matter was acting on this radiation.

The problem was that this kind of matter is invisible. Its effect is felt through its gravitational force. Thus the name "dark matter" was proposed for this invisible matter. To make things a bit more complex, they have discovered a parallel thing called dark energy too! They have not been able to detect it through instruments either. The existence of dark matter and energy has been deduced based on the effects they have on the observable matter. These two mysterious entities have evaded detection for the last eighty and odd years.

Why is there so much concern about dark matter? You will be aghast when you know the data. According to the "calculations" of cosmologists, our universe consists of only 4.9% of visible matter! Repeat that – only 4.9%. The rest of the universe is filled with dark matter (26.8%) and dark energy (68.3%). Dark, dark, dark. In spite of the enormous progress of science, we know only about 5% of the universe. The rest is darkness!

Given the flair for his startling insights, it is natural that Bagdenborg should throw an illuminating beam of light into the dark recess where dark matter has been hiding. There is the much-worn-out expression, "hide in plain sight." The phrase acquires a refreshing meaning when we consider what Bagdimedes reveals. No more teasing; we are going to give you his astonishing and at the same time rib-tickling answer.

Space!! Space is the missing dark matter, which has been brazenly staring at us all along (and through which we too have been staring all along). Hiding in plain sight, indeed. Review Bagden's theory again, please, bearing in mind, especially the lopsided ratio between ordinary matter and dark matter/energy. First of all, there is the all-pervading, primordial mother space. Then, spaceniks arise out of it at hot spots. Next, the spaceniks begin their simple dance of combination and configuration. The rest is the cosmic opera of creation ("recreation"), which is the universe as we see it.

Now, the universe that we observe is, in essence, nothing but the "effect" of spaceniks. The essential point to note is that spaceniks are only a minute portion of the vast ocean of mother space. They rise out of hot spots, remember? In other words, the ratio between spaceniks and mother space is lopsided, just like the ratio between matter and dark matter (energy). That fact, by itself, should tell you the whole story. Nothing can be more convincing, more simple than this; space is that dark matter which the cosmologists have been searching for all these days.

Dark matter, it is said, affects the observed behavior of galaxies – and so on. It is said to be unreactive toward light and electromagnetic waves. So is space! It is said to be "invisible." So is space! (As technology stands now, space is only inferred by the presence of objects located in it.) Lastly, there is the clincher. Dark matter is supposed to possess gravity and thereby affect the behavior of the visible matter like galaxies, nebulas, etc. Recall here Bagdenborg's theory, that space is elastic, that is, that space itself possesses the property of gravity. There! There you have your dark energy, your dark matter – that is all. Those people ("the telescopic guys") have unnecessarily complicated things by avoidable classifications, like cold dark matter, hot dark matter, dark energy, yada yada. Club all those together, says Bagdenborg, and simply call it "infra matter." Infra matter is a far more elegant description, for space is just that. (See the analogy with the term "infrared.")

Concentrate on space (and spaceniks), Bagdimedes advises. Pour all your mathematical genius into probing it; you will reap rich dividends. That is Bagden's message to aspiring scientists. One word of caution – do not treat space as an abstract concept. Treat it as if it were matter in its ultimate state of refinement ("infra matter"). The mathematical treatment may be easier than the actual physical experimentation, given the present state of technology. But Bagdenborg is sure that within the next two hundred years, science would be in a position to handle and experiment with space and spaceniks. That is good news and bad news at the same time. Remember what we said a few pages back about the cataclysmal devastation that may happen in the event of "fracking" of space – if spaceniks are handled roughly. With that prospect in view, and respecting Bagdenborg's sentiments, we would not like to delve deeper into this topic – absit omen.

*Charge – this way, that way, no way

Regarding the characteristics of space, we discussed many of its interesting properties like elasticity, gravity, gradients, hot spots, memory, software, umbilical cords, and finally spaceniks. There is one most vital and fundamental characteristic that we have not touched upon until now; without it, there will be no universe and no you and I to observe it or participate in it. That characteristic is totally abstract, and yet without it, nothing is – a mysterious characteristic indeed! Guessed it?... Yeah, it is, "direction"! It rises simultaneously with the first act of creation, that of one becoming two.

Consider the simplest illustration that follows. Imagine there is a point A, and nothing else. We mean absolutely nothing else. In such a chilling scenario, there is nothing to talk about either. Now imagine that another point B rises up. The characteristic of direction immediately rises up (or is "born") along with the birth of B, coupled with its inseparable twin, "distance." And, as the great bard said, "Thereby hangs a tale." And, what a tale! The irony (or wonder, if you want to put it that way) is that these two characteristics are totally abstract. We cannot touch them or feel them, and yet without them, we cannot have the universe as we have it now.

Once a point B, distinct from A, is created, we have one direction: A to B, right? Concurrent with that, we already have its opposite direction; whether it is the inherent nature of Nature or of the human mind is a point left for you to quibble about in vicious loops. You can move from A to B or from B to A; we will take up this thread again later. Already, one more direction—the way to move—is born. It is angular movement; moving circularly. That action creates a plane, that is, a surface. B can now choose to rise at a point not lying on such a plane. This gives rise to the concept of three dimensions ("solidity"). See, just a simple action of the birth of the second point has created a host of abstract properties. We are so accustomed to this mysterious property of direction (and dimensions concomitant with it) that we are inured to the sense of "wonder." But if we really think of it, this mysterious property of directions should induce deep emotions of awe and mystery in us. (It is by contemplating it that some ancient Eastern Sacred texts declared that god created the six directions first—front, back, left, right, up, and down.) If you leave the opposites there, we have three directions and three dimensions. It is in these three dimensions that our universe exists. Why nature chose only three dimensions for creation is an unsolvable mystery. "Don't ask me," quipped Bagdimedes. We tend to agree with him.

A few lines back, we talked about the dual nature of direction, from point A to B, and from B to A. This is linked with force as well. A force can act along one direction and also in the opposite direction. Two forces acting along a line in the same direction on an object will have double the impact on its motion. If the forces act in opposite directions, they tend to "cancel" each other, in the sense that the body will be stationary. In the context of angular movement (rotation) too, there are two types: clockwise rotation and anticlockwise rotation.

This state of affairs seems normal to us as human beings since we inherently have a left side and a right side. But there is another property that nature exhibits, which is a bit more baffling. At the fundamental level, the particles in nature possess a property called "charge," which comes in three varieties: some particles carry positive charge, some carry negative charge, and others are neutral, carrying no charge. All the particles found in the universe fall into one of these three categories. Now, how do you recognize that a particle has charge? How do you define charge?

We are back to our old friend, "force." Charge is that property by virtue of which it exerts a force on another (charged) particle suitably placed near it. The force can be either attractive or repulsive. That is, the two particles either move towards each other or move away from each other. In the former case, the particles have opposite charges, and in the latter case, they have the same kind of charge. By convention, one type of charge is called negative, like that of an electron, and the other type is called positive, like that of a proton. Particles with neutral charge are not affected by the presence of either type of charged particles. Neutrons are an example of neutral particles.

All of this is common knowledge. But there is a ticklish point here if you come to think of it. Talking in terms of common, man-in-the-street language, you can say, "That is all well and good, but you know, force is force and charge is charge. Two persons may use force in opposite directions, as in a tug-of-war contest, or as in wrestlers pushing against each other. They may use force in the same direction, as in pushing a stalled car. The point is that the direction of a force may be different, but inherently it is 'force' only. It should be the same way with what you call charged particles. They may push or pull, I do not care. But 'charge' should be charge only, no? I mean, how can there be two types of charges when force is inherently force only?"

Good question, and a ticklish one to answer. But Bagdenborg has a cute answer to that one. Look at the figure below, and the answer will be crystal clear; it is self-evident.

A clockwise rotation of field produces one kind of charge
and an anticlockwise rotation produces an opposite charge

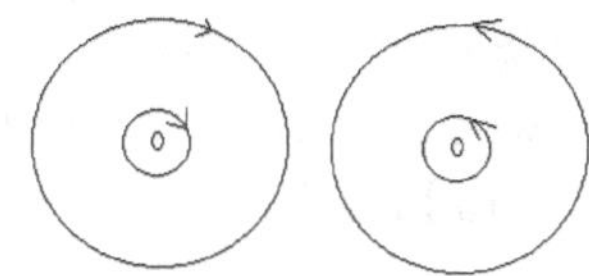

A - clockwise rotation   B - anticlockwise rotation

Figure 7

In the above figure, A and B represent the charges of two particles with opposite charges. The concentric circles represent the lines of the fields of the charges. The lines in A are rotating clockwise, and those in B are rotating anticlockwise. That is all. It is as simple as that. The charge-field rotating clockwise produces (shows) one kind of charge, let's say positive charge, and vice versa. Note that if a field is rotating, it produces a centrifugal force. That is the force associated with the charge of the particle. In other words, the force attributed to the charge of the particle is due to the centrifugal force of its rotating field. Also, whether the fields are rotating clockwise or anticlockwise, the effect of the "push" – the centrifugal force – is always from the center along the radial lines (outwards). Whether the particles have a positive charge or a negative one, the "push" in both of their fields is the same. In this sense, the "force" of both particles is the same. That neatly answers your doubt.

Then you will naturally ask the next question, "If both charges are the same in essence, how come they repel and attract each other? If 'force' is pushing out from both of them, then the particles should always repel each other irrespective of their charges!"

Again, a good question. Again, Bagdenborg is there to rescue you from your perplexity. Look at the figures below.

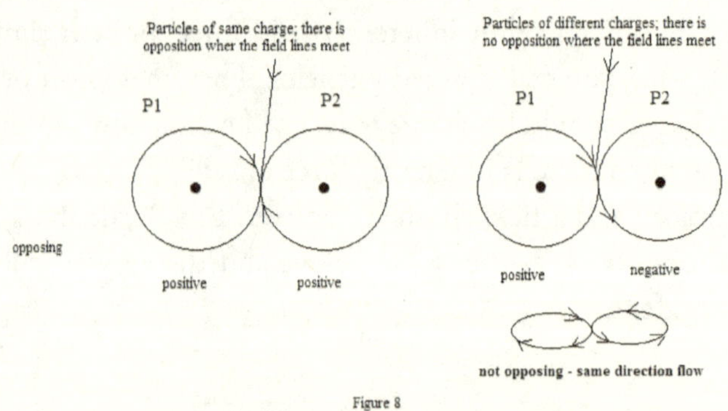

Figure 8

In Figure 1, P1 and P2 have the same charge. The field lines rotate in the same direction (clockwise). For convenience, only the outermost lines of force are shown. Mark the point where the two lines meet. They are in opposition, as are all other field lines of P1 and P2. Hence, the particles P1 and P2 repel each other. In the second illustration, the particles are of opposite charges; positive and negative. In this case, where the outer lines meet, there is no opposition. Hence, the particles P1 and P2 move towards each other (attraction).

Of course, Bagdimedes goes a bit deeper and shows that a similar action takes place at the level of the spaceniks too, so that spaceniks of opposite kinds rise from the bed of mother space. Bear in mind that spaceniks are linked to mother space through umbilical cords. The figures below illustrate the process of the birth of two kinds of spaceniks.

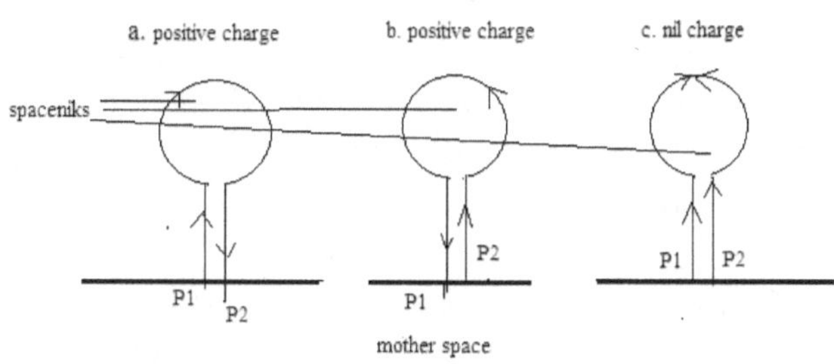

Figure 9

Consider the figure. As explained earlier, due to the formation of an energy gradient in mother space, Spacenik A is created. The two vertical lines are the umbilical cords that connect to the Spacenik. Energy flows from point P1, travels along the umbilical cord in a clockwise direction, and returns to point P2 of mother space. Note that P1 is at a slightly higher gradient level than P2. This process bestows a particular kind of property upon Spacenik A. At point B in the figure, P2 is at a higher potential than P1. So, the direction of energy movement is anticlockwise. This process bestows an opposite kind of property upon Spacenik B. Note also that, apart from the difference in directions, the "strength" (energy content) of Spaceniks A and B may also differ. Out of this basic process, mother space gives rise to different species of Spaceniks. In the third illustration, denoted as C in the figure, we see the origin of a neutral Spacenik. The two points, P1 and P2, are at the same potential. As can be deduced from the directions of the arrows, there is no circular movement—either clockwise or anticlockwise. The "bubble" of Spacenik C swells up uniformly from both sides. It has a neutral charge.

Once created, Spaceniks are free to move about in space. The umbilical cords attached to the Spaceniks do not in any way hinder their movements. In fact, the special feature of these cords is that they follow the Spaceniks like faithful shadows while maintaining contact (and communication) with mother space. To provide a visual analogy, they are akin to the shadow of an object moving above the surface of land. The object moves, and the shadow faithfully follows. In the figures provided here, the distances are highly exaggerated, of course. For example, in the figure, the sizes of A and B have been magnified to the tune of about a billion-billion times. Recall that Spaceniks exist far below the "threshold" of the Planck's length. Bagdimedes would like to add another clarification. When the Spaceniks, such as A and B in the figure, move about, the connecting umbilical cords do not stretch or get deformed, unlike shadows. The points P1 and P2 follow the path of the Spaceniks, maintaining the gradient differences. This uniqueness characterizes mother space. That is why Bagdenborg likened the primordial processes occurring in the womb of space to magnificent software programs. Indeed, the entirety of mother space is one cosmic software.

Now that Bagdimedes has solved the riddle of the two types of charges, he draws a beautiful corollary. His admirers have called it "The Bagdenbach Conjecture." As we have seen, the universe is populated by two kinds of particles: the positively charged and the negatively charged (excluding those that are neutral). From observing this, Bagdenborg intuited that mother space throws out the particles (spaceniks) at random, without specific preference. In such a case, the numbers of the two types of spaceniks must be equal, a "fifty-fifty" distribution. Thus, Bagdenbach instinctively deduced that the total amounts of negative and positive charges in the universe must be equal. This is known as The Bagdenbach Conjecture.

On Elements: Bagden in his arcane element

Physicists have sifted through all forms of matter on our planet and have discovered, so far, 117 elements. The search for newer elements has been as thorough and enthusiastic as possible. Until they manage to dig up to the central core of the earth (that is, excluding the quite big hollow space, discovered by Bagdimedes through his deiknymi methodology), we can assume that the number 117 seems to be a sort of limit for the elements on Earth. We can confidently assume that the same holds true for the universe too. Reports (and speculations) trickle in now and then that another new element has been "manufactured" in the great particle laboratories, and that it is possible there could be elements numbering up to 120, 123 (max); and so on. On this, Bagdenborg once facetiously remarked, "Of course, if you manage to sift through a sieve the whole of the material contents of the earth

– I mean, all of the earth ground to dust – you may possibly find three more new elements." His sense of humor cannot be classified.

There is another curious aspect to these numbers. Most of the elements – a vast majority – are found on our planet Earth. But in the cosmos, the population consists mostly of hydrogen and helium. Stars like our sun are made of these two elements. There is also carbon. Recently, astronomers have discovered a planet the size of Earth, composed of carbon, and structured like a diamond! Other elements like iron (meteorites), and gases (many planets) are also found, but when compared to the number 117 on Earth, those elements are a minority. How these elements were formed is a mystery. At present, the Big Bang theory offers its own solution. ("The godfather of science." – Bagdenborg) A broad, general idea runs like this: After the Big Bang, hydrogen atoms were created first. Out of them, stars were formed. In the intense heat of the stars, fusion takes place, in which process, hydrogen is converted to helium (that is, two hydrogen atoms combine to form a helium atom). The stars, after millions of years, die and become red stars or white dwarfs (or whatever). They explode. They are called supernovae. The heavier elements came out of the bellies of such supernovae. The elements we find on Earth are the debris of one such supernova. ("Yada, yada" – Bagdenborg.) Of course, the story is quite long, containing many more details and plenty of heavyweight mathematics. We have provided a short version here to help you grasp the basics. We want you to focus on the real issues.

Let us set aside the godfather's story ("modern fables" – Bagdenborg) of the bang and delve into Bagdenborg's more elegant insights. In the former story, the most challenging concept to grasp is the formation of the atomic nucleus, which contains protons and neutrons. Protons are, as you know, positively charged, and neutrons have no charge. Take note: Protons repel each other, and when left to themselves, there is no possibility of their forming a peaceful group. Neutrons, on the other hand, do not care whether another particle is positively charged or negatively charged. They have no inclination to cooperate or meekly co-exist with the protons. Typically, their population inside the nucleus is twice that of protons. If you look at it objectively, you will notice that the inhabitants within the nucleus make for strange bedfellows.

The tale gets "curiouser and curiouser," as somebody said. To begin with, the nucleus was alone, the tale declares. It was positively charged – the tale stresses that. A nucleus with one proton (strangely, it is the only nucleus without the strange bedfellow called a neutron) floated about lazily, positively charged, all by itself. It was able to catch a negatively charged electron into its orbit, and it became an atom of hydrogen, saying it had had enough of electrons and went away. Another nucleus with two protons caught up with the act, captured two electrons into its orbit, became an atom of helium, and said it had had enough of electrons and went away, eager to participate in the merry race of expanding space. Bagdenborg's admirers would like to ask questions here. We appear to be digressing from Bagdenborg's insight, but the questions are relevant and tenable, even if they sound funny. Funny questions are permitted in science. Oftentimes, they lead to astonishing discoveries. One question is, if neutrons (the strange bedfellows) can stay together with protons, why can't they do the same with electrons? That is, why don't we have a nucleus containing electrons and neutrons? Such a nucleus could have captured wandering protons, and they would have created an altogether new element not found in our periodic table! The question is not all that absurd, since the conceptual possibility of such a situation is tenable. This particular question can be answered in this way. A proton has roughly five hundred times more mass than an electron. A lighter body revolves around a heavier body; the way our Earth revolves around the sun and not vice versa. Then again, one can argue back by bringing the neutrons into the picture. The neutron is, in fact, a bit "heavier" than a proton – by a slight margin. (Footnote – If the mass of a neutron is taken as 1, that of a proton will be 0.9986, and that of an electron will be 0.005438. The actual masses of a neutron, proton, and electron are respectively, 1.6749286 x 10^-27 kg, 1.6726231 x 10^-27 kg, and 9.1093897 x 10^-31 kg.) The neutrons should not object, since being "strange bedfellows," they have no reason to show partiality between a positive charge and a negative charge. Once such a nucleus of two neutrons and two electrons is formed, there is no reason why they should capture two wandering protons into an orbit – making up an atom. Incidentally, such an atom will have the same mass as that of a helium atom, and its overall charge will be neutral. What would you call such an atom? Inverse helium (anti-helium)? In the initial "soup" of the Big Bang, if there were plenty of electrons, protons, and neutrons, then according to probability laws, such a kind of "inverted helium" – along with other inverted elements – should have been created. Extending this argument to a much later period of the Bang, the creation of similar 'inverted' elements corresponding to each of the 117 elements should have happened! (Hydrogen is an exception since it does not have a neutron in its nucleus). And, another vagary of nature can be observed too. The atom as a whole is generally neutral in charge. The negatively charged electrons are equal in number to the positively charged protons inside the nucleus. While such is the case, why should there be neutrons at all inside the nucleus? (Look at the normal hydrogen atom; it does not contain a neutron in its nucleus.) These are exciting questions, and if investigated in depth – from new angles – are sure to lead us to strange, serendipitous discoveries.

The other important question, which we touched upon earlier, is why should nature limit itself to creating 117 elements, and call it a day? Topping the heavy elements, plutonium contains 94 electrons, 94 protons, and 150 neutrons in its atom. Why can't there be atoms having 200, 300, or 400 protons, etc., inside the nuclei? Ask Bagdenborg, and he will tell you why.

Go back to your childhood days when you used to have fun blowing soap bubbles. Or to the day when you used to pop out thickly-coated bubbles from those bubble gums you used to chew all day long. Try as you may, these bubbles can swell only to a certain size, after which they will burst. This is because the bubbles have a property called surface tension. It is this surface tension that, in the first place, makes it possible for the air that you blow to be trapped and held inside the bubble. Depending on the strength of the material used (soap or gum, etc.), the bloated surface can stretch up to a certain point, and then it gets ruptured.

If you are wondering what this has got to do with the atomic nucleus, just flip back these pages and read the chapter on shells. You may recall that there, Bagdimedes showed that the atomic nucleus has a shell. Just as your soap and bubble gum bubbles have specific surface tensions, the shell surrounding the nucleus has a specific strength. That is why there is a limit to the number of protons and neutrons which can be crammed inside the nucleus. As the number of protons and electrons increases, the energy content of the nucleus increases. After a certain number (say 120 or 125 at the most), the energy content becomes too much for the nuclear shell to hold; it bursts open. ("The required mathematical equations can be easily derived." – Bagdimedes) The answer is so simple and intuitively correct.

Incidentally, this also explains why there is an abundance of lower elements with few intra-nuclear particles and why, as the elements get heavier and heavier, their occurrence in nature dwindles down. An analogy can provide a clear picture. Take two half-filled cups of hot coffee. Keep exchanging their contents by pouring from a height. Observe the froth that forms. Bubbles of smaller size predominate over bubbles of higher size.

In this context, Bagdenborg has made an interesting statement, drawing a conclusion from his fascinating study of analogies. If you compute the energy density of the heaviest possible element – say, element number 120 – you will find that it will be equal to the overall average energy density of the universe. When one of his admirers was skeptical about the statement, Bagden merely said, "You manage the mathematics, boy." After a minute of stunned silence, he said more softly, "You see, space outside is the same as space inside." The answer was in line with his methodology of descriptive science, the spirit of which, as he said, was soaked in deiknymi and gedanken experiment.

And then, as for the actual formation of atomic nuclei and the elements, Bagdimedes called it a minor detail. He said so because, in his view, the act of creation of the spaceniks is more fundamental. We touched upon this subject a couple of pages back while presenting the traditional explanations for the Big Bang. Bagdenborg looked upon those explanations as hazy, unconvincing, and speculative. We also touched earlier on the Bagdenborgian theory of configuration, which explains how fundamental particles are born ("come to effect"). That theory of combination and configuration of spaceniks is also sufficient to explain the formation of atoms of the elements. For example, a particular configuration of the spaceniks (say, C1) will produce an "effect" of a nucleus containing a proton, its protective nuclear shell, an electron outside that shell, and an overall second atomic shell. This effect appears to the outside world (we, the physicists) as an atom of hydrogen. Another kind of spacenik configuration, C2, produces its characteristic "effect" of a nucleus containing 2 protons, 2 neutrons enclosed in their nuclear shell, two electrons outside of the shell, and an overall atomic shell keeping all the six particles in their place. To us, this "effect" appears as a helium atom. Not only that, but also, the appearance exhibits all the properly observed behaviors and properties of a helium atom. You only have to step out from behind the (impalpable) screen of "effect" to this side of behaviors; you can carry on and carry out all the experiments (and technological acrobatics) to your heart's content. All the enormous scientific data collected so far about that helium atom will be left unscathed, intact. What more do we need?

Recall also that it was shown that energy rises out from the hot spots of mother space. The spurts of this energy come in varying amounts. These varying amounts correspond to the various spacenik configurations C1, C2, etc., the variation reaching up to a maximum of C120. Beyond that, the shell of the nucleus will no longer be able to contain the energy of its contents, and thus, the formation of the elements ends there.

Our natural curiosity impels us to ask that, even if new elements are no longer sustainable, should spacenik configurations beyond 120, such as C121, C125, C130, etc., occur? A good question, as the compeers of TV programs say. The answer is, "yes." Many more configurations beyond C120 are theoretically possible and do, in fact, occur. Bagdimedes investigated that angle too and found a remarkable phenomenon of nature. He found out that beyond a certain number, the configurations double back! A configuration, say C200, may occur, but it collapses back on itself and ends by replicating the first configuration, C1. He obtained this remarkable (in fact, awe-inspiring) insight directly through his deiknymi. And then, there is a more beautiful aspect to it. Beyond C200, almost all the configurations collapse back to C1! Can you guess the significance of that? That explains why there is an overwhelming preponderance of the element hydrogen in the universe, compared to the other 116 elements! The collapse of the higher configurations (collapse or splitting up) results also in C2, C3, C4, etc., which correspond to the elements helium, lithium, and so on. But the number of such occurrences is small compared to C1, that of hydrogen. This is why we find less and less amount of the heavier elements in nature. There is another aspect to the spacenik configurations above C120. Most of such configurations are unstable. That is, they exist for very brief periods of time. The periods range from a hundredth of a second to a billionth. These configurations are behind all those many short-lived particles which the scientists routinely find in their particle-collider laboratories.

Having arrived thus far, if we pause and look back, we can appreciate what a beautiful story the spaceniks have to tell. If the researchers are struggling to find the Golden Fleece of science – the TOE, the GUT – they need go no further than the spaceniks. Before concluding this exciting story, we would like to draw your attention to one final significance of Bagdenborg's discovery; a befitting finale. If you look at the concept of combination and configuration with a bit more concentration, you will realize that it knocks off the Big Bang theory from the pedestal it has been occupying till now. The most salient point to notice is that the process of combination and configuration of spaceniks does not demand a prolonged time process, as does the Big Bang theory of creation. The spacenik story does not need 14 billion years to evolve! (As does the Big Bang theory.) Note here that the BB theory was born from the seed of the so-called expanding universe. Bagdenborg's insight into spaceniks is unconcerned about the expanding universe. As we have seen earlier, Bagdimedes argued that the ("so-called") expansion of the universe is an intricate electromagnetic illusion. Moreover, there is no connection at all between the creation of matter and the expansion as seen from the viewpoint of the spacenik theory. As the astute reader can see, once the spaceniks come into play, matter (of all types and kind) starts forming everywhere in space. See the beauty of it. We don't need to belabor, forcing our unwilling brains (smother intuition into writhing agony) to imagine the grand universe shrinking and shrinking into utterly unbelievable sizes of pinheads, all the while sweating it out to travel back in time to reach the mirage of the zero point – the exact point at which the whole shebang started. As Bagdimedes says, there is no such thing as the starting point, since time itself is a make-believe software. Splitting time into smaller and smaller fractions is a never-ending futile exercise. That is why Bagdenbog drew a firm line between creation and recreation. Even in his theory of mother space and spaceniks, his story of recreation begins with the mother space and energy gradients. He simply refuses to go back beyond that.

Creation, as seen from Bagden's standpoint, now becomes a continuous, ever-present act. Time, in this scheme, is a useful tool for mathematical and technological enterprise – a highly useful tool, no doubt, but nonetheless, a tool only. If this sounds like a radical statement, you have to remember that even in traditional science, time is treated as a dimension. Time is not a property of matter, you can see. If you ponder deeply on that, you can appreciate why it does not matter whether the universe is billion years old or trillion years old. The only important thing is the very act of creation. Everything else after that is recreation (in bold letters, use the largest possible fonts there; the admirer adds). The beauty and irony of it is that, as Bagdenborg stresses, even that Grand Recreation – the play of the universe as we see – is just a matter of "effects." This idea may compel us to wonder what reality is if everything is an "effect" because that word, "effect," automatically connotes a sense of illusion. Bagden's advice on the subject of reality and illusion is quite practical. Forget about the difference! Because his "effects" are going to stay with us as long as you and I live, till the day of Dissolution. Play with it in full zest; drop it, if at all you get tired of it. That is as far as we can say here. Anything further takes us across, into the land of philosophy, which is beyond the scope of what we are studying in these exciting pages.

*An amazing answer

Well, back to hard science, then. Following the big bang theory, we found that for the creation – and completion – of the 117 odd elements, it took millions of years and many stages. In contrast, according to Bagdenborg's theory of spaceniks, the elements (all of them) do not need time to be formed. There is a catch here. If what Bagden says is true, then there should have been plenty of the heavier elements in the universe now – far more than what we observe now, by a factor of millions and millions. But we do not find such immense quantities of those heavy elements in the observable universe – elements like gold, lead, uranium, plutonium, etc. Then, what happened to all those immense quantities of such elements?

Bagdenborg has an amazing answer. He points at the standard, accepted scenario of the cosmologists. Gravity is the key factor in cosmology. Under the inexorable, persisting influence of gravity, stars and galaxies began to form out of the primordial cosmic dust. You know the rest of the familiar story. Stars of all sizes were formed. Among them, if the size of a star exceeds a certain mass C (called Chandrasekhar's limit), it finally turns into a black hole. This is all old hat by now. Bagden pulls out his magic answer from that old hat. He adopts the same cosmological scenario – with a twist. Look at it this way.

The "stars" need not necessarily require hydrogen or helium to gather mass. There were plenty of heavier elements in the beginning itself, he points out; heavy, in the sense of having more mass. They had more mass, and so their gravitational fields were stronger than those of the tiny elements like hydrogen and helium. So, naturally, their powerful gravity was more efficient in clumping the heavier elements together into huge masses, quickly shaping them into stars. Whether these mammoth stars gave out light (like regular stars) or not is of secondary importance. Of primary importance is that, owing to their heavy masses, the stars had enormous gravitational fields, so they began to pull in more and more of heavier elements (themselves having considerable gravity) into their voracious bellies. This is an escalating phenomenon. Thus, very soon, the mass of such a mammoth star crosses the Chandrasekhar limit. Presto, you have a black hole there! – and the amazing answer we promised. All the copious heavy elements have turned themselves into beautiful black holes. That is why, Bagdenborg says, the amount of heavier elements now observable in the universe is far less in comparison to that of the lighter elements like hydrogen, etc. Note also that once the elements enter the maw of the black hole, they – all of them of all denominations – lose their identity. You know the reason, of course. Under the unimaginably huge crushing power of a black hole's gravity, matter (that is, elements) is compacted into such small volumes that everything becomes a super-dense, uniform jelly. Your usual elements and particles simply do not exist inside it in their familiar forms. So now you know where all the heavy elements in the universe have gone.

A small corollary can be inferred from the above line of reasoning. Among all the grouped entities populating the universe, black holes were the first to be formed. The rest of the matter that failed to do so organized itself into stars, galaxies, nebulae, and so on. There must be plenty of black holes. It is a good bet that more than ninety percent of the matter of the universe is being held hostage by these black holes; dark matter apart. Nature is very good at hiding things from us. It also seems to enjoy the act.

PART II

JUVENILIA

Bagdenborg's creativity – like that of all great persons – began to flower at quite an early age. Even before he entered college, in his school days and early teens, he was in the habit of jotting down exciting ideas that cropped up in his fertile mind. In his works during the later mature years, we can see the attempt at a coherent synthesis. Naturally, that was absent in the early years. We are given to understand that Bagden tore up much of the copious notes he had written in his early years as he was not satisfied with them. Even so, the remaining notes can fill up the volumes of a couple of books – as his admirer confided. In this section, we present a few selected ideas since they are quite interesting by themselves, irrespective of their relevance to the mainstream of physics.

The Ultimate purist

Apple – bitten off more than can be chewed.

You sure are familiar with adjectives like die-hard, dyed-in-the-wool, hard-boiled, etc. Add "fanatic" to the list. Better make it more respectable, and say – purist, extreme purist, and ultimate purist. You may begin to suspect that we are slyly introducing politics here; God forbid. We are talking about science and the kind of possible scientific stances scientists can adopt. All the above descriptive words could have been applied to Bagdenborg's attitude when he was quite young. (Even "wild," "untamed," and "feverish" had their place). We give below a piece of his inimitable ratiocination that will leave you speechless with wonder. We prefer to enclose everything in quotes so that the reader can rest assured that what follows is a stream of Bagden's thoughts and Bagden's thoughts only. (He had not even reached his teens, then.):

"The Great Man2 has hastily bitten off more than he can chew when he took on the apple. The study and pursuit of science is not a joke. First of all, it needs a certain amount of intellectual sharpness. I am the first one to admit that the Great Man2 had an abundance of it. Then, one needs an unending supply of perseverance and patience. No hasty, on the spur of the moment conclusions. You need the patience of a Sisyphus. I want to repeat this a million times. A dozen or ten dozen experiments – to prove your theory or to conclude your observations – are not sufficient."

Follow me patiently, please. As the legend says, the apple fell down, and gravity was discovered. If you throw one apple into the air, the apple falls down to the earth. If you throw one stone into the air, the stone falls down to the earth. Well, that may be good news, but it is not the whole of the news. Sir, it is not a discovery yet. It is not the time to formulate a theory yet. One has to be THOROUGH. I will show you all what THOROUGHNESS means – the ultimate purity of it.

It requires an unprejudiced, completely open mind to understand (appreciation may come later. I am indifferent to it) my exposition. Let us get started. Please follow the logic carefully.

a. The apple fell down to the ground. Okay, fine. The next logical step is to pick it up and throw it again into the air. Let us assume it falls down to the ground again – as it most probably may. You have to pick it up again if it falls down and repeat the experiment. Do it twenty, fifty, a hundred times; you have to if you want to be thorough.
b. You are not to be satisfied if you throw it. You call someone else and ask him to repeat what you did a hundred times. A friend or your servant will be okay, but to be really sure, you have to call in a total stranger who does not know the three of you. You three will bear witness. Two witnesses are a must in all experiments. You may have to pay the stranger for his services – I do not mind.
c. By this time, you must realize that time is also a factor you have to take into consideration. You might have done the beautiful experiment in the morning. As confirmation, you've got to (sorry, have to) do it in the afternoon. Then, again in the evening. You close it by carrying out the same procedure at midnight.
d. We are not finished with the apple; we have a long way to go. You see, you might have inadvertently picked apples for your experiment from one tree. You have to pick apples (at least one) from all the trees in the garden to be thorough.

e. You must be careful to see that the apples are thrown to different distances and heights, naturally. Keep a record of the results if and whenever the apples fall down.
f. By now, you might be tempted to draw a hasty conclusion that all apples fall down to the ground when thrown up. Sorry, sir, it is a hasty and undeserved conclusion. You see:
g. You did the experiment in your garden. To be really thorough, you have to do it all over again in a different garden. After doing all that, you might say that all apples come down when thrown up.

No, sir, it is still an incorrect or incomplete conclusion. How many apples did you throw? One thousand? Ten thousand? In how many gardens did you carry out the experiment? Ten? Twenty? So, the correct thing to say – logically – is that ten thousand apples were thrown in twenty gardens, and they all fell down-to-earth. That is all.

From here onwards, our experiment has to move in the realms of imagination only, for conducting it with the thoroughness I need is not practicable. But practicable or imaginary, we have to keep at it. (Draw inspiration from Sisyphus). Taking inspiration from that mythical gentleman and with a strong determination to defeat me in an argument, you may now take up the huge project of testing all the apples at all places on earth.

That effort is well-appreciated. Still, alas, all I can say – I mean a pure scientist can – is that apples of different sizes were thrown to different heights and distances, at different places on earth, and were observed to come back to earth. (We are not even sure if one or two instances were not recorded, out of laziness, tiredness, or boredom.) That is not all – a lot more is left to be done.

How much time did it take to conduct these tests? You probably had a huge amount of resources at your disposal, like manpower, communication, and money. You completed the exercises in, say, three months. Good. The best statement we can now offer is that all apples all over the earth were observed to fall down for a period of three months. Three months only; not less, not more. There is no proof that apples will (or should) fall down-to-earth after that period. Many of you may say that I am being adamant, mulish, or downright stupid. Please think seriously about this, with an open mind, I beseech. Science is a serious business. The fact that a million apples fell down-to-earth yesterday is not a rigorous proof that apples will continue to fall down tomorrow also. By rigorous proof, I mean proof in complete purity – the ultimate purity itself.

Most of you may bet all your money that apples will fall down tomorrow too; you may most probably win the bet too. That is not an idealistic proof; that is only financial shrewdness.

If you want to be absolutely idealistic in your method of proof, you should continue throwing apples forever. At the end of it (if there is one), you are permitted to declare proudly that apples everywhere came back to the earth when thrown up. Please note the use of the past tense.

What I have briefly described above – omitting umpteen details – is, in fact, nothing compared to the unrelenting exhaustive work that is yet to be done. You too must have surmised it by now.

h. Apples fell down (for the past three months). You have carried out commendable experimentation on that score. Okay. But, for God's sake, don't rush into hasty conclusions. Please do not generalize the phenomenon by applying it in the case of other objects. This is a very dangerous trap into which many over-eager beginners fall. Have you conducted the experiment by throwing stones, instead of apples? How many stones, and of what sizes? For how long? Have you done it all over the earth, again? (Stones may fall down-to-earth in London but may not in New York or Tokyo). Did you try with bricks? Bats? Books?

You have to conduct the experiment on all the things that you see on earth to proceed towards a universal conclusion to declare with a pure conscience that all things fall down-to-earth. Oh, mind you, three months or three years will not do. You have to go on testing forever. If you are honest to the core...

This fantastic essay in theoretical inquiry was secretly copied and circulated among the schoolmates of Bagden. It happened in the hostel where he was staying then. (In Athens, as his admirer discovered recently. It was a fitting place for indulging in the purest of ratiocinations, a place to pay tributes to the great Hellenic thinkers of yore.) One boy pinned a message on young Bagdenborg's door, "If you don't believe in apples, jump down from the top of Pisa and record what happens." Bagdenborg wrote back below the lines, "My good breeding impels me to show hospitality; you first, dear guest."

The admirer seems to have been impressed by young Bagdenborg's intellectual rigor. He has furnished his own comments:-

I, for one, agree with young Bagdenborg. We can already catch glimpses of his budding genius here. At what stage can we totally accept the results of an experiment and make a theory out of it? How many tests have we to carry out? Will a hundred identical (almost) results do? Or a thousand? Where do we draw the line? At the root of it, you accept the results at a certain reasonable stage when a sufficient number of different people corroborate your results. Still, from Bagden's angle, it is not a theory. The corroboration only paves the way for new inventions, new technology. Then it becomes a matter of economics – big business. All further tests are being continuously and forever conducted on the people who use the new machines and gadgets! Yeah, airplanes crash, computers crash, machines break down, and even clocks run out of kilter. I am reminded here of at least one instance. Cell division continues to happen – from time immemorial. But as regularly, mutation manages to flash its mocking smile.

We conclude the discourse with Badenborg's words: "The all-pervading nature of technology in every walk of life makes us forget about the nature of the ultimate purity of inquiry. All knowledge is tentative."

The all-seeing eye

(Excerpts from young Bagdenborg's scrapbooks)

There is this phrase, the all-seeing eyes. The phrase may invoke different emotions in different people, in different contexts. But then I have to laugh when I think about it seriously. I say seriously because scientifically speaking, you have to add a qualifying number to that phrase – 360 degrees. (Admirer adds: We have learned from reliable records that when young Bagden wrote the final words of the sentence, "360 degrees," he abruptly stopped writing and went on laughing for half an hour at a stretch. Later, whenever his eyes fell on the lines, he was overcome by fits of chuckles. He was not able to continue the essay for one whole week.)

The field of vision of the human eye extends like a cone up to infinity. (Adm – obviously the boy had already read Da Vinci's notebooks.) The angle of the cone is limited, naturally. I want to extend the angle of vision to 360 degrees. See what happens! Conduct the experiment I am going to propose now – you will be blinded by the vision.

The experiment (not for queasy stomachs)

Remove the human eyeball and suspend it in mid-air. Hold it, I was just kidding; I am not a barbarian. For our experiment, the human eye will not do, even if you manage to suspend it in mid-air. It still has a limited angle of vision, you see. I want an all-seeing eye (ha-ha), a three-sixty-degrees eye! Prepare a synthetic eye which anatomically resembles the parts of the human eye, functioning physiologically similarly. Special photographic gadgets will not suit our purpose, for we want the visual experience to be authentic – the real thing as in life; a natural, biological experience. The eye will be suspended in mid-air. Next comes the real stuff – the eye shall have a 360-degree vision in all planes. That is, the eye shall catch images of the world, left, right, front, back, up, and down from all directions, from all planes, all angles – to make it unnecessarily clear to you what we want to be done. Don't worry about how such an eye can be constructed. Leave it to the technical wizards. They are extremely talented guys; they can build any gadget you want. On second thoughts, better make two of those eyes. They say two are needed to provide a real 3-D effect.

Now hook up this eye-set to the eyes of a normal human being. (Bio-tech experts can be asked to do it. They too are wizards, no less). What will be the experience of the person hooked up to such a pair of eyes? His are literally the all-seeing eyes. What do the all-seeing eyes see? They see everything and they see nothing. There is no use in turning left or right or up or down. The whole view is always there everywhere. So, what can the poor eyes do? Faced with the enormity of such an infinite (in a way, yes) view, the brain has two choices. It has to stall, like a computer, or it has to ignore a hefty percentage of the visual input. That is choice, that is focus. From this, I conclude, like my great predecessor Da Vinci (Admirer – see what we told earlier!), that the brain can only function in a limited sphere.

A natural concomitant to this conclusion is that knowledge itself is limited. How I wish Leonardo were with me now, by my side!

Big Bang; the unholy hurry

My argument is very simple; it is so simple that hide-bound traditional thinkers will recoil in horror at the conclusion. First, let me ask you to examine a couple of examples from actual life. Then, it will be easier to digest what I have to say.

You are watching a game of tennis. The game has just started. The players are top-ranked, equally matched. Can you conclude, at this point, how the game is going to end? You cannot. You can review the statistics: how many times the two players have faced each other before, how many times one or the other has won, the rank of the player, his physical conditions, his latest performance, all sorts of data. You can feed all that data into your supercomputer and make a prediction. However, it is only a prediction, and not the actual result. You have to watch the game till the end. You have no way of knowing the final scene. Even with all the computer analyses and the backing of all rigorous equations of physics, one (or both) players might just collapse and die on the court. (Such a thing is known to have happened).

Two chess titans are fighting it out on a board of sixty-four squares. They have just made two or three preliminary moves. Can you predict how the game is going to end? You cannot.

You are reading a top-notch thriller by the latest best-selling author. You have just come to the end of the first chapter. Forget about prediction. You do not know the full content of the book. If someone asks you to write a review of the book at this stage, what will you do? You will not even bother to give a reply to such an idiotic request. Please read the previous two sentences again and again, and then, what I am going to say next will become quite obvious.

Generalize the idea and consider an action, an event. You do not analyze an event until it is over. You can only collect and record all the data you want; you have to do it as long as the event lasts.

Most events are of short duration – like an apple falling to the ground, like the fall of a defenestrated body (an action often contemplated by the spooks or unfortunate souls in despair) or like an earthquake. There may be many events that last longer, no doubt: some chemical reactions, biological actions, the growth of trees and other life-forms, the orbits of planets around their stars, and so on.

But there is one event – the mother of all events, to use the popular catchphrase – that is longer than all the events you can think of... Take your own time... it started a long time back... got it?

Boy, it is the Big Bang! It is the big bang, my lord. The scientists (corrected spelling) say it began about 14 billion years back; give or take a few microseconds. (I am holding my stomach, rolling on the ground). Actually, it is not hours, but micro-microseconds because nobody knows exactly what happened just before that bang. Within a span of a few microseconds, fantastic, mind-boggling events are calculated to have happened. After a few odd billion years, something more happened, and the universe is supposed to be happily expanding steadily ever since.

Please note: it is still expanding now, even after the discovery was made less than a hundred years ago (again, I am rolling on the ground). My argument is complete. You are already thinking what I am thinking – as my favorite author, Alistair MacLean would say. Formality compels me to put it in words.

The Big Bang, boy, the big bang, lord, is still happening. It is not over. It is not over. It is not over. It is not an event that has completed its course. So, how can you theorize about it? How can you draw any conclusions about it? All conclusions will be premature!

My serious advice is this: Let us have patience. Let us go on observing and collecting data – I do not mind it. Let us wait until the Big Bang is over. Then, and only then, can we formulate an appropriate theory about the universe. I am not being facetious. I am saying this in all earnestness, as a staunch upholder of the true scientific spirit. All theories we formulate in the intermediate period, before the true ending of the Big Bang event, will be only tentative. They will be like the excited fantasies kids indulge in on the eve of the visit of Santa Claus.

The irony of the weak and the strong

My favorite pastime, as you must have guessed by now, is holding my stomach and rolling on the ground. I get the opportunity to indulge in it often, especially when I come across some funny paradoxes or ironies in science. I am going to ask you to have a good look at the table I am about to present. Before that, I want to prime you for the event. Please consider a couple of phenomena in our mundane world.

A candle is burning in the night, in the open. The atmosphere is clear, and there are no obstructions along the line of sight. Most people with normal eyesight can see such a candle from a distance of approximately three kilometers.

The night-lights of the city can be photographed from a satellite orbiting the Earth at a long distance.

The light from the sun can be seen by us, many millions away from it. Still brighter stars, which are light-years farther away, can be seen with the naked eye.

The other category of examples

The sonar explosions from your flatulence-prone friend can be heard by you (unfortunately) trapped in the same room. The man in the next building is unaware of it. If there is a collision between two bikes in the street, both of you can hear it. Those a block away will be unaware of it.

The shattering sound of a thunderclap can be heard by all of you. If there is an explosion of a nuclear bomb (god forbid), the apocalyptic boom can be heard many miles around.

The common thread across the above examples is that the greater the force (or intensity), the longer its range will be. Now, look at the table below. It lists the properties of the four fundamental forces discovered by science so far.

Force	Strength	Range (meters)	Particle
1. Strong	1	10^{-15}	Gluons
2. Electromagnetic	1/137	Infinite	Photons
3. Weak	10^{-6}	10^{-18}	Intermediate vector boson
4. Gravity	$6X10^{-39}$	Infinite	Graviton?

The scale for the strengths of the forces is prepared, taking that of the strong force as one. (The strong force is supposed to be the force that holds the positively charged protons inside a nucleus from flying away). The strength of the electromagnetic force is roughly 1/137th of the strong force. That of the gravitational force is the weakest. It is so small compared to the strong force that it is beyond imagination. A hint to help those unfamiliar with mathematical notations get an idea of how small that number (of the gravitational strength) is: The number, 10^39 means one followed by 39 zeroes! (You will have difficulty in finding how many billions it contains). The minus sign attached to 39 means that you have to divide the number one by that number, i.e., 1,000,000,000... (up to 39 zeros). It is so tiny, I repeat, that it is impossible to imagine. Now, that is the strength of your gravity compared to the first force in the list.

And now is the proper time for the stupendous joke.

The strongest force in the list, which is many billion-billion-billion times greater than gravity, has a range so small that you have to laugh and laugh. Its range is 10^-15 meters! That size is so small that you can't see it even through the most powerful microscope. By contrast, gravity, which is the weakest force, has an infinite range! CAN ANYTHING IN THE WORLD BE MORE RIDICULOUS THAN THIS? I am laughing so hard that I am busting my lungs.

Pardon me for repeating. Going back to our analogy of sounds, it is like making a solemn assertion that you cannot hear the cataclysmic roar of a nuclear bomb which has just exploded near your ear! At the same time, the scientific gentlemen who made the above assertion will take an oath that the boom of your friend's fart (to speak in plain but picturesque language) can be heard at the very distant-most edge of the universe!

Now, do you blame me if I am still rolling on the floor, busting my poor lungs? I deliberately gave an elaborate list of examples so that you can have a clear-cut idea of what I am talking about.

A word of warning here. Don't go to the boffins and ask them for an explanation. They will dump tons and tons of mathematics on your poor head, which will effectively bury you and suffocate you forever.

I am still a kid (in their eyes), doing my first year at the college. Someday, I hope to set right this topsy-turvy, ridiculous issue. I invoke the blessings of the Great Man3.

Gravity – A hilarious situation

Bagdenborg invariably placed the date and signature at the end of whatever he wrote. It appears he had developed this habit from an early age. The following notes, scribbled on loose sheets, were discovered by one of his admirers tucked inside an old, venerable edition of an encyclopedia. He had written, "I want to take up science as my subject at school so that I can solve riddles of this kind." Note the use of "can." Quite a bit of self-confidence indeed!

Instead of quoting verbatim, we will paraphrase his thoughts since the original version is a jumble of broken sentences containing many interrogative and exclamatory marks, dots, and dashes, the style being soaked in heavy doses of (unwarranted) humor. (Understandable, coming from a pre-teenager in his salad days.) For example, he began with the title, "The Sun Also Dies," a parody of a novel he had read just then. In his later years, Bagdenborg used to say that there are no such things as force and (by implication) energy. These scraps show that even in his young days, he was fascinated by the two fundamental entities that run the universe. That said, let us see what he has to say.

"The Sun and the Earth are secretly pepping themselves up with vitamin pills," was how young Bagden began his essay.

"Imagine this scenario. You are sitting in a chair. You have had no breakfast. The floor of the hall (in which you are sitting) is sloping downwards, away from you. There is a heavy stone, weighing about 200 kg, twenty feet away from you, with a rope firmly tied around it. The other, loose end of the rope is in your hands. You are to pull the stone toward you, up to the chair you are sitting in. Ah, of course, the chair has been firmly bolted to the ground – no need to mention that. The rock is equipped with well-greased wheels attached to its base, to offset frictional losses. After you pull the rock up to your knees, let go, pull it back again.

Remember, you are on an empty stomach. How many times can you pull the rock up to you? Thirty times? Fifty? A hundred? (You are a tough guy.) This goes on for some time. The smile on your face, with which the exercise started, gradually transforms into a grin and ends in a grimace. You also remember, then, that nobody had announced any reward for your act. And of course, since you have not been tied to the chair, you decide to reward yourself. You get up and go out, determined to gobble up a basketful of sandwiches, burgers, cornflakes, crispies, and as many bottles of milk as you can get hold of (And, you judiciously opt to take a good rest.)

If your poetically inclined friend is asked to describe the above scene, he may compose a mini Odyssey. But if a scientist were to do it, he will employ plain, bald language containing universally defined terms. At a certain time, T1, your body had a certain amount of energy, e. You applied force F to mass m, moving it a distance of twenty feet, taking time t to do it. Force applied over a time means energy expended. After time T2, your energy was depleted.

That is it. "Force applied over a period of time depletes the energy of the system. If the period of time is sufficiently long, a time will come when the system loses all its energy. In the above illustration, even if you replace the human being (who went in search of hamburgers) with a machine, you have to refuel the machine if it is fuel-operated or continuously draw power from the mains if it is electrically operated, and so on.

I want to reiterate what I have said so that the idea can sink in before I jump to the next scenario. It's a big, bold, and beautiful leap, I promise.

You pulled the stone a hundred times? Your muscles are sore? Your biceps are aching? (Did you get a Charley Horse by any chance?) You got so tired that you could no longer pull up the rock? No further energy, right? Good. Remember and relive that experience again and again. Have you had food and rest? Remember too that you got tired because you did work. It was physical work, and it was also 'work' as in physics textbooks – work done is equal to force multiplied by distance (twenty feet, in your case).

Now, take the leap with me. Let us go to the sun. (Just kidding – I am talking about a mental journey, of course). Just as you exerted a force back there, the sun too exerts a force. It is called the gravitational force. Hope you do not doubt it! Just as you started with a given amount of energy, the sun too started with a given amount of energy (that was about some billions of years ago). Your force was exerted using muscles and the rope. The sun's force is exerted by means of gravity, but force is force; remember that. You 'pulled' the stone for about half an hour, say. The sun has been 'pulling' all the planets in the solar system, apart from the many comets identified thus far (visiting professors), for billions of years. I have now given a broad picture – and even broader hints. The conclusion is inevitable.

I said that work done is the product of force multiplied by distance. The "force" of the sun is unimaginably greater than that of your arm. The distances of the many planets and comets run into millions of miles. The time involved—the billions of years—is also incomparably huge. Thus, if you compute the "work done" by the sun, the figure will be mind-boggling. Work done is another name for energy. When you (or machines or systems) do work, you expend energy. Recall the word "expenditure," and you will get a clear idea of what is happening to the sun. The sun is not an infinite entity. Even though it is about a hundred thousand times bigger than our Earth, it is still a finite object... OK?

So, by all reckoning, the sun must have gotten pretty tired by this time—just the way you did!! Think of all that stupendous work it has been doing for some billions of years. Notice that I mentioned only the planets and comets, leaving out other kinds of stellar objects. Our puny Earth itself has been attracting so many meteors—doing work all the time. Think how many more times than that the sun must have been attracting. Innumerable asteroids must have been swallowed by it, apart from other types of stellar objects. In addition to that, it has been doing work against itself! You know how? The sun, as you all know, is made of gases—hydrogen and helium mostly. Due to the nuclear fusion occurring on the sun every second, and the high temperature, the gases tend to fly away from the surface of the sun, and the sun is holding back an enormous quantity of all that by its force of gravity. Pulling, using force, doing extra work; you see. That is, the sun is spending its energy every second. Lest you be misled by that statement, I wish to point out that I am not referring to the fusion process of the sun, which is burning out its own nuclear fuel. I am specifically referring to the force, the pulling force it is applying on its planets and comets, et al.

If you are still thinking of nuclear fusion and the light coming out of the sun, come nearer home. Consider our own Earth.

The Earth has been "pulling" the moon for, say, some billion years. It has been "pulling" meteors and other forms of cosmic dust. It has been "pulling" the sun too; do you get it? And add to the list all those artificial satellites we have launched so far. Thus, the Earth too is pulling, exerting force, doing work, expending its energy! You've got to believe me; I am saying this in earnest. "So, what?" you may ask. That is a silly question, Mac. Did you already forget that you got so tired pulling that adamantine slab? I say again, that the sun and Earth must have gotten pretty tired by now. That is to say, a lot of their energies must have been depleted. But still, the apples continue to fall down. If you step off the hundredth storey of a skyscraper, you end up as widely spread pulp on the ground. What does that mean? That means:-

1. The sun and Earth must be pepping up themselves with a secret source of energy.
2. It is our duty to find out that secret source.
3. The other supposition is that the strength of the gravitational fields of the sun and the Earth were far greater when they were formed than what we find to be at present. The deduction is inevitable.
4. OR, gravitational force is not a force at all in the sense that we know of "force." It must be an anomalous behavior of either objects or space. I want to dig deeper into this when I enter school. I am going to solve it.
5. From the previous remarks, it may be supposed that if an object is kept isolated (from the rest of the universe), the strength of its gravitational field will remain constant, as long as it is isolated, since there would be no other object which it could try to 'pull'. Such may not be the case even in such an ideal condition because,
6. Consider the analogy of a candle. It is radiating energy in the form of light all around it. If another object comes within its range, that object is illuminated. But whether the other object is there or not, the energy of the candle is spreading out, expending itself. I strongly suspect that this must be the case with gravity also. The range of the gravitational field, they say, is infinite. That means that gravity is thinning itself out uniformly in all directions, at all times. I cannot help postulating that in the distant future – however distant it may be – all objects in the universe

will lose their gravity. (Size of the object has no bearing on the rate of depreciation, obviously). I wish to bring to your notice the phenomenon of radioactive decay. The rate of gravitational decay must be exceedingly small. Otherwise, by this time, all the planets of the solar system would have wandered off into deep space. And, of course, we human beings would not have been here to ponder such horrifying situations since Earth would not have had a sun to speak of.

7. While we are at it, I would like to contemplate on this very hilarious conundrum. I am laughing out loud as I write this, and my elder cousin is peeping down at me, breathing down my neck. (I can feel his breath not only as being hot but also hard and irregular.) Since I am loath to conduct actual experiments physically, I proceed with my thought experiments. (I have read somewhere that the great A.E himself trusted his thought experiments where real research was needed.)

Place a bar magnet on a table and move a small piece of soft iron toward it slowly. At a certain point, you need no more push the iron piece – the magnet will pull it to itself. You know that the great IN declared that action and reaction are equal and opposite. So, while the magnet pulls the iron piece toward itself, it is also being "pulled" toward the iron. You don't see it because of the friction of the table surface and the comparatively higher size of the magnet. Suspend your magnet and the iron piece by means of threads and bring the objects slowly nearer. You will surely notice then that both the magnet and the iron piece move toward each other, quickly effecting a union (like eager lovers).

My uncle often criticizes me that I never come to a point directly, that I pick up some other point and then move from there. It is a found foible of mine; I cannot help it. Of course, I can excuse him because he is not a man of imagination. You see, while making the journey towards the point under discussion, you often discover new things, apart from the fact that the journey itself is beautiful. Well, different folks, different strokes… Now to the point. (I make it slow and deliberate because at the end you will be unable to stop your fits of laughter).

You need not conduct the other experiment. It is already out there. The sun is your bar magnet. The Earth is your iron piece. Instead of the magnetic force, you have the force of gravitational attraction—mutual. (Note the word "mutual," please.) The sun and the moon are not even suspended by threads.

They are hanging free in space, all by themselves; so there is no friction or anything to hinder their movements. (At the risk of sounding facetious, I will say that nobody has grouted the sun with cement concrete, bolts and nuts to any firm foundation).

Visualize the grand picture once again. The sun and the earth are there in free space. The sun is attracting the earth with its powerful gravitational force, pulling it. Not to be outdone, the earth too is doing its best to pull the sun. They are in a mega-super-lubricated medium. Under these ideal conditions, the earth and the sun should meet each other, firmly getting themselves locked in an inseparable embrace – like true lovers. In fact, this should have happened long ago. That the earth will end up as smoke is a moot point as far as our purely logical quest is concerned. Ah, come to think of it, all the planets of the solar system should enthusiastically follow the earth. They should get themselves firmly embedded around the sun – vowing never to be separated. This is an awe-inspiring scenario, and I wonder again and again why the final act of mass self-immolation has not already occurred.

My future would be senior college mates may smile tolerantly at what I have so lucidly explained. They will console me in this way. The earth is revolving around the sun. The gravitational pull of the sun on the earth is real; it is acting on the earth all the time constantly. But the tricky point to understand here is that the earth is trying to move away at right angles from the sun's line of pull at the same time, and constantly. The earth is always – at every point – trying to move aside, and the sun is pulling it in. This results in an orbital motion. That is why, that is how, the earth is orbiting around the sun. Capisce?

Hell! Don't I know it? But they have not got to the core of my point. The earth may be going round the sun, or dancing or walking or somersaulting for all I care. I am talking of the mutual attraction between the two bodies. My buddies may even bring back those two gentlemen who retired three thousand years back – Atlas and Hercules – and ask them to hold the earth firmly on their puissant shoulders, thereby compelling the sun to orbit around the earth. I don't care. Mutual attraction, mutual attraction, that is my refrain. Even if the earth is orbiting the sun, the sun pulls the earth, and the earth pulls the sun. They cannot deny this basic fact. That is enough for me. And that is enough to bring the earth and sun together. (Comment from the admirer: - Notice the quaint and disquieting logic of young Bagden. Obviously, the seeds of his future fentologic had been sown at a very early age. Yet, I suspect he must have ingested peyote while he wrote these lines.)

On second thoughts, I think there may be a solution to this puzzle. You see, between the sun and the earth, there are no big objects like stars. The same goes with regard to the other planets too. So, all the countless number of stars on this side of the earth in our Milky Way must be pulling the earth, holding it from crashing into the sun. Also, the other stars and stellar objects must be pulling the sun, preventing it from smashing onto the earth... That must be it... I have heard rumors that resolving the combined gravitational effect of more than five mutually interacting objects is an impossible affair. So, I think my conjecture is on the right track. If we had accurate data on the distances between the sun and the earth and the other planets dating back to, say, ten or twenty thousand years ago, I think my conjecture would have been proved. A pity we do not have such records. Nevertheless, I am sanguine that our earth is going to crash-land on the sun at some point in the future.

La Terre, c'est creux

(From solid reasons to hollow solids via fluent logic)

Young Bagdenborg had plenty of quaint but startlingly original ideas. We provide here an extract from his "secret diaries," compiled during his initial years at the college: -

Nature is a great potter. Most of the time, a potter makes artifacts that are hollow; your ubiquitous pot is a most glaring example. Are you wondering what I am talking about? Well, you know Nature-made the earth and the sun. I hope that broad hint is sufficient.

Are you still bemused? Then let me spell it out for you. But first, hold on to your seat firmly and don't jump in the air dramatically, unnecessarily. Like our potter's clay pots, Nature's pots—the earth and the sun—are hollow! You think I am joking? Don't – I am dead serious. Come, follow me; let us visit Nature's pottering yard. It is not a long journey – you have to go back in time by only some 4.5 billion years. Come, hurry. Let us apply science diligently, in earnest, and gain new knowledge.

They say that the Big Bang occurred some 14 billion years ago. (Give or take a few hours). So, in that scale of time, 4.5 billion is not all that old. What they say is that around that period, roughly in the position of what we call the Milky Way today, a huge quantity of gas was present. You may call it gas, or primordial matter, or particles, or even soup for convenience. It does not matter much, you see. The great goddess of Convenience is very benevolent, and she impartially bestows her munificence on science too, in its times of need. Anyway, their point is that with all that enormous quantity of particles (read matter), gravity had a chance to play its hand handsomely. Random clusters out of the particles began to form, which gravity used as leverage to form bigger clusters, whose gravity increased further aiding them to grab more particles and so on. The Milky Way was born through such a process. As you are well aware, our sun and its planets are in the Milky Way, and they were formed by the process described. Minor details can wait – with the blessings of the aforementioned goddess of Convenience.

The point relevant to my thesis is that during its formative years – running into millions, note it – the earth was one huge ball of fire. They say so, and you better believe it; ipso dixit. Another important fact to which I wish to draw your attention is that the earth is spinning on its axis. The third point of interest to us is that since so much matter had gathered in one place, it had a good deal of gravity. That is it; matter in a fluid state (hyperlink it to the title of this thesis, please), and in a state of spinning, gravity acting all along. Out of these three pieces of data, we are going to construct a beautiful theory. Let us go at it slowly, step by logical step, relishing the elegance of it at the end of it all. Ready? Here we go.

A bit of geometry is involved. No worry – it is very elementary, and so basic that you need not fear to go back to your dust-laden textbooks of yesteryears. The geometry comes in the context of what is termed as 'the center of gravity' in physics. Please refer to Figure (12).

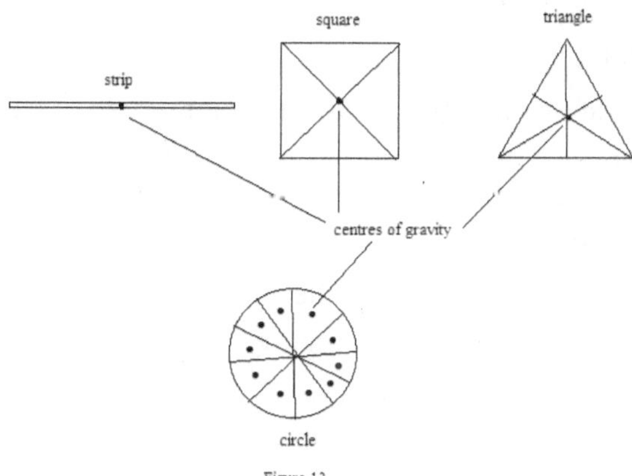

Figure 12

Consider a thin rectangular strip of any material. Its center of gravity lies at the middle of the strip. That is, the strip behaves as if all its weight is concentrated at that (geometrical) center. You can balance the strip with your finger placed beneath that point. If your location is accurate, you can even balance the strip using the tip of a needle. (The working principle of the old-time vendor's weighing balance.) Similarly, the center of gravity of a square-shaped plate lies at the center, where the diagonals cross, as shown in the figure. That of a triangular piece lies where the three bisecting lines from each apex cross, as represented in the figure. This is fairly common knowledge, as I said.

The next step in our inquiry is a bit subtle – but not deliberately clever, I insist. Examine the circle in the figure. A number of "diameters," lines passing from points of the circumference through the center to the opposite ends, have been drawn. Instead of looking at the circle from the outside, if you see it from the center, you will notice that the circle is made up of, is a composite of many triangles. (True, the base of each triangle is curved. But if you increase the number of triangles, the curve eases out, tending to become a straight line. Incidentally, this is how the great Archimedes calculated the area of a circle) Please note the center of gravity of each triangle; it lies away from the apex, more towards the base. We have drawn an inner circle connecting all such points – as a pointer to what comes next. That is enough of geometry for now. Bearing the inner circle in mind, let us again go back to that old 4.5 billion-year event when our earth was formed.

The earth then was a big ball of fire. There was no "solid" in it. Whatever it contained was fluid in nature. The earth has been spinning ever since. Now, the most intrinsic feature of a spinning object is that it generates centrifugal force. Centrifugal force is a force that acts away from the center toward the circumference. This force always exists in a spinning object. It is more strikingly evident if the spinning object is a fluid. The fluid (water, gas, whatever) simply starts flowing outward from the center toward the 'top,' outer surface. This is the principle on which those pumps that pump water to the overhead tanks in your houses work. We repeat for effect – spinning fluids do not stay at the center; they push up toward the periphery. You got the picture?

Well, gentlemen, consider the figure below for a few moments. For convenience, we have shown

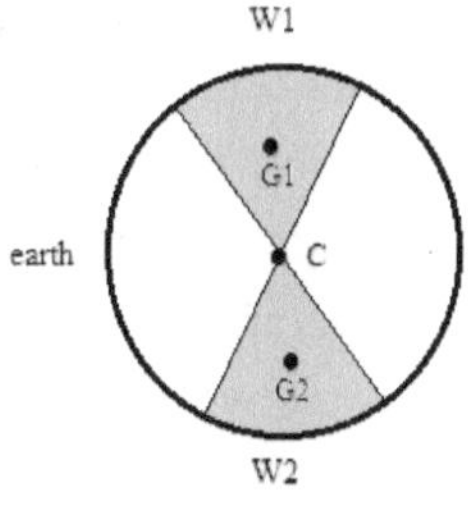

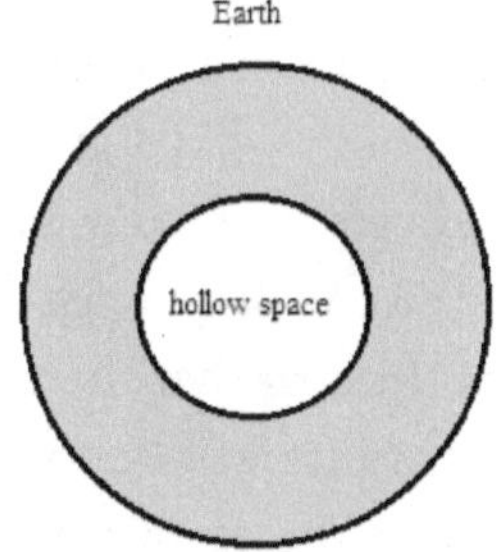

Figure 13

Consider the earth as a circle. Observe the two wedges drawn there, W1 and W2. They are three-dimensional masses consisting of primordial gas (or whatever they call it). Each wedge-shaped mass has a center of gravity. They (the centers) are marked G1 and G2 in the figure. The two wedges, W1 and W2, are shown for illustrative purposes. The earth-sphere can be divided into as many wedges as we like. Now, for the action part.

It consists of two forces. The mass, W1 has a gravitational force of its own and tends to pull any matter existing at the center, marked C, toward its center of gravity, G1. The mass, W2 too acts in a similar manner, pulling matter at the center C toward its center of gravity G2. The second force is the centrifugal force explained before. The earth is/was spinning continuously. So, the centrifugal force created due to this pushes all matter (gas, liquid, semi-solid, whatever) away from the center toward the outer surface of the sphere. Do you see what is happening? Both types of forces have no mercy towards any matter existing at the center. The wedges are pulling the matter from the center into their abdomens (G1 and G2). The centrifugal force is pushing the same matter upwards – aiding and abetting the wedges. As a consequence, all the matter at the center is being evacuated! What does this mean? It means that the center becomes hollow as time progresses.

The wedges and the centrifugal forces had all the time they wanted. Consider the time scale – millions of years for the earth to cool down. Under such circumstances, there is no doubt that a hollow (circular) space should have formed at the center of the earth – and for keeps. I confidently assert that the earth, our earth, is hollow even today, only waiting to be discovered!

Ah, and, you know something? The equatorial diameter of the earth is greater than the polar diameter. The earth has a bulge along its equator. That is a significant pointer to my argument about the centrifugal effect.

The same kind of arguments can be adopted to show that the sun too has a big hollow space at its center. Some people, especially those of the opposite camp, may doubt what I am saying. But time is on my side. My discoveries will be vindicated someday in the future – absolutely. The earth is hollow, I repeat. Si c'est le soleil. So ist der mond. Sic planetarum.

I know, I know that there will be many people who will raise objections. Their first instinct will be to argue like this: "This young tyro is considering a period when the earth was hot as a whole – inside and outside. More to the point, his description focuses on the period when the earth was gaseous or fluidic. When the earth cools down, and it becomes solid, the solids will definitely slide down to the center again, occupying the hollow region (granting that such a region has formed)."

To which, I offer consolation thus, "Solid, did you say, gentlemen? That is fine. Even better. Have you ever seen an arch, gentlemen? An arch is constructed out of many pieces of wedges. The bottom space, below the inner surface of an arch is hollow! You can even have a semicircular arch. Our earth is a giant semicircular (globular) arch with a vengeance. It is two semicircular arches supporting each other". The talk about arches is to illustrate and illuminate. In fact, our earth is made up of innumerable such arch-like slices held (and welded) together. And, ah, no doubt, you too must have heard of those things called tectonic plates! Thank you, gentlemen, for reminding me of solids.

Incidentally, since we are discussing contrasting temperatures (not idiomatically; just as a play on words), I would like to put forward another interesting argument. The accepted wisdom is that the interior of the earth is very hot, that only the surface has cooled down, formed into a solid crust of approximately 30 miles or something. It is on that crust that all our civilization of 8000 and odd years has been built: the pyramids, the skyscrapers, and the humble dwellings. Below the crust, (they say) is the 'mantle," about 1500 miles thick. The mantle is supposed to be very hot; hot enough to melt rock. It is this molten rock, lava, which regularly escapes up to the surface through the volcanoes. Beneath that (they say) is the "core," a huge iron ball hotter than the mantle. But the huge iron ball – the core – does not melt even though its temperature is around 9000 degrees, because of the enormous gravitational pressure of the upper layers (they say). Recently, someone else has claimed to have found another smaller core, around 360 miles in size, inside that core.

That is for the "blowing hot" part. How about the "blowing cold" part? Any takers? Well, let me take up the gauntlet. It is actually very easy and logical too when you come to think of it. Let us begin with a kid-stuff experiment.

Take a thick glass tumbler and fill it with steaming hot water. Thick glass is preferred so that the escape of heat from the sides and bottom of the tumbler can be minimized, allowing much of the heat to escape from the upper surface of the water, with the mouth of the tumbler being kept open. (The water need not be actually boiling. Thick glass tumblers may possibly crack due to a sudden temperature difference.) Wait for a sufficient time so that the surface of the water cools down enough for you to drink the water comfortably. Now go on drinking the water continuously. Do not stir the water. Watch carefully; you will notice that the upper portion of the water is warm while the bottom-most part of the water is already cold. This is natural. The hot molecules of water rise up from the bottom, like hot air rising in the atmosphere. The bottom line is (pardon the pun) that water at the bottom of the tumbler will be cooler compared to the top.

Now switch your view to that of the Earth as it was being formed 4.5 billion years ago. Like the hot water in your tumbler, the Earth contained hot gases (molecules, particles, liquids, whatever). The temperature of the contents might have been quite hot – very, as they say. But what of that? Look at the surface area of the Earth. The larger the surface area, the quicker the heat dissipation. And unlike the few minutes in the case of your tumbler, the Earth had, had, had had millions of years at its disposal to cool. So, what does that mean? Very simple. Just like the bottom of your tumbler, the bottom of the Earth – that is, the central space – had all the time in the world to become cool (cool, cool, cooler, coolest) than the top, which is the surface we live on. Cool, cool – many times all over. As I said, time is on my side. My bold conjecture will be vindicated someday in the future. It cannot be tested indirectly – like, by analyzing shock waves, seismic wave propagation, blah, blah. Who knows; man may one day actually get to the center of the Earth, and then my theory will be proved correct. On that day, a very broad smile can be detected above the grave of Jules Verne.

As a corollary to the cooling effect described above, we can arrive at an interesting conclusion. Since the upper layers are hot and the deeper layers are cool, it is necessary that the various elements (and compounds) that make up the Earth will be distributed in a vertically descending order. What is meant by that is that the lighter elements will float upwards, and the heavier ones will gradually settle at deeper and deeper levels.

So far, we have discovered about 114 elements, with plutonium being the heaviest. (Claims have been made for the discovery of the latest element, Ununoctium, a tad heavier than that; one, one, eight – 118). My prediction is that in the foreseeable future, the Earth-diggers will find at least a dozen more heavier elements – it is a certainty, in fact, if you think about it. They have not dug deep enough, that is all. When they do, they will be surprised to find elements with atomic weights of more than 300. I rightfully propose to name them Bagden, Bagdenborg, Bagdimedes, Bagnewton, Bagenstein, Bagalileo, and so on, not out of vanity but driven by a sense of official protocol… And of course, the central hollow space, when discovered, deserves to be called the Bagplatonic sphere.

By the same logic, the universe too has a big hole at its center; a hole that contains nothing. This, in fact, is the real white hole (in contrast with the black hole).

(The admirer adds, "I unabashedly admire the man's supreme confidence in himself.")

Diversity in Unity (The same, but not quite the same)

Excerpts from Bagden's diaries: Vol II, Period – precollege.

"In the field of scientific quest, no idea can be dismissed as being puerile or stupid." – Bagden in his teens.

Some ideas are so exotic that if they are presented point-blank in plain, bold language, most people – the scientific community too being no exception – will reject them outright. A lot of persuasion is necessary, in many cases, for the ideas to be accepted. Bagden did not mean persuasion in a cynical sense; he was aware that ideas, like goods, could be marketed. He meant it in a benevolent, humanitarian way – the way a seeker cannot hold to himself what he has discovered.

Even in those young days, he had found, by intuition, that the method of the pointing finger was the best – and unobtrusive – means of transmitting an idea. The pointing finger is, of course, an old philosophical metaphor. Bagden refurbished it by adding on more fingers. One finger (speaking in a scientific spirit) does not give the exact location of the object being pointed at. If two or more fingers are aligned at the object, there are no chances of missing the object. Bagden's favorite method has been to employ analogies as the pointing fingers. He was a great enthusiast in the study of analogies. He used to say, "The universe is teeming with millions and millions of analogies. A watchful study of them will reveal many interesting discoveries. I feel sad – and disappointed – that science has not fully appreciated the hidden riches contained in analogies."

So, in that spirit, let us examine a few analogies and discover what the pointing fingers are pointing at.

Go out and have a look at the seven and odd billions of human beings. Select any one among them. That person, as a generic representative, can be called a human being. At the same time, you can bet your last dollar that no one among those billions is identical to any other in terms of physical, mental, and psychological characteristics. That is obvious, even if you have not individually checked all of them.

Go out and examine the trees. Take it easy, just select one kind of tree, say, mango trees. Even though they are all mango trees, no single tree is identical to another tree in all respects – height, spread, number of branches, shapes. Almost all things vary from tree to tree.

In fact, even among animals, no two dogs are identical, no two elephants are identical...and so on. As they say, this is not such an earth-shaking discovery. The diversity is obvious.

Perhaps you might be thinking right now, as you are reading, that the differences are the essential characteristic of life. Perhaps you might (be tempted to) say that non-living things of a group might be identical. Do you? Well, apart from man-made artifacts, can you name any two things that are identical to each other in all respects? Rocks, hills, rivers, deserts...go on, ponder. The subject is warming up now. Be warned, when we are saying "exactly alike," we intend to use exacting standards!

If you are sensitive, you must already be experiencing a tingling sensation in your mind, wondering what the above "fingers" of Bagden are pointing at. (Young Bagden is a clever individual. He is teasing you before presenting the grand finale.)

"Strictly speaking," as the well-deserved cliché goes, we are examining here things found in Nature. During the intermission to Bagden's grand finale, we will take up man-made articles too, to show that our argument's scope extends to that area also. You can argue that if Nature is not willing to create two exactly identical objects, man can. You will naturally point at the manufacturing industry and the mighty capacity of technology. The manufacturing industry effortlessly spews out of its assembly lines millions and millions of identical parts and finished products. Take, for example, a motorbike of a particular brand and model. All motorbikes of that brand and model are identical, you may claim. If you do, then you would do well to remember our warming phrase – exacting standards.

Take two such motorbikes, as mentioned above, and weigh them. Remember, again, the exacting standards. Your weighing machine must be sensitive enough to measure even fractions of a milligram. Using such a machine, we are ready to bet our last dollar (Bagden is betting, we mean) that the weights of the two bikes will not match. You may now probably like to choose objects of smaller size, say, ball bearings. Still, our argument holds, and we are going to win the bet. Just hike up the sensitivity of the weighing machine a thousand times, and you will see that the weights of any two ball bearings will not match up to a millionth part of a gram! We (on behalf of Bagden) are not being mulishly argumentative. There is a fine point in all this nit-picking and hair-splitting. We are going to arrive there in the next stage of this argument – by making it more refined and more exacting. Let us assume that to win your argument, you are able to come up with two ball bearings with the same weight, matching up to a millionth of a gram.

Bagden would still argue that their shapes may not match. Oh, that is downright childish! He would be just teasing you playfully. What he wants to do is to take the exacting standard to its ultimate level. Here comes the kicker. Even if the two balls match in weight up to a millionth of a gram – by chance – the number of atoms, and the number of electrons in both will not be the same! Bagden is ready to bet his last dollar on that. You may begin to think by now that we are carrying the argument to ridiculous lengths.

And then, the intelligent reader will have a sudden brainwave. Bright brat Bagden was digging down to the level of electrons, wasn't he? ("Gotcha, you bragging geek.") He was talking of two identical objects. Well, take electrons. Any two electrons must surely be identical! "We will now bet our last dollar on that."...yak, yak, yak.

Stop! We have arrived there at last. Ironically, you started taking up the example of man-made things, and ended up with electrons, nature-made things. That is exactly what bright brat Bagden wanted. He wanted to talk about electrons – that is where his fingers were pointing at.

The pointing fingers were frantically signaling something else of importance also – powerful, compelling analogies. Having said that, we will leave the field entirely to Bagden now to present his fantastic conjecture. Conjecture it is from our point of view, but certainty it is to him, by conviction reinforced by intuition.

Back to our mangoes for one last time. Not only is one mango tree of a specific species different from another, but also, even one mango from the same tree is different from another (from the same tree). In the same way, Nature, even at the fundamental-most level, takes delight in variation.

Ergo, all electrons in the universe are not identical! This insight is sure to send a chill down the spines of many scientists. Ponder it deeply – there is no rule that all the zillions of electrons should be identical. Actually, if you are open-minded enough, you will appreciate the elegance of his theorem.

In case you want to argue against his conviction, you must be ready to face his invincible weapon – the battering ram of exacting standards. The problem of measurement and the standards of measurement have been extensively dealt with in the first part of this book (Chapter 4, "The Illusion and the Addiction"). It was shown there that there is nothing like absolute accuracy in measuring any quantity. You just agree to proceed up to certain numbers of decimal places and make your peace with the Goddess of Measurement. Seen from that angle, the mass of an electron can be defined as an average. Did we say an average? But, Bagden insists on two averages! Yes, two, you heard it right. See, it is like this. Let us suppose you proceed to measure the mass of an electron. You are very conscientious. You conduct many numbers of experiments, say, about a thousand. (After recording the values obtained in the thousand experiments, you may probably find that some of those values may tally. But it is a misleading temptation to accept those values as being the "correct" ones.) You calculate the average of the thousand values and define it as being the mass of an electron. In spite of your painstaking thoroughness, a subtle fallacy has crept in, in your experimentation. Unconsciously, you have accepted that all those electrons are alike. ("Electrons are electrons.")

Here, brat Bagden drops his bombshell in this shape: - Hark back to the analogy of human beings. All the seven and odd billions of humans that populate the earth are entitled to be called humans. Compare their height, then. The heights range from about two feet to seven feet plus. The factor of variation is almost four. Bearing this in mind, if you are truly honest with yourself, yes, honest with yourself, you have to collect samples of electrons from all over the world. The average you get from testing their masses is the second kind of average that brat Bagden is really interested in. The irony is that this average does not truly represent the mass of any electron at all. We have to expand a bit on this jaw-dropping idea. Follow carefully the ensuing streamlined (and super lubricated) reasoning of lean mean Bagden.

He pointed out that among human beings, the factor of variation in height ranged from one to four. The item of data to focus on is the total number of human beings on planet earth, i.e., seven billion. You may think that seven billion is a big number and that a variation (in height) of one to four is not all that surprising. A statistician may even say it looks normal. Quite; Bagden agrees; if you take only a thousand people at random, most probably, the ratio of difference may be less than one to four.

But friends, dear readers, and dearest scientists of the world, seven billion is but as a single speck compared to the number of electrons on the planet earth. Human beings dwell on a minor fractional area of the surface of the earth. Electrons, on the contrary, dwell not only on the whole surface of the earth, but also in every blessed atom of the earth and also in every blessed atom of the atmosphere. Can you count the number of electrons on the earth then? Count is an inappropriate word; estimate, guess, are more applicable in this exercise.

If there is a variation of one to four in such a pitiable number as seven billion, then how much more variation THERE MUST BE in a number – of a group – which is a zillion times more? It is anybody's guess. But even taking a ballpark estimate, the ratio should be at least one to one hundred thousand! Just to get your focus on what Bagden is talking about, we will put it in bland terms at the risk of repetition. Among humans, the ratio between the shortest and the tallest persons is one to four. Likewise, among electrons, the ratio between the lightest and the heaviest electrons is one to one hundred thousand!

Surely, this discovery must take anyone's breath away. (In an attempt to assuage your excitement nearing hysteria, Bagden says, "If that ratio frightens you, how about one to ten thousand?") After being properly outraged, if you are slowly simmering down, then take this punch to the solar plexus.

Seven billion, it was stressed, is but a single speck of dust compared to the number of electrons dwelling inside and outside the planet earth. We nominally called that number a zillion. But, dear readers, you have been unreasonably earth-centric. Lift up your heads and look up (and around) at the universe. Compared to the contents of the universe, the planet earth is but a single speck of dust. Think of the number of electrons in the universe! Compared to THAT number, your poor zillion of yore is but a single speck of dust. Statistically, if there is a variation ratio of 1 to 100,000 in a zillion, how much greater variation there must be among the zillion zillion zillion (yes, it's a godzillion) electrons of the universe! On the strength of pure statistics alone, there must be electrons of every possible denomination you can dare to conceive in the universe. (Oh, if only old Darwin were alive now! This vision would have warmed the cockles of his heart!) We will sum up the exegesis in plain, down-to-earth language. Go to a mountain and examine the rocks in it. You will find rocks of all sizes and compositions. The range in their differences is quite extensive. In the same way, there are electrons of different masses and properties scattered in the universe. It must be so. Nature guarantees it. Bold, brilliant Bagden assures you of that. What a thrilling revelation!

Yet, traditional hide-bound science – propelled by a knee-jerk reaction – will raise objections. The objections will be two-fold. First, if there is really such a tremendous variation in electrons – as that braggart boasts, how come we have been investing in and utilizing innumerable electronic gadgets and instruments that have been working infallibly all these days? Many of them are calibrated to a high degree of accuracy. Almost every other gadget in the present day is built on the properties of electrons. Secondly, if there were such infinite denominations – as that juvenile lunatic claims – how come we have not found them so far?

In fact, young Bagden had anticipated the objections and answered them. To offer the readers a flavor of his reasoning, we will partly reproduce his own words.

"Objection #1 is not really so bright. Consider the data. The radius of an electron (as they claim) is about 2.82x10-15 meters. The mass of an electron is about 9.10938291x10-31 Kg. Keep it in a corner of your mind while we jump to a related concept – the operating word is "tolerance," as used in the manufacturing industries. To illustrate, suppose a machine part is required to be 2 inches in diameter; they allow a "tolerance" of ± (i.e., more or less) 1/50th of an inch. That means the required part, while being manufactured, could be either 1/50th of an inch thicker or thinner than the designated 2 inches. The part will work satisfactorily. Almost all parts (and machines assembled out of such parts) in practice conform to this procedure. The point is that as per mathematical calculations, while designing that part, the answer would be 2 inches, but in actual practice, a tolerance of ± 1/50th of an inch does not hinder the machine from working perfectly. Thus, objection #1, citing the smooth working of machines, is a very lame one, besides being untenable.

The second objection is far more lame. It is premature, in fact. Look at the objection – "How come we have not found electrons of different denominations so far?" If I were a politician, I would have replied, "It is not my fault!" If I were a philosopher, I would have reminded them of the Biblical advice about seeking. (It is more than advice in this case; it is an assurance.) Being a scientist (granted that I am still a fledgling), I would recommend the three Ps – passion, perseverance, patience. The important thing to keep in mind is that all these days we did not have any inkling that electrons could come in different shapes and sizes. Once we are convinced, the next step, that of discovering such electrons, will be realized sooner or later. Such has been the case in many a discovery. I congratulate in advance the future discoverer of my electrons. Every neuron in the intuitive part of my brain screams that Nature has not limited its grand plan of diversification to the biological species alone but has extended it into the realm of inert matter too. If it were not so, Nature would have created one single electron as a sample and stopped there, just as it would have produced one single human being as a sample and called it a day. Can anything be more obvious than this? This is logic at its highest intensity. This is intuition unstoppable.

Further tidbits (Marginalia)

What we have presented above is a highly condensed version of young Bagden's exegesis on the topic. As is his wont, he had further thoughts on the subject, now and then, while studying books on science, and scribbled them in the margins. Many of the books have been lost, but his admirer was able to salvage a few of his marginalia: -

*It is possible that my thesis may be mistakenly equated with that of a famous concept in quantum physics. What I have discovered is poles apart from the Uncertainty Principle.

*The idea that electrons come in all sizes and shapes has got no relation whatsoever with the probability-waves theory. In the heart of my hearts, I dislike that theory; it is neither here nor there. Science can take a new turn only when it is able to drop its unreasonable addiction to that theory.

*If an electron – in the zoos of the laboratories – has a mass of one emu, then, I predict there must be at least ten billion electrons that have a mass a million times more out there in the universe. Those having masses in between will be at least a hundred thousand.

*The reason for their not having found (stumbled upon) my electrons is simple. The rogue electrons (from their point of view) are scattered randomly throughout the universe. They are not clustered, that's why. I urge the modern-day Columbuses to go forth and seek. Rich rewards await them at the end of their voyages.

*Extrapolating the analogy taken from biodiversity, I predict that just as there is mutation among living cells, mutation occurs in electrons too!

*The "mutant" electrons must possess different properties than those of the normal ones. But they would retain the generic properties of electrons. For example, their electric field strengths may differ, but the field will be there. Moving, they produce a magnetic field, but the strength of the field will be different. When they are discovered, many other attributes will be unveiled.

In my original exegesis, I solely concentrated on the electrons. But the core idea can be generalized to include all the fundamental particles... obviously. ("In for a penny, in for a pound!")

Even through purely intellectual reasoning, it can be shown that there are electrons and electrons. For instance, take the Big Bang. (It is purely as an instance only. The Big Bang is a Damp Squib as far as I am concerned.) Assume that a quantum of energy was responsible for the creation of electrons. By applying Fourier analysis to that quantum Q, it can be shown that electrons of different denominations will naturally emerge. QED! I leave the math part of it to you.

Admirer's explanation à la popular science: What young Bagden means can be illustrated in non-mathematical terms for the general reader as follows. Suppose you have a box of fixed size, say, one-foot by one-foot, by one-foot-high. That is one cubic foot. Now, if it is required to fill up the box with balls, there are many ways of filling the box. You may put one single ball of one-foot diameter inside it. You may put more balls of a smaller, suitable diameter. (Incidentally, it is one of the trickiest problems in mathematics). But the more relevant point is that you can fill the box with many numbers of balls, each having a different size. This is the purport of Bagden's quoting the Fourier analysis. The bundle of energy, the quantum, can be mathematically broken up to include the equivalent energies of many types of electrons. That is what he means here. Besides, it stands to reason that at the time of the Big Bang, "quanta" too must have been released of various sizes, which further bolsters Bagden's insight.

*Scholium: Personally, I do not like to indulge in experimentation. But I would like to suggest a simple one here. The techies, no doubt, can come up with more sophisticated ideas. The core of the idea is like this. Create a beam of electrons and shoot them at a target screen. The beam should preferably be wide and divergent. The stream of electrons should be as dense as possible, containing copious electrons – say, in the range of at least billions. Deflect the beam employing magnetic coils or electrically charged plates. In place of the target area, put as many sensors as possible, capable of detecting electrons, their deflection, and intensity and so on. If they (the techies) analyze all the parameters involved in the experiment, they are most likely to come across some anomalies. By carefully analyzing the anomalies, they will be able to detect the presence of my "rogue" electrons. The experiments may have to be conducted for at least two or three years continuously. More importantly, the experiments have to be replicated in selected areas covering the geographical surface of the earth to the maximum extent possible. They should use as many kinds of sources as is possible to produce electrons for the beam.

There is an alternative way to conduct the same experiment with a variation. Instead of a diverging beam, we have to use a straight beam. A bit farther away from the deflecting coil, place another coil in the opposite direction so that the deflection from the first coil will be exactly canceled. The resulting path of the beam now should be on course with its original direction. Now, place the sensors above and below the calculated (expected) "target" area. Normally, the sensors should not register there if all electrons are identical. But I predict that my 'rogue' electrons will seek out the sensors – which are out of the path of the beam. The other stipulations concerning the period of experimentation and geographical coverage do apply, of course. A period of three years for the experiments is an optimistic estimate. Probably, we may have to wait for ten years.

An improvisation, as an afterthought. In the second experiment on the parallel beam, we will be able to detect those electrons which have less mass and size than the standard normal ones. The effect of the magnetic coils will be more pronounced on the smaller electrons; that is the reason. What about the heavier, giant electrons? To detect them, we can adopt the first experiment with the divergent beam, with an improvisation. Use two magnetic coils on both sides of the beam ("up" and "down"), but the magnetic polarity of the coils shall be such that they will attract the negatively charged electrons (weakly, just a wee bit, of course). This will tend to increase the width of the beam. A bit farther away, along the route of the beam, place again two more similar coils. The beam widens further. Repeat the process 3-4 times, carefully selecting the positions of the magnetic coils at each step. The distance between the source of the beam and the target screen shall be so arranged that when the beam finally arrives at the target, its width shall be about a hundred to two hundred times greater than that at the point of the source. By this arrangement, almost all the 'normal' electrons will be concentrated near the outer surface of the beam. The heavier, rogue electrons will tend to travel along the central area, in a straight line. So, if you keep your detectors/sensors at the inner area, the chances of finding the bigger and heavier electrons will increase. We can employ a smart trick – that of tuning in. You see, in radio and TV we use a "tuning" mechanism to select the particular channel we are interested in. The same method can be employed in designing the sensors/detectors. They can be designed in such a way that they can ignore normal electrons striking them and respond only to electrons of higher denominations. The same principle can be used by placing sensors away from the periphery of the beam; these sensors having been designed to detect only electrons of smaller sizes than the normal ones. The technology men are quite a gifted lot. Just give them the specifications of what you want, and they will come up with a dozen equipments. What I am going to say is not a scientific statement, but it sure works. "Search and you shall find." So it is with my electrons.

This is so because, as I said, the Earth is less than a speck in the universe. I am fully convinced that we can get almost immediate results if the experiments are conducted in various galaxies – as many and as far away from one another as possible. Oh, if only there were some way to conduct such experiments! Note that we have to conduct the experiments "in situ," as the expression goes. Analyzing the particles reaching us from the distant galaxies may appear to be far more easy and "practical." But that won't do. Why? Because, as the distance from a source increases, the surface area is squared. (Remember the Great Man's law.) And so whatever particles that reach us represent only trillionths, quadrillionths of the original source. The exercise of searching for my electrons in such a context will be futile – like searching for the proverbial needle in the haystack. Only, the haystack will be as large as the universe!

My electrons exist, I insist. They will be discovered one day. I only hope that the lucky discoverers will remember the prophecy of a certain young lad in his teens. A gentle reminder. In your excitement (which, I can quite understand), don't forget what I said about the other particles like protons and neutrons! They too come in all sizes and shapes…Happy hunting.

Bagden's Universal Law of Creation

See what an exciting journey we have made thus far. We hope you will agree that young Bagden's grand finale was one heck of a presentation. But a magician always has one last trick up his sleeve. Bagden has one final surprise for you – The Bagden's Dictum. We will sum it up in as few words as possible, since the Dictum is a generalization of what we have already covered. It is the boldness of the generalization that makes one's jaws drop in incredulity.

From the previous experiments, and the theoretical reasoning before that, the reader may get a slightly distorted – or incomplete – idea about what young Bagden really meant in the deepest depth of his heart.

Bagden's initial foray was into the province of the rogue, mutant electrons – and other fundamental particles. But he was not satisfied with the discovery. He saw the scope for moving further – beckoning him like the enticing voices of the sirens. He pondered the subject for a while and then, unhesitatingly arrived at a grand conclusion – his Dictum. That electrons come in different sizes and shapes was no big deal to him. In a flash of brilliant perception, he saw that the rogue electrons did not form a percentage of the total number of electrons in the universe. He knew that every electron was a rogue electron, that every electron in the universe is unique, different from every other electron!! "It has to be so; it cannot be any other way," he declared.

Think of it this way. Every human being out of the seven billion is unique. Forget it. Think of the number of human beings nature has created from the beginning of human evolution. As said earlier, Nature could have produced one human being and stopped there. Nature wants to diversify, and that is why it proliferates. (Try to imagine a world where all the seven billion people are all of the same size, shape, and color!) This analogy holds true in every sphere of Nature's creation, either biological or physical. From such considerations, it can be clearly seen that no object in the universe is identical to another object. That is Bagden's Dictum. Now we will close the topic with Bagden's commentary.

"The human mind is a funny mechanism functioning in contradictory modes. Take inertia. If an object possesses great inertia, it requires a commensurate effort to start it moving. Also, once it is in motion, it is very difficult to stop it. Oftentimes, the mind sees the obvious and does not see the more obvious. The mind sees the big objects of the world and accepts that there is immense diversity. All objects directly perceivable by the eyes are different from one another with regard to size, shape, mass, and many other attributes. But somehow, it (the mind) "believes" that there must be uniformity at the smaller – microscopic – levels. It is just a fond belief only, not a fact. When you dive into the depths and reach the seafloor of intuition, you will see clearly that there cannot be absolute uniformity. Differentiation and thus diversity are the very seeds of creation."

An addendum by the admirer: In the practical world, we are flooded with electronic goods day in and day out. They all seem to be working perfectly, without any hitch. A doubt may arise in the minds of the readers that if each electron is different, as Bagden claims, then all those gadgets and goodies must have broken down long ago. The readers need not be unduly worried about it. The differences that Master Bagden is talking about are at the scale of the Planck's length – just above and below it. (Planck's length is set at 1.616199X10-35 meters). On that scale, there is enough scope for all electrons to choose their own sizes. The Planck's length is so small that it has no effect whatsoever on the level of our mundane machinery and gadgetry. To offer a perspective, even such a small object as a molecule will appear to be bigger than a galaxy when compared to the Planck's length! A concrete example can be offered in a different way. Imagine a hundred-storey skyscraper built out of concrete slabs. If the sizes of the slabs differ by fractions of a micrometer, the skyscraper will still be intact and serving its purpose perfectly well. The rogue electrons, naturally, differ by a far greater amount; some even by a million times. Yet that is nothing when compared with the thirty-fifth power of ten.

Therefore, there is nothing to worry about on account of Bagden's discovery but much to wonder about.

A conjecture: The mystique of 128

Excerpts from young Bagden's scrapbook, written down when he had attained the ripe young age of six:

"I think I have found today what could be a unique number: the number 128. Pythagoras might have discovered the perfect numbers, but in my considered opinion, I think I have discovered the COMPLETE number. I will adduce reasons for that qualifier by and by. I was able to come across this number because of analogies, which are a significant source of inspiration. In my opinion, the study of analogies helps one to expand one's mind. How endless they are, and how beautiful! Oh, I am digressing. The mind wants to leap in all directions at the same time. As a serious student of science, I must hold it in check. But it is also a blessing – this unstoppable rush of ideas. I am handicapped by mathematics. I must make amends. I hope to master mathematics by next year. But the handicap is also a blessing in disguise since ideas can flow forth from the mind uninterrupted (and uncensored!). Oh, there, I am digressing again.

I was espousing the greatness of the number 128. The context is my study of the elements. They have discovered 117 elements so far. Discovering new elements is a tough job. I guess that by the time I attain the age of sixty, they may discover another two or three more elements. My curiosity is this; after the discovery of the 120th element, will they find one more, or two more? Will the maximum number of elements be 121, 123, or 134? My bet is on the number 128!"

You will naturally ask me, "why?" Follow the logic thus. Things multiply by doubling. One becomes two, two becomes four...4-8, 8-16, etc. Continue the series, and you will arrive at our number 128. The series stops there. There is no further multiplication. That final number, 128, is the limit to the number of elements nature creates. The next number in the series is 256, and that is too ridiculously large a number for the elements. You cannot even imagine in your sci-fi books that scientists have found 256 elements. So, we accept 128 as the final limit. That is, nature itself has put a limit on itself. Obviously, there has to be a limit to the number of elements in the world; otherwise, if 256 can become 512, the argument can be stretched all the way up to infinity. Then, you know what will happen? There won't be any place in the universe for molecules! Everything will be made up of elements only. Again, you know what will happen? No molecules, no chemistry, no biology, no life, no you and me! What a thrilling argument!

There! I am digressing once more. What I actually found out was why nature should stop at the number 128. Analogy, dear boy, analogy. Go to biology. Observe how cells multiply. In the same fashion as I said before – by dividing themselves into twos. Cells multiply fast, and soon you will have more than enough if they keep up the act. You see, cells, after a certain state of multiplication, die. Nature has adopted the same strategy for diversification of the number of elements; the multiplicity stops at 128. That is why I call 128 a complete number. Of course, there are uncountable numbers of atoms – just as there are uncountable numbers of cells. But the diversification of the atoms stops at 128; that is all.

This analogy propels me to move further. Count the things of which our universe is made. For example, planets, satellites, stars, asteroids, galaxies, nebulae, black holes, pulsars, quasars, supernovae, red giants, white dwarfs, and so on. Apart from such grouped formations, the universe contains stray entities like hydrogen, helium, etc. My intuition, backed by the analogy of the elements, tells me that the above list must contain 128 items! I am willing to bet my last dime on that. If astronomers have not yet found 128 items, I urge them to search more diligently. If they have already found more than 128 items, I recommend that they revise their list and drop a few rogue items from it. (I have a sense of humor too. I am a boy, after all, and I have my privileges, you know.)

A final quiz for the day. Which is the biggest molecule? I mean big, size-wise. I am well aware that in biochemistry, we come across many complex protein molecules. There are even chains of molecules containing thousands of individual molecules linked together. I accept even such a chain as a giant molecule. Recently, I read somewhere that a DNA chain can be stretched from here to the moon! I am ready to accept that as a mega-giant molecule. Well? My molecule is a trillion trillion trillion times bigger than that! Got it? Yeah – the universe! As far as I am concerned, the whole universe is one cosmic molecule containing infinite quantities of the 128 elements we discussed just now. Well, joking apart, it is a concept worth pondering."

Absurd contradictions.

I love science; I am fascinated by it. You may say I am even addicted to it. What I like most about it is the severe logic, the process of reasoning running through it. But at times, science becomes too much, even for me. You know what I mean? Now and then, you come across a contradiction – I dare say, even an absurdity – that is too much to bear. Take this, for example.

*Heat: Let me use the word "temperature" here. Because when you handle a block of freezing ice, those guys will talk about the amount of heat energy it contains! Isn't that itself an irony to begin with? Leave it at that. Let me warm up to my topic: temperature. (I want to insert an emoticon here.)

Study what temperature does to objects. If you heat a solid object, it melts. Most solids do, anyway. A block of ice melts when heated. Metals melt at certain temperatures. If you raise the temperature further, the molten liquids vaporize. The progression as the temperature rises is from a solid state to a liquid state to a gaseous state. If you raise the temperature of a gas, and if there is nothing to hold back the gas – like a metallic cylinder – the molecules of the gas fly apart at great speeds. Mark that again. When the temperature is high, things (particles) do not stay together; they fly apart. Hope you got the drift of my logic. OK? Now hold it there for a sec. Then, look at this confusion. This confusion has got a specific name; it is called atomic fusion. (Ha, ha.)

In what they call nuclear fusion, two nuclei of an element fuse together to form a heavier nucleus, and consequently, a heavier element. (That is too smooth, very glib. I will take it up anon). In the process, a good deal of energy is released (pep talk, to soften you into acceptance). As against this, there is also what is called nuclear fission, where the nucleus of an atom (plutonium, for example) splits up into two lighter nuclei. In this process too, energy is released. As we all know, historically, the first atomic bomb was created using this knowledge. Very soon, the fusion bomb too was born; it's called the 'hydrogen bomb' since, in that device, hydrogen atoms were made to fuse together to form a new element, helium. Now, fission – breaking up of the nucleus – I can accept. It is reasonable, since, as we saw, temperature breaks up/splits up/shatters things. But fusion, by God! When temperature moves things apart (that is a very mild word), how can it make things come near? You may argue that under normal circumstances, two different metals, even mixed in powdered state, remain apart, but if they are heated sufficiently, they melt and combine to form an alloy.

Good, let me laugh before continuing. For one thing, the temperatures you are talking about are like cold ice when compared to the temperatures of nuclear bombs! Leave it aside. Secondly, if you compare the proportionate distances between two adjacent nuclei, you will be aghast. Talking in terms of meters (to give you an idea of the scales involved), if one proton of a hydrogen nucleus is right in front of you, the periphery of the atom of that element will be at an equivalent distance of ten kilometers! So, the distance between the two protons of two adjacent atoms will be twice that. Now, go ahead and imagine them rushing toward each other in a headlong embrace of love when they are heated like hell. I urge you to sincerely try your best to imagine such a scene. Things scatter apart in heat, I repeat. They do not even hug one another, let alone merging together.

There is more. Let us assume that the improbable and implausible thing happens – that the contents of the two nuclei fuse together. That is, one proton fuses with another proton of a second nucleus. Fuse, dear sir, fuse; note that. Then you should get one single proton of twice the size of a single, normal one! (I am, as those net addicts say, LOL and rolling on the ground.) To this remark, the serious-faced, frowning scientist will reply with barely held-back contempt, "The mass of a proton is fixed. Therefore, the bigger lump will naturally split into two protons." Yeah, I know that; that is why I was laughing. But my rolling on the ground was for a different reason. If the bigger mass splits into two protons, then, where is the fusion you talk of? (Confusion compounded.)

But wait. Listen to this. If the bigger mass splits up into two protons, why should the two protons stay together like inseparable lovers? As a reply to this, they (you know, who) will fall back on the stock hypothesis – that the strong force will naturally keep the protons together. To me, that answer is weak, naïve, and ridiculous in equal proportions. Bear with me, and imagine the scene. Imagine two circles sitting side by side. There is one proton in the center. There is another, identical. If one proton, somehow (God knows how), enters the other circle, then that circle can be, for the sake of argument, called the nucleus of a helium atom. Then, what happens to the first circle, which is blank?! (I am laughing again.) The circles, as I said, can only fly apart, not come together. There is another bizarre explanation offered by them. The circles (nuclei), under the intense heat, collide, smash into each other, the energy due to the temperature being sufficient to overcome the internal barriers of sub-nuclear forces, bla, bla. For one thing, the probability of such a head-on collision of two nuclei is extremely small. Bear in mind the unimaginably small sizes of the nuclei. Modern particle smashers achieve it by employing elaborate technical equipment, costing millions and millions of dollars. For another thing, even if such a head-on collision occurs, our two circles – which I gently asked you to imagine – will be smashed into non-existence!

To my independently thinking mind, this explanation of nuclear fusion is a fable; a modern fable couched in appropriately masquerading terminology. But the fusion of hydrogen to helium does happen. So, the obvious conclusion is that there must be a different explanation for it – the real one. I intend to discover it someday.

I am still not done with the fable of fusion. There are other perplexing considerations too. Apart from the proton, there is the mysterious character, neutron, which has no business to be nestling inside the nucleus. Normal hydrogen does not have a neutron in its nucleus; it contains one electron orbiting outside the nucleus and one proton inside. (Incidentally, hydrogen is the only element that does not contain a neutron. A deep mystery lies behind this. I will dig it up someday). A helium nucleus has two neutrons in it. So, two normal hydrogen atoms cannot combine into a helium atom since they do not have neutrons. We need the second kind of hydrogen atom – the deuterium, H_2 – for that to happen. Well, back to the neutrons. In the collision/confusion of the two circles, I said, we have to give a thought to the neutrons too. The coming together (the peaceful co-existence) of two protons is itself a highly improbable event. Now we have to believe that the same thing happens with the two neutrons also. Meanwhile, remember that neutrons do not carry any charge, which makes the probability of their coming together even less. To make the improbable even more improbable, you have to appreciate that the two events – that of protons intermingling, and of neutrons agreeing to stay together – are supposed to happen at the same time. I will show you the yet more improbable occurrence. Let us be highly credulous for the time being and accept that two protons came together and stayed put, that two neutrons did the same. Please appreciate the nuance here. A proton and a proton made friendship. Good. A neutron and a neutron made friendship. Good. But, dear sirs, dear gentlemen, scholars, and skeptics, a proton-proton pair is free to go its own way, just like a neutron-neutron pair. The funny part of the fable – a breath-knocking improbability – is that the protons and neutrons get inspired by the atmosphere of mutual entente, and they agree further to come together and stay together. (It is as if two separate nations were overpowered by feelings of love and sealed a covenant to merge into a single nation!) This story makes excellent content for a comedy, but we are talking science here; we have to view it with somber and sapient faces.

Oh, I forgot. I am still not done with the fable. Haven't we forgotten something? Electrons, of course! There can even be an atom without a neutron, like your standard hydrogen atom, but there cannot be an atom without an electron. (At least, as far as our present knowledge of science goes.) In the previous paragraph, I dealt with the double improbability. For what I am going to present now, I have run out of words to specify the improbability of the event. (Something like improbability raised to the power of improbability?)

Back to our two circles again. Imagine an electron furiously orbiting the circle (that is, the nucleus). When the two circles (nuclei) collide in the myth of fusion, God only knows where exactly the two electrons are located. Even God may not know, if you believe in the uncertainty principle – the New Testament of Science. In the mighty bedlam of the thermo-nuclear (con)fusion, you have to believe that electrons somehow manage to exchange signals of eternal love, cross the borders of the two circles to stay together. No, not exactly; they agree to act together. Their agreement to do so is, of course, inspired by the merging of the two nations (P-P and N-N). So, they celebrate the historical event by orbiting the new nucleus! I am too exhausted to laugh anymore.

There must be some other explanation for the formation of a helium atom out of two H_2 atoms. My intuition also tells me that temperature has got nothing to do with it. To find out the real answer to this mystery, we have to knock at new doors. I intend to find the answer before I die. (My willpower is so strong that I intend not to die if I do not find the answer!)"

Comment by the admirer: Well, the precocious fellow did possess willpower. He succeeded in his search. Elsewhere in the notes of his mature years, we find his discoveries of the spaceniks, the "effects," and space-software. His theory of spaceniks and effects adequately explains the fusion of elements – apart from many other phenomena of nature.

Considering his age and his irrepressible enthusiasm, his somewhat acerbic language can be excused.

How neutral is neutral?

Young Bagden's scrapbook follows two styles. Often, he wrote as if he were having a monologue with himself. His writings also appear, in some instances, as if he were trying to explain something to others, though he did not perhaps intend to compose a full-blown article. What follows below is an example of one such style.

"The other day, I was struck by a casual remark that I came across in a textbook on magnetism. The author says that there are no magnetic monopoles. That set me thinking furiously.

All of us know that a magnet has two poles: a north pole and a south pole. (Imagine me holding my tongue in check, there. I saw an old flick yesterday in which Charles Bronson introduces a horse to his Japanese partner with, 'This is a horse.' Ergo.) But seriously, the poles of a bar magnet come in a pair because the magnetic lines of force move from one pole to another, as the textbook explains. It is analogous to the way electricity flows—from the positive terminal of a battery to the negative terminal. (To confound you, the book further clarifies that the actual current, that is electrons, flow from the negative to the positive!) Back to our magnet with the north and south poles. As you know, if the magnet is freely suspended, its north pole always points toward the north pole of the earth. That is how the names for the magnet's poles came to be designated as north and south. One of the oldest inventions of mankind, the compass, was created using this property of the magnet. (Oh, boy, there I go again, shooting off my irrepressible mouth). Back again to the magnetic poles. The lines of force emanate from one pole (say the north) and terminate at the other (the south) because the potential at one end is higher than that at the other end. A magnetic field surrounds the magnet, and you can measure the strength of the field at various points and see that the field strength varies from point to point. The main point is that we have two poles. A monopole naturally means a single pole. So, when the textbook says that there are no magnetic monopoles, it makes sense. You need two poles: one from where the magnetic field starts and the other where it ends. The concept, to my mind, is eminently sensible. I intuitively feel that this phenomenon must be universal.

Let us take a leap from here and examine something strange – the field of electric charges. (Pun intended.) The subatomic particles are of three types: those with a positive charge like the protons, those with a negative charge like the electrons, and those that are neutral like the neutrons. This is a very peculiar and mystifying state of affairs. Did you notice it? If you adopt the terms of magnetic poles (+, - or N, S), you will see that whereas the magnetic poles come in pairs, the fundamental particles do not. They are either positive or negative. To make it worse, there are the alien neutrals – the neutrons. The magnet has a magnetic field, and the subatomic particles have a field (charge). So, why this anomaly? Every cell in my brain screams that such a disparity should not exist in nature. I think the neutrons hold the clue. (They are marginally "heavier" than protons).

My answer to the riddle of the neutrons' neutrality is this. The normal explanation that a neutron carries no charge is incorrect! The neutron covertly carries two charges: a positive and a negative one. The plus and the minus add up to zero! My intuition tells me that it must be this way only. Then you may wonder how a positive and a negative field (charge) can co-exist. Look at the figure below, and the concept will become as clear as daylight.

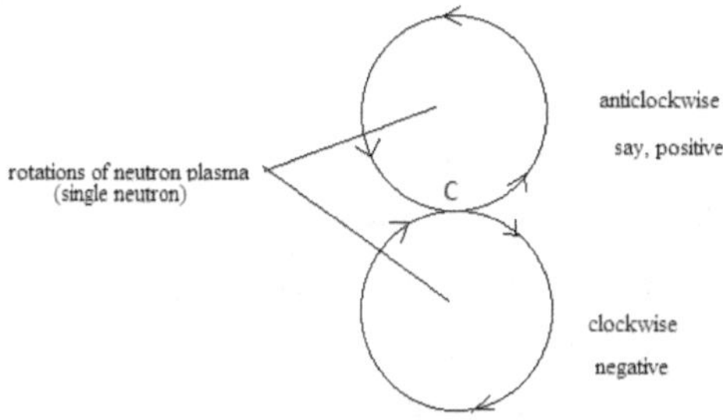

The positive and the negative cancel each other; neutron as a whole is neutral.

Figure 14

Start from the center point 'C' of the figure of eight. The arrows indicate the directions of the lines of force along the upper and lower loops. If the upper half follows an anticlockwise movement, the lower one follows a clockwise direction—and vice versa. Therefore, if the top half represents a positive charge, the lower half represents a negative charge; and vice versa. The net result will be a null charge—that of the neutron. This must be the mechanism underlying the mysterious behavior of the neutron.

Note here that the "lines of force" were introduced to convey the concept. Their rotation and direction are the important properties we have to focus on. The positive and negative charges arise because of them (the rotations). The natural question that crops up here is that if the concept of lines of force is discarded, then what is it that is rotating? The simplest answer is that it is the content of the neutron itself which is rotating—somewhat akin to a whirlpool. To give you an analogy, the movement of electrons produces a magnetic "field". In a similar fashion, we can conceive that the whirlpool-like rotation of the contents of a neutron produces a "charge" around it. Two charges, note it; the upper and the lower. This scenario offers us a new model for the neutron. It is not a spherical "blob". In one sense, it is a single blob, and in another sense, it is two blobs. The two blobs, for practical purposes, are a single unit. Imagine a balloon. By holding it in both hands and carefully manipulating—twisting, for example—you can create a three-dimensional figure of eight. The content of the neutron can be called "neutron plasma," to keep it simple, and we have now a fairly beautiful new model for the neutron.

There is also an elegance here. In the analogy of the magnet, the lines of force leave one pole and end at the other pole—two points, please note. Look at our figure again and notice the central point 'C.' The lines of force in this diagram start from one point (C) and return to the same point. Thus, we do not need two poles. That is how a single charge is created.

One more advantage can be seen in this model; it can explain better the mechanism by which neutrons stay together inside the nucleus of an element. The nuclei of all elements contain neutrons. This is a very peculiar (anomalous) situation since the neutrons are chargeless, and therefore, under normal laws, they have no business staying together inside the nucleus. (The same can be said of the protons too, the anomaly being greater). At present, they explain this situation by bringing in complicated—in my personal opinion, unnatural—interactions, exchanges of some other kind of particles like mesons, gluons, and so on. I question why we should have to bring in more and more particles. A far more natural explanation exists.

Look at the figure eight in the previous illustration. The top and bottom halves, I said, have different charges. Yes? Now take a second neutron and place it upside-down next to the first one—something like putting two number 6s together, with one of them being upside-down. (My somber apologies there.) Under such a condition, the positive half of a neutron will be facing the negative half of the other neutron, and vice versa. I need not explain the obvious now. The positive and the negative attract each other, and thus, the two neutrons stay together. A similar mechanism can be envisaged in the case of three and more neutrons.

I think the above explanation of mine is really brilliant. Normally, I should feel bashful for saying so, but in the fiery passion I am carrying for scientific research, bashfulness has no place. The fury of my thoughts is propelling me further now. You see, the mechanism I offered for the neutrons can be adopted in the case of protons too!

Yeah. This is a beaut. I said that a single, isolated charge is an anomaly. (Link it up with the magnetic monopole.) The proton, as observed, measured, and tested, etc., carries a positive charge. But I surmise that the proton too, like my neutron, carries both charges—positive and negative. But the proton behaves like a positively charged particle. But, but, but. Hold on, friends; I am about to expose the card up my sleeve. First, answer my simple questions concerning practical matters. If your monthly expenditure is 5000 dollars and your income during that period is 6000 dollars, are you not on the positive side financially? If you earn 6000 dollars and spend 7000 dollars, are you not in the negative? That is all. Similar is the case with the proton! Look at the familiar figure of eight once again. The upper and the lower lobes, each lobe representing an opposite charge, are of equal size. Yes, no? Now, just make the upper lobe 90 times bigger than the lower. In that case, if the upper half represents a positive charge and the lower, a negative one, the overall charge of the figure will be overwhelmingly positive. There! That is your proton. Reverse the situation, and in that case, you will have an overwhelmingly negative charge on hand. That is your electron.

As they say, one thing leads to another. This new model of mine for the proton can explain beautifully why protons stay together inside the nucleus. Just as we laid two neutrons in the uroborous fashion (I am bashful to use the simile of numbers six and nine for a second time), we can put two protons too in the same fashion. The positive lobe attracts the negative lobe of the other proton. The negative lobe of the same proton is attracted by the positive lobe of the other proton. Thus, mutual attraction is assured. The simplicity of this explanation is that we can do away with extraneous assumptions like gluons. Even the so-called "strong force" can be discarded!

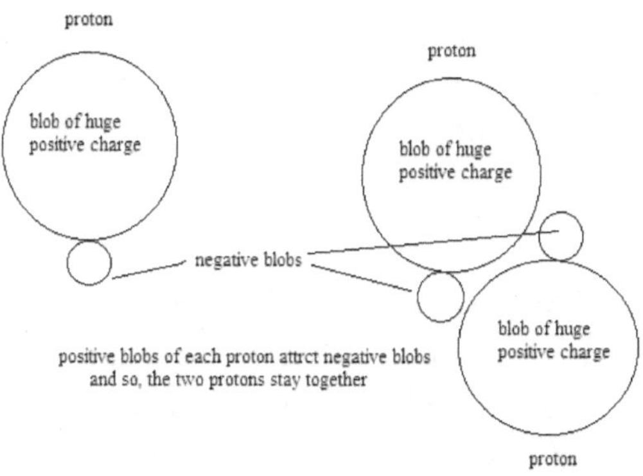

Figure 15

We can extend the same analogy in the case of electrons too. But I guess the proportionate sizes of the upper and lower lobes will be different—probably in the ratio of 99:1. Actually, my desire is to submit a thesis on this topic, but at present, I do not have the necessary mathematical knowledge, without which nobody will accept an essay on theoretical science. I intend to master mathematics soon, though I confess that I do not love it much.

Since I have come this far, I can as well move further. Guess what? It is gravity, dear pals! The gravitational force is one of the great mysteries in nature. As you know, other kinds of forces are dual by nature; force can be attractive or repulsive. Like magnetic poles repel each other and opposite poles attract each other. The same happens with electrically charged particles. Even in the case of mechanical (that is physical) force, there is a push and there is a pull. But gravity, the quirkiest force, always attracts. They have posited the graviton as a messenger across the gravitational field—the way photons are messenger particles for the electromagnetic field.

That concept of the graviton is very convenient for my theory! I know you have already outguessed me. But let me spell it out, anyway. Just like my neutrons, gravitons too have two lobes of equal size and opposite charges. I have already explained how by the soixante-neuf method, two neutrons get stuck to each other. Apply the same principle to the gravitons. Presto! you have two gravitons that attract each other. (In case you have any doubts on this, please go back to the figure of eight for my neutrons and study it once more). I ardently hope that they will soon detect and confirm the existence of gravitons. Then my explanations will be truly vindicated.

I have scribbled all the ideas in a fury of inspiration. My only regret is that I am unable to provide a solid mathematical skeleton. There are many numbers of brilliant mathematicians out there. I am sure that if they are willing, they can easily build up such a firm skeleton. Amen.

Tailpiece

My friends say that I have a great sense of humor. I agree. The only problem is that my humor is erratic and unpredictable. Now and then it encroaches into the serious (and dignified) field of science. Personally, I do not mind it. And seriously, humor often provides you with new insights. What I am going to propose now may sound like fiction or fantasy to you. But I am serious. Here we go.

Till now, we have considered the inter-nucleus elements as invariables. That is, the nuclei of all elements contain protons and neutrons in varying numbers and proportions, and only those two particles. I am proposing this bizarre idea – why not the third and equally important particle, the electron? Are you shocked? Not me. Think of it this way: Protons repel one another, but yet, they are found bound inside the nucleus. Neutrons have no reason at all to stay together, yet they are found bound inside the nucleus. So, why not electrons do the same? The idea is thrilling (and spine-chilling to some of those square nerds in the labs). There is one possible objection to my proposal. Electrons being negative and protons being positive, they may mutually interact and destroy one another, giving birth to new particles, and so on. Such a possibility can be overcome by hypothesizing another field like your strong force. The gluons are supposed to hold the protons together, according to them (Glue – gluons; see, they too have a sense of humor). Well, let me introduce a variant of that strong force. Let there be repellons, à la gluons. Only, the repellons help in keeping the electrons and protons from coming too close, short of a fatal embrace. From the descriptions I have read so far, the gluons have been doing their job very diligently for the past 14 billion years. Give my repellons a chance, and you will see wonderful nuclei everywhere with three nations in peaceful co-existence – protons, neutrons, electrons, et al. In fact, if you re-examine my figure of eight, you will see that the gluons and repellons can be represented by a single, composite messenger particle with two lobes. The upper part can act like a gluon, and the lower one can act like my repellon. Such a composite particle can hold the protons together with one lobe while at the same time, keeping the electrons at bay by the efficacy of its other lobe. An atom playing host to three particles in its nucleus must possess extraordinary properties. There is no objection if some electrons orbit around the nucleus. In the normal world, the count of protons and electrons is equal. So, in my new atom, half the electrons can stay inside the nucleus along with protons, and the other half of them can orbit the nucleus. I have no objection. In fact, that will be convenient, as otherwise, if there are no orbital electrons, we cannot get electricity!

The above idea is not wacky or far-fetched. Since the discovery of the atomic nucleus and the three particles, we have been accustomed to that concept (the old model of the atom). We have not searched deep enough and far enough. In the vastness of space, there must be some riches where my kind of atom would exist. I am saying this because the conditions just after the big bang were imponderably hot. Anything could have happened there. Search, and you will definitely find one day, atoms with three particles inside – protons, neutrons, and electrons. Just a matter of time. I am saying this also because I have observed quite an interesting thing in scientific research. If you conceive a reasonably tenable concept, somebody or another is going to actually discover its existence! Please do not think perversely and construe the above statement as damaging. My observation has been uttered in a positive, optimistic spirit. The meson, the god's particle, deflection of light in a gravitational field, the black holes are just a few among a plethora of examples which support my assertion.

Addendum: Oh, I am not finished with it yet. While we are at it, we may as well conceive of other exotic elements whose atoms do not contain neutrons in their nuclei. We already have one such representative among us – the normal hydrogen atom (It does not have a neutron in its nucleus). Since the Big Bang has already created one such atom, there must be an atom with two protons and two electrons, but no neutrons. If you are in the mood, you can call it "lame helium"! There must be many more such atoms out there in the deep recesses of unexplored space.

Boy, I am shivering with excitement again. Look at the solar system. There is only one sun, having a huge mass. There are many planets orbiting the sun, with the planets being far smaller than the sun. Okay? The point of interest here is that eight to nine planets (leave alone comets) of smaller size can (and do) revolve around one central object of very heavy size. Carry the analogy to the inside of the atom. (After all, the Rutherford model too is a similar analogy). The proton is far heavier than the electron, about 200 times, roughly speaking. Now, let us stick to the "one nucleus, one proton only" principle. We can construct the following scenario using that principle. In the beginning, the Big Bang created a simple nucleus with a single proton. (Search and replace 'the Big Bang' for 'god'.) The proton, being positively charged, begins to attract electrons in its vicinity. Considering the mass ratio of 2000:1 between the proton and the electron, we can safely assume that at least 100 electrons could be captured by one proton into an orbit. Considering also the unimaginably chaotic conditions at the time of the Big Bang and being fair in our assessment, we can surmise that a single proton need not necessarily capture all the 100 electrons it is capable of doing. So, what happens? There will be many categories of our "one nucleus, one proton" system. Atoms will be created containing electrons ranging from one to one hundred—all atoms possessing one proton only in the nucleus. What wonderful properties must such atoms be endowed with! They must all be good conductors of electricity, for starters.

Such a situation, as I have described above, is possible. You see, Nature delights in its play of permutations and combinations. We can call such atoms "alien atoms," if we wish. Why have we not found them? It is simply because we have not bothered to search for them. The infallible slogan, "Search and you will find," is eminently applicable in this case. We have been spending so much energy and time searching for aliens. A fraction of that will suffice to discover my alien atoms. No "LOL," please; I am serious.

Comment from the Admirer: Young Bagden might have something of interest there. The idea per se is quite intriguing. But we think he made a serious omission. While comparing the proton and electron, he took their mass into consideration. Mass plays a major role in gravity. He should have compared the relative strengths of the charges instead. But then, on second thoughts, we can see that the charges of the electron and proton are equal (and opposite) – about 1.60 X 10-19 C. That is why the precocious brat kept schtum on this point!

Manufacturing of elements: - Atomic cloning

I am speculating here, but I think it is worth doing. Note that the word is "manufacturing," not "transmutation." Alchemists through the ages have dabbled in transmutation only. They did not have access to the kind of extreme knowledge of matter (and materials) that we of the present day are fortunate to possess. I think that the transmutation of one element into another is no big deal. We now accomplish it through fission and fusion. Nature does it through spontaneous decay. (Some of the mysterious figures in the history of alchemy might probably have succeeded in their efforts.) My intellectual venture is of a quite different kind. I mean, manufacturing an element out of nature's building blocks – the three fundamental particles present in all elements.

If we are able to actually manufacture an element using protons, neutrons, and electrons, I think that would be the next greatest step in science and technology. I am fairly confident that it is possible to achieve that goal. Come to think of it, it is more a matter of technology than of science. Everyone knows that all matter consists of the three particles: P, N, E. The real problem is how to bind them in one place (and in the desired proportions). A kind of analogy already exists. We have been able to manufacture new materials that never existed in nature before – thousands and thousands of them. Chemistry, metallurgy, and physics have been able to achieve that by using the existing elements. The next step, as I said, is surely that of being able to "build" the elements themselves out of the fundamental particles available in abundance.

Of course, nature already did it billions of years back, as the Big Bang theory claims. The main difficulty in duplicating nature's creation is that we need unbelievably enormous temperatures (and energies) to bring about fusion.

Having said all that, let me now proceed with my speculation. It is based strongly (very) on intuition (but logic is not far behind). I will argue my case from two angles—theirs and mine. First, examine their "strong force" postulate. It is a postulate as far as I am concerned. The strong force is one of the four fundamental forces as per the generally accepted standard model. You know one funny thing? The strong force is supposed to be the strongest among the four forces. It is stronger than the electromagnetic force by a factor of thousands. And yet, whereas the weaker of the two has a theoretical range of infinity, the stronger one is supposed to be limited to not an infinite but an infinitesimal range! I simply cannot swallow it, even if it is forced (yes, the force) down my throat. But that is a different issue not particularly relevant to my argument. OK, let us accept the strange strong force. But my intuition is that the strong force is not "boxed in" inside the nucleus only. It exists everywhere; it must. For what is a nucleus, anyway? Is it a box, a tin can? The "nucleus" is designated so because, in a particular location in space, protons and neutrons stay together, with electrons orbiting them at a safe distance. If you argue that the 'strong force' is existent only between protons and protons (whatever), then the strong force is not an independent force at all, and therefore we can reject it and adopt my figure of eight configuration, with all the concomitant explanations I have offered! Ergo, like a good sophist, I say the strong force exists in space independently. My second line of argument—with relevance to the manufacturing we are discussing—is, naturally, my figure of eight configuration for the protons and neutrons. (I have written down the whole shebang in my diary last week).

These ideas are the groundwork for my next proposal. Bring enough protons and neutrons together and patiently wait it out. Sooner or later, some of them will group themselves into an atomic nucleus. The law of probability guarantees it. There is a subtle, refined aspect to my proposal, which is diametrically opposite to that of the conventional method. You see, at present, it has become a rage to experiment with particles by boosting their energy. I say that is unnecessary for my type of experiment. I say, invite the particles to a conference, figuratively speaking, and then you go away, leaving them to manage their own ways of interaction. To use a different metaphor, you do not do the cooking; the cooking will take care of itself. Once the cooking is done, you just add the spice. What I mean is, after allowing sufficient chance for the protons and neutrons to group into nuclei, you introduce electrons amidst them. The same law of probability guarantees that atoms will be formed (manufactured) at random. I provide below a schematic diagram with a few explanatory notes to give you a clearer picture of what is involved in my proposal.

SP in the figure is the source of protons. They have already mastered the art of isolating protons. The simplest of the hydrogen atom, H1, has one proton and one electron. If you take hydrogen atoms and knock off the electrons, you are left with protons. The next step is to direct the protons towards the Seed Chamber. The seed chamber is where we expect new atoms to grow. Plates P1, P2, P3, etc. (duct, in the figure) are charged positively. Since the protons

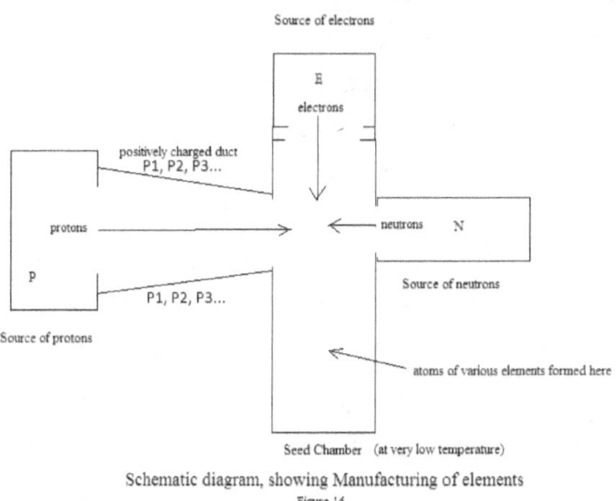

Schematic diagram, showing Manufacturing of elements
Figure 16

are also positively charged, the plates reflect back any wayward protons. The plates thus serve as a guiding tunnel through which the protons arrive at the seed chamber. Two minor details are to be noted here. The plates are just sufficiently charged positively so that the protons are not unduly accelerated. We need our protons to be in as low a state of energy as possible. To aid it, we arrange the passage through P1, P2, P3, etc., in such a way that the temperature drops down starting from the source towards the seed chamber.

On the other side of the seed chamber, we have SN, the source of neutrons, from which we introduce neutrons directly into the chamber. Managing neutrons is a tricky business since they have no charge. Producing them is no problem. There are many ways. Atomic fission is one example. (They have even invented the so-called "clean bomb" which produces a zillion neutrons, sending everybody into a silent grave in a clinically sanitary way). Directing the neutrons into the seed chamber should not pose much of a problem for the techies. It is their job, after all, to prepare blueprints and working models, once we scientists feed them with the basic ideas.

After this is done, the protons and neutrons meet in the seed chamber. You may even call it the womb. As I said, the strong fields (note the plural, please) exist inside the chamber. Since their range (read, size) is unimaginably small, there should be more than plenty of them inside the chamber. Here is where the law of probability plays its role. When protons and neutrons enter this zone, it is the job of the fields to grab them, forming different kinds of nuclei. The size of a nucleus is roughly in the range of 10-12 cm. The ingredients are a thousand times still smaller. We have to bear this in mind and ensure that we cram plenty of protons and neutrons into our chamber of conception. We leave the rest to nature and the laws of probability. Both are very potent and efficient, so there is no room for anxiety on our part. Patience is the main key. We wait. I am opting for both choices here, as I said. If the strong fields choose to play hard with the laws of probability, then the second choice, my figure of eight theory, is there waiting to show its hand. So, one way or the other, we have to get enough—and more than enough—of nuclei of elements, the proton-neutron congregations. We keep the seed chamber at as low a temperature as possible. The bottom portion, we keep at even lower temperatures, for reasons which I will tell you just a bit later. As regards the waiting period, I prefer one week (or at least twenty-four hours if you are impatient).

Now we proceed to the final act. After the "incubation" period, we pour electrons into the chamber. SE in the figure is the source of electrons. Since the techies have mastered the art of producing and manipulating electrons, this part of our experiment is a breeze. Just keep pouring electrons into the chamber. Inside the chamber, the proton-neutron congregations are eagerly waiting for this event. When the stream of electrons enters, it is a dead cert that a sizeable percentage of the electrons will be captured by the newly formed nuclei. In spite of the low temperature inside the chamber, the particles will be in a state of highly random motion—obviously. Therefore, not all the electrons will be able to 'seed' the nuclei. The speeds and angles at which the inrushing electrons and the nuclei meet one another are important. But still, the laws of probability are on our side. Nuclei will begin capturing electrons in such a way that electrons will begin orbiting them.

Naturally, there will be various combinations of protons and electrons, which means that atoms of many elements are going to be formed inside the chamber. So, it is better to design the height of the chamber to be greater compared to its length and width. The lighter elements like hydrogen and helium tend to float up, so, in such a design as above, the segregation and detection of the newly created atoms will be easier. Needless to say, the heavier metallic atoms will collect at the bottom.

This, in short, is the methodology for manufacturing the elements on our own. By trial and error, the design of the three main units, the SP, SN, and seed chamber, can be perfected. A few tips may serve handy. The obvious one, of course, is that all three units must be vacuumized to ensure that there shall be no atoms of any elements at the beginning.

The seed chamber too is suitably charged positively so that the protons are kept herded inside. The neutron source may even be kept inside the seed chamber if it is found difficult to control the stream of neutrons.

The experiment that I have outlined may seem far-fetched to some people. But my every nerve of intuition is screaming that the experiment will succeed if we persevere. It has to succeed; if not today, at least tomorrow. Then it will herald a new political and economic era.

Afterthoughts

I want to ask you some questions. Is the total number of electrons in the universe constant? To clarify, suppose that 121 electrons were created by the Big Bang 14 billion years ago. (I am suggesting 121, to make it easier for counting—tongue-in-cheek.) Even after 14 billion years, are we left with only 121 electrons, not an electron more? Electrons (in a free state) may possibly react with other particles and be destructed, as when they meet other positively charged particles. Besides, modern gadgets of all sorts are employed to knock off rivers of electrons from suitable materials. That means the population of electrons in the universe is decreasing. I took electrons as an example; you can add other fundamental particles to the list.

Actually, my main question is different. Were 121 electrons created at the time of the Big Bang and were they not created further on? Did creation stop there? From the way the cosmologists describe it, it looks as if nature was inspired by a burst of inspiration (for a very brief second) and thereafter went to sleep, forever!! (I am reminded of the old phrase, "flash in the pan.") I simply cannot swallow such a concept.

So, creation expired very fast indeed. If you study the literature of the Big Bang, you will appreciate the subtle logic that the one true act of creation was the Bang only, which lasted for less than a nanosecond. Everything else that has followed after that, for these 14 billion years, is only fallout!! It is a detritus of the Bang! Seen that way, we are all—along with the universe—dead things moving along out of sheer force of momentum!

I repeat, I cannot swallow such a concept. I strongly feel that creation is a continuous process. That is why I say that (at least) the fundamental particles like protons, neutrons, and electrons are still being created. We can discover that fact if only we are willing. But mere local, laboratory experiments may not be enough in the attempt to search for them. The reason is obvious; just compare the size of your biggest laboratory with that of the universe. In one way, if my suggested experiment for manufacturing elements succeeds, at least it will indirectly vindicate my postulate that nature too must be doing it, unbeknownst to us. Hunt, hunt, hunt, that is all I can say for now.

The questions naturally arise: if creation is still happening, will it keep on forever, will it end, and if so, when? I close this discussion by simply dubbing such questions as futile or even unwarranted.

Turin there, Turin here

What I am going to propose in this short essay is fueled by a spirit of defiance. But be assured that it is not perverse. You just need a bit of patience and empathy. Tune in to my frequency, and it won't be difficult to follow the apparently bizarre idea I am going to place before you.

The whole ballyhoo starts with a very disconcerting idea proposed by Alan Turing. (Nobody calls his idea perverse, you see.) The core idea proposed by him runs thus: Suppose there is a machine designed to mimic the behavior and responses of a human being. Then we can claim that there is no difference between the two! The idea is about seventy years old by now, yet it has not become stale. A good deal of literature exists on the topic. The computer was just being born in those days, and robotics had not advanced to the extent it has now.

To take the present day example, imagine you are carrying on a conversation with a robot. To make it look more real, the robot's appearance resembles that of a human. The robot can even move its limbs, neck, eyes, mouth, and so on. You pit your wits against the robot, trying your best to fool it. No go. The robot has been perfectly programmed, and it carries on a conversation with you just like a human being.

The machine (that is the word they dote on) is thus not distinguishable from a human being. You may argue that you have a soul, that you have an "ego," an "I," and so on. The machine courteously claims that it too possesses all those very things! You cannot disprove it, actually! Those who are obsessively fond of this subject go even to the length of saying that the machine can be said to have consciousness too! I am not introducing this subject for fun; a lot of scientists are studying it seriously. So, you too, better take it that way. That is my advice.

Of course, my advocating the advice has an ulterior motive. It supports and abets my proposition! In the man-and-machine conundrum of the above paragraphs, the underlying principle is the identity of behaviors. The actual, physical construction (of either man or machine) is almost of no importance. My proposition shamelessly adopts that principle, transposing it onto another platform. I am not teasing you deliberately; I am priming you gradually so that when you hear me out, you may not jump out of your skin. Here we go.

Have you ever seen an atom – I mean, one single atom – with your naked eye? Of course, nobody can ever do so since an atom is ludicrously small. Even imagining its tininess is difficult. If you thought my question was ridiculous, consider this – I propose to build an atom big enough to be visible to the naked eye, without the aid of any kind of instrument. In fact, with suitable technological support, you may even see my atom from a distance of a hundred feet, maybe a kilometer, or more. (No distance limit, ideally). The way to build such an atom is to borrow the Turin Concept and suitably transform it.

Well, structurally, an atom has a nucleus at the center, with one or more electrons orbiting the nucleus. The nucleus contains one or more protons corresponding to the number of electrons and a slightly smaller number of neutrons cohabiting with the protons. This is the essential structure of an atom. Okay?

Well, just build a physical model of the atom – only on a large scale. (Working on such a model will be far more convenient and easier since you do not need costly and super-delicate instruments.) Yet, the job is not as easy as it sounds. Think of the proportionate sizes of the parts involved, and you will see what I mean. We have to preserve the scales if our virtual atom is going to represent the real atom (and, hopefully, duplicate it in every way). Ponder the sizes and masses of the ingredients involved.

Electron, size – 2.82 X 10^{-15} meters, radius

Proton, size – 1.11 X 10^{-15} meters

Atom, size – about 10^{-8} cm

Nucleus, size – 10^{-12} cm

Neutron, mass, 1.6749286 X 10^{-27} kg – charge = nil

Proton, mass, 1.6726231 X 10^{-27} kg – charge 1.60 X 10^{-19} C

Electron, mass, 9.1093897 X 10^{-31} kg – charge = 1.60 X 10^{-19} C

Virtual atom:

So, our virtual atom will have a nucleus – say, a sphere containing tiny balls representing protons and neutrons. If you wish to have the tiny balls with sizes of one centimeter to make them visible, the nucleus sphere will have to be a thousand times bigger. That is, one thousand centimeters – 10 meters! Then, the electrons should be roughly a hundred kilometers away from the center of the nucleus! In view of this, I suggest we better (wisely) discard the scaling of our virtual atom in terms of distance. Most probably, it does not distort or alter our model. But we should stick to the masses and charges correctly. Charge-wise, there is no problem since the proton and electron are of equal strength but of opposite kind. Mass-wise, our virtual proton (and neutron) should be about 1900 times heavier than the electron. If you go at it in a straightforward way, you will face an insurmountable difficulty. Notice the sizes of the two particles in the above table. The proton is just twice the size of an electron, but its mass is 1800 times more. That means the density of the material out of which you are going to construct your "proton ball" should be roughly about 4000 times more than that of your electron's material. The restriction is that both "materials" should be the same! So, a practical solution is to use a suitable gas such that, in the "proton ball," the gas can be sealed in under very high pressure. Naturally, the gas in the electron ball should be of negative ions, while that in the proton ball should be of positive ions. I am sure that our brilliant technology can solve such minor problems quite easily. The neutron is only marginally heavier than the proton, but of neutral charge. If you want to build a complex atom (apart from hydrogen), you will have to fill up your neutron ball with the same gas, under the same pressure, but with a neutral charge. It is better to start our experiment with the simplest atom: that of hydrogen. For building the nucleus of any other atom, you will require two or more proton balls. Since they are positively charged, they will repel one another. Nature uses the "strong force" to keep protons together in the nucleus. We may have to use mechanical devices like strong glues or clamps to keep our virtual proton balls (and neutrons) as one compact assembly. We can safely leave it to our techie friends to achieve the desired configuration. (They welcome such challenges; they thrive on them!) After you build the nucleus, you have to make the electron balls revolve around the nucleus ball – at a reasonable distance. It is just one more job for our pals. Keep in mind, too, that what we are describing is not a "flat" model of two dimensions. We are constructing a three-dimensional model; a sine qua non.

To cut it short, let's imagine we have actually constructed a three-dimensional model of a hydrogen atom, imitating it in every way. Then, the Turin Dogma asserts that there is no difference between such a virtual hydrogen atom and the real one. I wholeheartedly support it. The same applies to any virtual atom created by us. Our atom may be one-inch in diameter, one-foot, or even the size of a ten-story building; it makes no conceptual difference. I think this is a very exciting concept that may open new avenues for further research in many branches of science, ushering in new technological innovations as well.

We have to note here that since the advent of computers, simulation has become as easy as child's play, but what I am suggesting is a different ballgame. We are simulating by employing actual physical entities.

There are further intriguing possibilities to pursue, to actually test and verify. For example, if we bring one virtual (how about the word "artificial"?) hydrogen atom in contact with another virtual atom of oxygen, will they combine to form a molecule of water, as it happens with real atoms? I dare to speculate that the two should give birth to a molecule of water - artificial water, naturally!

If only we can test the possibility and see!

I am serious by nature, but I have a healthy sense of humor too. Suppose you actually carry out an experiment as suggested above and you do not get an artificial molecule of "art water." What could possibly have gone wrong? The answer lies with Nature, which loves to play with us, clever human beings, now and then. The secret is hidden in the old "ratios and proportions"! Go back and notice the proportionate sizes of the proton and the distance from the center of the nucleus to the outermost electron. To be faithful to nature, if you build a virtual proton of one cm size, your virtual electron should orbit it roughly at a distance of 100 kilometers! Manage to build such a model first, and then ask me questions.

If you still have doubts about my virtual atoms theory, consider a simple analogy. You can construct a watch with a one-inch dial. You can make a clock with a one-foot dial or one having a face as large as that of Big Ben. Hypothetically, you can even have a clock that's ten kilometers in size. The fundamental operation is that the clock should tick once in a second, the minute hand should make one revolution in an hour, and the hour hand, once, in twelve hours. Materials used for the construction and sizes are of secondary importance. As the bard would have said, a clock of any size... I hope you have stopped your remonstration by now.

Extensions and generalizations.

Actually, what we discussed above is, as the good old trite phrase puts it, "only the tip of the iceberg." The doors to many exciting possibilities lie open ahead of us, beckoning us alluringly.

We begin with a grand generalization, the BST – Bagden's Simulation Theorem, if I am permitted to pat my own back. The theorem states that any system that simulates an existing system is equivalent to the existing system except in terms of actual physical identity. The possibilities of simulation are limitless. Even flights of fancy cannot be excluded from its ambit. I would like to entertain you (but seriously) with one example before we close the topic.

A flight of fancy: We select a plant as a case in study. We proceed to create a virtual plant using the simulation technique at every stage. The bare essentials will be as follows:

*First, we create a central processing unit (à la the CPU of a computer). Our CPU can physically manufacture whatever is demanded by the plant for its growth and productivity. The CPU is located just above the ground on the spot where we wish to grow our VP (it could even be a pot).

*Roots: Simulating a plant, our CPU sends its tentacles boring into the earth. Naturally, the CPU is able to manufacture appropriate synthetic materials suitable for specialized parts of the plant, like roots (with semi-permeable membranes), trunk, branches, shoots, leaves, flowers, etc. We just help the plant by sprinkling appropriate chemicals ("fertilizers") in its bed.

*Leaves: Synthetic leaves grow out of synthetic branches. They are capable of photosynthesis, like nature's leaves. (On the sly, they work like solar batteries too, replenishing the energies of the CPU).

*Flowers, fruits: These are optional, but our CPU shows off its prowess by manufacturing them. (Our virtual plant does not need pollination, for a change).

*Oxygen: What is a cricket batsman if he does not score a century? Our plant is well aware of that. So, it sucks in carbon dioxide from the air and sends out oodles of oxygen into the (grateful) atmosphere.

And so on and so forth. We can simulate all the details. Then, our virtual plant is equivalent to a natural plant in functionality.

Note: I have deliberately omitted one important function of a natural plant, as you might have already noticed – reproduction. But that is not really all that important for my argument. If we simulate the functionality of a plant, just for once – I mean, one plant vis-a-vis one plant, then we have demonstrated our theorem. We can declare we are satisfied. Besides, even the day of simulation of reproduction is not far away. The way genetic engineering is progressing, that day may come sooner than we expect. Apart from all that, our main concern is not about technological achievements; we focus on core concepts. The aesthetic satisfaction obtained from an exciting (and sound) concept is far superior to that of its practical realization at a later date.

A Reconciliation

The duplicity in the behavior of light is an old affair. The topic itself may seem stale to many veteran readers. So, we will make a brief statement and proceed. Light behaves like a particle under some circumstances and like a wave in other circumstances. When it takes the avatar of a particle, as in the photoelectric phenomena, it is a photon. Otherwise, as in the interference phenomenon, it is an electromagnetic wave. Particles are discrete entities. Quantum physics was introduced to explain the mysterious behavior of energy propagating in discrete "packets," called quanta. All of this is old news, as every graduate student knows.

I want to attempt a new interpretation here. The other day, I was reading a book when the phrase "the sun's rays" caught my attention, and I was enlightened! (Pardon the pun; the temptation was irresistible.) Allow me to develop the idea in my own freestyle way.

Normally, we do not actually "see" light. We see light when it reacts with another object, like passing through it, being reflected off its surface, and so on. You "see" the ray or beam of light because of the minute particles that exist in its path. That is the core of my idea. Light reacts with another object. We can extend the example and apply it generally to all waves.

Now, imagine a wavefront (energy) meeting an object in its path. This is an abstract, generalized statement, but it is the basis of all measurements and acts of detection. To put it another way, you cannot know the nature of light unless it reacts with another object, small or big.

When the wavefront encounters the object (the term "hit" is quite mild when you consider the speed of light), there is a mutual reaction, and the wave is also affected. An example will illustrate this clearly. Imagine a stream of water flowing steadily at a constant speed, smoothly and unruffled. The water is uniform and smooth everywhere. If the stream encounters a rock in its path, then along the surface where the rock and the stream interact, you can clearly discern a change in the pattern of flow. What I am proposing is that something analogous happens when light waves encounter a particle on their path. You can distinguish a pattern, a shape. This pattern defines the characteristics of the light striking the particles. My conjecture that this pattern could be what we call a quantum – a concept entirely apart from the grandiose mathematical formulations concerning the official "quantum" – deserves some serious thinking. Generally, when two boundaries (of any kind) meet, something special occurs near the common area where the two intersect. This is a broad-spectrum generalization.

Zooming in on the particulars, consider electromagnetic waves. Their behavior may be dual, depending on the object they interact with. For example, if the wavefront encounters an individual particle (or anything of microscopically small dimension), then a 'quantum' may arise at the point of impact. The results of such an encounter, when studied or measured, will be amenable to traditional quantum mathematics/analysis. If the object is comparatively large, like a TV dish antenna, the behavior of the electromagnetic wave will conform to that of a wave.

I would like to venture further. The concept is quite exciting, and I cannot stop hypothesizing. I think my kind of quantum could be of two types – the microscopic and the macroscopic. Let me clarify. What I described in the previous paragraphs was the genesis of a quantum of the microscopic kind. Now, think of the ray I spoke of earlier and view it from an entirely new angle.

I said that at the point where the wavefront touches the particle, a singular event occurs, creating a quantum. Now, this action involves a reaction at the source of the wave. The moment the "quantum" is created, a ray of the wave is generated all the way from the source to the particle. It is a kind of reaction to the action of the wavefront impinging on the particle. We can define this creation of the ray as a form of communication. The phenomenon can also be seen as a broad generalization of what happens when two entities react, with the generalization being the well-accepted principle that action always begets a reaction. Recall also that the Great Man2 showed that action and reaction are equal and opposite. From these principles, I have surmised that a ray will be created between the source and the point of impact where the source's wave meets the particle on its path. The ray would actually be a ray of the substance of the wave only, existing for the shortest imaginable period. You could say it is destroyed the moment it is created! If the source is active for a period of time, the ray is continuously wiped out and re-created again and again. The process continues as long as the source is active. This kind of ray is what I meant by a "macroscopic quantum."

I intuitively believe that this macroscopic quantum ray is a form of communication between the two objects involved – the source and the receiver. Incidentally, I conjecture that this macro quantum ray – the ray of communication – may hold the key to explaining that mysterious and puzzling event known as quantum entanglement.

By the way, we can deduce a beautiful (and breathtaking) generalization from quantum entanglement. Everything in the universe, every single particle, regardless of its nature, is connected to everything else. This concept, of course, is widely discussed in many popular science books. Here, I propose to make this connection more scientifically precise. In its simplified form, quantum entanglement states that if two particles, A and B, originate from the same source, and if you alter the state of one particle, A, then the state of B is automatically altered, even though the two particles are spatially far apart and isolated. Innumerable experiments have been (and are still being) conducted on this phenomenon. Recently, they have succeeded in achieving a kind of teleportation of particles using this effect. Now, you just have to take the next logical step.

You see, according to the Big Bang theory, the entire universe originated from a single source. Therefore, if the entanglement effect is true – and there is no doubt that this effect has been firmly established experimentally – then it naturally follows that all objects in the universe are mutually interconnected, or quantum entangled, if you prefer a scientific term. An action performed on a single particle affects the whole universe! The idea is truly breathtaking. Deriving this mathematically may be impossible, as of now. The reason is that the gravitational effect (entanglement) between two bodies can be calculated fairly easily. I am given to understand that calculating the same effect (entanglement) when five bodies are involved is almost an impossible task, let alone countless bodies in the universe. We might as well stop aspiring to calculate the effect in such a complex situation. Nevertheless, an intuitive conclusion can be safely drawn that such a universal entanglement exists.

A brief redux. (I am shamelessly using that word as it is much in vogue, especially in scholarly-sounding writings). We began with the observation that light exhibits the dichotomy of being both a particle and a wave. Our insights in the paragraphs above showed that light was solely a wave, but it can also be considered a particle, a particle in the sense of a discrete bundle of energy (a wave). The essence of all intellectual inquiries lies in performing perplexing somersaults! Yes, let us revisit the wave. A wave is not really an object at all when observed closely. A wave is a shape only. A water wave is a description of the behavior of water, which is matter. The same applies to sound waves. Therefore, when we say light is an electromagnetic wave, the emphasis is on 'electromagnetic.' If you inquire about what 'electromagnetic' refers to, you receive the answer that it refers to a field – magnetic field, electric field, and so on. We have merely been provided with a new name, a synonym, "medium." This medium has been elusive, like the Cheshire cat, until now. Nobody knows what that medium is. At one time, it was assumed to be ether, but that idea was abandoned in frustration.

The bottom line is that we have perpetually oscillated between two words – particle and wave. My intuition tells me that we have been ensnared by these two words. Our minds have been conditioned to think in these two terms. I feel that if we discard these two words, we might discover something new, something strange and thrilling.

Such a discovery will usher in the Fourth Generation in Science. The first generation was the Hellenic period. The second generation thrived during the Newtonian era. The Einstein generation paved a new path with its strange, previously unthinkable concepts. A century has passed since then. It is high time that science should explore new frontiers. To do so, it must free itself from the confinement of particle-wave duality. We must re-examine our concepts of forces and fields. It is not an easy task, I admit; but it must be undertaken. We may even have to devise new forms of logic and mathematics. As a great man once said, if you are on the wrong path, even a journey of a million miles will not lead you to your destination. I have a gut feeling that the pursuit of particles – even if they are "god's particles" – will be futile. The same applies to the frenzied search for strings and the pounding of imaginary membranes in even more imaginary multi-dimensions.

The birth of a new messiah in science is the dire need of the hour.

PART III

HIS MONOLOGUES

This section may be read as an extension of the Juvenilia. Young Bagden jotted down many ideas with the intention of developing them later. We have selected a few to provide a glimpse into the young lad's feverish (almost feral) activity in exploring new and strange insights. The contents can be seen more appropriately as his soliloquies.

1. Gravitation cannot be considered a property of the things they are studying. They are on a false trail. Magnetism, electric charge, chemical reactions, even inertia – all of these are studied as properties of matter/things/whatever. However, gravity is universal to all things/matter, whatever they may be. That is a clue flashing at us like a desperate neon sign. What is common to everything? Space! Everything floats and moves in space. Space holds the secret of gravity – not the numerous kinds of particles they are diligently studying.
2. Present scientific knowledge posits four types of forces – electromagnetic, gravitational, strong, and weak forces. In their outer appearances, these 'forces' appear disparate and separate. I intuitively believe that this should not be the case. I think there is only one force that operates across a broad-spectrum. Gravity (the weakest) and the strong force (the strongest) may lie at opposite ends of this spectrum. Due to their positions on the spectrum, these forces 'exhibit' different properties. The analogy of light may illuminate this idea. The behaviors of UV and IR lights are vastly different. It may require some sound mathematics to work this out.
3. The most famous equation in science is, of course, $E=mc^2$, which demonstrates the equivalence of matter and energy. Matter is condensed energy, akin to quanta. I prefer to use the word 'localized.' So, when energy becomes localized as matter, the equation provides us with the equivalent energy that has 'condensed' there, locally. We are aware of the

immense power of mc^2 – exemplified by nuclear bombs. I believe that is just the tip of the iceberg compared to what I have in mind. I strongly feel that space is also a form of energy. If, in the future, another Great Mind4 discovers this equivalence, I speculate that the equivalence may extend to the 20th degree – something like E=Sc^20, where S stands for space. (Comment from an admirer: Young Bagden had a profound intuition. He was to further develop his concept of the localization of space in later years, leading to his famous Spacenik Theory).

4. No orbits, please; we are electrons.
We have all been told that electrons orbit around the nucleus of the atom. I vehemently question this concept. The solar system was readily available to inspire such an idea; planets orbiting around the sun in various zones, you see. Once you convince yourself of an idea, it's not too difficult to construct a mathematical model from it.

What are my objections? Well, they say that where there is electricity, a magnetic field must follow it. (There must be thousands of gadgets in the market utilizing this principle.) Electricity is the flow, the movement of electrons. So, if electrons are constantly orbiting the nuclei of atoms, the atoms should exhibit a magnetic field. All materials in the world consist of atoms (you doubt it?). Therefore, all materials should be magnetic!

The main problem is this: If the planets stop orbiting the sun, they will be drawn in toward the sun, and the sun will engulf them. To avoid this fate, the planets must keep moving around the sun. A similar situation applies to electrons. If they cease moving around the nuclei, the nuclei will consume them. Furthermore, since protons are positively charged and electrons negatively charged, there will be mutual destruction. Then, there won't be any atoms to speak of. I believe this is a flawed analogy. I can propose a simple solution. Electrons are simply stuck – without the obligation to orbit – to the nucleus without coming into contact with the contents of the nucleus. How can such a thing be possible? It's possible if the nucleus has a cover, like a shell! The shell need not necessarily be a "material" shell but a kind of field. I suggest we conduct thorough research on this matter.

5. Black holes cannot be 'solid' throughout. They must be hollow inside. For that matter, any celestial body (like a star) composed of gases must contain a central hollow space. The rings of Saturn's planet amply prove my point. The

formation of a hollow space is quite logical. When visualizing the formation of a black hole – or any immense gaseous object – we are automatically tempted to think about the crushing force of gravity acting from the periphery towards the center, with the crushing effect increasing as one moves deeper towards the center. However, consider this perspective. Take an object. Its gravitational force acts all around it, attracting other objects in a 360-degree plane. To be specific, the object attracts other objects both 'above' and 'below' it. Imagine a massive mass roughly halfway between the center and the periphery of a sphere. That mass 'pulls up' the relatively smaller mass at the center naturally. Symmetrically, the same logic applies to the other side of the center. Therefore, a hollow space must form at the center of a fluid, whether it be a star or a black hole. Yes, black holes must have holes – quite literally! I'm willing to bet we can even create a computer program to substantiate my point.

6. Is there a limit to the size of the universe? By limit, I mean one observable or measurable by instruments. I believe there is a limit, and here's my deduction. The universe, as they say, is expanding; that is, galaxies, etc., are receding from us as observers. What they have discovered is that the farther objects are from us, the faster they are receding. This should provide a clue because objects farther and farther away will approach the speed of light. However, no object can move faster than light. Therefore, that critical distance must be the limit of our universe. You may wonder about the space beyond such a critical distance. My guess is that the expanding universe may simply begin to fold back on itself after reaching that point.

You can also calculate the size of the universe in a different way. We know the strength of the uniform cosmic background radiation. Calculate the energy level (theoretically, of course) at the time of the Big Bang. I'm sure they must have already done it. The ratio between the two energy levels may offer a clue to the size of the present universe.

7. The God of Science
Quantum mechanics is simply great. As poets say, words fail to do justice to its greatness. With quantum mechanics, anything can happen—literally anything. Using it, you can explain anything. Science has found God at last. Nobody understands God fully; so it is with Quantum Mechanics. In one way, QM is greater than God. You can live your life without God. But you cannot have science without QM! (As far as things stand now).

8. Why can't we have science without mathematics? Is math absolutely indispensable? I am seriously contemplating amending the situation. Actually, doing science without math is far tougher than doing it with the help of math.

(Comment by the admirer: There is a good scope for "smart quotes" here. Fact was, Bagdenborg was very good at mathematics! So, it seems you have to master math first to be able to discard it later).

9. It is fashionable to bandy about the multidimensional universe. You know, like the 4th, 5th dimensions, etc. They are all concepts only, not reality. We live in a three-dimensional world, that is all. About three hundred years ago, Nature itself threw a broad hint at us through an agent, but we have not been able to appreciate it fully. The agent in question is Fermat! The broad hint is the famous Fermat's Last Theorem (slightly altered by me). Assuming that some readers may not be aware of that theorem—a very rare possibility—I will explain it briefly. It is about numbers. You can always find three whole numbers such that $a + b = c$. (Very silly to state it because it is so obvious.) For example, $1+2 = 3$, $2+3 = 5$, and so on. This demonstrates the existence of (one) single dimension. Next, the equation $a^2 + b^2 = c^2$ is also possible for whole numbers (integers). For example, $3^2 + 4^2 = 5^2$. This demonstrates the existence of the second dimension. And then, the equation $a^3 + b^3 = c^3$ is also realizable for whole numbers (if not theoretically, at least practically! Justification follows). The superscript "3" demonstrates the existence of the third dimension ("volume," say). Fermat's last theorem states that for the above superscript (i.e., for the number 4), there are no whole numbers fulfilling the equation like $a^4 + b^4 = c^4$. This famous theorem lay unproved for nearly 300 years—till very recently, in spite of the best efforts of thousands of brilliant mathematicians. So you can understand the greatness of the theorem. But the great hint I spoke of lies in the number 4. To repeat, there are no whole numbers such that $a^4 + b^4 = c^4$. The number "4" stands for the fourth dimension. The equation thus clearly proves that there is no fourth dimension at all. If purists are afraid of the word "prove," they may substitute it with "a broad hint."

Further (superfluous) clarification

For one dimension; $a + b = c$, is realizable. You can take 4 marbles, add 6 more to them, and have 10… One dimension is okay.

For two dimensions; $a^2 + b^2 = c^2$, is also realizable. A plane represents two dimensions. You can draw a right-angled triangle on it. Then the Pythagoras theorem states that in such a triangle, the sum of the squares of two sides opposite to the hypotenuse is equal to the square of the hypotenuse. Or, you can draw three squares such that the sum of the areas of two of them will be equal to the area of the third one... Two dimensions too are okay.

For three dimensions; $a^3 + b^3 = c^3$, is also realizable in practice. A cube represents three dimensions. You can construct cubes in three dimensions, see. You can make one can of 1 cubic liter of capacity, another of 8 cubic liters, and a third one of 27 cubic liters, such that, if you pour the contents (gas, gas, gas, please note!) of x and y into z, z will be exactly filled up to the brim. (My sincere and sympathetic apologies to pal Fermat, if his soul is mortified. He has to blame the famous Charles' and Boyle's laws for gases, here! I want to leverage his theorem to serve my purpose in a beautiful, fentological way.)... Three dimensions are okay.

Four dimensions; $a^4 + b^4 = c^4$, is unrealizable. You simply cannot construct an object having 4 dimensions... Four dimensions not okay. Forget it.

(Admirer: I have to appreciate the chutzpah of the brat there. His acrobatics with the cubes is a class by itself. Recently, when I had the opportunity to bring this to the notice of the professor, he grinned boyishly at me and said, 'I just channelized logic, that is all. Anyhow, what is fentologic for if it does not come to our rescue in such situations!')

10. I think the much-touted phrase, "curvature of space" is a fancy phrase. In my opinion, it is not proper (sober) science. Curvature of space is usually attributed to the influence of matter on space—a roundabout way to avoid using gravitational force. Perpend. What does curvature of space imply when you imagine it? It implies that space is an object, like an elastic membrane! Does it mean that space is matter? It should, ha-ha! It really should, if at all you are honest to the core. If space is matter, or matter like, then there is no such thing as space! I think it is best to treat the curvature of space as a convenient mathematical entity, a tool to explain certain kinds of motion of matter. In that case, space does not really curve, you know. What a relief.

(Admirer's comment: The brat, later on, in his more mature days, made a volte-face. He treated space too as a form of "matter," but of an entirely subtler kind on a vastly refined scale).

11. The sun's wicks: You have an oil lamp with a wick, oil, and all. You light the wick, and the lamp burns steadily and for a long time. If there is no

wick, no enclosure for the oil, and you ignite the same quantity of oil (as in the lamp) in an open pan, the whole thing will go up in a flash. Any doubts there, gentlemen? The same reasoning is valid for any combustible material. Right?

Now, what is the most super-duper fuel we know? The hydrogen atom, naturally (the heavier one). Ignite even a ridiculously small amount of it under proper conditions, and you will have a god-almighty explosion. (Remember Bikini Atoll?)

Take this punch, then. You know the sun, the gent who so kindly has been lighting our days for billions of years, at a calm, steady pace? The sun, (they say), is crammed with billions and billions and billions of far more fuel of the same kind than your puny Bikini Atoll bomb. No doubt there, what say? Then, if atomic fusion takes place in the body of the sun (as they say), why does not the sun blow away as a whole in an instant? The sun is a damn lazy fellow. He should have blown up himself some billions of years ago.

But the fact is that he did not. He has not, so far. Most probably, he may not. Therefore, I deduce that the sun has provided itself with billions of wicks—just like the good ole oil lamp.

If you put the above question to the physicists, they will sandbag you physically and also with weighty mathematical equations. Better not approach them. (Better torture yourself for a lifetime, in private with the question). But seriously, something else, apart from atomic fusion, is occurring on the sun. Only, nobody has bothered to search for it since the bikini (Oops! Forgot to put 'b' in capitals!) has provided us all with a convenient, readymade (and smug) answer. Let there be hydrogen, let there be helium on the sun; I do not mind at all. What I suspect is that something else, an X-factor, is hiding there. Who is going to find it out?

12. Inside, outside: The word "insider knowledge" can only exist in thriller books and politics. It has no place in science. Perhaps I may have confused you just a wee bit. Rewrite "insider" as "inside," and my meaning may become clearer. More yet. Knowledge of the 'inside' is what I mean. Follow my reasoning thus, please.

When you look at an object—say a tennis ball—you are seeing it from the outside. That is, you are standing away (or apart) from it. In fact, standing away from an object is the only way of being able to "view" it. This leads us to a funny game of infinite regression. You see a solid object from outside. You are not satisfied. You claim you can go inside. You do and see particles. Again, you are not satisfied. You go inside and 'see' la, la, atoms…la, la…nucleus… la, la, protons…la, la, quarks… You can go on until you are either sick of it or get totally tired of it.

At the end of it all, the original conundrum prevails impishly. You see what you see from outside. The end.

13. Pulling apart: Remember the good old days when a person's limbs were tied with ropes to four horses, and his limbs were torn apart as the horses were driven radially outwards? Don't shiver; I am not contemplating bringing back that civilized practice. I have got a fancy idea of testing that procedure in science. Not on homo sapiens; God forbid. The basic idea is that of pulling apart. Why not choose electrons or protons as candidates?

Take a proton, the positively charged particle. Place powerful, negatively charged plates around it at a suitable distance. Go on increasing the negative charge of the plates. What happens? The proton is being pulled—uniformly—in all directions. So, logically there must come a stage when the proton will be torn apart into pieces.

I intuit that there will be a release of energy. I feel that the whole of the proton will be converted into a burst of energy. I strongly urge the techie geeks to attempt the experiment. The reason is simple; the energy released will be incomparably greater than that in a nuclear fission (or fusion). In the present nuclear reactions which we know, only a minute part of energy is released as compared to the mass of the participating particles. In my experiment, the whole of the participating particle will (must) be converted as energy. A hundred-percent energy conversion is unheard of—it is mind-boggling. That is why I am so excited about the 'pulling apart' experiment. The proton is a better candidate since its mass is higher than that of an electron.

They have been trying for more than seventy years to create a controllable, commercially viable method of nuclear fusion, without success. Why not try my method? It will surely be more profitable to mankind.

14. Dark secret: You all know that the amount of dark matter is predominantly overwhelming that of 'visible' matter. By "visible," we mean detectable. Dark matter is concealing a dark secret. Dark matter has not been detected so far – that is the irony of the situation. Well, then, Sherlock, what do you deduce from this?

"Elementary, dear Watson. Visible matter is the tail of dark matter! What I mean by this is that visible matter was created by dark matter. Dark matter transforms itself into the visible kind. This process is still going on even now. Naturally, that implies the amount of visible matter should steadily increase. Of course, it does. We have not been able to detect the growth in the amount of visible matter because, primarily, we did not think of it. Secondarily, it is almost impossible in view of the timescale. The universe, as they say, is 14 billion years old, and you have to compile and compare data on matter for a minimum of a hundred thousand years to get viable results!! By the bye, since dark matter is being converted to visible matter, we do not need the Big Bang theory.

"Lastly, dear Watson, do not ask me what the exact process is that enables dark matter to come to light. I have planted the seed idea, and it is up to the big boffins to get going.

"My personal pessimistic prognosis is that we may never be able to discover that secret process. Dark matter has been justly (and unwittingly perhaps) dubbed as dark, and it is going to remain dark forever, I guess."

15. Memory is essential for any repetitive act. Nature has endowed us with memory. It is, in fact, a reflection of the Original Memory of nature. What we call the 'properties' of matter is just another name for that innate Memory of Nature. Otherwise, how can an object behave identically an infinite number of times under identical circumstances? You throw the tennis ball at the wall a million times, and it bounces back. You drop Newton's apple from the top of the Empire State Building, and every time it reaches the ground. And so on, and so on. You get me?

16. We interpret matter as matter because of the structure of our bodies. Our bodies are not 'solid' by any means. They are like sieves (of enormous holes). But the size of the sieves matches that of the external matter, like air, water, and dust, etc.

17. We have to thank Nature that there is so much empty space inside the atom. (Compared to the overall size of an atom, the size of its contents, like electrons, protons, and neutrons, is so small as to be almost negligible. The ratio is roughly a hundred thousand to one. Or more.) Compare this with the earth and moon. The size of our earth is about 14,400 km. The distance

at which the moon orbits around the earth is about 384,400 km. The ratio of the distance to the size (of earth) is approximately 30:1. Imagine the same ratio existing inside the atom. That means that the density of such an atom would be thousands of times more than that of a normal atom. Under such circumstances, if a drop of rain falls on your head, your skull would crack open! What is a pleasant breeze now would (then) be like a bombardment of a million bullets! There is ample scope in this scenario for an exciting sci-fi book.

Thank God (sorry, I mean Nature) that atoms are as empty as they are now.

17. Limits and limitations: Why is there a limit to the speed of light? Why can't objects move faster than light? Light – let us look at the lighter side of it. Take the first case. If light were to travel instantaneously across any distance, then we will have to scrap the yardstick of the light-year! It would be almost impossible to measure the size of the universe – conveniently, that is. Imagine the number of zeroes you will have to place after the decimal point in measurements pertaining to the intergalactic distances! Assuming the nature of the light waves has not changed, then the frequency will have to be infinite. There will be no such thing as an expanding universe. Light waves are, in fact, electromagnetic waves. So, can the other forms of electromagnetic waves, like radio waves, etc., keep quiet? They will imitate light. Still maintaining proper fear of the Einsteinian decree that they cannot reach the exact speed of light, they may nevertheless reach speeds just a mile or two less! Then we will have a hell of a problem with electronic tuning devices. The list can go on and on.

Actually, Nature wants us to experience the concept of vastness. You enjoy your trekking experience across the universe one-foot at a time – metaphorically – and go on tramping for 14 billion years and more.

Secondly, if objects (we) are able to move at the same new (or nearly the) speed of light, then distance will lose its meaning. We will be able to reach the edge of the universe and be back in a jiffy. The universe – let alone our earth – will lose all its charm and awe.

18. That reminds us about the other limit. Science has seriously proposed a limit to length at the short end of the scale. There is the famous Planck limit beyond which length loses its meaning. (The length is unimaginably smaller than the smallest subatomic particle.) If we accept that idea, then we should naturally extend it to the other end. There should be a limit – by the

same logic – to the greatest length. Infinity will not do. We want a concrete number, similar to the Planck length. I propose to name it the Bagden Length (modesty apart). We can derive it empirically thus. Taking the meter as the normal yardstick, the Planck length is defined as 1.6169226 x 10^-35 meters (real tiny). Take the light-year as the normal yardstick for the universe. Then the Bagden length would be 1.6161926 x 10^35 light-years. It is as simple as that, besides being compellingly logical and appealing!

If we accept that (PL), we must accept this also (BL). As for size in three dimensions, there is no problem. They have already calculated it. Above a certain size, things collapse (into themselves) under the force of gravity – and become black holes! Thus, something unimaginable should happen if the universe exceeds the span of the Bagden length. Mathematicians, get busy! By the way, there is also the Bagden Ratio, which is equal to the diameter of the electron divided by the diameter of the universe.

19. Gravitational currents – Bagden's Conjecture

A field is a field; you have to agree with that. It is elementary knowledge that when a metallic object – like a piece of wire – moves inside a magnetic field, there is a flow of current. Electricity is produced. In the history of mankind, this can be said to be the single most important discovery that changed civilization forever. Hold the picture in your mind and savor it for a minute or two.

Now you are ready for Bagden's Conjecture. Let us repeat the mantra 108 times – a field is a field. There is the sun. The sun has a huge gravitational field. Right? Then there is the earth moving in a field. A field is a field. Since the earth is moving in a field, something analogous to electricity must be produced in the earth. Let me christen it as the gravitational current! I am thrilled at this idea. Right now, it is only a conjecture. But...!

Now that I have spilled the beans, it is up to the science geeks to get going. I am sure that they will discover some new phenomena in nature. Of course, the current in the wire moving in a magnetic field is produced because of the build up of voltage – the equivalent of pressure or force. So, something similar must be happening to our planet earth; and naturally in the other planets of the solar system. I am excited at this idea. I really am. Let some enterprising soul come forward and find out exactly what is happening! (The bottom line here is experimentation. As all my friends know, I am allergic to that.)

It need not be the case with the planets only. On our earth itself, we have an inexhaustible source of moving objects (moving in gravitational fields, I mean). Faster objects are likely to yield comparatively measurable results. We have many of them too: planes, rockets, bullets, satellites.

I am sure that this (so far) undiscovered effect of the gravitational field on (inside) moving objects, when found out and studied, will solve many puzzles in science. Happy hunting. My advance salutes to the would be Faraday of the future.

20. For better or worse, modern science was totally transformed on the day Young did his double-slit experiment. Many new variations of the experiment have been carried out since then. The interpretations of the results are not meant for the weak-hearted! I just wonder here whether anybody has carried out the experiment using Wilson's cloud-chamber, or the latest improvement on it. The idea is to track the individual particles, slyly, marching towards the twin slits. I take it that they generally use detectors to detect the individual particles. I feel tracing the tracks would provide more insight into the mysterious phenomenon. The particles would be in a quandary if they want to play their usual hide-and-seek games in such a set-up.

21. That reminds me of another historical experiment carried out to detect ether, the hypothetical medium in which light waves were supposed to travel – the great M-M experiment. The experiment triggered in me the memory of another demonstration carried out by Galileo. He dropped objects from the mast of a moving ship to show that the objects always fell at the foot of the mast, thereby demonstrating that the movement of the ship had no effect on the path taken by objects falling down; objects which are a part of the moving system as a whole. If ether really exists, I also wonder whether it could be a part of the moving system, the earth! In that case, we will have to retry the M-M experiment. Place two of the mirrors far away in outer space not affected by earth's gravity – or at least at a distance where the effect of earth's gravity would be empirically negligible. Any takers?

22. I strongly feel that there may not be such a thing as a gravitational wave. Field, yes. But waves, no. My reason? Waves, as you all know, invariably exhibit the phenomenon of interference – the way dark and light bands form when light waves interfere. The dark bands represent the areas where the light

waves cancel one another. So, if there are gravitational waves, they too must exhibit interference. At the "dark areas" where the gravity waves cancel one another, there should not be any gravity! Objects moving across such a band of interference would behave very oddly indeed. As far as I know, nobody has detected such odd behavior of bodies in movement, either earthly or heavenly.

(Note by the admirer: It is probably after such reasoning that Bagdenborg, in his later years, theorized that space itself was elastic).

23. Faster than light?

If one end of a lever is pressed down, the other end rises up. Just imagine a lever that is more than a million miles long. The lever is in outer space, so that it need not bend down or break into two under its own "weight". Press one end of the lever. The other end should move in the opposite direction. The million-dollar question is, "Will the other end move immediately, or after some time?" If it moves immediately, then the accepted law that nothing can move faster than light will be broken! (Force would have been transmitted immediately, you see?) I think only an actual, physical experiment can settle this question. Using light beams, etc., is of no use. I want a real, solid lever made of solid matter.

If nothing can move faster than light, then, even in the case of a small lever – say one-meter long – on Earth, the other end will (should) rise only after a lapse of some time when the active end is pushed down. The lapse could be so minute as to be imperceptible, or un-measurable, but a lapse there must be. Care to experiment on this? Any takers?

24 Spin it does – if not, it should.

Follow these analogies, please. The next sequence will become obvious to you without me parting my lips. Take a bucket filled with water. Introduce a spinning rod or an object into it and start spinning. What happens? The water will also spin; what else? Survey your bedroom. It is now filled with air. Look above, and you will espy the ceiling fan. Switch it on. What happens? The fan will start spinning, naturally (assuming the power is on, obviously). What else happens? The air too starts spinning; what else? Consider next a slightly more technical machine. There are what are called magnetic coils – or field coils – in the electric generator. The "field coils" will act as magnets, with a magnetic field surrounding them. When the generator starts, the coils rev up.

The magnetic field begins to rotate. All the above examples are simple, easy to grasp, and an obvious part of our daily experience.

You have been doing fine so far. So, don't flinch when I throw the next sequence (in the series) at you. Be honest and accept the natural conclusion. Ready? Ponder about the planet Earth. It is spinning on its axis, as you and I and all of us know. Next, ponder about what surrounds the Earth – apart from the air we have managed to pollute so profusely. Space, dear soul! Space is all around the Earth, in complete contact with its surface. Now, add two and two. There is the Earth surrounded by space. The Earth is spinning.

So, space too is spinning! If not, it should. (Repeat it, write that in rubric.) Only, we have not been aware of it till now. Only, we do not have, as at present, suitable detectors equal to the task of detecting that spin. Do not think of this as a hare-brained idea. When a great man (truly great) showed that space could bend (curve), you were all aghast but accepted it in due course; did you not? If space could curve, it could spin as well, is all I am saying.

Congratulations! You just added two and two and came up with four.

25. Zeno's arrow, horse, and snake

Old Zeno was a clever guy. Of course, you know about his famous arrow, but permit me to spell it out. The arrow has been shot from a bow, and it hits the target. Zeno puts forth a clever argument to prove that the arrow does not travel at all! In his chain of argument, there is one particular sentence whose truth you cannot deny – at any point in time, the arrow is occupying a space exactly equal to its size. The remark appears to be totally logical, true, and unquestionable.

Well, my granddad used to say that when one chooses to be too clever, one's area of focus becomes very narrow. Zeno probably had an obsession about arrows. He probably must have forgotten that such things as horses and snakes existed. Why am I bringing in horses and snakes when we are discussing such a famous paradox as Zeno's arrow? I am doing it because horses and snakes also move – not just arrows.

Let us drop the humor bit and get serious. The key word here is movement. Consider two analogies. I am obsessed with analogies. We can learn a lot of new things by studying them carefully. I have said this umpteen times, and I am not ashamed to repeat it. Consider how a horse moves. First, it keeps its front leg (legs) forward. Then the rear leg follows. Look at the slithering snake. A minute section of its belly stretches forward. Then the snake drags up the section behind the first one, and so on. There is a common course of action in both cases. A part of the moving body stretches forward, and then the hind part follows up. Stretching, pulling up, stretching, pulling up – that is the essence of movement. In this context, review what Zeno said about the arrow, that the arrow occupies an amount of space equal to its size at any and every point in time (while moving). Obviously, we cannot apply the statement to the context of horses and snakes. Their bodies stretch; they occupy more space, for a brief period of time. Of course, arrows are inanimate objects, and animals and reptiles are animate objects – that is the immediate response Zeno would throw at us. After these two thousand odd years, you and I too would agree with him.

Hold it there for a second; immerse yourself in the analogy of (moving) snakes and horses. Let the image sink in. Replace the words "stretching and pulling up" with "expanding and contracting." There you go! Inanimate objects do expand and contract, don't they?

That is precisely what I am proposing in my theory of how objects move. Objects – including your smallest discrete particles – move by expanding and contracting. The figure below is self-explanatory. It is so simple. You do not even need a figure to understand what I mean. Just imagine the particle as a snake slithering forward – in space.

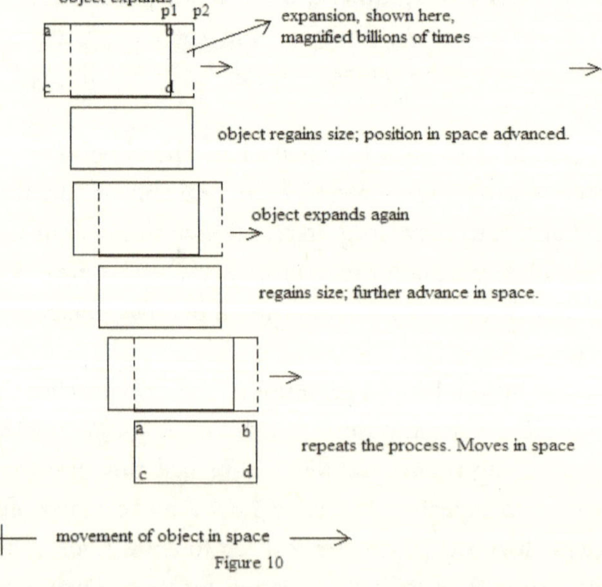

Figure 10

The surface of the particle in the forward-moving direction extends up to point P2. The expansion is infinitesimal, naturally, which is why you cannot detect it. In the very next fraction of a second, the particle regains its original size by contracting. That fraction of a second is also infinitesimal. The particle has now occupied a new position in space. The process continues as long as the particle keeps moving.

One finer point, for the sake of the ever-doubting Thomas in you. (Doubting is good, of course.) You may ask, from where does the body (particle) get the energy for expansion and contraction? Good question, easily answered. The energy comes from the original impetus given to the body; the way a soccer ball gets its from the kick it receives. It may also come internally, the way a rocket gets its from the burning fuel. When the moving body meets an obstacle and comes to a stop, expansions and contractions stop. Thomas may again ask, "What about the object moving freely in space, without meeting any opposing force? It will keep on moving. Will the expansions and contractions go on forever?" No problem there either. Expansion will follow contraction indefinitely as long as the body keeps moving. There is no other way for objects to move.

Remember the swinging pendulum. An ideal pendulum will keep on swinging forever if there are no frictional losses of energy.

Whew! I am terribly excited by this idea of mine. The only thing left is the mathematical part of it; formulating equations for the tiny expansions and contractions, the time involved, and so on. It may not be a difficult task for all those mathematical whiz kids out there. I generously invite them to embrace my theory and work out the mathematical framework.

If only Zeno were alive!

Postscript: what I have explored above is not connected with the Lorentz contraction. Please note the difference. The Lorentz contraction deals with what happens to a moving object. My theory goes deeper. It explores how the object moves. A private whisper in the ears of those unfamiliar with LC. Lorentz put forth the concept that when an object moves, it contracts. There are formulas to calculate the amount of contraction, and so on. The famous theory that time moves slowly for a moving object is based on the Lorentz contraction phenomenon. And so on and so forth. You must surely be familiar with those strange stories about time-shortening, floating in the air for nearly 100 years, following the fallout of the Theory of Relativity. One of the twin brothers sails out into space, traveling at very near the speed of light, and he returns sixty years later, still fresh and young, while the other brother has become an old decrepit dotard being pushed around in a wheelchair. And so on, and so forth.

To repeat, my adventure in thought deals with how an object moves – to the very basics, gathering inspiration from analogies in nature, analogies which, alas, Zeno had overlooked. My theory of the expansions and contractions of the moving object is unique. They exist independently of all the known and established laws of dynamics but do not interfere with the concomitant mathematical equations.

A horse wink and an aside to those Lorentzian votaries, enthusiasts, nerds, and geeks. If you managed to hear what I whispered in the previous paragraphs, wipe out your amused smiles. By all means, make your Lorentzian contraction calculations. But you better make up for the required corrections on account of the (infinitesimal) expansions predicted by my theory. Your calculations will be more refined, then.

26. Why objects have to travel at less than the speed of light.

One of the most famous statements in science is that no object (anything) can travel faster than the speed of light. It requires enormous guts (or mild insanity) to challenge that statement. (I intend to pick up the gauntlet one of these days).

The equations of the Great Man3 demonstrate what happens to an object when it reaches speeds near that of light. The mass of the object increases and so on. I wish to put forth a simple concept in this context. Don't panic when you read the next sentence. Objects may and can travel at speeds faster than that of light, but we cannot either see them or detect them in that mode! My argument is simple; it follows the old (but clever) Zeno's methods of ratiocination. Study the simple figure given below.

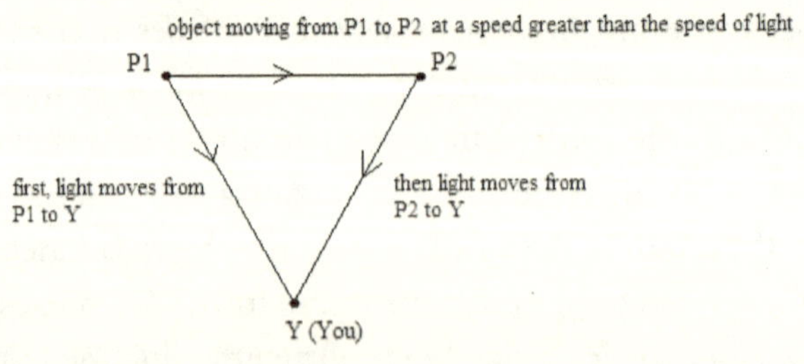

Figure 11

Let us take a normal case to begin with. The object starts at point P1 and moves towards point P2. Y is your position as the observer. Initially, light – or any signal – has to reach you (Y) from point P1. That is basic: otherwise, you will not know if the object is at P1 or even whether the object exists or not. Similarly, when the object, in its travel, reaches point P2, light reaches you at Y, and you can determine that the object is indeed at P2. You conclude that the object has traveled from P1 to P2. You have timers and all, and if you know the distance between P1 and P2, you can compute the speed of the object. Now, in normal circumstances, the speed of light is immensely greater than that of most objects that move. Yet, you have to note that even light takes some time, however small, to travel from P1 to Y or P2 to Y (that is, you).

What happens if the object travels faster than light? It's simply obvious. First, light travels from P1 to you at Y. You conclude that the object is at P1. Good; then you scan for the object at P2. The act of shifting your scan too takes some time, however infinitesimal it may be. Even if we ignore it and assume that you look directly at point P2 immediately, the object would have already traveled beyond P2, since its speed is faster than that of light. (We are assuming a simple case where the distance between P1 and P2 is less than that between P1 and Y). That means, the object has vanished out of sight, out of detection! You have to conclude that the object traveled faster than light. If you do not want to accept such a proposition, you will be forced to admit that the object has vanished into nothingness – an idea more unpalatable.

The triangle P1 P2 Y in the figure holds good even if you imagine the object to travel any distance (P1 to P2). Every schoolboy knows the basic Euclidean theorem that P1Y + P2Y is always greater than P1P2. Explaining in common-man's language, you may say that light has to travel two times, from P1 to you and P2 to you. As the good old reliable Greek used to say, QED.

There is a secondary by-product of understanding from the above theorem. Speculate in the sci-fi fashion. There is an audio world where communication exists only through audible waves. There is no light. There are no other kinds of electromagnetic waves too. In such a world, you can stipulate that no object can travel faster than the speed of sound. Our syllogism for light holds good for this scenario too. The same triangle in the figure can be used the show that objects vanish or become untraceable when they overshoot the speed of sound.

This directly pushes us into another thrilling speculation – into the land of sci-fi, as things stand now. But who knows? What is sci-fi today can become a mundane – almost boring – affair tomorrow. There are copious examples in the history of science to prove it. So, speculate further thus. In the previous case, we took the example of an object moving in air. In actual experience, we know that when the object crosses the speed of sound, there is a stomach-churning sonic boom. Right? Apply this analogy to our object traveling faster than light. The object should produce a photic-boom á la the sonic boom when it crosses the speed of light! The analogy is very enticing. I think some such thing like a photic-boom will really happen. The idea is not all that far-fetched. Light from a moving object does suffer changes – recall the famous red-shift phenomenon of the receding galaxies.

If we do extensive research on this speculation, I feel many a puzzle that has been tantalizing scientists, especially in the fields of astrophysics and cosmology, may be solved. We may even discover new secrets that have been lying hidden until now. All those enthusiasts who derive pleasure in experimentation are welcome to share my intuitive speculation. I am eager to get feedback from them.

* Goodbye, for the present, dear readers. Hope to meet you all again in more pages like these.

AN ABRUPT ADIEU

We were able to compile this remarkable book (with minimal editing) because the admirer of Bagdenborg used to dump the notes of the professor on our table periodically and enthusiastically. Alas, the admirer too vanished quite recently, following the untraceable path of Professor Bagdenborg – most probably being inspired by him. Luckily, the material offered was enough to form a coherent whole. The last act of the vanished admirer was to send us a final, valedictory-like note taken out of the last page of the Bagdenborg Notes. Since the missive serves as a fitting closing note, we would like to reproduce it below.

Where it all ends

"Last night I was struck by an ironic and funny observation. Science, as we know it, can be said to have begun with the Greek thinkers. Then it almost lay dormant for six hundred years. It picked up momentum from thereon, going through a phase of frenetic frenzy during the early 1900s, culminating in the steady robotic methodology of the present times. In the early stages, only very few individuals here and there contributed to science. On the contrary, in these modern days, thousands and thousands of people all over the world are engaged – round the clock! – in scientific research. The (saddening) irony is that we are still far from obtaining a comprehensive, unchallengeable, and indisputable understanding of the universe. The situation truly makes one feel desperate, sad, and, I confess, disheartened.

The famous Planck's limit imposes a limit on the size of meaningful measurements of length. I am afraid that, in the same vein, there must exist a limit to the "meaningful" employment and manipulation of thought itself – thought as expressed though scientific words and symbols. With due modesty, I would like to call it the Bagdenborg Limit.

There is another most valid aspect to this business of scientific knowledge. Science, to put it in a nutshell, is an endeavor to understand the world we live in, following certain rigorous unique methods. In essence, it is the human mind's response to the challenge of the universe man lives in. The important thing to keep in sight is that the response of the human mind is a manifold activity. Literature, poetry, philosophy, art, ethics, sociology – all these are various forms of human response. All of them are valid. Therefore, there is nothing special about science.

Talking of the response by the mind, it is not strictly an independent function. First, there is the physical response, automatic and almost unnoticed. The physical organism – human in this case – first registers the presence of the environment around it. The organism accomplishes this act through the five sensors it is endowed with, classifying the data received as the sensations of light, sound, touch, smell, and taste. Then the mind takes over – immediately, almost – and builds up its fantastic, elaborate, and intricate webs of responses. Even in the field of science, the million splendid instruments it employs are nothing but extensions of the five primary sensors (organs) of the human body. Seen from that perspective, even science is only a way of interaction of the organism with the environment. If you zoom in, through this funnel of understanding, you will recognize that the most basic riddle is that of differentiation – the organism (that which senses) and the other thing which is separate from it, the environment (that which is "sensed"). The organism has to "separate" itself from the environment in order to "sense" it. Billions, trillions of organisms are doing it all the time. And yet, the supreme irony is that the organism is always a part of the environment! Here we are confronted with a logical deadlock. If the organism senses itself as separate from the environment, and if it is part of the environment, then the environment itself is sensing itself as separate from itself! If my scientific colleagues would excuse me, I would like to remark that our previous statement about the environment and the organism sounds like one of those good old Zen Kōans.

Recognition and separateness go hand in hand. They are part of some mysterious, unfathomable phenomenon of creation. What I am expressing is not a flight of fancy. Even in the biological (non-human) field, an organism first "looks" at the environment as being separate in order to feed on it. I dare to go further and pronounce that even the so-called inert matter too possesses this quality of recognizing separateness. A hydrogen atom "recognizes" its separateness from an oxygen atom in order to react with it. It has to do so.

These and other more intense considerations propel me now to forsake science. Not forsake; to go beyond is a more apt way of saying it. I wish to delve deeper into that fount of intuition on whose shallow surface only the most refined logic dares to sail.

Au revoir, I am going away from all this. Whither, I know not, since I am relying solely on my intuition to guide me. Even if this involves severance from all that is old, including human contact, I am not daunted. I leave the legacy of my researches to my beloved admirers and go.

A final word to my dear admirers. Do not feel vexed. Who knows, I may even come back someday to do justice to many of my scientific intuitions that are yet to find external expressions.

RECOMMENDED READING

There are two stages in reading books on science. In the first stage, you get terribly excited and inspired. You go on reading as many books as you can grab. Sooner or later, you reach the second stage where you begin to feel frustrated because there are no indisputably final answers. If you are still in the first stage, here is a list (very small indeed) of books you may want to read – assuming, of course, that you have not already read these books:

"The Mysterious Universe" by Sir James Jeans
"The Nature of the Physical World" by Sir Arthur Eddington
"Cosmos" by Carl Sagan
"Men of Mathematics, Vol I and II" by Eric Temple Bell

(The above two volumes deal with the great people who built the vast empire of mathematics. Since science is inseparably linked with mathematics, I have mentioned these two books. The books have been admirably written. They make for fascinating reading and will surely inspire everybody who reads them.)
The Fabric of Cosmos: Brian Greene
The Elegant Universe: Brian Greene
The Emperor's New Mind: Roger Penrose and Martin Gardener
The Hitchhiker's Guide to the Galaxy: Douglas Adams
An Uncommon Knowledge: Al McDowell
Dancing Wu Li Masters: Gary Zukav
The Cosmic Blueprint: P.C.W. Davies
A Brief History of Time: Stephen Hawking
ABC of Relativity – Bertrand Russell
The Mind's I: Douglas Hofstadter

Einstein: His Life and Universe – Walter Isaacson
Maya in Physics: Narasinga Charan Panda
Superstrings: F. David peat
The Hidden Reality: Brian Greene
The Sphinx and the Rainbow: David Loye
The Tao of Physics: Fritjof Capra
Sci-fi and general:
Lateral Thinking: Eduard di Bono
The Mechanism of Mind: Eduard di Bono
A Fantastic Voyage- Isaac Asimov
The books of Robert Sheckley
2001, A Space Odyssey: Arthur C. Clarke
Journey to the Centre of the Earth: Jules Verne
Man's Search for Meaning: Victor Pranks
The Edge of Physics: Anil Ananthaswamy
Pale Blue Dot: Carl Sagan
The Universe in a Nut Shell: Stephen Hawking
The Grand Design: Stephen Hawking
Edge of the Universe: Paul Halpen
Jestus: V.S. Sury
Jestus on Rampage: V.S. Sury
(These two books, the second one especially, will give you a very good idea about the fascinating ways of the incomparable Professor Bagdenborg.)
Surely You're Joking, Mr. Feynman!; Richard Feynman & Ralph Leighton
Gödel, Escher, Bach; An Eternal Golden Braid: Douglas Hofstadter
The Particle at the End of the Universe: Sean Carroll
Four Laws That Drive the Universe: Peter Atkins
One, Two, Three… Infinity: George Gamow
The Feynman Lectures on Physics: Richard Feynman & Robert B. Leighton
Dated : 16th June, 2015

www.ingramcontent.com/pod-product-compliance
Lightning Source LLC
LaVergne TN
LVHW091253150826
845673LV00006B/1406

* 9 7 9 8 8 9 1 3 3 4 2 9 8 *